Nina ...
Boon—ever s...
...cks of M... & Boon ...
to this dream Nina acquired an ...English degree, a hero of her own, three gorgeous children and—somehow!—an accountancy qualification. She lives in Brighton and has filled her house with stacks of books—her very own real library.

Since 2002, *USA TODAY* bestselling author **Judy Duarte** has written over forty books for Mills & Boon True Love, earned two RITA® Award nominations, won two Maggie Awards and received a National Readers' Choice Award. When she's not cooped up in her writing cave, she enjoys travelling with her husband and spending quality time with her grandchildren. You can learn more about Judy and her books on her website, judyduarte. com, or at Facebook.com/judyduartenovelist

WHISKED AWAY BY THE ITALIAN TYCOON

NINA MILNE

STARTING OVER WITH THE SHERIFF

JUDY DUARTE

MILLS & BOON

Falkirk Community Trust	
30124 03145621 5	
Askews & Holts	
AF	£6.99
GM	

ISBN: 978-0-263-29978-6

0521

MIX
Paper from
responsible sources
FSC C007454

www.fsc.org

Printed and bound in Spain
by CPI, Barcelona

WHISKED AWAY BY THE ITALIAN TYCOON

NINA MILNE

To Philippa—
for being an amazing friend and for all the
(socially distanced) support whilst I wrote this book.

CHAPTER ONE

LUCA PETROVELLI SNAPPED his cufflink on. The simple design—a house that encompassed a cocoa bean—touched him with a familiar sense of pride. The logo represented his business—Palazzo di Cioccolato, an upmarket, growing chocolatier that Luca would one day take global.

Yet that ambition had been diluted, impacted by the death of his father. The man who had deserted him when Luca was only five years old. James Casseveti had left his pregnant wife and five-year-old son to marry another woman. An English aristocrat, with wealth and connections. His father had never looked back, had used the riches and contacts to set up his own company—Dolci, a dessert company that was a global success.

And as the young Luca had watched this success unfold, seen the glittering heights his father had reached, he'd made a vow. His success would surpass his father's and one day he would find James Casseveti and demonstrate that superiority. He'd been so close, planned to launch a new product and open a flagship London store, had envisaged hand-delivering the invitation to the glittering opening party. Tried to picture his father's face. The expression of surprise, shock, regret, pride... *No!* Luca didn't want his father to feel proud—he had no right.

In any case, now that would never happen. Because eight months ago James Casseveti had died, robbed him of that opportunity. Taken away Luca's chance for... revenge, justice, to ask the questions that had burned his childhood soul.

How could you leave me?
Why won't you see me?
What did I do wrong?

His own pride clicked in as he snapped the second cufflink. Of course, he would not have asked those questions, the idea of his father believing he gave a damn horrific. In any case he knew the answers, at some point he'd figured it out. There must have been something intrinsically wrong with Luca—after all, what parent left a child they truly loved, and then never came back, never so much as called or wrote or sent a postcard? He knew what his mother would say, had said, in fact—that it was nothing to do with Luca, that it was James Casseveti who was wrong. He could picture the fierce look on Therese Petrovelli's face as she said the words and Luca tried to believe her, told himself she was right, but deep down there was the sear of absolute certainty that the blame was his. A knowledge he'd worked to bury. To counter by a determination to show his father that he'd been wrong, that Luca had survived and thrived without him.

But now that couldn't happen and since James' death Luca had found himself in a state he did not recognise. Emotions strove to surface and he wanted none of them; he'd spent his life controlling his emotions, had long ago decided not to give his father the satisfaction of his feeling grief or anger or pain. So he'd subdued those emotions, then honed and focused them into a burning ambition and a desire for revenge.

A desire that had been thwarted and his conflict heightened by the irony of ironies that in death James had done what he hadn't done in life. Reached out to his first family. He'd left Luca and his sister, Jodi, a third share each in Dolci. With the remaining share going to his daughter from his second marriage, Ava Casseveti. A half-sister Luca had never even met, though he had followed her charmed, glittering life in the gossip columns—the life of an heiress-cum-supermodel-cum-businesswoman.

Then a month ago Ava had turned up unannounced to his business headquarters and forced a meeting. And to his surprise and chagrin there had been an instant sense of connection. Plus an admiration that she had gone against all advice and reached out to 'the enemy'. But despite the positivity of the experience Luca retained his natural wariness—instinct told him Ava was on the level, but experience told him to never show blind trust. Ava was James Casseveti's daughter, after all.

Yet here he was in a plush London hotel room, about to attend Ava's engagement party to celebrate her impending marriage to Liam Rourke. When he'd accepted the invitation he'd told himself it was a business decision. Dolci was floundering with the death of its founder and the uncertainty caused by the will. A show of unity would help calm the waters, and whilst a part of him didn't care if Dolci went under, he did care that it would take the livelihoods of many if it did.

But there was another reason he was here: a curiosity about this half-sister of his. For years he'd watched her grace the celebrity pages as an heiress, an aristocrat, and a model, the girl who had replaced him so comprehensively in his father's affections. The child James hadn't deserted. Hadn't left behind to face poverty, to endure the schoolyard bullies who had delighted in taunting the child whose father had 'desserted' him. Even now his fists clenched as he remembered the acrid taste of fear, the writhing sense of self-loathing because he was too weak to fight back. Along with the knowledge that the bullies were right—his father had abandoned him.

The father Luca had adored, looked up to…loved and never seen again. Yet Ava had had James in her life for twenty-seven years; for all her life she'd been loved and wanted. Innate justice told him it wasn't her fault and yet he couldn't help but wonder what did Ava possess that he didn't?

As if on cue there was a knock on the hotel-room door. 'Come in,' he called, even as he knew who it would be.

The door pushed open and—no surprise—Ava walked in, her amber eyes friendly but guarded. No doubt she was here to ensure he really would come downstairs, to attend the party due to start shortly.

Since their one meeting they had communicated by email and in that time Luca had worked hard to diminish any sense of kinship. After all, they might share a father but that did not make them family in a real sense. Luca's family was his mother and his sister and for them he would do anything. Ava was family in name only, by genetic mischance.

'Hey.' They said the word at the same time, and both smiled with the same degree of awkwardness.

Ava stepped forward and again there was the twinge of recognition, a familiarity that made little sense. 'I thought I'd check you were…'

'Here?' he asked, the quip half in earnest. 'I told you I would attend—I do not break my word.'

'Actually, I was going to say OK. I came to see if you were OK. I know you don't particularly want to be here. So I wanted to thank you because it is my engagement party and I want my brother to be here.' Her gaze met his with more than a hint of challenge and against his will he found himself admiring her stance. He knew it took guts to admit that, knew too that she felt deep regret for her father's actions and he wished he knew what to say.

Ava must have sensed his turmoil—not hard as a quick glance at his reflection showed a terrifying scowl etched his face. One he attempted to replace with a rictus of a smile and, perhaps emboldened by this, Ava inhaled deeply and continued. 'I wish Jodi could be here too. Have you heard from her?'

'No.' His voice was clipped as the ever-present worry resurfaced. After James' death Jodi had thrown in her job and gone travelling. At first she had stayed in touch, kept him apprised of her travels through Thailand and India. Had been excited to visit the Indian island of Jalpura, home to the cocoa farm that Palazzo di Cioccolato had recently signed up to provide beans for a new product. Whilst there she'd got involved with the Royal Film Festival held on the same island. But her communications had changed, become briefer and at longer intervals. She'd sounded *different*. Then two months ago she'd said she needed some space and she'd be in touch soon. Whatever that meant. Had made him promise not to try and find her, do anything 'dramatic' or go into 'overprotective overdrive'.

Ava moved a little closer. 'I know you're worried, but Jodi has told you she is OK. Given everything, it's understandable she wants space.'

'Yes.' But Luca knew that wasn't true. Because he knew his sister and this was not like her. To shut him out. Something was going on—he knew it, suspected Jodi was in trouble. But this was nothing to do with Ava. Jodi's feelings about their half-sister were even more ambiguous than his own and so he only told Ava the minimum, just enough to explain why he couldn't make any decisions about what to do about his share in Dolci.

Nodding, he forced a smile to his face. 'I am sure you are right.' Then, wanting to change the subject, 'Thank you for your email with the guest list.' Ava had sent him the list along with details about 'friendly faces'. Something he appreciated but didn't need. Luca had no qualms about his ability to navigate a social gathering, even if it would contain people who didn't like him. People who resented the fact he and Jodi now controlled Dolci. And as he looked at Ava he realised that this woman, the one who had the most right to resent them, didn't. Was actually concerned about his welfare. Almost against his will the knowledge touched him.

'No problem. I thought it would help.'

Luca smiled. 'It will. Do not worry about me, Ava. Enjoy your party, be happy.'

'I am happy.' Now her smile was radiant. 'Truly happy.'

'I'm glad.' And part of him was, though it went against the grain to wish happiness upon this half-sister he did not know how to feel about. If only he could simply decide to hate her, to transfer his anger at his father to this woman. But he couldn't, knew it was not Ava who had done wrong. 'I will see you later. At the party.'

Emily Khatri looked round the glitter of the ballroom, the theme of love clear in the setting. Candles, white flowers intertwined with red, the pop of champagne corks and the background strains of the orchestra. And for a second a tiny taste of bitterness invaded her. Because for a brief period she had believed in love and romance and happy ever after, allowed herself to be deluded, conned into a belief in fairy tales.

Well, no more. Her marriage had been a disaster of epic proportions and had ended in betrayal and misery. Remembered grief over her miscarriage twisted inside her, the grief made even worse by its lateness, at a time when she had believed her baby to be safe, had felt him kick inside her. On instinct she placed a hand over her now flat belly, remembered the swell of pregnancy, and she closed her eyes to ward away the pain as a stab of sadness hit her heart.

A sadness she had borne alongside the sheer humiliation of the discovery during her pregnancy that her husband had been having an affair.

Enough. The all too familiar haunt of guilt threatened. If she and Howard hadn't had a row over his infidelity would she still have lost the baby? Had the miscarriage been caused by the emotional fallout? Been caused by any action of hers? *Not now.* Those questions had hammered at her incessantly. She had spent months in an abyss of misery and despair, one she had slowly and excruciatingly pulled herself out of. This was a happy occasion and she would embrace it. For Ava's sake if not her own, she could and would still be happy for her best friend. Ava literally glowed and there was no way Emily would rain on her parade.

Plus it was time to get her life back together, to try and barricade against the might-have-beens, the gutwrenching knowledge that right now she should be holding her baby in her arms. That was not to be; all she could now do was throw herself back into work.

Though that was proving easier said than done; so far all her efforts had been to no avail and now anxiety threw itself into the emotional churn. Because it seemed as though her marriage to and divorce from Howard had alienated a whole load of people. Howard's pernicious influence made itself felt as people she had believed to be friends avoided her calls and emails. Perhaps she shouldn't be surprised that people had taken Howard's part so readily. Howard, of globally renowned fame, winner of numerous awards and accolades for his hard-hitting photography from all over the world. Howard, presenter of wildly successful documentaries, Howard in talk with Hollywood producers… As such her ex wielded a whole heap of influence, had a network of friends in high places ready to believe him or make excuses for him. And in the aftermath of the miscarriage Emily hadn't cared about anything, had left the field to Howard, who had spun rumours and lies and somehow made himself out to be the hero of the hour, a persecuted husband who had done his best. After that sheer pride had prevented her from even attempting to tell her side of the story; she would not use her miscarriage to garner sympathy.

The only silver lining was that they had never announced her pregnancy—Howard had decreed it to be a private thing. Hadn't wanted it to distract from his imminent book launch, or so he'd said. When there had been speculation in the press he had denied it, without so much as consulting her. Turned out it was because he didn't want the other woman he was sleeping with to find out; he'd been lying to her as well.

Not that she would deign to try to prove that it was Howard who had been the cheat and the liar. She suspected that no one would believe her if she did. Instead she'd decided to somehow put it all behind her and tonight she would try the face-to-face approach, see if she could talk her way into a job.

Yet for a debilitating moment as she looked out at the crowd panic rooted her to the spot, stretched its tendrils round her nerves, caused her heart to pound against her ribcage and her breathing to turn shallow. Oh, God. Not now. Ever since the miscarriage panic assailed her, held her hostage at a whim, but she'd thought she'd tamed it, or at least learnt to hold it at bay.

But this was her first public foray, her first attempt to navigate the real world and she wasn't sure she could manage it. Especially without the comfort of her camera in her hand to hide behind; she missed its familiar shape, the protective mantle of invisibility it threw over her. People tended to only see the lens, not the person behind it, and tonight she hated feeling so visible. *Enough*; she forced herself to move forward, hoped, prayed that if she launched into the fray she would stave off the panic before it took hold. One blind step, straight into the path of a fellow guest.

Instinctively she put out a hand to balance herself, the high-heeled shoes an added liability, and her palm landed on an arm. An arm hard with muscle under the super-soft fabric of his tuxedo.

'Sorry.' She let go, nearly leapt backwards.

'It is I who should apologise. I did not see you behind the pillar.'

As she looked up at the owner of the Italian-tinged voice, *Wow* sprang to the forefront of her brain and flashed in neon. This man was seriously gorgeous. Obsidian-black hair, a little bit overlong with a rebellious spikiness. Silver-grey eyes, a face that demonstrated strength, the nose a broad arrogant jut, the jaw square and determined. His body was solid muscle packed into a beautifully cut tux that moulded to said muscles.

Emily blinked, realised the wow factor had derailed her. Completely. On the plus side the hormonal surge seemed to have also shocked panic into retreat. *Say something.*

'I was just…' *looking at your muscles* '…preparing to enter the fray.' *Really, Emily? Great opener.*

'So this evening is a battle? An ordeal?' There was a hint of amusement in his voice but for a mad moment she also sensed an empathy.

'No. Of course not. I am thrilled to be here to celebrate such a happy occasion.'

'But?'

'There is no but. Or at least… I guess I am a little nervous. I haven't been on the social scene that much recently and…' And now she needed to stop talking. 'Anyway…'

'Let me introduce myself.' The deep Italian-tinged voice sent a trickle of warmth straight through her even as her brain registered its meaning and finally managed to put two and two together. His identity clicked as he held out his hand. 'I am Luca Petrovelli.'

Of course—clearly her brain had turned to mush. The accent should have alerted her as soon as he spoke and, now she knew, she could see some elusive fleeting resemblance to Ava. Though she wasn't sure how or where— Ava was blonde, beautiful and an ex-supermodel. Luca's hair was midnight dark and his face was all lines and planes, his body all muscle. Solid, compact breadth of muscle. There was that word again and this was ridiculous. Her interest in the opposite sex was currently non-existent; her libido had buried itself under layers, strata of misery. Yet this man had poleaxed her. Comprehensively.

And she still hadn't shaken hands. 'I'm Emily.'

Luca's brow creased for a second. 'I know we haven't met, but you look familiar.'

Emily sighed. She was used to this, even when she

omitted giving her surname, as was her wont. People 'knew' her because of her parentage—because she was the daughter of Marigold Turner and Rajiv Khatri. One of the world's most iconic models and a Bollywood film star respectively. Emily was the product of their brief marriage. Clearly brief ill-fated marriages ran in the family. At least on her mother's side. Marigold was currently on husband number five; Emily would have the sense to stop at one. Alternatively, Luca might know her because of Howard.

'It's likely something to do with my parents or maybe my ex.'

As she said the words he snapped his fingers. 'Got it! I visited the Dolci head offices this morning. I think Ava has a photo of you in her collage of photos on the wall.'

Oh. 'Sorry. I am so used to people asking me about my famous parents or what it feels like to have been married to a genius that I assumed that's why you would recognise me.' After all, why else would he?

'In which case, I promise not to ask any of those questions. Tell me instead how you met Ava.' Surprise touched her—Luca wasn't even going to ask who her parents were, though, thinking about it, she supposed it was natural for Luca to ask about Ava. They were siblings, however complicated the situation was.

'A few years ago, back when Ava was a model, I was one of the fashion photographers on her shoot. We just clicked.'

Now he smiled and Emily blinked. The man had already awoken her long dormant hormones—now his smile had them doing aerobics. 'It's good when you just click,' he said, and his voice deepened to a rumble that slid over her skin. Was he flirting? Could she blame him? Somehow, without even noticing, she seemed to have closed the gap between them, was, oh, so close, too close. Near enough that the expensive hint of his soap tickled her nostrils, close enough that she could see the faintest hint of five o'clock shadow, study the thick gloss of his dark hair. And again her thought processes were derailed. Quickly she stepped backward.

'Yes. Yes, it is. What do you think makes people click?' No, no, no. That had come out all wrong. Now it sounded as if *she* were flirting. Was she? What was happening? How and why was this man affecting her so powerfully? She could almost feel more of her hormones yawn and stretch as they woke up for the first time in months. She ploughed on hurriedly. 'With Ava and me, we shared a sense of humour, found it easy to talk to each other, so we grabbed a coffee together and then it snowballed from there.'

'I agree a sense of humour is important and, of course, ease of conversation. For friendship *or* any sort of relationship. Though, of course, other things are important too.'

'Such as?'

'First impressions. A sense of instant connection. In a relationship, mutual attraction.'

'Pah!' The noise somewhere between a snort of derision and a puff of exasperation left her lips and he raised his eyebrows.

'Pah?' he repeated.

'Yes. You are talking about how a person looks.' Her mother had been feted and glorified for her beauty. Men tumbled head over heels for Marigold Turner but it never lasted, no relationship ever made it past the attraction— once reality kicked in they slowly faded away. Yet with every man Marigold waxed lyrical about 'instant attraction', 'magnetic pull' and, of course, 'love at first sight'.

Hell, Emily could date her childhood years by hus-bands' number two to four. At the start of each 'magi-cal romance' Marigold had 'known' this was 'the one' and Emily had been relegated, encouraged to fade to the background of her mother's life. Remembered pain at the sense of isolation, the hurt at knowing she was seen as an obstacle, tingled inside her.

'Darling, I need you to keep out of the way. I don't want Kevin to think you're a nuisance.'

'Sorry, sweetheart, I know I promised I'd read you a bedtime story...come to Sports Day...but Alex is more important.'

Yet when each relationship ended in the slam of the door as each husband left, Marigold would turn to her daughter for solace and comfort and Emily would help pick up the pieces of her mother's shattered heart. Time and again 'instant attraction' had translated to 'later misery'.

Now she glared at Luca. 'Looks don't matter.'

'I disagree. First impressions count. Do you not judge people by the way they dress or the way they cut their hair or…?'

The size of their muscles? asked a small sly inner voice that she shushed instantly.

'Of course, I don't. Because if you get all caught up in that you forget what is important. And that's what is inside. Attraction isn't enough to make a relationship work. Not in the long term.' Her father's second mar-riage was proof of that. Neela was the antithesis to his first wife; she wasn't beautiful, just…ordinary and the marriage had been content. They had five children and she knew her dad was happy. So happy that Emily felt a bit redundant. Someone he'd seen once or twice a year during her childhood, and during those visits Emily had

felt out of place. In the hurly burly rough and tumble of a
real family life, she'd been an invisible outsider, an extra
accorded a politeness due to a guest.

But that was beside the point. 'Attraction is too…
distracting.' Which presumably explained why her gaze
continued to dwell on the breadth of his chest, the lithe
swell of his forearm, the clean strength of his jawline. If
she could kick herself, she would.

Luca watched her carefully and now his lips tipped
up, his grey eyes lit with a hint of amusement. 'A happy
distraction, or a start point—that initial spark is…exhil-
arating.'

'I…' Now their gazes seemed to mesh; her lips went
suddenly dry and it felt as though the edges of the world
fuzzed, to leave only Luca and Emily in the room. Mad-
ness. But, mad or not, she couldn't seem to break free of
the sheer tug of desire that pulled her feet, urged them
to move closer to him. 'I suppose so.'

She forced herself to break the gaze only to find herself focused on his lips, firm, strong and such a defined
shape. She'd never studied the shape of a man's lips before, the contours, never wanted to touch, to smooth her
fingers over a mouth.

Enough. There was going to be no clicking of any kind
going on. 'So,' she said. 'I guess it's time to circulate.'

'To enter the fray,' he said in echo of her earlier words.

'Yes.' Reluctance gripped her and without meaning
to she sighed. Once again she wished she had a camera
with her to render her invisible.

'You have no need to be nervous.' The nerves she'd
alluded to, the nerves that had completely vanished during their conversation. Replaced by the cartwheel of her
hormones, the spark of attraction and the sparkle of an

interesting conversation with an undercurrent of simmer. A happy distraction indeed.

'I think I do. There are a lot of people out there with a preconceived opinion of me, who have already made judgement.' Her voice was imbued with a hint of bitterness as she scanned the room. Recalled the number of people who had already avoided her emails and calls.

'Does it matter?' His tone was serious now. 'Surely the only people whose opinions matter are the people you care about. And who care about you.'

In theory that held good, but, 'You're right. I know you are, but when I see the pity or the judgement in people's faces I...'

'Crumble inside a little?' he offered.

'Yes.' How did Luca know? And how on earth had this conversation with a stranger got so personal? The idea sent unease through her—no way should she be sharing on a personal level with a complete stranger, even if he was Ava's half-brother. In this case *especially* because he was Ava' s half-brother.

'When you feel like that you need to remember it is their problem, not yours. Show them they are wrong. Wrong to pity you and wrong in their judgement.' There was a resonance in his voice and a shadow crossed his features. Then, as if he too sensed that the conversation had edged into deep waters, he shrugged and there came that smile again. 'It also helps to imagine the people you are most worried about making silly faces or dressed in absurd costumes. Or in embarrassing situations.'

'Do you do that?'

'Absolutely.'

Now she chuckled. 'Is that what you are going to do now?' It sounded as if he spoke from experience, yet she couldn't imagine this man being worried by anyone.

'If need be, absolutely. I am sure there are plenty of people out there who have judged me too, as the evil villain, the usurper of the Dolci inheritance.'

'Ava doesn't believe that.' She knew her best friend didn't hold Luca to blame at all.

'Perhaps, perhaps not. But either way I am here to try to help further Dolci business interests. But now I have also had the pleasure of meeting you.' He smiled and held out his hand. 'I wish you luck in the fray.'

'Th…' She placed her hand in his and bit back a small gasp, told herself that electricity could not be generated by touch. Yet she saw an answering awareness flicker in his eyes. Her hand remained in his and for one mad second she wondered if he would kiss it in some quixotic gesture of gallantry. The idea tingled her skin and of their own volition her feet took a step closer to him.

The noise of a throat clearing broke the spell and she pulled away her hand as Luca let go and they turned towards the man who now stood next to them. Emily flushed as she realised she hadn't even noticed his approach.

'Liam,' she said hurriedly as she moved towards Ava's fiancé, kissed him on one cheek and then stood back. She had a lot of time for Liam, knew him to be a good, honourable man who truly loved her best friend. 'It's lovely to see you.'

Was there a glint of speculation in his eyes as he glanced from Luca to her? She could only hope not as she watched the two men shake hands, sensed the wariness in Luca's stance. Knew from Ava that the two men had only met once, that it had been Liam who had taken Luca around Dolci headquarters that morning.

'Ava asked me to tell you her mum has arrived, and

she wondered if you want to get the introductions out of the way sooner rather than later.'

Now Luca's wariness froze into something Emily couldn't identify, though she imagined his feelings could only be negative about Karen Casseveti, the woman who had supplanted his own mother. As for Karen, it was well known that she couldn't stand Luca or his sister, Jodi. So this meeting wouldn't be welcome to either.

'Of course,' Luca said.

'I'll leave you to it…'

'Actually no,' Liam intervened. 'Ava thought it may look more natural if we mingle as a group. If you both don't mind?'

Luca hesitated and then gave a decisive nod. 'That makes sense. If that is OK with Emily.'

'Of course.' Emily knew how good her friend was at orchestrating publicity and managing social occasions. 'I'm happy to help.'

'Then let's go,' Luca said.

CHAPTER TWO

LUCA CONCENTRATED ON keeping his expression neutral; this was a moment he had known would come. The meeting with Ava's mother, the woman who had taken James Casseveti away. It was not Karen Casseveti's fault, he reminded himself; it had been his father's choice to walk away, his father's choice to not even visit his children from his first marriage, to paint them out of his new life. Yet it was impossible not to feel some animosity.

Probably best to focus on something else, or perhaps someone, and a person came all too easily to mind. Emily, the woman at his side. From the minute he'd seen her he'd been a little on edge, a little too aware of her. Too caught up in her smile, the elusive scent, and the ripples of awareness, the undeniable tug and pull of attraction. One he'd do best to douse. Emily was Ava's best friend; that put her strictly out of bounds. It was all complicated enough. But still his curiosity was piqued. Why did she see this crowd as a fray? Why hadn't she been on the social scene for a while?

And in the here and now he could feel the warmth of her body next to him, and somehow it helped as they made their way through the throng of people—Emily's own reluctance to 'enter the fray' made her feel like an ally.

One he was in need of as they approached their destination and anger surged and simmered inside him. *Grow up, Petrovelli.*

Luca tried to remember his own mother's advice. 'Do not show anger or hatred or bitterness, Luca. This woman is much to be pitied right now. She has lost her husband and in truth I am not sure she ever had him.' His mother had shown him the letter she had received on James Casseveti's death, a letter etched on Luca's memory.

Dear Therese,
I am sorry...
    Sorry I behaved as I did.
    Please know I have thought of you every day since I left and never stopped loving you. I know I did wrong, and sometimes I imagine the life we could have had...wonder if I could have started Dolci with you by my side, or whether that even matters.
    I gained wealth and business success but I lost you. As I have grown older I realise that in the end I also lost out. On watching our children grow up, on growing old with a woman I truly love.
    All I can do now is to try and make amends with an apology to you and by leaving Luca and Jodi a legacy.
James

As he'd read the words, he had felt a surge of protective love for her, laced with anger at James. An apology that was too little, too late because Therese had never got over her husband's desertion. She'd tried a few relationships but had never been able to commit. He'd heard her once tell a man that she couldn't put herself, couldn't put her children through the possibility of another break-up.

Not unless she was sure it was really worth it, and she couldn't see that any man was.

Turned out no woman was worth it either. His own first and only love had left him for a man more sophisticated and wealthy than Luca. A repeat of history with a twist. The lesson reinforced: people he loved abandoned him. Wealth and position trumped love. Always. An image of Lydia shimmered into his brain and he banished it. All she had been was proof that love was a crock—nothing was worth that level of pain if you lost it.

Per carità, Luca. Not now, for goodness' sake. This was not the moment to dwell on the past; as the thought crossed his mind he was aware of the gentlest of nudges from next to him. 'You OK?' Emily's voice was whisper thin.

'I'm fine.'

'Good. You've got this.'

He glanced across at her and she smiled and for an instant the word 'arrested' took on new meaning; this woman literally stunned him. Shoulder-length straight hair, near black with a tinge of chestnut highlight, flawless brown skin and eyes with a depth of umber. Her nose gave her face character, her mouth generous. Then even as his brain registered bedazzlement her expression morphed and he blinked as she crossed her eyes and stuck out the tip of her tongue.

His puzzlement switched to instant understanding, her funny face a reminder of his own words from earlier—in a difficult situation imagine whoever is giving you grief pulling a silly face or in an embarrassing position. Now he couldn't help but smile back at her, warmed by her gesture of solidarity and a strange sense of camaraderie, given she didn't even know him.

He braced himself as they approached Ava and Karen;

Ava stood next to her mother and he could see the family likeness, though he could also see an unsettling resemblance in Ava to his sister Jodi. Suddenly he wished Jodi were here by his side, instead of God knew where after her trip to Jalpura. *Not now.* He'd figure out what to do about Jodi later. Plus his sister would hate this gathering with every iota of her being. Edginess lined his gut as he forced his lips into a parody of an upturn.

'Luca, this is my mum, Karen. Mum, this is Luca.'

He managed to keep the smile in place and although he saw the swiftly veiled venom in the older woman's eyes, to her credit her return smile was faultless, before she turned to Emily. 'Hello, Emily. It is good to see you again.'

'And you, Mrs Casseveti. Especially at such a happy occasion.'

'Yes.' The word was said with emphasis, yet the warmth felt cloying in its falsity and he knew that if these were medieval times he would suspect a poisoned chalice at the table.

With that Ava managed to launch the conversation into fashion and Luca swiftly turned to Liam and asked about business, the next ten minutes an orchestration in small talk that successfully minimised contact between Karen and Luca whilst giving the interested guests a show of unity. A necessity to show the world that Dolci was still viable. The knowledge enabled him to play along until finally the strains of the orchestra announced the first dance. Gave them all an out. He turned to Ava. 'Perhaps if you and Liam and Emily and I head to the dance floor together for the first dance it would be a further demonstration of *family* unity.' And if the word 'family' held more than a tint of bitterness he didn't care. Took satisfaction from Karen's barely perceptible wince.

A hesitation and then Ava nodded. 'Good idea,' she said, and the four of them headed to the dance floor as Karen's attention was claimed by another guest.

'I hope this *is* OK,' he said to Emily.

'Of course. I know how important it is to show that you and Ava are working together and I know people are watching.'

'Yes. Absolutely.' Problem was that wasn't actually why he'd suggested it—he'd *wanted* to dance with Emily. Wanted to hold her in his arms, wanted to continue their conversation, find out more about her. The depth of the desire triggered a sense of alarm, as he realised just how much this woman had hit him bang between the eyes. This was not a good idea on many levels. Emily was Ava's best friend; every word he said to her would be filtered back, possibly analysed and discussed. The idea brought his eyebrows together in a frown. Equally he had little doubt that Ava would be super protective of her friend, which would complicate an already complicated situation.

Chill, Luca. He wasn't planning on proposing to Emily—one dance could do no harm. 'So I guess we'd better get on there.'

Doubt widened her dark brown eyes for an instant, almost as if it was only now the real dangers had occurred to her. Before either of them could change their mind he stepped forward and pulled her into his arms.

He held in a gasp, heard Emily's intake of breath and tried to regulate his own breathing. The scent of her shampoo tickled his nose, the span of his hand on her waist, seemed to suck the air from his lungs. The soft silky sheen of her dress, her sheer closeness and warmth played mayhem with his senses as the haunting notes of the melody lingered in the air.

And she felt it too, he knew it, could see it as she lifted her gaze to his, surprise in the depths of her deep brown eyes, her lips rounded in a small circle as she moved a step closer, her body swaying in a natural rhythm with his. Now surprise morphed to awareness and he could see a desire that matched his own. And now his entire focus was on Emily, the two of them lost in the moment, so attuned that they barely even needed the music.

As the dance continued she moved even nearer, her body now, oh, so close, her arms looped round his neck and she looked up at him, lips parted, and he knew he wanted to kiss her, knew she wanted it too and his head spun; every instinct urged him to lower his head and meet her lips. Until a small alarm of self-preservation pealed, told him that if he kissed this woman he would step over the edge of an abyss.

Break this spell, whatever it is.

But how? Somehow he had to inject some form of normalcy, to ward off this insidious desire. 'So you're a photographer?' It was all he could think of to say and his tongue twisted around the words, but he could see the relief on her face that he'd instigated any form of conversation. Even as he could see and empathise with her struggle to formulate an answer, and wondered if, like himself, Emily felt as though she were emerging from a fog of desire.

'Yes.' A pause as she straightened her spine and gave her head a small shake as if to clear her brain. 'Yes. I am. Ready and available.' Now her eyes closed momentarily and she gave a small groan. 'For work, I mean. Obviously. What else could I mean? Don't answer that.' Her inhalation was audible as she moved a little further from him within the movement of the dance. 'I meant

I took a…a sabbatical for a year and a half but now I'm looking for work. Really looking. My plan tonight is to network.'

Luca heard the hesitation, the small catch in her throat when she mentioned a sabbatical, wondered what had made her step away from a successful career path. If she had been involved in Ava's shoots, he had little doubt her credentials would be A grade. His half-sister had graced the cover of the world's top magazines as well as modelled for exclusive brands. Yet Emily had taken time out, and now as she surveyed the crowd of guests he sensed her anxiety was real. 'With the fray?' he asked.

'Exactly.'

'Surely you could contact all your old clients.'

'Yes. But unfortunately it's not that easy.' Her voice was clipped now, and he sensed a simmer of frustration.

'Why not?' It was true that he wasn't supposed to be curious but, hell, curiosity had at least down-notched the attraction factor. Plus he wanted to know what had brought that frown to her brow.

'I am a bit persona non grata in the industry at present.'

As she spoke the music came to an end and Luca guided her off the dance floor as a matter of priority, before he succumbed to the temptation of keeping her in his arms for the next dance. Knew that now was the perfect moment to separate, to say, *Thank you for the dance. I'll let you go and network. Good luck.*

But his brain and his voice had some sort of mix-up and instead he found himself saying, 'Why is that? Why don't we go and sit down and you can tell me? *Then* you can go and network.' Told himself there was no harm to it. In two days he would be on a plane home. Back to Italy. So surely it didn't matter if they helped each other get through a difficult evening. He gestured to a small table partly shielded by a pillar and a luscious large-leaved plant. 'Shall we?'

It was a good question. For the second time Emily hesitated—was this a good idea? *Should they* go and sit together in a secluded corner? After a dance that had nearly caused her to spontaneously combust. Yes, yelled her hormones. But it wasn't only her hormones. It was so long since she had felt attractive, that someone was genuinely interested in her, and the knowledge fizzed adrenalin through her body. Howard had been the master of the understated barb, had an uncanny ability to undermine her confidence, and she'd been on tenterhooks the entire time she was with him. Had despised herself for craving his approval but had found herself desperately seeking it nonetheless.

Tonight for the first time since she had fallen pregnant, lost her baby, gone through the pain of discovering Howard's infidelity and the strain and misery of the divorce, for the first time in month upon month she felt a little lighter.

So perhaps in the here and now she should take a few moments of light with this drop-dead gorgeous stranger. Perhaps she could harness the confidence boost into networking successfully. Perhaps she would even feel better if she explained the situation to someone not involved, someone she wouldn't see again after tonight.

'After you,' she said now and followed him towards the table, allowed her eyes to linger on the breadth of his back, the width of his shoulders, the sheer compact muscular strength of him impossible to ignore.

Once seated she sipped from the glass of champagne he'd taken from a passing waiter.

'So,' he said. 'Tell me what the problem is?'

Emily considered. No way was she telling Luca the whole story. Her grief, the pain, the misery and humiliation were still too raw to share with anyone, let alone a complete stranger who had no reason to give a damn.

'The problem is I married a man who has a huge amount of clout in the magazine and entertainment industry. Our divorce was a bit acrimonious and as a result people are choosing not to employ me, or are ignoring my emails.'

'Who is your ex?'

'Howard McAllister.'

Luca raised his eyebrows. 'I have heard of him. He did a phenomenally successful TV series. My sister loved it.'

'That's him. He has also won numerous photography awards, is in talks with Hollywood about a film and is feted and adored by all and sundry. Hence I am not flavour of the month.'

His frown held a fierceness. 'That does not seem fair. Could you not call people out on this?'

'There is no point. No one has come straight out and said that's why there is no available work for me. They have other plausible reasons: I've been off the scene for too long, my skills aren't quite the fit they need for a particular project, blah blah blah.'

'Could your parents help? You said they are famous—are they part of the fashion industry?'

'I'd rather not get a job just because they demand it for me.' That was matter of principle. All her life she'd loathed being courted or feted simply because of her parents' fame and status—no way would she use that. Emily had vowed from a young age that she would stand on her own two feet, come what may. At some point she had realised that she wasn't necessary to her parents, that they didn't love her in the same way other parents loved their children.

They didn't abuse or dislike her, indeed they were quite fond of her, but both would have been perfectly happy if she had never been born, a reminder of their disastrous brief romance. Marigold Turner didn't have a maternal bone in her body; her primary concern was the pursuit of love and keeping her looks. Her father's priority was his second family, the five children he lived with, the product of a successful union.

So Emily had decided to accept her place in the pecking order, but had also vowed to make her own way in life, find her own niche, without using her parents' fame or wealth. 'Using them seems just as wrong as people not giving me a job because I'm Howard's ex-wife.'

'That is not so. Are you a good photographer? I am assuming you are, given you worked with Ava on a number of shoots.'

Emily opened her mouth to assert that she was good, but the words wouldn't come. Instead an image of Howard flitted across her mind; his voice rang in her head, belittling her portfolio as 'good if you can count that sort of thing as real photography'. Gritting her teeth, she pushed the memory away. Her photography, her career, was one thing she did have, the one area of her life where she could hold her own and her head high. She might never reach the pinnacle of her profession, or transition to serious photography, never have Howard's stature, but, 'I'm good. I worked on shoots for *Theme*, *Star's Market* and *Genie*, all top fashion magazines.'

'Then use what influence you have, use your parents. If you are being discriminated against you should use every weapon you have. All you are doing is fighting fire with fire.'

'Perhaps. But all my life I have been known as the daughter of Marigold Turner and Rajiv Khatri. I will not use my name or their status—I want to stand on my own two feet.'

His whole body stilled. 'Your father is Rajiv Khatri, the Bollywood actor?' An expression she couldn't interpret flitted over his face and she frowned. Usually people were more interested in the fact she was Marigold Turner's daughter.

'Yes. He's a superstar in India, though not that many European people have heard of him.' She tilted her head to one side. 'Obviously you have?'

'Yes.'

She waited but that appeared to be it. Though she sensed he wasn't being rude, just distracted.

'How? Have you seen one of his films?'

'No.' As if realising how abrupt he'd been he shrugged. 'Sorry. It is not a very interesting story. As you may know, I founded a chocolate company, Palazzi di Cioccolato. A year ago I found a new source for cocoa beans. On the Indian island of Jalpura.'

Now she understood. Jalpura hosted a biannual film festival that showcased both Indian and European films. 'My father is pretty popular on Jalpura.'

'Yes.' But somehow she suspected there was more to it than that. 'Has he ever attended the festival?'

'Once, I believe, a few years ago.' She'd read an article about his trip—'Rajiv Khatri and his family attended the festival…' The words had held a barb—he hadn't even asked her, had taken his second wife and their five children. She knew she was being oversensitive—those children lived with him; she had been in her mid-twenties; he would have taken her if she'd asked—but for some reason it still stung. The knowledge she wasn't really family. 'The island looks beautiful, a photographer's dream.'

'It is also a chocolatier's heaven. The cocoa beans were an amazing find—we are about to launch a whole new brand.'

A whole new brand of chocolate; the idea piqued her interest, as did the note of determination and enthusiasm in his voice. 'How does that work? I take it the beans taste different? Make a completely different-tasting chocolate?'

'Well, a potted version is that, yes, different beans do definitely create distinctive tastes—because of climate, processing and sometimes, I believe, the personality of the grower. I may be being whimsical but I always prefer beans grown by people I like, with fair value and work practices and ethos.' He shook his head. 'But that is obviously not even remotely scientific.'

'No, but I think you're right. Creativity and growth come from inside. It sounds like the beans are really important to your brand.' She tucked a strand of hair behind her ear as ideas sparked her professionalism. 'Maybe you should use photos of them in your promotional material. Or have some sort of documentary on your website? About Jalpura—it sounds like a fascinating place. Complete with a royal family—you could even have a fairy-tale theme. Beauty and the Bean'

She stopped, she could almost hear the whir of his brain before he gave a long slow smile. 'You're a genius.'

'I am?'

'You are. Tell me, would you like a job?'

CHAPTER THREE

LUCA BARELY REGISTERED Emily's look of confusion, his brain too busy running with its brilliant plan. Because Emily's suggestion was advertising genius and it had sparked an idea in his head. He could plan an advertising campaign to launch his new brand and shoot it on Jalpura—Emily was right, it was a magical location and the source of the bean that had inspired the chocolate. The campaign also presented him with a legitimate reason for going to Jalpura and whilst there he could discreetly retrace Jodi's footsteps, figure out what had changed his sister and where the hell she was now. So far so good.

And Emily was the perfect person for the job—she had come up with the concept and it made sense for her to run with it, she was immediately available, she had the skills he needed and she needed a job. Plus, as an added bonus, she was the daughter of Rajiv Khatri, Bollywood star, and therefore holder of hero status on Jalpura. If he needed to talk to anyone associated with the Royal Film Festival her name would open every door. But would Emily be willing to do that? She'd been adamant that she didn't like using her name to gain advantage. But this was different—this wasn't to help herself, it was to help Jodi.

The obvious thing to do would be to ask her. Problem

was he knew Jodi would loathe her business being told to anyone. Especially Ava's best friend. Yet the idea of asking Emily to do a job without full disclosure didn't sit well with him.

Belatedly his radar kicked in and he realised that his wannabe travel partner had no idea what he was talking about.

'A job?' she asked. 'What sort of job?'

Luca made a decision. For now he'd leave Jodi out of it. For a start Emily might not even take the job, second he might not need to use her name. Therefore he'd keep the Jodi angle out of it. For now. 'I love the Beauty and the Bean idea and I want to go with it. Shoot the ad campaign on Jalpura. To launch the brand.'

'Just like that?'

'Yup. What do you think?'

'I don't think anything because it makes no sense.' Her voice was tight. 'Why would you offer me a job when you haven't even seen a portfolio of my work? Or a single picture I have taken? When I am a *fashion* photographer?' Emily rose to her feet. 'I am sorry if I gave you the wrong impression, but I am not interested in whatever it is you have in mind.'

Oh, hell. She'd got hold of completely the wrong end of the branch and he couldn't really blame her. Not after the dance and the sizzle of awareness that had pervaded the air since they had laid eyes on each other. Even now he sensed an undercurrent of fizz that her anger simply added to. For an instant he felt an almost visceral tug of regret, that by offering Emily a job he was effectively closing the door on any other type of relationship. No matter. The attraction could never have gone anywhere. Emily was Ava's best friend—it was complicated enough between Ava and himself without adding extra mud to the water. Plus, Emily was just out of a messy divorce and therefore she was way too emotionally vulnerable. And Luca would not risk hurting anyone.

'I understand that this seems a little off the wall and I understand why you're suspicious. But this is a genuine job offer with no strings attached. Not a single one.' Different expressions chased across her face, suspicion still held the upper hand, but she didn't move away and he kept talking. 'I love the idea of an advertising campaign on Jalpura. I'd like to make it happen.'

Her brown eyes narrowed. 'That still doesn't explain why you want to use me as the photographer.'

'Because it's your idea and I like the vision you created. You're looking for work—so why not?'

'So it is nothing to do with...?' Heat touched her cheeks but she held his gaze as she gestured towards the dance floor. Closed her eyes, then reopened them. 'Whatever happened out there.'

'What happened out there was due to a mutual attraction. The click factor, if you will. But that now needs to be clicked off. I would never mix business and pleasure, would never offer anyone a job because I expect some sort of sexual quid pro quo.' The idea caused his lips to press together in distaste. 'If we decide to go ahead with a professional relationship, that is exactly what it would be.'

Emily shook her head; her brown eyes held his, searched them. 'So there is no ulterior motive? Is this some sort of pity thing? Because I explained my situation to you. Or did Ava put you up to this?'

'No one put me up to anything.' Yet the question reminded him anew of how close Emily and Ava were and he knew he needed to be wary of that. Especially when it came to Jodi. But that didn't change the fact he wanted Emily for this job. Instinct told him she'd bring the skills he needed, plus now he had this idea he wanted to run with it and, as she herself had said, she was 'ready and available'. And, of course, there was her name, always assuming she'd agree that he could use it.

'It still doesn't make sense. How can you offer me a job without seeing my work? You may hate it.'

It was a fair point. Instinct and convenience were all very well, but... 'You're right. So let's meet tomorrow. Bring your portfolio and we can discuss it. No strings, no commitment. If I decide you aren't suitable for the job or if you decide it's not for you, then we can both walk away. No hard feelings.'

Her fingers drummed on the table and he could see the trouble in her eyes, then she scanned the room and turned to him. 'OK. When and where?'

'Brunch meeting? At Zelda's? It's a bit off the beaten track. I'll ask for a private table.'

'I'll be there.'

The following day Emily approached the agreed upon venue; anticipation vied with anxiety and she glanced down with trepidation at the portfolio she carried. This whole idea was surreal in the extreme; in fact, the more she thought about it, the more her instincts told her this was a bad, bad idea. Too far out of her comfort zone. She wanted a job that she would find easy, preferably working with people she was familiar with.

But what choice did she have? Her networking last night had been an unmitigated disaster.

Phrases filtered back to her. From the indirect *'So sorry, daahling, but I've just put a new team together.'* To the more direct, *'Sorry, Em, but if you will take eighteen months off to play wifey then you can't expect to waltz back in.'*

Incipient panic threatened yet again and before it could take hold she pushed the door of the restaurant open and entered, scanned the occupants and spotted Luca at a large corner table. Holy Moly. Against all odds the man was even hotter in smart casual than he was in a tux. Shower-damp jet-black hair showed a hint of unruly curl, his shirt sleeves rolled up to show tanned muscular forearms that she had a sudden urge to photograph for posterity. Forced herself not to do just that.

He looked up and smiled and she blinked, wishing he didn't have this unsettling effect on her. She didn't like it, didn't want it; it made her feel uncomfortable that she could be so aware of a man. The very idea had seemed impossible a few months ago and somehow it still felt wrong. A near betrayal that she could feel something as primal as desire when for so long all she had felt was the raw ache of grief for her baby, the dull layer of misery blanketing her from all other emotion.

Not now. All too often the slightest thing could trigger a wave of misery, a surge of panic. But somehow she had to suppress it. Forcing a smile to her face, she walked towards Luca as he rose to greet her, saw those silver-grey eyes scan her face. 'Hey.'

'Hey.'

As she sat he pushed the menu towards her, and she looked down, glad of something to do, to distract from the wave of sadness that was about to wash over her. A part of her wanted to succumb, to allow herself to drown in it, to float in the waves and think of all she had lost, all that her baby would never have.

'Are you OK, Emily?' The concern in his deep Italian-tinged voice was palpable and jolted her to the present.

'I'm fine.'

'If this place is not to your liking, we can go somewhere else.'

'No. It's not that.' The restaurant was lovely, vibrant and busy with the hum of people having a weekend brunch. Friends catching up. Families out on a Sunday.

The kind of place she'd always loved but now somehow seemed wrong, seemed designed to show her what she couldn't have. The sight of every baby, every happy family an emphasis of what she'd lost before she even had it. Did a career even matter compared to the precious life she'd lost? Because deep down she knew it was her own fault. She should have taken more care, not been so blithely confident. She shouldn't have let Howard bully her into hiding her pregnancy, shouldn't have been so intent on trying to make him happy, shouldn't have attended parties, dressed to the nines, in high heels to try and disguise her pregnancy. The sense that she'd somehow jinxed her pregnancy was irrational but unshakeable.

'Emily?' Luca's voice recalled her to the present, reminded her to get a grip. Her career might no longer feel relevant but she needed a job. And she would not let her own personal situation impact on her professionalism any more. If she did this job she would give it her best, however tarnished that might be. 'This is perfect. Truly. I'll have the pancakes. With bacon and maple syrup.'

'Good choice.'

A waitress came and took their order and soon reappeared with their drinks.

Emily sipped the foam of her cappuccino and said, 'So…how would you like to do this?'

'Would you like to show me your portfolio first?'

'Sure.' The idea of displaying her work filled her with a sudden sharp surge of dread, and frustration filled her. What was wrong with her? Two years ago she'd been an up-and-coming fashion photographer. The stuff in her portfolio was excellent and she knew it. Or at least she had known it once, before Howard's ongoing critiques had dulled the gloss of her pictures, distorted the way she saw her work. Picking up the slim folder, she handed it across the table, tried not to let her gaze linger on the strong shape of his hand, the deft, competent grip of his fingers. Photographer's eye, she told herself. Or an over-reaction due to nerves. 'I've brought a small printed port-folio and I'll show you a digital gallery as well.'

As he opened the leather-bound binder, she couldn't watch, almost didn't want to see his reaction, busied her-self with booting up her netbook.

Finally she knew she couldn't stare at the screen any more so she looked up and across at him. Saw the binder still open, though his gaze was now on her.

'Obviously, as I said, I am a fashion photographer, so my portfolio mostly consists of examples of fashion photography. I did include a couple of still-life pictures I did for a National Trust campaign. But I do think you should consider taking on someone with more experi-ence of commercial photography.'

What? What are you doing, Emily? Talking yourself out of the job? Pressing her lips together, she focused on not talking. At all.

'I appreciate your honesty and I get it's a risk but it's one I'm willing to take.' And again Emily wondered what was going on, why he was so set on employing her with-out even considering anyone else. She was sure it wasn't anything to do with the latent smoulder of attraction that had sparked the previous night; she'd believed his asser-tion that he would never mix business and pleasure. Yet instinct, finely honed instinct, still warned her there was something else. Some reason he wanted to move so fast.

'Why? Why would you take that risk?'

'Your photos show vibrancy and flair and original-ity. I love how you use shape and colour and background effect. Plus the two different pictures of Ava showcase how you can use the same model to portray completely different things.'

The sincerity in his voice was evident and relief swathed her; the job wasn't a sinecure. He'd studied the pictures and grasped what she'd tried to do and he liked it. The knowledge sparked a small, unfamiliar surge of confidence. 'Ava was a great model to work with.'

'Yes. But the idea, the lighting, the captured image is down to you. In the perfume ad you have conveyed the essence of flowers and lightness in a way that's difficult to explain—but it works.'

Emily frowned; she had been particularly proud of that photograph, yet it was one that Howard had targeted as frivolous and dismissed as cutesy. And she'd accepted that criticism as just, but now, as she looked at it again, her frown deepened.

'I would like to know how you did it.'

'The original plan was to have Ava sitting in a meadow of flowers with the sun shining down on her, but that seemed a little too clichéd. So I persuaded the director to give my idea a go. To be subtler.' She'd kept it simple, Ava bathed in the light of a setting sun, wearing a floaty summery dress, a circlet of flowers in her hair and a daisy chain around her wrist. Looking almost ethereal.

As she spoke she remembered the person she had been then: a woman confident in herself and her ideas, happy to offer her thoughts and opinions. A woman who'd be-lieved in herself. Where had that Emily gone? Right now she truly didn't know. Somewhere along the way her faith in herself had seeped away—but as she studied the photo, listened to Luca's words, she could feel a small trickle of pride.

He nodded. 'It worked. Perfectly. And it encapsulates what I want for my campaign. Something that captures the essence of my chocolate and where it comes from. You somehow made the viewer want to smell like the perfume. I need you to make the viewer want to taste my chocolate. Can you do it?'

The questions preceded the arrival of their food and as the waiter busied himself with serving their pancakes and refilling the coffees it gave her time to think. As she did so her mind began to play with ideas, a familiar spark that she hadn't felt for a long time. Brought on by having her work valued. By someone uninfluenced by Howard or by past association of any sort.

And so, once the waiter had left, she leant forward and said, 'I don't know if I can do it and that's the truth. But I'd like to try.' She picked up her knife and fork. 'Let me see if I can come up with an idea.'

'Is there anything I can do to help?'

Emily took a mouthful of pancake as she considered. 'I need more information.' She glanced at him. 'I know this may sound nuts but I need to know about Palazzo di Cioccolato, about your company ethos, about all your chocolate and, of course, as much as possible about this particular chocolate. When I did this ad I spoke to the perfumier who created it. I knew absolutely everything there was to know about that perfume. The circlet of flowers in Ava's hair was made up of the flowers in the scent itself. But I also wore the perfume myself, spoke to people who wore it. Got my friends to wear it...'

There was a silence and she wondered if she'd blown it. 'Sorry. There was no need for you to know any of that. Give me a few days and I'll get back to you with an idea.'

'No need to apologise. I like your enthusiasm.' His voice was deep and there was something in his silver-grey eyes, a warmth that heated up her insides, a balm to her soul lacerated by Howard's put-downs. 'And it obviously gets results. So I am happy to provide you with as much company information as you need. How about I start with an overview? In terms of ethos I always try to use the best ingredients possible—no hidden rubbish. I want my product to be affordable, but I won't compete with supersize mass-produced products. I know it is possible to buy a huge bar of chocolate for a low cost. I'd prefer people to choose to spend the same amount for a smaller bar because it's worth it. I see chocolate as something to be savoured, a luxury, a treat that is worth looking forward to, spending time on.'

His words held a depth and a tone that seemed to epitomise the chocolate itself, and Emily was sucked in by the words, and his sheer charisma, the delicious sexiness of a man speaking of chocolate with such appreciation. She cleared her throat. 'Sounds good. What about the new range?'

'I want this to be a little different, an experiment with fruit and spices. I want it to feel decadent and new. I've spent the past year tasting, mixing, thinking, tasting again, sourcing… I am hoping this will be a major player in the premium chocolate market.'

Decadent and new…the deep rumble of those words sent a sudden rush over her skin, the animation in his voice, the fact that he got so involved. Her gaze lingered on his hands as she pictured him intent over the recipe, stirring, tasting, and now her eyes moved to his lips and she pictured him tasting the chocolate. Jeez. Get a grip. Think.

'That's all great,' she managed. 'That gives me a real feel for what you represent.'

'Good. So what do you think about the project? Are you interested?'

The questions seemed to take on too much meaning.

Her gaze kept returning to the lithe muscle of his forearm, the way his shirt glided over the breadth of his chest, the allure of his eyes, the jut of a nose that proclaimed both confidence and arrogance. But it was also his aura—there was something powerful and scary about his air of contained energy, the feeling that he was a man on a mission, a man who would carry out his agenda whatever that might be. A man who most likely didn't suffer fools gladly, and a momentary doubt struck her. She questioned whether she had the strength to take that on, risk being assessed and found wanting. Again.

Throughout her marriage with Howard she had tried so hard to win his praise for her work, had wanted so much to prove she had the talent to move into a different sphere of photography. To no avail—in the end she'd had to accept she simply wasn't good enough, and somehow that had transcended so her belief in herself had been diminished. And now the pressure to succeed, to fulfil Luca's unexpected belief in her, felt almost too much. Almost.

Because she would not give in, would not return to the despair of the past months, despite the temptation, the enticement of cocooning herself from the world because it made her feel closer to her baby.

Not happening, because the world had intruded in its reality, the ping of unpaid bills arriving in her inbox. She needed a job—the alternative would be to turn to her parents for help. The idea was unacceptable.

Perhaps they would help, but they hadn't thought to offer. Had given her practically no emotional support throughout the past months. For her mother infidelity and divorce, smashed dreams and the failure of love were the norm. As for the miscarriage, for Marigold, a woman who had never wanted a family, she simply didn't get it. She had tried—descended on the flat with expensive gifts, wine, chocolate and flowers—and in truth Emily had appreciated the gesture, accepted it was the best her mother could do. Her father had called her a couple of times, expressed his sympathy, the conversation full of encouragement about how he knew Emily would move on. 'Other fish in the sea.' 'So many women have a miscarriage and go on to have many children.' And Emily had concurred—knew that her father too was doing his best. But then, duty done, her parents had both gone back to their normal lives.

And that was the point: she was peripheral to their lives, and as such her independence was a matter of pride to her. She would never ask for anything, just accept what they could give.

So now, she met Luca's gaze and nodded. 'Yes. I'm interested.'

'Excellent.' He sipped his coffee, drummed his fingers on the table top. 'I've got an idea.'

Emily glanced at him, wondered if she could deal with any more of Luca's ideas, sensed that this one would be another humdinger. 'What's that?' she asked as trepidation prickled her spine.

CHAPTER FOUR

LUCA DID ONE last quick recap of the pros and cons and then, 'It's a way for you to learn more about Palazzo di Cioccolato. Come back to Turin with me tomorrow and I'll give you a tour of the factory and headquarters. I really like the way you immerse yourself in everything to do with the product and I think the best way to get a real feel for the business is to see it for yourself.'

Emily put her coffee cup down with a sudden *thunk*. 'Tomorrow?'

'Why not?' Now he had a plan, he *wanted* to move fast, wanted to find his sister. Because whilst Jodi was a grown woman, and more than capable of looking after herself…he was her big brother and part of his job, his role in life, was to look after her. Ever since his father had walked out Luca had vowed, sworn to himself, that he would be the man of the family. And when, seven months after his dad had gone, Jodi had been born, a deep, deep protectiveness had come over him. A sense of responsibility so profound he could still remember the weight of the mantle he'd gladly accepted. So right now he couldn't see any reason to wait. 'My idea is we spend a couple of days in Italy and then head straight to Jalpura from there.'

Now Emily stared at him, her brown eyes wide, and

he suspected she was evaluating his sanity levels. 'Whoa. Hang on a minute. How exactly is this going to work?' Emily raised her hands in a gesture that conveyed bafflement and he couldn't help but note the fluid grace of her movements. His gaze lingered on the elegant shape of her fingers, the supple delicacy of her wrists. *Focus, Luca.* 'Do you know how an ad campaign works?'

'Of course, I do.' He shrugged. 'Well, maybe not the detail. I have an agency that usually deals with that.'

'Well, I am not an expert, but I do know how to do a photo shoot. Usually I work with a production company. You need to do a massive amount of research, decide on the campaign and how it would work. We need to find a location, a model or more than one model. Once we find that we need to figure out clothing, we need a stylist, a make-up artist, someone to make the location look right, a lighting expert. I can't just go to Jalpura and pluck a person out of thin air, hand them a bar of chocolate and take a photo.'

'I get that.' And he did—realised he hadn't fully thought this through. 'This trip to Jalpura would be preliminary, a research trip, to give you some ideas.'

Her eyes narrowed. 'Why do I get the feeling you made all that up on the spot?'

'Does it matter if I did? I want to run with this.'

'Enough that you want to drop everything to research an ad campaign yourself that you only thought of yesterday.'

'Yes. There is no point in wasting time once a decision is made.'

'But why? Surely you have a marketing director or someone else who would usually do this.'

'I do. But I'm also a hands-on CEO. I work across all departments. I do stints in packaging, delivery, tasting, everything. Otherwise I think it's too easy to get distanced from reality. I want to produce chocolate for everyone and for me to do that I need to understand every facet of my business. I don't want to end up consumed only by admin and spreadsheets and profit margins.' All true. 'This feels right—I want to get it done. Yes, obviously, I have some stuff scheduled but I have a very efficient team of people and I can manage to be away for a few days.' He paused. 'Though we'll need to sort out a visa for you. Mine is still valid from my last visit.'

'I have a valid visa already. I got a five-year one that hasn't run out as yet.' He could hear reluctance in the admission.

'So how does this sound? We head to Turin tomorrow afternoon. Next day the factory tour, after that we fly to Jalpura. Stay there a few days and we'll be back in a week.'

'A week?' There was a small catch in her voice, her brown eyes wide with doubt, her upper lip caught in her teeth. His eyes lingered and caught on her mouth, before he wrenched his gaze away, stared into the dregs of his espresso and tried to dismiss a sudden niggle of doubt. A week with Emily. Seven days, seven nights... With a woman who impacted him in a way he didn't understand.

His glib words of the previous night mocked him. *Instant connection, mutual attraction, click factor.* It was all that and more.

Resolutely he stopped the thoughts in their tracks. The die was cast and once this had become professional the attraction factor was irrelevant.

'A week,' he repeated firmly. 'That should be enough.'

More than enough. He wasn't sure if she'd actually said the words or he'd imagined them. 'OK.' She nodded and he sensed she was trying to convince herself. 'It's not as though we will be spending every minute together. I'll get on with my own thing; I don't need hand-holding.'

His gaze dropped to study her hands, the slender length, the short unpainted nails, the faint line where her wedding ring had once been. *Stop looking.* But as he wrenched his eyes away he saw that Emily's gaze loitered on *his* hands, her eyes wide. She pressed her lips together as if to moisten them and desire gave a fierce tug in his gut.

Sufficientemente. Enough, Petrovelli. Professional, remember?

'Excellent, as I don't plan to hold your hand.' The words were too harsh and he did his best to smile. 'Because you won't need me to—I trust you to get on with it. So, do we have a deal? I propose to pay you a flat fee of five thousand pounds for this week and all expenses paid. After that you can invoice me for the hours you put in.'

A silence and he'd give a lot to know what was going through her head. Then she nodded. 'That sounds more than fair. We have a deal.'

Relief mixed with satisfaction—Mission Jalpura was on. Which meant perhaps now was a good time to tell Emily about Jodi, ask her if she would be willing to use her name to help him in his search. But the words wouldn't come; instead an image of his sister filled his mind. Dark curls, fierce-eyed. And the words of their last conversation.

'Please, Luca, let it be. I am OK, I just need to figure some stuff out and to do that I need space and time.'

'But—'

'No buts, Luca. This is my business, not yours. I appreciate your concern, but please leave it be. No big-brother stuff. My business, OK? Got it?'

Her lips had turned up in a smile as she'd said the words, but the underlay of seriousness had been clear.

It was Jodi's business and he'd done his best to stand by his sister's request. Had held back, done nothing, but now he couldn't do that any more, not when he sensed there was something wrong, that Jodi needed help. And this opportunity to take action had come along. But if Jodi didn't want to confide in Luca or Therese, she'd definitely recoil at the thought of Emily knowing anything. In which case he owed it to Jodi to try and find the answers on his own; he'd bring Emily in only if he needed to. So there was no need to tell her anything now. For a second discomfort edged him and he dismissed it. He'd tell Emily if and only if it became necessary; in the meantime, he was employing her to do a genuine job.

'Great. I'll get a contract drawn up.'

She held her hand out and he hesitated, told himself not to be an idiot. What did he think would happen if he shook her hand? He'd combust? His hand would light up? He reached out and took her hand in his, resisted the urge to instantly drop it. Because the simple touch did affect him, pulled back the memory of their dance yesterday, enough to conjure desire right back up.

Dropping her hand, he cleared his throat. 'Right. I'll try and get you on the same flight.' He pulled his phone out of his pocket and a few minutes later nodded. 'As luck would have it there is a seat free. We can travel together. Can you meet me in the first-class lounge tomorrow afternoon?'

'I'll be there.' Emily's voice seemed taut and, in all truth, Luca couldn't blame her.

Emily walked through the busy airport lounge, pulling her suitcase behind her, gripping the handle so hard it hurt as she battled the sense of surreal. Until now she'd focused on packing, on getting here on time, but, now that she had made it, as she approached the meeting point her nerves fluttered and she tightened her muscles to counteract them, felt the insidious flick of panic.

She braced herself against the fear that she *couldn't* do this job. Somehow when she'd been with Luca it had all seemed possible. The ideas had buzzed, caught up in his own clear enthusiasm for the project and his equally clear strength of feeling for the product and for his company. This man would expect the best, deserved the best, and now all of Howard's jibes rang and danced in her brain, told her she'd bitten off more than she could chew.

Emily gritted her teeth. This was the only job on offer. Striding forward, she raised an arm in greeting, forced herself to project a confidence she didn't even feel a flicker of.

'Hey.'

'Hey.'

'Shall we head to the departure lounge? We've time to grab a coffee before boarding.'

'Sure.' But she could feel her steps lag as they started to walk, as the flutter of nerves turned into a pirouette. For the past months she had spent nigh on every waking and sleeping minute in the sanctuary of her home. Now here she was about to embark on a global trip. And now the panic began to build, to twist and layer itself into knots of tension that tangled inside her.

She tried to focus, found her gaze riveted to Luca and decided to give in and be shallow in the hope his sheer aura would exert a soothing calm. So as they walked she studied him as she would a model, the jut of his jaw, the swell of his biceps and the tantalising strength he exuded. The kind of strength that would blanket and cocoon you in safety. And, politically correct or not, that carried her through the process of boarding, finding their seats and getting settled. Allowed her to try and suppress the growing, escalating swoosh and whoosh and pound of irrational dread.

Until the flight actually took off and the anxiety whirled in her head, turned and twisted her stomach in a nauseating spin. Closing her eyes, she concentrated on her breathing, on slowing her pulse rate.

'You OK?' Luca turned to her and she tried to speak, her hands gripping the arm rest as she forced her vocal cords to work.

'Fine.' The syllable sounded strangled but she hoped it would be enough.

'Hey. It's OK.' His deep voice held concern but also a calm reassurance that at least didn't escalate the numbing fear that had sent her fight-or-flight response into dead-lock. 'I'm guessing you have a fear of flying.'

It was a fair assumption but not true; this was a panic attack, brought on by the inescapable knowledge that she was heading away from the sanctuary of home, co-alesced with the sudden realisation and guilt that she had taken this first step to moving on with life. All she wanted was to go back home, to the almost comfort of the abyss of despair that kept her close to her lost baby. What was she doing? How could she move on from him, the being whom she had loved so much?

None of this was anything she could or would share with Luca, even if she could speak, which right now she couldn't. All her effort was concentrated on staying put, and not running up and down the plane in an attempt to get out.

He continued to speak, his tone soothing and almost conversational. 'Jodi used to be terrified on planes—

NINA MILNE 55

she'd hold my hand as tight as she could during take-off. She said it helped, stopped her from running to the pilot and begging him to take the plane down. We can try that, if you like.'

And so she gripped his hand, with all her might, focused on the cool reassuring strength of his grasp, the scope of his palm, the feel of his fingers encircling hers, closed her eyes and tried to think soothing thoughts. Time seemed to slow and ebb, but slowly the wave of panic stemmed and then subsided, as if his touch somehow soothed the tangle of chaos inside. Unknotted her insides and now, instead of panic, a different sensation pervaded with a gooey warmth, invaded her veins with a liquid heat. Now his hold encircled her with awareness, charged her with desire and she released him as tell-tale heat flushed her cheeks.

A sideways glance revealed an expression of shock flitting across his face as he looked down at his hand and she wondered if he'd felt something too.

Quickly she burst into speech. 'Well, that was embarrassing. Especially when I said I didn't need hand-holding.' She tried a smile, hoped it didn't wobble too much and he smiled back, the smile full wattage, and it curled her toes.

'Don't worry about it. Truly. How are you feeling now?'

'A lot better. Thank you—I didn't hurt you, did I?' She studied his hand and again a frisson ran through her; his fingers combined strength with a masculine beauty that fascinated her, the breadth of his palm, the compact sturdiness of his wrist. This had to stop. All she could think was that this was some sort of aftershock, a reaction to her panic, but her awareness of the man next to her had grown exponentially.

Her gaze roved upwards; she saw the shape of his tanned forearm, the curve of his biceps, the width of his shoulder. Continued to take in his face, the angle of his cheekbone, the jut of his determined jaw and now her eyes lingered on the shape of his mouth.

Oh, God. As she forced herself to meet his gaze she saw something in his expression, a spark, and she sensed he had clocked and understood her scrutiny.

'No. You did not hurt me at all. Please feel free to make use of my hand again.' The deep undertone had a layer of suggestion, just the smallest hint of a double entendre, and she looked at him with a small question of wonder. Had she imagined it?

'Thank you. But I think I'll be OK.'

'Do you often suffer from a fear of flying?'

'No.' Realising the abruptness of the answer, Emily wished she had simply claimed that as the reason. 'This is the first time so hopefully it's a one-off. Plus, the prospect of seeing Turin cancels any panic.'

For a moment she thought he'd pursue the topic but instead he clearly decided to accept her disinclination to discuss the issue further. 'Have you been to Turin before?'

'No, but I am looking forward to it. I haven't had a chance to do a lot of research, but I do know that it is meant to be an amazing place. Full of history and tradition.'

'It is. Turin has a real sense of tradition and the past. It is also, of course, the capital of chocolate. The very first chocolate bar originated in Turin. And in 1678 the Queen of Savoy granted a chocolate maker from Turin a licence to open the first chocolate house, so like a tea or coffee house today. And today the Piedmont region produces about eighty-five thousand tons of chocolate a year.' He came to a stop. 'Listen to me. I sound like a tour guide.'

Emily shook her head. 'You sound like someone who is very proud of their city. A city that sounds like chocolate heaven. I'll make sure I make time to look round, get some photos. I can see that Turin itself is important to the essence of your chocolate and I think we need to get that idea in somehow, even though we will be shooting in Jalpura.'

He hesitated. 'If you would like I could take you around Turin, if that would help.'

A thrill of anticipation shot through her, one she quelled instantly. This was work related, nothing more. 'That would be wonderful, and it will really help to see Turin through your eyes.'

'Then I'd be happy to be your guide. We can start tonight. I'll pick you up from your hotel at seven.'

'Perfect. Thank you.' There was that sense of looking forward. Again. And she hadn't even noticed that the plane had begun its descent.

CHAPTER FIVE

EMILY GLANCED AT her watch: five minutes to seven. She surveyed her reflection in the hotel mirror, reminded herself she was done with dressing for a man. Any man. Before Howard she'd never dressed to be noticed, had preferred to blend into whatever scenario she found herself. Knew that as a photographer it made sense to be as invisible as possible and Emily was good at that. Invisibility was her watchword. Much of her childhood had been spent relegating herself to the background, tiptoeing around her mother and the man de jour. As she'd got older she'd disliked being feted because of her famous parents. So she'd learnt to dress to not be noticed.

Until Howard. Once she'd met him somehow she'd ended up dressing to please him.

'How you look reflects on me. I need you to be beautiful, elegant, poised and attractive...'

'Emily, sweetie, of course I love you for you, but I am a photographer—I need to be surrounded by beauty and I have an image to uphold. My wife cannot be a dowd.'

And somehow Howard had started to dictate her wardrobe and from there it had descended into snide criticisms and put-downs if she had so much as a hair out of place. Worse perhaps had been his habit of studying her and then emitting a small frustrated sigh, a shake of his head and then, 'Honestly, Em. Why can't you ever get it right?'

Never again would she dress for a man, so she should be happy with her appearance tonight. Smart casual black trousers and a plain demure button-up blouse with a collar, complemented by a pair of boring but serviceable, smart black pumps. Hair pulled up into a businesslike bun. Professional, boring and invisible. Perfect.

So why did she look so glum? Why was she wishing she'd packed a dress from the Howard era? Why was her hand hovering over her make-up? Why did her fingers itch to pull her hair loose?

The answer was obvious—dark haired, gorgeous, as sinful as the chocolate he created, Luca Petrovelli. Which was ridiculous. But something had happened on the plane—perhaps it was his instinctive ability to ward off her panic without belittling it as Howard would have. Or his clear enthusiasm and love for his home city. Or perhaps it was the thought of a night out, a chance to see a city she'd never seen, guided by a man who had succeeded in waking her hormones from a sleep she'd believed to be permanent.

Whatever it was it was time to go; one last glance in the mirror and she headed for the door. Reminded herself that this was a business meeting, a chance for her to work out how to incorporate elements of Turin into the ad campaign. And get to know the founder of Palazzo di Cioccolato better.

She scooped up a lightweight jacket and headed out of the elegant hotel room. As she entered the marble lobby she saw Luca by the front desk and her heart skipped a beat. He looked positively scrumptious—black hair, shower-damp and spiky. Shirt and chinos and a jacket hooked on one finger over his shoulder—he could have stepped out of a glossy magazine. In fact her fingers itched to capture the image. Itched to do way more than that—the tantalising V of his chest made her head spin and she forced her feet to maintain a steady pace towards him. Even as she fought the urge to race past him, find a boutique, buy a dress and transform herself.

Really, Emily? Shallow, much.

'Buonasera.' The timbre of his voice washed over her as he smiled at her. 'I hope the hotel is OK?'

'It's wonderful. The room is beautiful and it's got a marvellous view of Turin.'

'Good. I plan to show you the sights a little more personally. I thought we could walk the streets for a little, then I will take you to Silvio's, a cocktail bar where I used to work. They do the best cocktails in Turin and the food is pretty good too.'

'That sounds lovely.' She couldn't remember the last time she'd gone out for cocktails and dinner and the idea filled her with an unbidden sense of excitement. 'So tell me about your cocktail-shaking skills.'

'I am a pro. I can make a martini shaken or stirred. I invented at least three pretty brilliant mixes. Silvio still serves them today.' Emily suspected that whatever Luca turned his mind to he would be the best at, the knowledge both potent and ever so slightly intimidating. After all, Howard had been excellent at what he'd done and it had made him both arrogant and cranky. *Stop.* Tonight she didn't want her ex-husband to intrude—instead she wanted to try to enjoy this evening. The idea was a novel one, brought about by being in a new place, the scent of Italy…the buzz of a different language around her.

As they stepped out into the balmy air Emily inhaled. 'I love the smell of Italy.' Though truth be told she'd swear she could also catch Luca's scent, a crisp, deep note of bergamot and citrus that added to the sudden heady feeling. This unfurling of enjoyment had been absent for too long and she suspected it would be a short-lived burst before the shadows set back in. For a moment the rawness of grief and loss cast a darkness; it shouldn't be like this. She should be home, with her baby, celebrating the milestones: a first tooth, a smile…all things her baby hadn't had the chance to experience. *Not now.* Instead she pulled in air, refocused on the smell and the sights around her, allowed them to create a bubble that insulated her from the might-have-beens.

Luca's gaze rested on her face and she saw the dawn of concern and knew she must head it off. 'I can smell garlic and oregano and chocolate.'

'My chocolate in particular, of course.'

'Of course.' She returned his smile. 'It must feel amazing to be part of Turin's history. Part of how chocolate has evolved through the years.'

He looked struck. 'I'm not sure I ever thought about it like that. Thank you.' His smile was genuine and he looked absurdly youthful and it touched her even as she wondered how he did see himself.

Absurd shyness overcame her and she took refuge in what she knew best. 'Would you mind if I take pictures as we walk?' The camera was her equivalent of a safety blanket.

'Of course.'

As they walked she looked round, snapped away, took in the wide tree-lined boulevards, the buildings of varying sizes and shapes that oozed history and colour. Elegant gardens vied for attention with a proliferation of formal beds that looked centuries old.

Luca seemed content to walk beside her, occasionally pointing out a place of interest.

Until, 'We're here. This is Silvio's.' Emily gazed around at the square, absorbed the sheer feel of the history of the buildings, shops and cafés. In the middle was a church, an architectural mix of bell tower, walls, domes and a neo-classical face that combined to create an awe-inspiring awareness of how long people had worshipped here.

Following her gaze, Luca said, 'This is one of Turin's most loved places of worship; it has been added to over the centuries and is said to be a place of healing.'

'It's beautiful,' Emily said softly. 'It all is.'

Luca nodded towards a small café. 'That has been there since the mid-seventeen-hundreds. We should come here tomorrow for a cup of *bicerin*.'

'I'd like that. Layers of espresso, chocolate and milk, right?'

'Right.'

She smiled at him. 'It's a date.' The words seemed to echo softly round the square and she hastened to clarify. 'Not a real date, obviously. Just a business date.'

'Of course.' His voice was smooth but laced with amusement and she felt heat flush her face. 'Shall we go in?'

Luca looked round the familiar, eclectic interior of the bar he had worked in for years. The walls were a vibrant blue, and empty bottles were suspended from the ceiling in an eye watering zigzag display. Small mosaic-topped tables were scattered over the wooden floor, the air hummed with conversation, and the scents of fruit and food and a sheer vibrancy that always gave him a buzz.

'Luca.' The waist-coated man moved from behind the bar arms outstretched and Luca moved forward, clasped hands and exchanged a hug before turning to Emily.

'Emily, this is Matteo, my old manager.'

'Your old boss,' the Italian corrected with a beaming smile.

'Matteo, this is Emily Khatri, a business colleague, here to get some photographic inspiration on Turin.'

'Enchanted to meet you.' Luca saw the appreciation in his old friend's eyes as they rested on Emily and felt a sudden absurd stab of emotion. Whoa. What was that? Jealousy? That was both irrational and ridiculous. Emily was not the type of woman he would enter into a relationship with; she was just out of a relationship, she was clearly vulnerable, she had got married, which implied she believed in the fallacy of love and, as icing on the proverbial panettone, she was Ava's best friend. In other words, he had no claim on her whatsoever, yet a stab of irritation jabbed him as Matteo smiled at Emily and engaged her in a flirtatious conversation.

Luca gave his head a small shake. He knew exactly how negative an emotion jealousy was—it had been the downfall of his first relationship. He had been so terrified Lydia would leave him he had smothered her in love, hated it when she so much as looked at another man. Ironically enough, in the end, she had left him for another man. A rich, handsome, charming man who 'knew how to have fun'. Just as his father had left him for a rich, aristocratic woman who had financed his path to success. The parallels were impossible to ignore and he'd learnt a lesson he would never forget. Do not get involved; if you don't feel love, you can't fear its loss, can't let that fear generate negative emotions, take over your every waking moment with dread of the inevitable. Even better, you couldn't experience the pain of loss when the inevitable happened. As it inescapably would.

Never again. And in truth, since Lydia, no woman had

ignited so much as the smallest spark of jealousy—he'd always been in control of his liaisons. Luca shook his head. Jealousy was a mire of negativity that would have no place at his table. Certainly not now. Matteo was one of his dearest friends. And Emily was a business colleague. And if for some inexplicable reason attraction was distorting into feelings of jealousy it was time to rein the attraction in. Fast.

They were both looking at him. 'Is all well, Luca?' Matteo asked and he'd swear he saw a smile lurk in his friend's eyes.

'Yes. Sorry.' He pulled a smile to his face. 'I was daydreaming about my many hours behind the bar.' Now he turned to Emily. 'Have you chosen a cocktail?'

'Not yet. I was going to see if I could have one of your signature ones.'

'Better yet,' Matteo said. 'Why don't you mix it, Luca? Show Emily how it is done. You are both welcome behind the bar. In the meantime, I had better serve some customers.' He waved a hand to one of the other staff. 'Keep a table for Luca.' He smiled at Emily. 'It will be good, I promise. Luca was the best in the business.'

As Matteo moved away Luca knew how foolish he'd been. Presumably the misplaced jealousy was simply another symptom of his current emotional state—a state he *would* supress. As he would suppress this attraction. Yet he sensed perspiration form on the back of his neck as he eyed the somewhat small space behind the bar. Forcing his jaw to unclench, he managed a smile as he gestured to the area. 'Come, I will show you how to make *martini cioccolato di Luca*.'

'Luca's chocolate martini?' she asked, with the faintest gurgle of laughter.

'It sounds better in Italian,' he conceded. 'Try it.'

She repeated the Italian words and then grimaced. 'I sound ridiculous. I have no aptitude for language.'

'You need to say it with more emphasis, make each syllable more dramatic, more passionate. *Martini cioccolaaato.*' His over-emphasis brought a smile to her face and he felt ridiculously pleased. 'You have a go.'

'*Martini cioccolaaato.*' She stopped and gave a small delicious chuckle. 'Like that?'

'Excellent. Now come, let us get started.' He paused. 'As long as you are sure you would like this particular cocktail. It is a little decadent—a bit like having dessert before your main course.'

'I can do that,' she said. 'In fact, I'd like to do that.'

'Sometimes it is good to do something a little bit sinful.' The words fell from his lips without intent, as if his vocal cords had been taken hostage. Created a shimmer of awareness, carried on the waves of noise and chatter and the clink of glass.

'Then let's get started.' Her words were low as her breath caught.

He led the way behind the bar, to a secluded corner, and now he was, oh, so aware of her proximity, the scent of her vanilla shampoo, and a subtle refreshing hint of her perfume. *Keep it together.* 'Have you ever shaken a cocktail before?'

Emily shook her head. 'Nope. And I feel I should warn you now that my culinary skills are not particularly good.'

'No worries. I'll run over the basics. Then just copy what I do.'

He was aware of her studying him as he set out the ingredients, suspected she wanted to take photos. 'So we have vodka, we have a *bicerin* chocolate liqueur, we have an espresso and we have my secret ingredient.' He picked up a grapefruit. 'This adds a sour kick to counteract the sweetness of the chocolate and the darkness of the coffee.' Quickly he cut the grapefruit in half and juiced it.

'That sounds divine. So what now? We put all the ingredients in with some ice and shake?'

Luca couldn't keep the pained expression from his face and Emily gave another gurgle of laughter. 'Sorry. I am guessing that's like someone saying to me "so I just point and click"?'

'Exactly. Mixing a cocktail is an art. You need the measure of ingredients to be exactly right, the perfect combination of strength and sweetness, depth and light.' As he spoke he was aware of her gaze on him, the widening eyes, felt his own pulse ratchet up a notch at the undertones of his words. 'Sometimes you need a cocktail with a bit of spice, like a chilli, or other days you may feel like something a little more bland, but with a kick, like a vanilla martini. Different moods call for a different touch. But the most important thing is to get the balance right.'

Her breathing quickened and heat flushed the angles of her cheekbones to a red-brown glow. 'It sounds almost Zen-like.'

'And the art of the Zen master is to make sure every cocktail, whatever the mix, brings satisfaction.'

Their gazes locked and the surroundings no longer mattered, the voices on mute, the blue of the walls seeming to fade as his lips tingled with the urge to kiss her, to lean forward and taste her lips.

The spell was broken by the bartender, who stepped in and reached up for a bottle of spirits. 'Sorry, mate,' he said, in a cheerful London twang. 'I need the spiced rum.'

'No problem.'

They spoke simultaneously and Emily took a small step backward.

'Right,' Luca said, knowing he had to use words to bridge the awkwardness. 'So, we need to very carefully measure each ingredient.' Relief touched her expression as she concentrated on the amounts and he continued to speak. 'So this is a two-piece shaker. It's made of stainless steel, which I think is better than glass. It creates a purer cocktail. You put the ingredients in the smaller cup. And now we need the ice. I use ice straight from the freezer to reduce any possible dilution factor. The ice goes in the top half.' Her forehead creased in a small frown of concentration, he saw a glimpse of her teeth as she bit into her upper lip, her whole body taut as she copied his actions, and desire tugged inside him again. 'So now we get ready to shake. Tip the top half over the smaller one as quick as you can so you don't spill any ice.'

She hesitated and he saw doubt cross her face. 'What if I miss?'

'Then we start again. It's no big deal.' Yet it seemed as if to Emily it was. 'Hey, no one is expecting you to be perfect. Honestly, when I started I made at least a million mistakes. But I think you've got this.'

She raised an eyebrow but he saw a hint of a smile. 'Somehow I doubt that, but thank you for making me feel better. Here goes.' In one fluid movement she did as he'd said.

'Perfect. Now tap the top to form a seal and you're ready to shake.'

Now a smile did tip her lips and he could tell the success had given her a small thrill of satisfaction. 'So are there any special moves?'

'Of course.' He walked over to the music section and chose a track. 'Caribbean drum beat for twelve seconds. Ready, set, go.'

He started to shake, keeping the rhythm of the drums.

For a moment she stood as if mesmerised and then followed suit, closed her eyes and he allowed himself to watch, the sway of her body, the entranced look on her face as if she were lost in the movement. And he sensed this was an instant of escape, wondered what she was escaping from. 'Now we strain it and then we're done.'

A few minutes later Emily surveyed the two glasses, tipped her head to one side. 'They look beautiful,' she proclaimed and, no surprise, she pulled out her phone and took a picture. 'Now how about we taste them?'

He led the way to the small square table in the corner and placed his drink down on the mosaic top, moved round to pull her chair out before sitting down. 'Cheers,' he said and she raised her glass, full of the dark rich liquid. Carefully she tasted it and closed her eyes in sheer delight. 'It's incredible. I can taste the hint of grapefruit but it's not overpowering, just the teensiest bit astringent.' She took another sip. 'The world of chocolate may have benefited but the land of cocktails definitely missed out.'

She smiled as a waiter approached and her eyes widened as a wooden platter was placed on the table between them. Cold cuts of salami and thin slices of Parma ham, bowls of plump olives, sliced rustic bread, cheeses, were all laid out beautifully.

'This is incredible. I hadn't even realised how hungry I was until I saw this.'

'Usually this would be a pre-dinner snack. *Aperitivo* originated years ago when a man in Turin invented vermouth. He claimed it was a good thing to drink pre-dinner. Then it all evolved and now all over Italy people have pre-dinner drinks and snacks and most bars serve something. Today I asked Matteo for enough for a meal.'

'No wonder you love this city,' Emily said as she picked up a piece of bread. 'When did you move here?'

'When I was eleven.' A shadow crossed his face as he recalled the reason for the relocation from England. For the previous six months his life had been made a living hell by a gang of schoolyard bullies. The daily rituals of taunts and humiliations, pain and misery still occasionally populated his dreams. Worst of all had been his anger at his own weakness, the soul-churning knowledge that he couldn't stand up for himself. A weakness he had refused to reveal to anyone.

But eventually the situation had escalated and his mother, once alerted to the problem, had gone into characteristic action. Had changed their name to her maiden name of Petrovelli and whisked the family to Italy to live, away from England where Dolci and the new Casseveti family continued to flourish. 'Mum said it was a new start. She got a job here and we never looked back.' The words sounded hollow even as he said them; in truth you could argue he had spent his whole life looking back.

As if she sensed the demon on his back she reached out and placed her hand over his. The warmth of her touch, the sense of her fingers shivered a small shock through him. 'It's hard not to look back,' she said gently. 'And there is nothing wrong with looking back, staying close to the past. There are some things we should never forget.'

And he saw such sadness in her eyes that pain touched his chest and he covered her hand, so it was sandwiched between his. Wondered what demons populated her past. 'You're right. Because what's behind us is what shapes our present. We make decisions based on what has happened to us. Learn from it. But you shouldn't dwell on it. You need to focus on the future, on your goals and dreams.' Yet that hadn't worked for him. Because now the dream, the goal he had worked towards, was out of his reach for ever. And that sucked.

'What happens if you fail?' Now her voice held a bitter undertone and her fingers curled around his palm; the touch shivered through him.

'Then you try again or you reset the goal.'

'That's not always possible.'

'No. It isn't.' His plan could never now be fulfilled and, it seemed, neither could hers.

They sat silent and he sensed a shared frustration, an instant of empathy he knew he had to dispel. He had no wish to get embroiled in anything emotional, yet the urge to do just that was nigh on overwhelming, told him to ask, to delve, to offer comfort. *Stop.* That was not his way and he could not let Emily under his skin. Instead perhaps it would be better to try to distract her, bring back the smile to stave off whatever it was in her past that had brought such sadness to her face.

'How about we set ourselves an easy-to-achieve goal? Let's walk the streets of Turin in moonlight.'

His reward a small smile and a decisive nod, the downside the bereft feeling as she gently pulled her hand away. 'That sounds wonderful.'

CHAPTER SIX

As THEY EMERGED into the dusky streets of Turin, Emily glanced up at Luca's broad outline next to her, and curiosity surfaced as she wondered at the complexity of the man. He'd been the perfect host, charming and fun, but at the end she had sensed the depth of emotions that lay behind the charming façade, wondered what had brought shadows to darken his silver-grey eyes.

As if he sensed her gaze he turned and her breath caught—he looked ridiculously handsome. Moonlight glinted his dark hair, his chiselled features etched with strength, and for a crazy moment she wanted to hurl herself against the breadth of his chest, hold him, talk to him, kiss him.

But she wouldn't. This wasn't a viable attraction. Luca's emotions were his to guard and she sensed he guarded them as fiercely as she did her own. That he too held a hurt, a dream unfulfilled, a failure he had to live with as she lived with hers. Her failure had led to tragedy, the loss of the baby she had wanted so much. Pain hurt her heart as the image of her lost baby hovered.

But she knew tonight he didn't want to dwell on it or look back, and for now neither did she. Instead she'd absorb this city with its life and laughter and traditions, focus on getting the ideas she needed.

As if his thoughts walked with hers, he gestured around. 'It's beautiful by day but it's a different sort of beautiful by night.'

Emily nodded agreement. 'A city is different by night, by day, by season…by weather. Sometimes it's happy, sometimes it's sad—I think places are fascinating and capturing different images of them is a hobby of mine. You can show such different facets—the tourist haunts and sometimes the grittier undersides.'

'I see what you mean but it would never occur to me to take a picture.'

'Of anything?' She turned to look at him, aware that incredulity had pitched her voice high. 'When is the last time you took a photo?'

'Um…' Luca frowned. 'I scanned a business document on…'

'Doesn't count.' Emily came to a halt in the middle of the street. 'Seriously, I genuinely want to know. I mean, you must take photos—nowadays you don't even need a camera. Surely you take pictures of…something. When you look around you and see such beauty don't you want to record it?'

But Luca didn't look round. Instead he looked at her; his gaze held a molten spark that tugged desire in her tummy. 'Perhaps you are right,' he said, his voice deep and decadent, and she felt a delicious sizzle of knowledge that he was saying she was beautiful. 'But sometimes I prefer to simply look at beauty. Absorb it.'

She gulped, realised she was hanging on his every word now, tugged into the depths of his eyes, intoxicated by the words, by the play of moonlight on his strong features. The catch of his accented voice added to the spell and she knew danger loomed. But somehow she couldn't bring herself to care. 'But a picture captures that beauty.'

'Or I can put it into my memory banks.'

'Memory distorts things, a picture doesn't.' Her voice sounded breathless and she realised she had stepped closer to him.

'Not true. A picture can tell a lie. Think of all the fake smiles, pictures taken to pretend everything is all right.'

'A good photographer bypasses that. If you look closely you can see the fake, it's something in the eyes, or the tilt of the lips.' Now her eyes fell to his lips, the firm contour of them, and she caught her breath.

'Fair enough, but if you are always recording a moment you aren't living it. If you look at life through a lens, then you always have something between you and reality. You're experiencing it at one remove.' The dip and cadence of his voice sent a shiver over her skin and she moved forward another step. 'It is important to experience the moment.'

'Like this?' She couldn't have stopped herself if she tried; she took one more step, placed her hands on his shoulders and kissed him. Had meant it to be a quick brushing of the lips but she hadn't reckoned on the impact, gave a small gasp of sheer delight.

And then he cupped her face gently and lowered his lips to hers again, let out a small groan and now she tasted a hint of grapefruit and the sweetness of chocolate. Then her arms went round his neck and he deepened the kiss and she was lost. The scent and sounds of the Turin night seemed to dim and mute and condense until all she was aware of was Luca and that she wanted this to last for ever.

But it couldn't. Eventually reality intruded into the bubble of sensuality. They broke apart and Emily stared at him. What had she done? Why, oh, why had she kissed him? And how could it be so sinfully wonderful? How could she have been so swept away that she'd forgotten everything: professionalism and, even worse, her grief? How could she have allowed such joy to fizz through her—not only allowed, but actively sought it out? The betrayal of her grief appalled her even as her whole body still buzzed.

'I… I have to go.' Turning, she stumbled through the crowd. A cascade of horror at her actions ran through her as her brain relived the kiss, caused her to barely see the crowds around her, the glare of the lights, the exclamations of annoyance. All she wanted, all she needed, was the sanctuary of her hotel, where she could retreat to bed and try to block this from her mind.

'Emily. Wait.'

The sound of her name permeated the fog of regret and she recognised Luca's voice. She halted and spun round so quickly she almost collided into him. Braced herself, hands up to avoid so much as an accidental touch.

He moved to the side out of the way of passers-by. 'Emily. I am sorry.'

'You have nothing to apologise for. I kissed you.' Anger at her own actions mingled with the swirl of guilt that she could have been so shallow.

'And I kissed you back. That is not acceptable behaviour.' He took a deep breath. 'I want to make this right.' Emily could see the trouble in his eyes as he ran his hands through his dishevelled hair.

'*I* want to make it not to have happened. To erase it from our memory banks.' Something she suspected wouldn't be possible however much she wished it. How could she have let attraction trump common sense and simple common decency? She was grieving and her baby deserved a time of mourning. Work had become a necessity but the pursuit of pleasure had been wrong.

Luca exhaled. 'We can't pretend it never happened but…'

'We can make sure it doesn't happen again. It won't. I can assure you of that.'

He hesitated, raised a hand and dropped it again and it occurred to Emily that Luca was rattled. Clearly the kiss had affected him too and it would appear he regretted it as much as she did.

He settled for a nod. 'In that case I will meet you tomorrow morning for the tour of the factory.'

Turning, she walked almost blindly, her mind churning with regret, her body aching with guilt. Tears threatened and she increased her pace, desperate to return to the hotel where she could lie down on the cool sheets and simply weep.

CHAPTER SEVEN

LUCA WAITED IN the hotel lobby, watched the lift doors open and Emily step out, disconcerted anew by how her beauty affected him. But today as she approached him that impact was instantly diluted by worry. There were smudges under her eyes, eyes that had a washed-out look. Had she cried herself to sleep?

And if so why? The kiss had been a mistake. He'd be the first to acknowledge that; guilt still prodded him at his own stupidity. But it didn't warrant tears. He studied her face covertly, wondered if perhaps he'd been wrong. Wished he didn't care so much, didn't feel so angry with himself that he had clearly hurt her. *Stop.* Hell, she could have got shampoo in her eyes or just slept badly.

'Good morning.' He focused on keeping his voice steady.

'Good morning.' Her voice gave nothing away, but her expression held wariness as she crossed the lobby, and as they walked through the revolving glass door he saw the effort she made to hold herself aloof so as not to risk even the smallest chance of accidental contact.

Actions he mirrored as they both climbed into the back of the car that would take them to the factory, the idea of stopping at a café for a *bicerin* now impossible. Once inside she scrunched herself as close to her side window as was humanly possible as the car pulled away from the kerb and the weight of silence descended.

Luca cleared his throat. 'The weather is a bit cloudier today.'

'Yes. Especially for this time of year.'

That seemed to cover the weather. 'I hope you will enjoy today,' he said.

'I am sure I will find it useful.' Her voice was tight, each word propped up by stilts. A pause. 'I'm looking forward to seeing where your chocolate is produced.'

Luca recalled the previous evening, the ease of their discourse, and tried to equate the woman who had shaken cocktails to the beat of Caribbean drums with the woman sitting so far away from him, her whole body taut. Regret ran through him as he cursed his own lack of restraint— he might not understand why, but the kiss had impacted her profoundly. *Come on, Luca.* It had impacted him hugely too. That kiss had broken all his own rules; in one fell swoop it had crashed through the fundamental basis of his relationship cornerstone. Do not act on attraction, do not get involved on any level until the rules were on the table. It was time to acknowledge what had happened, properly.

'No,' he said. 'You aren't looking forward to it and I wish you were. I am sorry I spoilt our professional relationship.'

'You didn't. I will still do my job to the highest standard.'

'I am sure you will, but I think what happened has made that harder.' Which was exactly why mixing professional with personal was so stupid. 'I would like to try and clear away this…awkwardness, try to make it right.'

She shook her head. 'It's hard not to feel awkward. To say nothing of embarrassed.'

'There is no need to be embarrassed. What happened between us was—'

'Unfortunate, unprofessional, unnecessary, stupid, and mortifying.'

At least this was a proper conversation. 'It was also natural.'

Suspicion frowned her face. 'What do you mean?'

'At Ava's party we clicked, did we not?'

For a moment he thought she'd deny it, then she gave a small reluctant nod. 'I suppose so.'

'I know we decided not to act on it and I know we shouldn't have but I will not be embarrassed by something natural. There is nothing wrong with feeling attraction. I agree we need to put it behind us but there is no need to be ashamed.' He studied her profile, saw that for some reason his words had had no effect. 'Look at me.' She did as he asked and he reached out and touched her lightly on the arm, pulled back fast. 'Truly, do not feel embarrassed. I do not.' That was true; he felt chagrin, surprise and annoyance and true regret at his lack of control, determination to avoid a repeat performance, but there also lingered a different regret that there wouldn't be one. Now he frowned—there were way too many feelings in the mix. So, 'How about we agree to try and be natural around each other?'

'I thought you said that was the problem in the first place.' Her tone was wry and he belatedly remembered his words of a moment ago.

'Touché,' he said and he couldn't help it, his lips turned up in a smile and suddenly she gave him an answering smile.

'But I know what you mean so, yes, let's try and put it behind us.'

'Agreed.'

The remainder of the journey was achieved in a silence, but this time it felt more comfortable. Once at the factory they climbed out of the car and she gazed at the loom of the factory building, pulled out her camera and started to snap.

Once inside he led the way to an office. 'The contract should be in here,' he said, then picked it up from the desk and handed it over to her. Emily read it carefully and once again he found himself studying her, the smallest of creases in her forehead, the bent head supported by the graceful column of her neck.

She signed quickly and he followed suit.

'Right, let's start the tour.'

As he showed her around the factory he watched her expression, felt a sense of satisfaction at her genuine interest as he led her round the different machines and explained how each one worked. With each step, the atmosphere relaxed a little more and he could see her immerse herself in taking pictures, admired her focus and method as she made sure she got every angle.

After a while she came to a halt and, although he could still sense a slight rigidity in her posture, her expression held only interest as she returned to stand by the conching machine.

'The sheer quantity of chocolate you produce is mindboggling... I mean, I could practically swim in it. And to think it all starts with a cocoa bean.' She glanced down at her notes. 'And so much happens to those poor beans. But, if I have it right, how they are fermented is crucial, and so is the roasting process and the conching. I'm not sure I understand that last bit.'

'Basically the mixture is stirred to extract any water that remains and to distribute the cacao butter evenly. This is what gives chocolate its taste, its texture, even its smell. The name comes from the word concha, which means shell. In the old days chocolate was conched in a vessel that was shell-shaped.'

'I really like that. I'll try to incorporate conch-shaped shells in the ads, and maybe something natural that represents the roasting and fermentation as well.'

'I'd like that.' Admiration touched him at her creative process, for the idea that the ad would embrace the actual process, would hold hints and clues that tied it all together. 'Now I see why this is so important to how you work. And now for the last bit of the tour—the tasting.'

He led the way out of the factory to the café he'd installed for meetings and tastings. Flowers hung from the rafters over the tables and the air was scented with a mixture of floral and chocolate. Once Emily was seated at one of the small wrought-iron painted tables he put together a selection of Palazzo di Cioccolato products.

'This is one of our best sellers, this is a midnight-dark bar, here is my version of a nuts-and-raisin bar and finally here is a prototype for the new brand.'

She popped the first sample in her mouth and closed her eyes as she savoured the flavour. Luca couldn't help himself, he allowed his gaze to rove over her beautiful face, the length of her dark lashes, the slant of her cheekbones, the hue and glow of her skin. And, of course, the lips that had joined his in that explosive kiss just hours before.

Her eyes snapped open and he instantly dropped his gaze. 'What do you think?'

'These are freaking amazing. Why can't I buy your products in the UK?' She picked up the next one and took a bite. 'You are missing an enormous opportunity.'

The question was a reminder of his plan, thwarted for ever now by the finality of death. Now he would never visit Dolci headquarters, march into his father's office and issue a personal invitation to the opening of the Palazzo di Cioccolato flagship London store. Satisfy his need for revenge.

A dish best served cold and now a dish he would never get to serve at all. His dad had died and now he'd never get the chance to tell him anything. And without the idea of vengeance to fuel him the whole idea of a London store seemed pointless, filled him with a sense of flatness. Not the excitement and drive he needed to launch.

'I am planning to open in the UK. I am looking for premises in London and then I will expand to regional high streets. It's a balance between being a bit more exclusive and boutique and reaching a wider market.' He also had to summon up the enthusiasm from somewhere.

'Sure. You have already achieved so much.' She gestured towards the door that led to the factory. 'This is a massive operation. You made this happen. How? What's your story? I did look on the website but there's nothing there. What inspired you?'

Revenge. That was not an answer he would share. That he had been inspired, driven, by the need to outdo his father.

'I've always understood the importance of chocolate.' Keep it light. Give a little, but not too much. 'My mum was pregnant with Jodi and she craved chocolate. But only very good quality, expensive chocolate. I used to watch her savour the tiny squares and even then I could see that good quality chocolate was the answer.' And so the first seed of becoming a chocolatier had been planted in the close aftermath of his father's desertion, when all he'd wanted was to provide his mother with what she craved. At a time when affording basic food was a problem, and Luca could remember the gnawing pain of hunger in his belly.

Sometimes they had imagined a feast and always in that illusory meal had been chocolate; the two of them would sit and imagine the taste of it, list the ingredients, savour the imaginary taste on their tongues. The memory unsettled him and he shifted on his chair, aware of Emily's eyes on him, saw a question in hers.

'I went on a tour of a chocolate factory with school and I decided then and there that this was what I wanted to do.'

He'd looked round and wondered if the Dolci factory looked like this, full of the smell of sweetness and the churn and grind of machinery. Known he didn't want to copy his father or follow in his footsteps, he wanted to rival him.

'I managed to get a meeting with Lucio Silvetti, one of Turin's foremost chocolatiers, and he agreed to train me. I worked hard, at the cocktail bar and various other jobs, and in the end I started small and then grew the business.'

'You make it sound easy, but I know it can't have been.' Her frown deepened and she tucked a strand of hair behind her ear. 'In fact, you're making it sound boring. I don't get it. When you talk about your products and your company ethos you are full of enthusiasm. And pride. Surely you're proud of how you achieved such success. Your story?'

'Of course, I am. But there isn't much to say about it.'

'There's loads to say about it.' A quick sideways glance at him as she picked up a crumb with her fingertip. 'Plus you don't have a photo of you on your website. I could take one now, if you like. Maybe you on the factory floor, a hands-on CEO surveying your domain.'

'No need. But thank you.' After their conversation last night he felt stupidly vulnerable, as if all his mixed feelings about his company would show in his face, in his stance, in his eyes. And maybe he could fake a smile, but Emily would know it was fake and he wasn't willing to show that to her discerning eye. For her to pick up the nuance and emotion he'd rather remain hidden. Hell, that he'd rather not feel at all. 'I prefer for my products to speak for themselves. I am more of an invisible presence.' For a moment he thought she'd protest but then she gave a small rueful smile.

'Fair enough. I guess I get that.' She placed the last piece of chocolate in her mouth and her eyes widened.

'This is absolutely amazing. I've never tasted anything quite like this.'

'That's the idea,' he said. 'I wanted to make this different—I know some people may hate it but I'm hoping lots of people will love it.'

'I am definitely in the latter camp. It somehow combines decadent richness with refreshing lightness. How have you done that?'

He smiled and gave a mock bow. 'I told you. I'm a Zen master, remember?'

Now she laughed. 'How could I forget? But do you also think it tastes different because of the actual cocoa bean? Because it's from Jalpura and the others aren't?'

The question with its mention of Jalpura jolted him, a stark reminder of Jodi and that for the past twenty-four hours he'd barely given his sister a thought. Guilt straightened his lips into a grim line. What the hell was wrong with him? Yes, the ad campaign mattered, but not as much as Jodi. He had to keep his eye on the goal.

'I think Jalpura is definitely part of it,' he said firmly. 'So I think it's time to go there.'

CHAPTER EIGHT

EMILY SNAPPED HER seat belt on and took a deep breath as she glanced around the aeroplane. The first-class section was relatively empty of passengers so she and Luca were effectively alone, which at least meant that if her panic returned she would be free from observation. For a moment she wondered if he had deliberately orchestrated their privacy, told herself not to be foolish.

'You OK?' As he spoke he reached down into his briefcase. 'I got you this from the airport. Just in case you needed it.'

She accepted the paper bag he handed over and peered inside and a trickle of warmth touched her as she saw the content—a red squishy stress ball. 'Thank you. That is really thoughtful.' The kind of thing that would never have occurred to Howard in a million years and for some reason the gesture prickled her eyes with tears. Pulling it out, she squeezed it as the plane took off, held on tight and focused on her breathing, told herself that the sooner she got to Jalpura, the sooner she would get back.

'I hope your evening was productive?' he asked.

'It was, thank you.' She'd elected to work in her hotel room the previous night; by tacit consent neither of them had wished to spend the evening together, had no wish to risk a repeat of the kiss. 'I've put together some ideas for the ad campaign and then I sorted out my photos of Turin.' She gave a sudden smile. 'Could I be any more boring?'

'That is not boring. What do you do with all the photographs? You must have taken hundreds of images.'

'I go through, keep the best, in case I need them in the future. If I ever get asked to do a photo shoot in Turin they'll be helpful.'

'What made you choose fashion photography? I can see that you are very good at what you do but over the past days you have taken pictures of food and buildings and people, but not once have you shown any interest in actual fashion. Or gone shopping, or even window-shopped in any of the boutiques.'

His perception surprised her; the fact that he had even noticed gave her a jolt. Howard had always been focused on himself; his only concern with Emily had been how she reflected on him. Her mother's priority was always herself or her current 'love'. 'I didn't really choose it. I kind of fell into it. I've always enjoyed photography.' Her camera had been like a security blanket, a way of making invisibility a positive. She'd grown up constantly being told to 'not get in the way', 'not be noticed' by her mother. At her annual visits to her father's she'd had no idea how to fit in, had felt redundant, embarrassed, had *wanted* to be invisible. Taking photographs gave her something to do and she'd figured out that most people liked having their picture taken. And so she'd taken family photos of her dad and his second wife and their happy brood of children, all the time aware of the irony that, as the photographer, she wasn't in the snaps. A fitting representation of her role in her father's life.

'But becoming a fashion photographer was sheer dumb luck. I was at a party and the host asked if I could take some informal photos. I took one of a model and she loved it; I thought it was the booze talking but next day she called me up, told me she'd used her clout to get me a job. It all went from there. So fashion chose me really.'

'But you could have changed course if you wished.'

'It's not that easy.' She had wanted to. Had wanted to do more serious photography, the type that documented real life. The sort of work Howard did, that genuinely made a difference, showed the world the ravages of war, the injustices of poverty. That was how she and Howard had first got together. She'd somehow found the courage to approach him at a party, asked for a critique, been in super-fangirl mode. Had been stunned when he'd agreed, hadn't even cared that he'd said it was the least he could do for the daughter of a photographic icon like Marigold Turner.

'Why not?' Luca's blunt question interrupted her trip down memory lane. 'Why is it not easy?'

'It turns out my talents are better suited to the fashion industry.' Ironic but apparently true, according to Howard, and whilst her ex had many flaws Emily had understood and accepted his original critique as spot on.

'How do you know that?'

Emily glanced away, could still remember the nervous anticipation before she'd met Howard to discuss his 'verdict'—that she simply didn't have what it took, her style was too light and frothy. 'More serious stuff requires a versatility, a technique, an eye I don't have.'

Luca frowned. 'Did someone tell you that?'

'Yes, but I agree with them.'

Howard had explained it. *You are good at what you do, Emily, in the same way an actor who is good at comedy will not be able to play Hamlet. But you should not*

despair, and I am sorry to be the bearer of bad news.
Let me make it up to you with dinner.'

And so it had begun.

'Photography isn't only about the type of camera or the lighting or the lens, it's about an instinct, an eye and a God-given talent. You can practise and practise and practise, but those things give you the edge. It's probably the same in the world of chocolate—not everyone can come up with the types of recipes you can. However hard they practise.'

'I get that. There are some chocolatiers born with an ability to taste and mix and judge that you can't learn. But that doesn't mean everyone will love their chocolate, because it's a matter of taste. And each person is unique—photography is not like a game of tennis where someone has to win. I don't understand why you wouldn't be able to use your talent for any type of photography. Your photographs show emotion and convey mood.'

For a second she was carried away by the force of his words, remembered vaguely that once she'd thought the same. Had held out hope that Howard might have been wrong, a hope that had eroded during the course of her marriage, under the onslaught of Howard's continued critiques, that had worsened when she'd given up her own job to be his assistant.

Until she'd accepted the truth—Howard had been right from the start—she didn't have what it took.

She shook her head. 'There is no point raising unrealistic expectations, trying to dream your dreams into reality. It's important to be realistic. I am happy with the talent I have. And I'd like to use that talent to do a good job for you.' She injected finality into her tone; she'd made her decision and she would stick to it. All her life she'd been surrounded by people of immense talent, top of their field; it had been hard to accept that she wouldn't do the same. But she had come to terms with it—decided the fact she had any talent for photography was amazing in itself; there was no need to aspire to be of Howard's calibre. 'Speaking of which, what is the plan in Jalpura?'

His gaze flicked away from her for an instant. 'I've arranged to visit the cocoa-bean farm, so you can have a tour, and we'll need to scout some locations.'

Emily studied his face, sensed a certain flatness to his voice and wondered where his usual enthusiasm had gone. 'I've already done some research into locations. There's a place where the sunsets are spectacular, and also some incredibly lush gardens and, of course, the palace. I was wondering about introducing a hint of royalty into the campaign seeing as Jalpura has a royal family.'

'That sounds great—and as though you are completely on top of it all.'

Yet again the words lacked depth, a genuine interest, and she wondered why. This project was Luca's idea, yet he looked as if his mind was focused elsewhere. Not her business. 'Speaking of which,' she said brightly, 'I'll get on with a bit more research.'

The rest of the flight was uneventful and Luca was grateful that Emily seemed content to crack on with some work, hoped she didn't notice his distraction as they approached Jalpura. Where he hoped to find answers. As they landed, went through customs and climbed into a taxi his determination grew. He would discover what had happened to Jodi.

Once they arrived at the resort, Luca looked around. He'd chosen the place because of its proximity to Jodi's last known location, a youth hostel she'd told him she'd stayed at. Though this was a far cry from a hostel. Instead of a conventional hotel a selection of thatched cottages, all side by side, surrounded an opaque turquoise swimming pool, fringed with palm trees. The air was scented with flowers and the whole place emanated an atmosphere of tranquillity.

'This is amazing.' Emily let out a small sigh of appreciation.

'I'm glad you like it. Let's settle in and meet for dinner in about an hour.'

She glanced at him, presumably surprised at the terseness of his voice, but he couldn't help it. Somehow in the past few days he'd been sidetracked from the true purpose of this trip. Had got caught up in Emily, in her company, her conversation and, of course, the fateful kiss itself. He had seen some of her vulnerabilities even if he didn't understand them and in so doing he'd lost sight of his goal to find his sister. *Not good.* His family meant everything to him. More than that, he would not break the promise he'd made himself after Lydia and the pain and humiliation of her rejection—never again would he get involved in any depth at all, never again would he put his feelings on the line.

'Dinner sounds good,' she said.

He nodded; it would give him time to contact Samar, the cocoa-farm owner, and ask him again about Jodi. See if he had remembered anything else about how she had been, whether she had mentioned anything about friends or acquaintances or plans. He would also need to request that Samar didn't mention Jodi to Emily. At this stage there was no point—after all, he might be able to discover what he needed without involving Emily at all.

Once in his cottage he pulled his phone out. 'Samar. It's Luca…'

Preliminaries over, Luca segued into what he really

wanted to talk about, 'I was wondering about Jodi's visit to Jalpura. She mentioned a friend's name and I wanted to look them up, but I've lost the message Jodi sent me and I can't get hold of her at the moment. Did she mention anyone to you?'

There was a pause as Samar clearly gave the matter some thought. 'She spoke a lot about the film festival and her job there and I believe she did mention meeting the royal princess. I got the impression it was more than a meeting, more of a friendship, but I am sure you wouldn't forget that. Plus it wouldn't be that easy to just look up royalty.' A laugh travelled down the line. 'I am sorry, Luca. I cannot remember anyone else.'

'Don't worry. It isn't that important.' Royalty? Luca's brain whirred. Jodi certainly hadn't mentioned meeting royalty.

'Perhaps you could ask Jodi for an introduction,' Samar continued. 'Get royal endorsement for your chocolate.'

'I'll do that. Thank you. And, could I ask a favour? Please do not mention Jodi in front of Emily tomorrow. There is a slightly complicated situation going on and...'

'You do not need to explain, my friend. Women are complicated.'

Goodbyes said, Luca disconnected and began to pace as he tried to figure out what to do with this new information, wished that Samar had recalled it when he'd spoken to him weeks before to question him. It was a slim lead that might lead nowhere but it was better than nothing and he would definitely follow it up.

A glance at his watch and he headed to the door, exited his cottage and headed for Emily's. He'd keep dinner quick and get back to do some research into the Jalpuran royal family.

He knocked on Emily's door, braced himself for the impact. She truly did stun him anew every time he saw her and he wished she didn't. Didn't understand the visceral punch and it unsettled him that he couldn't seem to douse or control it.

'Ready?' he asked.

'Ready.' Dressed in black smart trousers and a tunic top, she looked perfectly presentable in her usual understated way. He sensed it was deliberate, that she dressed to eschew attention, to deflect notice.

She picked up a small evening bag from the table by the door and stepped outside into the balmy scented evening, pulled the door shut behind her.

He led the way to the outdoor terrace where tables dotted the mosaic tiles and it was only now, as a waiter materialised, pulled out their chairs, lit candles and provided menus, that he really took in the setting and its implications. The scent of frangipani rode gently on the air, the flicker of candles added to the twinkle of the fairy lights that artfully bedecked the surroundings. The tables were placed discreet distances apart and as he glanced around he saw the place was full of couples. And for a crazy moment he imagined that he and Emily were here together as a couple, that he had the right to lean across the table and brush his lips against hers, to hold her hand as they chose their meals, to play footsie under the table.

Resolutely he turned his attention to the menu just as the waiter approached, held out a basket filled with garlands of flowers. 'Would you like to choose one for your beautiful lady?' he asked.

He saw Emily open her mouth to deny the need but all of a sudden Luca wanted to choose some flowers, wanted her to put them in her hair or round her neck. To jazz up the plainness of her outfit and show off her beauty.

'Of course,' he said and studied the different choices, settled on a white jasmine, took it out and leaned across the small intimate table and carefully tucked it into her hair, felt his fingers tremble at the feel of her silken strands, heard her breath catch too.

Leaning back, he surveyed his handiwork. 'Beautiful,' he said. The waiter beamed at them both and moved away.

'You didn't need to say that. I mean, you're right, it's probably easier to let them think we're a couple like everyone else here. But there's no need to overdo it.'

'I wasn't. I was simply stating a fact. You do look beautiful.'

He'd swear she shifted slightly on her seat, looked more than a touch uncomfortable. 'Thank you. I guess.'

'It's not an insult.'

'I know.'

'Then why has it made you so uncomfortable?'

'I told you, I don't think looks are relevant.'

'So, if we were a couple you wouldn't want me to say you look beautiful?'

'I…' Her eyes narrowed. 'It's a moot point. Because we aren't a couple.' That was true enough, so what was he doing? Yet she was beautiful and for some reason he wanted her to know that. But Emily continued to speak. 'Unlike everyone else here. It's like Romance Central, Cupid's arrows darting everywhere.' Her voice held more than a hint of disparagement and he decided to go with the opportune change in subject.

'Perhaps those arrows are missing their mark. Or these people could be here desperately trying to spice up a dead marriage, or this is what they do every year and they are utterly bored, or they could be plotting a divorce or a murder…'

'OK, Mr Cynic. I'm guessing romance isn't your thing.'

'No.' His gaze rested on the flower he'd just put in her hair. 'It's not.' The words almost over-emphasised, a reminder to himself.

She raised her glass of water. 'Good call.' She tipped her head to one side. 'So this isn't the sort of place you'd bring a partner on holiday.'

'I wouldn't bring a partner anywhere on holiday. That's not the way my arrangements work.'

'Arrangements?' Her nose wrinkled as she looked at him questioningly, tucked an errant strand of hair behind her ear, the movement fluid and familiar, and for some reason it tugged at something in his chest. His gaze lingered on the flower in her hair, the contrast of colour, the delicate shape of the petals against the silky softness. And a memory of their shared kiss suddenly blasted his brain. Perhaps this would be a good time to remind himself of his relationship rules, demonstrate exactly how far out of bounds Emily was.

'Basically I date women who fit a certain criteria, who are looking for the same things that I am. A relationship where we enjoy each other's company every so often but without clinginess or neediness on either side. No expectations other than an entertaining dinner companion, a bed partner, someone to take to social functions. The occasional night away but definitely not a holiday.'

'But how do you keep it like that—surely if its long-term you get to know each other better over time, start to like each other more?'

He shook his head. 'I'm talking about meeting up once, maybe twice a month. Not keeping toothbrushes at each other's place. The essence is that it's low-key, not intense. Fun and easy. Nothing heavy.' It was a system he had perfected after his break-up with Lydia. A system devised to ensure no investment in deep emotion, dependency or love. That way there was zero risk of hurting or being hurt. One thing was certain: Luca Petrovelli would never open himself up to the risk of abandonment again. He could spot a pattern when he saw one: first a father he had loved and then a girlfriend he'd adored. 'That way no one gets hurt.'

'But you can't guarantee that.'

'I can try. I take care to only date women who are not emotionally vulnerable. For example, I would not date someone who has recently been in a relationship.'

She waited until the waiter came and took their orders and then leaned forward. 'But what if a woman wants something different from you?'

'Then she shouldn't date me. I am upfront from the beginning as to what I can offer and what I want in return. And I do my best to make sure any woman who I date truly wants the same.'

'But how can you be sure of that? You seem to want a fun, low-maintenance woman with no emotional needs at all. Does that exist?'

'Yes. There are women who are not interested in a happy ever after. I don't want to get caught up in anyone's desire for love—I won't hold them back on their quest. Neither will I pretend or con them into believing I am something I'm not. That I'll be there for them on a weekly or daily basis. Equally I don't expect them to be there for me. It works and there are plenty of plus points. Enjoyable dates with no pressure, relaxed conversations, sharing a nice time.'

Worry etched Emily's features. 'Are you in one of those relationships now?'

'No. If I was then I would not have kissed you.' In truth he should not have kissed her anyway; she didn't fit his criteria, was not a woman he had discussed his relationship rules with and yet it hadn't stopped him. Even now as he looked at her across the table the desire to kiss her again simmered inside him and he clenched his jaw in frustration. With Emily he was breaking rules; worst of all they were his own rules. 'My arrangements may lack emotion, but they involve fidelity.' That was important. 'I would never betray that trust.'

'So what happened with your last arrangement?'

He sipped his beer. 'Georgia worked for an international company—she got an assignment overseas.'

'And you didn't mind?'

'Not at all. I was happy for her—it was a promotion she'd worked hard for and she deserved it. We said goodbye and wished each other well.'

'How long had you been "together"?'

'About eighteen months. But we'd probably only seen each other twenty times in total over that time. She travelled a lot for work.'

'And before that?'

'Marina broke it off—she met someone else.'

'And that didn't bother you?'

'No, that's the beauty of this. No one gets hurt.'

'But it's also sad. The idea of these women moving on and not having made enough of an impact on your life for you to even care.'

The comment jolted him; he'd never thought about it like that and for a moment he felt strangely diminished inside, as if he lacked something important. A notion he dismissed promptly. 'But that's way better than them moving on and I am left devastated.' This he knew.

'Has that happened to you? Have you been left devastated?' she asked.

'Just the once. It falls under the young and foolish category, so perhaps devastation is a bit of an exaggeration. I was twenty, I fell in love and Lydia moved on to someone richer and more successful.' An echo of his father's actions.

'That sucks.'

'It did, but I really only had myself to blame.' He should never have lost control of his feelings, should never have let the feelings flourish and grow into love.

'Had you been together long?'

'Six months. I was working at Silvio's and she used to come in for a cocktail. We got talking and it spiralled from there.' He'd fallen and fallen hard, tried to resist but in the end he had succumbed, decided that he and Lydia were the exception to the rule, that happy ever afters were possible. 'Unfortunately she didn't feel the same way I did. I walked into work one day and she was kissing one of the customers. Harry Chisholm. His dad was a millionaire and he lived a way more exciting lifestyle than I did.'

He could still feel the raw pain he'd felt then, as he'd stood rooted to the spot, watching the kiss. It had been Lydia who had spotted him, who had broken away. She had taken Harry by the hand and they'd approached him.

I'm sorry you had to find out like this. I've been trying to work out how to tell you.'

Harry had left them alone and Lydia had continued to speak. Luca had been unable to say anything, the rawness of his pain new, yet all too familiar. There had been sadness in her voice.

'I'm truly sorry, Luca. But you're so serious, so focused on your business and your training and work. Harry is fun and exciting and—'

'Rich.'

He'd managed the syllable, infused it with all the bitterness he'd felt.

'*And he's charming...and he doesn't take life so... personally.*'

The words had cut him to the heart, a reminder of his childhood self. This was his fault—just as it had been his fault his dad had left. There was something wrong with him.

'I'm sorry, Luca.' Emily's voice, gentle and full of compassion, pulled him to the present.

'Don't be. It's an old story—it happens all the time to millions of people. It was no big deal, but I will admit it put me off love and romance.'

'I understand why. But I think there is a different solution to your arrangements.'

'Such as?'

Before she could reply the waiter approached their table.

CHAPTER NINE

AS THE WAITER put the aromatic plates in front of them Emily reflected on what Luca had shared; it might be an old story, but she sensed that eighteen-year-old boy would have been devastated by Lydia's behaviour. Sensed too that he would rather walk on hot coals than admit it, and wanted to give him a bit of a time out to walk away from the memory of Lydia.

Emily looked down at her plate, inhaled the delicious scent of spices, garlic, fresh green chilli and cumin and couldn't help but admire the presentation of her *sadhya*—a variety of curries and dals and pickles in small stainless-steel pots all arranged on a banana leaf. She looked across at Luca's choice, a rice-flour pancake filled with a curry that emitted the waft of ginger and coconut.

'Do you mind if I take a picture of yours as well as mine?'

'No problem.'

A few minutes later, she gave a small sigh of satisfaction and took her first taste. 'This is beyond amazing.'

He nodded. 'Mine too. Do you want to try some?'

'Yes, please.' She waited whilst he sectioned off a bit of his and moved it onto her plate, 'And help yourself.' She tore of a piece of chapati and handed it over, watched as he dipped it into one of the pots and she revelled in the strange intimacy of sharing food.

For a few moments they savoured the dishes, and then he wiped his mouth on a napkin. 'So what is your solution to relationships? You tried marriage so I assume you believe in the happy-ever-after theory. Or at least you did.'

'Definitely past tense.' There had been no happiness in the ending with Howard. Even now the sequence of events was a horrible blur. Her pregnancy had been a surprise but to Emily it had been a welcome one. To Howard it had not; and as her pregnancy had progressed his displeasure had only increased. His insistence she conceal it, his growing impatience, his disparaging remarks. All had culminated in her discovery that he was sleeping with someone else. The scale of her anger at his betrayal still shocked her, their confrontation a humdinger that she regretted with all her heart, because two weeks later she'd lost the baby and a part of her believed that somehow the sheer raw pain and exhaustion could have caused it.

Her pain must have shown on her face because Luca leaned forward and, oh, so gently took her hands in his. 'I'm sorry. I didn't mean to bring back memories or hurt you.'

'It's OK. Truly. It was a painful break-up but I have put Howard behind me now.' Not her baby, she would never ever be able to do that, would never want to. 'And I won't repeat past mistakes, I'm done with love.' She wouldn't make the same mistakes as her mother. 'But your type of arrangements wouldn't work for me. If I am with someone I want to feel I am important enough that they would at least miss me if I were gone. Or at the very least notice—it doesn't sound as though Georgia or Marina impacted on your life at all.'

He shook his head. 'They didn't in the sense that they

had the power to hurt me. But I did like them, and they liked me—we did have good times together.'

'But they didn't matter.'

'No,' he agreed. 'That was the point. Once a person matters to you then you open yourself to pain and hurt.'

'Agreed.' She'd seen her mother hurt time and again and after each disaster she'd got back up on her feet and entered the fray again, her quest for love undimmed. 'It's no secret that my mother has been married multiple times and it seems to me that she never learns; she opens herself up time and again to the same type of man in her search for love.'

When Emily had remonstrated, Marigold had simply pointed out that she wasn't a quitter.

'I'll never give up on true love and my happy ending.'

'But my father—he did learn from his marriage to my mother. His second marriage works perfectly. He and Neela do matter to each other but not too much.' Rajiv Khatri had married Neela very soon after he split with Marigold and his second wife couldn't be more different from his first.

'How so?'

'Their relationship works because it isn't based on grand passion, or whirlwind romance. It's practical and nice and comfortable—they care about each other but without the angst.' There were no fights, no raised voices and a sense of calm politeness. 'They like and respect each other and they are both happy doing their own separate things. Neela goes with him to some of the Bollywood parties but she doesn't mind if he goes on his own. Neela is involved with charity work and Dad helps out with that if he can. But she spends a lot of time on that. And, of course, they have a family.' The words were a reminder of what she had hoped for just months before, and what she'd lost—the chance of a family of her own. *Not now.* 'That is definitely Neela's priority. And Dad's. They put their family first.'

As a child she had watched the loving, nurturing bond Neela had with her children, realised that she prioritised them, thought about them, planned for them. And it had been nearly impossible not to compare it with her own relationship with her mother. It would never occur to Marigold to put Emily first. At the start of each new relationship, throughout each marriage, Marigold put her man first, relegated Emily to second tier. There was the time she had been bundled off to boarding school, only to be taken back out to comfort Marigold when the marriage collapsed. The time a live-in nanny had been employed, until said nanny had an affair with husband number three.

'What you are describing…in a way your father and Neela have found love.'

'They have found affection. That would be enough for me.' Along with a family. The beauty would be that she would be able to prioritise her children, put them before romantic love. Put them first in a way she never had been by either of her parents. In some ways, she hadn't put her baby first—instead she had been swayed by her misplaced love for Howard.

'So really you want an arrangement too. But with a bit more depth.'

Emily considered the words, then acknowledged the truth. 'A lot more depth. I want to be with someone I like and respect and who will be a good father to our children. Will put them first. It would be a good arrangement. Maybe you should consider it.' Belated realisation of how he might take her words hit her. 'Not with me, obviously.'

Amusement glinted in his eyes. 'So that's not a proposition?' The words were said with a smile that curled her toes and the mood morphed and suddenly the air seemed heavy with possibility.

'Of course not!' Yet scenarios triggered in her imagination—herself and Luca surrounded by a brood of children. A dark-haired boy with brown eyes, a dark-haired girl, hair in plaits, with Luca's grey eyes. Emily sat holding a tiny baby in her arms, Luca looking down on them with a smile in his eyes.

Holy Moly. Where had all that come from? Yet as she looked at Luca, desperately tried to keep any vestige of her thoughts from her face, she saw something in his eyes and for a treacherous moment she wondered, hoped, that it was a mirror of her own stupid vision.

Enough. For the first time in twenty-four hours panic started to ripple in the deep dark pool of guilt. How could she sit here picturing a new family, a new baby, in such vivid detail? It was only a year since tragedy had struck. Since the miscarriage that had sent her spinning downward.

'Emily.' Now Luca's voice was laced with concern. 'I apologise—it was simply a joke and a bad one at that. I know you are not propositioning me.'

'I know you know.' Seeing the dawn of questions she didn't want to answer, the flash of concern in his silver-grey eyes, she pulled her unravelled thoughts together, pushed back at the panic until it subsided, sank a little towards the depths. 'I just thought maybe you should consider a different type of arrangement, one that allows you to have a family.'

'Nope. It's still too high risk. For me, as a man. If my wife were to leave the odds are that she would take the children, would have custody. And maybe I would not deeply love my wife, but I would love my children. That love would give any woman too much power over me. The power to take them away from me.'

Emily heard the depth of passion in his voice, knew he meant it. That this man would rather not have children at all than risk losing them. And how could she blame him? His father had abandoned his family; why wouldn't his wife abandon him? And he was right. Her arrangement would work better for a woman; she would most likely have custody of any children.

So, 'I get that.' Her voice was quiet and he looked at her with raised brows.

'You do?'

'Yes. You don't ever want to settle for being a part-time father.' As her own father had been. In truth Emily knew she was a redundant child—he had five others and his interest in Emily was a duty only. 'And you won't risk the pain of having your kids taken away from you.' She looked down at her empty plate. 'I understand, but I think you're wrong.'

'Why?'

How to explain it? Explain that despite the pain, the misery, the gut-wrenching, soul-searing sense of loss she wouldn't undo her baby, wouldn't take away her pregnancy? She couldn't explain that without telling Luca of her grief and she wasn't ready to do that.

'Because I believe the chance to be a parent is worth any risk. And because I believe, even if you were a part-time father, you'd make it work somehow. If you wanted to.' This man would make anything work. If he wanted to.

There was a silence and then he shook his head. 'I don't want to and the best way to ensure that is not to start that sort of relationship. I think I'll steer clear of love of any kind.'

'I am not advocating love. Love is a chimera and an illusion, the holy grail that people chase, a word they bandy about when really it's all about attraction, or money, or fame... I've always known that. But when I met Howard I forgot the rules, forgot what I know deep in my bones. I got conned by the illusion. Never again.' She gave a sudden laugh. 'Listen to me. In the most romantic place in the world, denouncing love.'

He raised his glass. 'To non-romance.'

'I'll drink to that.'

Once they'd clinked she said, 'Now how about we talk about something completely different? What's the detailed itinerary for tomorrow? Cocoa-bean farm in the afternoon? And I was thinking about visiting the royal palace gardens in the morning.'

Luca's reaction was palpable; his forehead creased into a frown and his lips thinned.

'Unless that doesn't work for you? There's no need for you to come to the gardens.'

'It's not that. You simply reminded me of something.' Something important, clearly. 'Samar, the owner of the farm suggested I get royal endorsement for the chocolate.'

'That's a great idea.' But it did not explain the reason for the grim set to his lips or the fierceness of his scowl.

'I just need to work out the best person to approach.' His frown intensified as he glanced at his watch. 'If it's OK with you I think I'll call it a night. I'd better get on with some research and putting a proposal together for this endorsement.'

'Sure.' She tried not to feel hurt at the abruptness. 'I've got work to do too.'

Ten minutes later she said goodbye to Luca and entered the cottage, looked round the clean, cool, uncluttered interior. Wicker furniture and white cushions, a sleek wooden desk and a sumptuous double bed.

But she wasn't tired—a mix of jet lag and a reaction to the conversation she'd just had. Perhaps work would help; she could research tourist spots or finish putting together her Turin photos. As she booted up her computer and pulled up the images she paused, she hovered over a rare shot she had got of Luca. He'd been in the shot accidentally and in fact that made it way better than a posed one. He had been explaining something in the factory, the art of roasting a cocoa bean, and you could see passion and integrity and pride in his stance and features. It would be perfect for his website. Whatever he thought.

Emily frowned and quickly pulled up the website of Palazzo di Cioccolato to study it again, as an idea gathered in her mind.

Luca awoke the following morning, aware of a strange sense of anticipation. As he swung his legs out of bed he assured himself his mood had nothing to do with Emily Khatri and everything to do with having done something constructive about Jodi.

The previous night he had researched the royal family and the recent film festival. Nowhere had he found any mention of his sister, but he now understood two royal family trees. The Jalpuran one and that of the Mediterranean island of Talonos. The Royal Film Festival was held on each island biannually and covered both Bollywood and European films. The royals from Talonos fronted the European side.

So in terms of friendships, assuming Jodi had been befriended by the younger royals, this narrowed it down on the Jalpuran side to Prince Rohan, Princess Alisha and Princess Riya and on the Talonosian side to Prince Carlos and Prince Juan.

Obviously contacting royalty wasn't straightforward

but he had emailed the royal representative to ask for a meeting about an endorsement. At the meeting, what could be more natural than to mention Jodi? And the beauty of it was there would be no need to involve Emily at all, no need to use her name.

So now he could go and enjoy his time with Emily with a clear conscience. The words replayed in his head. Enjoy his time? No. What he meant was he could focus on the ad campaign. This was business, not a date. He and Emily wanted diametrically different things from a relationship and he would not forget that. Would never risk hurting someone else, especially Emily, who had clearly been hurt badly before. The memory of the sadness in her stance and face brought a frown to his face. If it had been Howard who had caused such hurt, he would take great pleasure in kicking the man round Jalpura, globally renowned photographer or not.

Once dressed in chinos and a T-shirt he left the cottage and headed to the outdoor restaurant area, which had been transformed from its night-time ambience. Now the sun shone on the grass-thatched canopy that trailed flowers down the stilted sides that propped it up. The air was replete with the smell of coffee and an aroma of spice emanated from the heaving buffet table set up to one side.

He waved as he saw Emily emerge from her cottage and soon they were seated. He glanced at her, sensed a certain lightness in her mood and he smiled. Her return smile was so sweet he blinked, felt warmth touch his chest. 'This looks sumptuous,' she said. 'I can't believe I can even eat after last night, but I can.'

They headed for the buffet and returned with heaped plates. 'It's strange to eat spicy food at breakfast but somehow here it works.' Emily spooned tomato chutney onto a piece of her *dosa*.

'Last time I came here I vowed I'd learn how to cook some of these recipes.'

'Have you?'

'Unfortunately not.' He'd got home and soon after that his world had imploded with the death of his father.

'Do you cook a lot?'

'A fair bit; I like coming up with new recipes, but nothing on this scale.' He looked down at his plate with the *idlis*—rice flour cakes served with a spicy *dal sambar*.

They ate in silence after that, both savouring the tastes until, once replete, Emily spread a map of the island on the table.

'Right, the Royal Palace Gardens are here. I reckon we've got time for a couple of hours there before we head to the farm.'

'Sounds good. Let's go.'

Half an hour later they approached the lush green hill and looked towards the apex where the palace sprawled in an ungainly beauty. The red-orange walls were dappled with flecks of sunshine and the multi-faceted windows reflected myriad motes of light.

For a moment Luca wondered if Jodi's friend was inside somewhere, a person who could give him the answers he sought, and then he was distracted as Emily made a sweeping gesture that encompassed lush landscaped meadows, flowering shrubs and bamboo thickets.

'This definitely has potential.'

'Yes.' He looked down at her and for a bittersweet moment it seemed to him as though her words applied to them, that somehow in a different universe and time they had potential to be something more than business colleagues. But not in this one, for all the reasons they had enumerated only hours before.

'Especially if you want the hint of royalty. Either

way I'll take some good focused shots of the palace and grounds.'

He watched as she clicked away, camera shutter whirring. She paused, looked up at the palace. 'I wonder what history those walls have seen. And what sort of life goes on in there now.'

So, ironically enough, did he.

'Anyway, I think I've got enough. Are there any particular angles you think I may have missed? Would you like a shot of you?'

'No. I'm good, thank you. I'm sure you have it covered and I'm sure we don't need a picture of me to sell chocolate.'

Emily took a deep breath. 'Actually, I want to talk to you about that. I…well, I've had an idea.'

'Go ahead.' He indicated a bench and they sat down.

'I think you *would* sell your chocolate.' She pulled her phone out of her pocket and quickly scrolled down to a photo of him in the factory in Turin. 'This would look great on your website. It could be part of your story. It shows how much you care, your passion for what you create. I think that will make people buy your products. People like the personal touch. You could have a photo of you with your mentor, the famous chocolatier, pictures of you mixing ingredients, on the cocoa farm. I'm happy to do it.'

He watched her expression, the way the light played on her skin, her excitement at the idea, the expressive wave of her hands and he wanted to encourage that, wanted to agree, but he couldn't. He had always vowed never to do what his father had done—bind his product to his name. 'I told you, Emily, *I* don't want to be on the website. I prefer being an invisible presence.'

'But why?' Now she twisted to face him, her brown

eyes studying his expression as her forehead creased in puzzlement. 'You have achieved so much, Luca. It's... incredible and, damn it, I bet loads of people want to know how you did it, want the personal touch. The Petrovelli brand. The Petrovelli story.'

'I prefer to remain out of the public eye,' he said.

She shook her head and he could see hurt dawn in her eyes. 'It's OK. Obviously you have your reasons and you don't want to share them. I thought it would be a good idea. Sorry I overstepped.'

Damn it. Luca tried to tell himself he hadn't asked Emily to waste her time on this, that this wasn't his fault. But as she stood up and hitched her camera onto her shoulder he knew he wanted to erase the hurt from her gaze. He suspected she'd been hurt enough recently, knew she'd taken the rejection personally as a slur on her ability.

'You didn't. And I truly love your ideas. But I can't do it—tell the Petrovelli story. You think I should do what my father did, and I understand that it's a great marketing strategy.' Dolci's success had been part founded on marketing the Casseveti name, the entrepreneur husband, the aristocratic beautiful wife, the cute Casseveti heiress, the celebrity lifestyle. 'But the whole Casseveti fairy tale was built on a foundation of betrayal, on my mother's misery and abandonment. The Petrovelli story is the flipside of the Casseveti coin. When my father left we had nothing.' His mother had refused to take anything, had too much pride, 'Then my mother realised she was pregnant. That chocolate I told you about that she craved—do you want to know why she was so restrained when she ate it? Because there was only one small bar, and even that I begged from the shop owner. When it was gone, we sat and listed the ingredients together, closed our eyes and imagined the taste. That's how my love of chocolate started. And I'll be damned if I put that on the website.'

She sat back down on the bench, turned towards him, her focus now solely on him. 'I'm sorry. I assumed your father supported you, or at least made some sort of settlement.' The compassion on her face was almost painful and he didn't want it. This was exactly why he didn't share his background. He did not want pity, remembered it etched on the man who owned the chocolate shop all those years ago, on the faces of anyone who ever discovered they were Cassevetis, the pauper outcasts of the Dolci brand. Remembered the bullying, all brought about because a playground thug had seen an article on the Cassevetis.

But all that was over. 'There is no need to be sorry. It doesn't matter any more. It is best forgotten.'

'No, it isn't. Because it makes your story all the more amazing. You built Palazzo di Cioccolato from nothing, built it on a foundation of guts and determination. And I bet your mum is proud of you.'

Now he was on easier ground. 'She is amazing; I couldn't have done it without her. She didn't let what my father did make her bitter. And she always put us first. Looking back, I know how terrified she must have been, how lost and lonely. I do remember her crying a lot but always when she thought I couldn't hear her. And somehow she picked herself up and supported us. Found a way to put food on the table. She worked in some terrible places, but she also studied, did evening courses and now she is a high-flying lawyer. And somehow through all of it she was always there for us, to help with homework, to talk to us, to support us.'

'She sounds wonderful.'

'She is. Jodi and I are lucky.'

'Yes, you are. Truly lucky.' For a second she looked away into the distance and her wistful voice made him wonder what her own relationship with her mother was like. 'So why not put that on your website? A tribute to your mum, a picture of you and her, part of your story to honour her strength.'

'No. I won't do that; I won't do what my father did, spin a sugary story of love and devotion and family. I do love my family—I would do anything for my mother, for Jodi. Anything. But I will not use that love and turn it into a publicity stunt to sell my product. Our family life is private.' Even now he wasn't sure he understood what his mum had gone through, but he knew he wouldn't expose her or Jodi in any way to the public eye.

'I didn't mean it like that.' Emily's voice was small and he realised he'd sounded harsher than he meant. 'I meant I truly think your mum is fantastic. Not all mums put their kids first.'

He recalled her words from yesterday, the allusion to her mum's multiple marriages, her desire to have the type of arrangement where she put her family first, and he spoke without thought, 'I guess yours didn't?' He shook his head. 'Sorry. Now *I* have overstepped.'

'It's OK. You're right. Don't get me wrong, my mum loves me, she does, but she didn't put me first. Not when it came to her relationships—she seemed to always fall for men who had no interest in children. So I became a nuisance; she was worried I'd get in the way, drive them away, and she wanted to focus her whole being on her new man.'

'That can't have been easy.' The idea of a young Emily being shunted out of the way, made to feel like an unwanted impediment, made him both angry and sad.

As if she sensed this, she gave a quick shake of her

head. 'It wasn't, but it wasn't the end of the world either. In all fairness to Mum, she had never planned on being a parent, and she does her best. When she isn't pursuing love or getting over a broken heart Mum is loads of fun to be with. I have plenty of good childhood memories.' She met his gaze, her chin jutting out. 'So there is no need to be sorry,' she said, echoing his own words of a few minutes before, and he realised she wanted pity as little as he did.

'I understand that, and I am glad you and your mum do have a positive relationship.' He admired the way Emily took the good and didn't bemoan the bad.

'And I am glad that you succeeded and now you can provide your mum with as much chocolate as she wants. You started a business off your own back with strength and resolve, not helped by family friends or inherited wealth. And you should be proud of that.' She tilted her head to one side. 'But you aren't, are you? When you talk about your company, your passion and pride is unmistakeable. But you must be equally proud of yourself.'

Her words jolted through him. 'Of course, I am.' But the words lacked conviction even to him. Even if that didn't make sense. He'd been driven all his life to be a success, to rival his father, and until this moment he'd have sworn he was damn proud of his journey. Just because he didn't want to publicise his story didn't mean he wasn't proud of it. Did it? Emotions began to swirl inside him, triggered by the sincerity of Emily's gaze as she continued to speak.

'What you have achieved is…superlative. You've built your company up on talent, guts and determination.'

Luca listened to the words, saw admiration in the depths of her brown eyes and the truth hit him: the realisation that he didn't deserve admiration or accolades from this woman. From anyone.

His voice was harsh as he spoke. 'Palazzo di Cioccolato isn't built on guts and determination and talent. It's built on revenge. All I wanted was to outdo my father.' The whole raison d'être of this company was to defeat James Casseveti.' And now bitterness pervaded his voice as he realised that, whilst he'd prided himself on getting over his dad, in truth his whole life's work had been governed by James. Frustrated anger roiled through him.

'Then you made something positive out of something negative.' She leant forward, placed a hand on his arm, and he caught his breath; her touch diminished the anger as warmth entered the mix. She looked up at him and his heart twisted at the serious look in her eyes, the depth of belief. 'What your father did to your mother, to you, was wrong. You could have taken that negativity and desire for revenge and done something bad with that. Instead you did good. You found a talent inside yourself and you have made a success of your life. Of your company and yourself.'

How he wanted to believe her, but emotions twisted his gut. How could he be proud? Because in the end he'd failed. Death had robbed him of the revenge he'd dreamed of and he was left knowing his life's purpose could never now be achieved.

Her hand moved from his arm and slipped into his and she squeezed gently. 'Be proud of your story, Luca. I would be.'

'Even if it ended in failure. In the end I never had my chance to show my dad that I made it. Without him. He'll never see me set up my flagship London store. I'll never send him an invite to the opening party.' He gave a small mirthless laugh. 'It sounds stupid, does it not? That was my life goal.'

'No. It doesn't sound stupid. But you didn't fail. The very act of living your life as you have, of being a true family with your mum and Jodi, all you have achieved despite what he did to you all—that is success and you mustn't let anything take that away from you.' She continued, 'Set up your London flagship store and dedicate it to your mother, to your own success. Full stop.'

As he saw the conviction on her face for the first time in a long time he felt a small buzz of enthusiasm about a London launch, a faint sensation, but it was there, and he took her hand in his, squeezed it gently. 'Thank you. I will think about it.'

'I'm glad.' Her smile was so warm it seemed to envelop him with a sense of well-being, a lightness that prompted him to lean forward and brush his lips against her cheek. Her closeness, her scent, the tickle of her hair all combined to whirl his head, the impact somehow equal to when he had really kissed her.

He heard her intake of breath, knew he had to break this spell, had to change the dynamic to one he actually understood. Pulling away gently, he rose to his feet, made a show of glancing at his watch. 'We'd better get going. The farm awaits.'

CHAPTER TEN

THE JOURNEY TO the farm held Emily speechless; the sheer verdant lushness of the landscape took her breath and all her energy as she frantically tried to capture it on film, relieved to have something to do, something to focus on other than Luca. Something had happened back there—somehow they'd both ended up sharing and she wasn't sure how or why.

'Don't forget to also look and take it in,' Luca recommended from beside her and after a while she did just that. Hills gently undulated against a background of majesty where mountains loomed in the distance, the rush of water from a waterfall vied with the cacophony of the wildlife and in the end she simply watched as the vivid, vibrant scenery flashed past. Forest dark and thick with deciduous green, the dip and rise of dense valleys spun her head with the sheer force of nature.

Until they reached the farm itself, where she took in the sweet fragrant scents of coconut and the rich smell of soil and earth. She walked with Luca to the whitewashed house where she knew Samar lived and worked.

Before they could knock the door swung open and a man emerged. Grizzled salt-and-pepper hair, dark, weather-beaten skin and deep-set eyes creased with laughter lines, he stepped towards Luca, a smile on his face.

'Welcome, Luca.'

Luca moved into a quick embrace, stood back and the two men clasped hands, and instinctively Emily held her camera up, snapped the picture even as she asked permission.

'No problem.'

Luca gestured to Emily. 'This is Emily. Emily, Samar.'

'I am happy to meet you,' Samar said, his English fluent and his smile wide.

'Me too. I am so excited to see your farm; from everything Luca has told me, I understand that your beans inspired his new brand and I am stoked to see where it all started.'

'I am happy for Luca to show you around and then please come back here for tea and cakes.' Samar turned to Luca. 'All the staff have been told of your coming and your requirements.'

Emily frowned. Had there been some sort of secret message, an emphasis on the word requirement, or was it simply because Samar spoke English as a second language?

Luca smiled easily. 'Thank you. Is it OK for Emily to take photographs anywhere or are there any areas we should stay away from?'

'Feel free to go anywhere. Many of the workers do not speak English but I can answer any questions you have later.'

'Thank you.' Emily smiled, instinctively liking the middle-aged farm owner, his face weathered from the sun and the callouses on his hands indicating that he did his fair share out in the fields. She followed Luca back to the car and they drove down a dusty track that led to the farm itself and groves of trees.

'The taller ones are coconut trees,' Luca explained as

he parked on the verge and they climbed out. 'They provide shelter for the cocoa trees that have been planted between them. The trees are quite delicate and keeping them thriving is a huge part of Samar's responsibility. They need to be protected from wind and sun, the soil needs to be fertilised correctly and any sign of damage or disease has to be dealt with quickly. Samar once said to me that he sees these trees like his marriage. He has been married for forty years…since he was seventeen.'

'Wow.' She contemplated the idea, and for a scant second she envied it.

'Samar believes that marriages need work and effort to thrive and bear fruit. He says nowadays people give up too easily.'

Emily thought of her mother on marriage number five, of her own disastrous marriage to Howard. 'The problem is that it takes two people to do the work. It can't all be done by one person.' Her mother had put so much effort into each relationship, made sure she always looked perfect, relegated Emily to the background, thrown herself into every husband's hobbies, tried to support them all to no avail. And, irony of irony, Emily, having vowed she never would, had followed exactly in her mother's footsteps.

'Exactly. That's why I stand by what I said yesterday. On your own you are in control, in a partnership you have to rely on someone else. Samar relies on these trees to respond to his care, he relies on the weather, on luck, on so many variables. Plus he has to put a lot in before he gets anything out. These trees don't yield pods at all for a few years.'

'What is their yield?'

'A typical pod contains thirty to forty beans and there

are about thirty pods per tree. It takes about four hundred dried beans to make one pound of cocoa.'

She stopped and looked at the trees, studied their shape, the clusters of pink and white flowers that dotted the branches and trunks, the green pods that dipped from the branches. She wanted to take photographs that emphasised their beauty, productivity and fragility, how susceptible they were to nature. That they needed care and nurture to flourish.

'I wish I could get up closer. I mean, I can zoom in, but I want to actually touch the pods, get the texture and the feel. Do you reckon I can climb it?'

'No.' His voice held a hint of amusement. 'The bark is soft and quite fragile. At harvest they use long-handled steel tools to reach and cut the pods so they don't damage it.'

'Hmm. Climbing is definitely out.'

'Not necessarily. You can climb up and sit on my shoulders.'

She knew, with absolute certainty, he'd spoken without thinking, simply made a practical suggestion.

There was a silence and she eyed his shoulders, their breadth and strength, imagined sitting astride them, legs dangling over his chest, him steadying her by wrapping his hands around her calves, and she gulped, looked up at the tree and then across to him. Considered her options. If she refused it would be awkward. After all, she wouldn't give it a thought if someone else had suggested it.

'Fine. What's the best way to do it?'

Luca inhaled a deep breath. 'I'll squat down...' he suited action to word '...and you...hop on.'

This was the world's worst idea but if either of them acknowledged that it would mean they didn't have this attraction under control and she was damned if she'd admit that.

Before she could change her mind, she 'hopped on' and tried to ignore how that meant effectively wrapping her legs round his face. Tried not to notice the muscle of his shoulders, the easy grace with which he rose and balanced her weight.

Focus on the damn tree, Em. Pretend he is a chair, an inanimate object.

Not possible when she could sense the vital strength of him; he stood sturdy and strong, unbowed by her weight. His hands encircled her calves, his grip gentle but it steadied her, so she didn't sway. Calves were not a sensory part of one's body. They weren't. Or surely they weren't supposed to be. But her brain had clearly got it all mixed up because all she could feel was his hands on her, branding her.

Focus. On the tree, on the living, flourishing tree. Somehow Luca's touch, the warmth and strength of him, seemed to make the tree come alive to her eye. Made the green more vibrant, the bark softer to her gentle touch, every sense heightened because of him. As she looked at the pod ripe and full of life, inhaled the tang of the fruit, the delicate scent of the flower, her head whirled. But she knew it wasn't only the force of nature, it was something to do with Luca, and all she wanted was to slide down, feel the strength of his chest, stand toe to toe with him. To touch and hold and kiss him.

But she wouldn't, couldn't.

Aware that at some point she had stopped taking pictures, was simply balanced on him, she forced her voice to work. 'I'm done. Thank you.'

Slowly he lowered himself to the ground and she scrambled off with as much dignity as she could, turned to face him and suddenly realised how close he was, and her heightened senses soared.

The sound of someone clearing their throat caused them both to turn, the moment broken as a woman stepped forward, an apologetic smile on her face.

She started to speak, the Indian language of familiar cadence to Emily, but she had never learnt it and now it was her turn to smile apologetically as she shook her head and turned her hands up.

The woman pointed to the camera round Emily's neck and then at herself before putting her palms together and holding them up in a gesture that clearly indicated 'please'.

'Of course.' Emily smiled her understanding and took a few pictures of the smiling woman, including one with Luca.

With another beaming smile the woman left and Emily turned to Luca, relieved that the interlude had hopefully eradicated the previous atmosphere. 'I'll develop the photos and give them to Samar.' She glanced at her watch. 'We'd better head back for tea and cakes.'

Fifteen minutes later they sat in a cool white-walled room, decorated with family pictures, some clearly from a previous era, garlanded in fragrant chains of flowers. Samar had introduced his wife, Shamini, a slender petite woman with grey-streaked black hair and a serene smile.

'These are delicious,' Emily said as she bit into the sweet, crumbly round *laddu*.

'Thank you. I am pleased you like them.'

'Was your tour successful?' Samar questioned.

'Definitely,' Emily said, and sudden heat touched her cheeks at a memory of being astride Luca's shoulders. 'We met one of your employees, a woman called Priya.

She asked for a photograph of her and Luca. I'll get it developed and send it to you for her if that's OK.'

'Of course.' Samar nodded. 'I too have a request. If you have time whilst you are here and Luca can spare you, would you perhaps take on an additional job, take some photos of the farm for our website?'

Emily hesitated, glanced down at her plate, picked up her cup of tea and put it down again as doubts pervaded. 'Um…to be honest that isn't my speciality. The pictures I took today are more for inspiration and ideas for Luca's ad campaign and…' And in truth she didn't want to do it, could see Howard's slow head-shake, the incredulous rise of an eyebrow that she was even considering it. It was one thing suggesting a few pictures of Luca for a website, but this was…an actual job. Plus Luca hadn't taken her up on her offer—true, he'd explained why but…somehow insidious doubt crept in and there was Howard's voice now. *Stick to what you know.'*

Countered, she realised, by the very real and present voice of Luca. 'That sounds right up your street, Emily.' He turned to the couple. 'Emily took some wonderful photos already and earlier today she came up with some amazing ideas for my website. I think she'll do a great job.'

Now she was torn, between her inner doubts and pleasure at the endorsement. 'Of course, I'd like to help,' she said.

'Excellent.'

Now Shamini beamed at her. 'And I too have a request. Would you be able to take a family portrait for us to put on our wall? We have four children and eight grandchildren and we have no picture of us all.'

'No problem.' That she could do.

'Thank you. We will, of course, pay you.'

Emily shook her head. 'For the website pictures, sure, but I will not accept payment for the family photo. I feel like you have paid me in cakes.'

'I can go one better than that.' Shamini clapped her hands together. 'You and Luca come with Samar and me to the local dance tonight. There is a performance by a visiting dance troupe and then it becomes a bit of a party.'

'Um…' Emily exchanged a quick glance with Luca, read in his gaze that, not only would it be impolite to refuse, but an evening in company would be much safer than a dinner *à deux*. A whole village would surely act as an effective chaperone. 'That sounds marvellous.' She took a deep breath. 'Would it be OK if I got started on the website pictures now?'

'Good idea,' Samar said. 'As long as Luca can spare you?'

Luca rose to his feet. 'No problem. I'll meet you back at the resort and we can walk down to the dance, grab some food on the way.'

Later that evening, Luca looked up as Emily approached the entrance to the resort, noted the lithe grace of her walk, and to his own chagrin his heart pitter-pattered at the sight of a woman he had seen mere hours before.

'How was your day?'

They asked the question at the same time and she smiled, a smile that stopped him in his tracks. 'You go first,' she said.

Luca hesitated. In truth he'd spent his afternoon looking for clues as to what Jodi had done whilst on Jalpura. He'd secured a meeting with Pradesh Patankar, the royal representative, in two days' time. The exchange of emails had been brief and to the point and all related to Luca's request to apply for royal endorsement of his chocolate.

There was no indication from Pradesh that the Petrovelli name was familiar, but perhaps that meant nothing. Perhaps the royal representative had simply assumed it was a common name, or a coincidence. Next Luca had gone to the hostel where Jodi had stayed, followed up his previous calls, but he'd drawn a complete blank. The proprietor thought he had a vague memory of Jodi, but given the volume of visitors he couldn't even be sure of that.

'Luca?'

He heard the concern in Emily's voice and blinked, erased the frown from his forehead. 'Sorry. I was thinking about work. I caught up with the office. And I have a meeting set up with the royal representative to discuss the endorsement.'

'That's brilliant.' Her smile of approbation deepened the sense of wrongness at not sharing the whole truth. And for a moment he was tempted to do just that, explain about Jodi, tell Emily of his worry for his sister. But that was the point, he wouldn't only be sharing his worries, he'd be sharing Jodi's business in the sure knowledge that Jodi would see that as a betrayal. Hell, Jodi would be mad enough that Luca was here on Jalpura, let alone if he involved Ava's best friend in his capers.

'How was *your* day?'

'I took some shots for Samar's website.'

He heard the flatness in her voice and frowned. 'You don't sound happy.'

She shrugged. 'I'm not. If I'm honest I kind of wish I hadn't agreed or that…'

'Or that I didn't push you into it?' he asked, and she nodded.

'I'm sure you meant well but…' He heard doubt as to his motives and he frowned.

'I did mean well—you have taken so many pictures

since we've been here and I've seen how much energy you put into them, how enthusiastic you are. I thought this was an opportunity for you. To try something different.'

'I told you already that I don't want or need to do that.'

He decided to try a different tack, still didn't understand why she wouldn't follow her dream. 'Can I see the pictures?'

'Um…sure…at some point… I guess. I haven't had a chance to look at them, pick out the best ones, and you'd only be able to see them on a screen right now, which isn't the same as—'

'So you could show me them on your phone now.'

'Well, yes. I can access them from my phone but…'

There was genuine discomfort in her stance now, her shoulders had drooped and one arm crossed her waist, her gaze averted from his, and he came to a halt, oblivious to the people who thronged round them.

Glancing round, he spotted a small low-walled courtyard and he made his way over and perched on the stone ledge. Reluctantly she followed, and he risked a smile. 'That's the first time I've understood the phrase dragging your feet,' he observed. 'What on earth is wrong?'

'Nothing.'

Luca watched as she sat on the wall; her expression showed a worry that verged on fear and he frowned. Perhaps he should back off but this didn't make sense, plus it occurred to him, 'Ever since we got to Turin you must have taken hundreds of pictures but you haven't shown me a single one. Apart from one of me.'

'You haven't asked,' she countered, and then bit her lip as she realised the opening she'd given him.

One he instantly took. 'I'm asking now.'

'I'd rather show you the finished products. It makes more sense.'

'I can just about see that if it's for the ad campaign, but why can't you show me the pictures of the cocoa farm? I'm interested.'

'I can.' Emily sighed. 'Of course, I can.' But he sensed the tension that still emanated from her body as she pulled out her phone and tapped a few buttons. 'Here you go.'

She handed him the phone, and turned away, arms folded across her middle.

This really didn't make sense; he'd expected her to want to show them to him, had looked forward to her enthusiasm, the gestures, the smile. If he were completely honest he would have welcomed the closeness, the tickle of her hair as she leant over to point something out.

Now he remembered her trepidation in the London café, but that had been when she was touting for the job. Then he had understood her worries. But surely not now; why would she fear his judgement now? Yet he could see doubt and fear in her brown eyes and in the tap of her foot and the slump of her shoulders.

He looked down at her phone; her fear was infectious and for a mad instant he was sure he'd see a mishmash of out-of-focus images on the screen. He studied the first photograph, a glorious picture of a woman next to a cocoa tree, reaching up to check one of the ripe pods. The woman wasn't young yet her body, the slightly calloused tips to her fingers, showed the suppleness of a woman used to hard work. Somehow the wide smile on her face, the vivid colours of her sari, the browns and verdant colours of the trees, the intense blue of the sky, all combined to show joy in her work, and in the beauty of her surroundings.

Luca continued to scroll down, marvelled at how Emily had captured the essence of the farm, beauty combined with a place of work, growth and productivity.

The lush ripeness of the pods, the sheer quirkiness of the coconuts, the wave of the tree fronds, the movement of people going about their tasks, the casual intimacy of two women laughing as they worked, the concentration on the face of a young man pruning a tree.

He turned to her, saw she hadn't moved, her stillness rigid as if she braced herself for his verdict.

'These are absolutely bloody brilliant,' he said. 'You've brought the farm to life for everyone to see. As an overview and in the detail. I can almost smell the trees, feel the sun on my face. I want to meet these people.'

Very slowly she relaxed, and he was rewarded with a tentative upturn of her lips, though her eyes still held scepticism, her frown one of disbelief. 'You don't have to be nice.'

'I'm not being nice. I'm being truthful.' He studied her expression. 'Surely you can see how good they are.'

'Honestly? No, I can't. All I can see is what I may have done wrong, wrong perspective, angle, feel, colour... I'm terrified to show them to Samar. I don't even want to show you anything I've done for the campaign. I think I'm just all ideas—all snap-snap-snap, all mouth and no follow through.'

Their conversation on the plane came back to him, her conviction that her metier was fashion photography and she didn't have the talent or ability to move into a different sphere.

'Look, I know I am not an expert, but I don't need to be—I am the target audience. I promise those photos will appeal to anyone looking at Samar's website. But I believe they are worth more even that that—I think you could do a photo documentary on Jalpura. On the life on this island. You said yourself it is a fascinating place—an independent Indian island with a royal family.'

'I told you—'

'I know what you told me, and I profoundly disagree.' He eyed her closely. 'What expert told you that you don't have what it takes?'

She hesitated, then, 'Howard.'

For one incredulous moment he stared at her. 'Your ex-husband.'

'Yes.' Her eyes narrowed at his expression. 'But he wasn't my ex when he told me. It's how we met—he agreed to do a critique, an assessment of my work. He told me the truth. He didn't have to—he could have strung me along because he wanted to date me, but he didn't. And the points made sense.'

'Perhaps he believed what he said, but that doesn't mean he is right.'

Emily looked at him. 'He is a globally renowned photographer. He's won every award there is.'

Luca waved his hand. 'That still doesn't make him infallible and you can't trust that his opinion wasn't coloured by his relationship with you.'

'I get that, and I spent months trying to prove him wrong. In the end I gave up my career to be his assistant because I hoped I'd learn from him.'

'And did you?'

'No.' Her voice was small now. 'He tried but it was frustrating for him. To be fair to him he genuinely saw fashion as an inferior branch of photography, something frothy and frivolous, so to him my work was…not very important.'

'But what you do is part of a billion-dollar industry.'

'Howard doesn't care about money. And I can't blame him for criticising my work. It was full of flaws, in my technique, the angles, the light. Sometimes he'd take a picture of the same thing I had and he'd point out the differences.'

Anger began to rise in Luca, but he kept his voice even. 'Just out of interest, did he ever say anything positive?'

'Of course.'

'Let me guess—it was always followed by a "but" or was a backhanded compliment.'

Luca forced himself not to rise and pace. 'It sounds like he wanted to undermine you, and it sounds to me like his voice is still in your head.'

'Of course, it isn't. Or at least not in a bad way. I'd be a fool to discount his opinion on photography.'

'No, you wouldn't. I am not dissing Howard's talents, but I do think his perspective was warped by your relationship.' Plus the man sounded like a bully and he suspected Emily's marriage had been marred by a bullying she wasn't even aware of. Because she was so star-struck by the man's talent she believed his words to be gospel. But it explained her fear of showing her work, the way she expected criticism, the fact she still had Howard's words in her head. Just as the taunts of those schoolyard bullies had echoed in his.

'Perhaps.' Emily shrugged. 'It doesn't really matter.' She rose to her feet. 'Shall we walk?'

'Sure.' He followed suit, looked down at the sudden pinched look on her face and he knew it did matter, that he had to try and convince her that Howard was wrong. 'We can talk whilst we walk.'

CHAPTER ELEVEN

AS THEY STARTED to walk the thronged noisy streets, redolent with the scent of spices and rich with the sound of chatter, the honk of horns and the cries of street vendors hawking their wares, Emily considered Luca's words, wondered if he could be right. When she'd taken the pictures at the farm it had felt...'right'. As she'd snapped she'd felt in the zone, as if everything had come together.

It was only when it came to showing them to Luca that doubt had assailed her and she'd prepared herself to be put down. But that wasn't down to Luca, that was down to her—she'd grown to assume and believe negativity from Howard, not just on her work, but on everything. She had been sure during their marriage that he had become more and more judgemental because of her inability to learn from him. That that inability had made him see only her flaws and not the things that had presumably made him marry her in the first place.

But how could she question whether he was right? He was Howard McAllister.

Luca glanced down at her and his voice was quiet now, his grey eyes dark with purpose. 'Those photos are good, Emily. Don't let Howard's voice stay in your head telling you they aren't.'

'It's not that easy. If you went to your mentor and he said you only had the talent to produce mass chocolate what would you have done?'

'Gone away and produced the best mass-produced chocolate in the business and gone back to the drawing board. I'd have proved him wrong.' He shrugged. 'But there is a big difference here. My mentor is a gentleman. Yours sounds like a bully. And bullies have power. I don't think Howard's opinion of your work was unbiased.'

'You can't know that.'

'No, but I do know a bully when I see one. And I remember what it is like to be taunted and put down—not in the same context, but I know how much it can hurt. I am telling you this so you know what I am saying is not just empty words.'

Now she focused on him, saw the remembered hurt in his eyes and knew this was a trip down memory lane he didn't want to take.

'I told you that when my father left life was tough. But after a while my mother pulled us through the toughest bit, there was more money, I was settled in school, life became more normal. But then things began to change. As Dolci grew so did the publicity around the Casseveti name. A boy at my school figured out who I was and he latched onto it. Asked where my dad was, why I never saw him, told me my dad didn't love me because I was so weak, came up with different reasons and made me repeat them…and soon it caught on and then it escalated. Into relentless bullying.'

'That's awful.' Her heart cracked as she imagined the young Luca, a small boy having his vulnerabilities displayed and exploited; she could almost feel how much each taunt must have seared his soul. And to force him to list reasons why his dad had left took cruelty to a new level, was tantamount to Howard listing out all her faults and flaws and making her repeat them. At least he had stopped short of that. 'I'm sorry you had to go through that.'

He shook his head. 'I didn't tell you because I want your pity. I told you because I know what that treatment does to you. It undermines you and makes you insecure and miserable. It eats away at your soul and makes you crumble inside. It erodes your confidence and it can make you doubt everything about yourself. I endured it at school, you had to live with it. Howard forcing you to spot the difference, his constant put-downs, his dismissal of your achievements as frothy and frivolous. He is a grown-up version of the boy who made my life so miserable.'

His words made her pause. Of course, she knew Howard was a full-scale cheating rat, a man who had cheated on his pregnant wife, a man who had quite simply not given a flying fish for his unborn child. Yet because the man's photographic talent could not be questioned, she'd still accepted that all the put-downs, all the criticisms of her work were justified.

Just as she was sure Luca would have believed the awful cruel taunts of his persecutor. Would have believed his father's abandonment was his fault. The idea heated anger in her veins as well as compassion for the child he'd been.

'I hope that boy got what was coming to him, or at least some help. I hope he saw the error of his ways, but before he did I hope someone bopped him on the nose or something.'

His expression crinkled into amusement and she frowned. 'It's not funny.'

'I know it's not, but I guess we are both displaying a

violent streak. I was just thinking how I wish Howard were here so I could kick him round Jalpura.'

They both contemplated the idea and then she turned to him and without even realising it she slipped her hand into his. 'What happened?' she asked. 'With the bullying?'

'Nothing. I endured it. I was too ashamed to tell my mum. Things were finally going well for her. She'd qualified as a lawyer, she'd even started another relationship. And I didn't want to tell her. I was meant to be the...' He broke off and she completed the sentence.

'The man of the family.' And her heart cracked a little more even as anger surged at James Casseveti for leaving his son so heartlessly.

'Yes,' he acknowledged. 'And to be frank the whole situation was far from manly. I couldn't tell anyone, so I endured it. Until one day I snapped. They decided to take it a step further; they brought my mother into it, started trying to make me say filth about her. I saw red. I went for the leader. I'd love to say I won but I didn't. But he did get bopped on the nose—my only satisfaction is that I did get in a good few punches and kicks and I certainly surprised him. But he was bigger than me and had a couple of friends there too. The teachers pulled us apart and obviously after that adults were involved. I didn't tell the whole of it, but other kids were questioned and they did. I wish they hadn't.'

'Why?'

'Because it made me feel weak. As though I needed to be looked after.'

'You did need to be looked after. You were a child.'

'I get that, but it didn't feel like that back then. It felt humiliating and as if I'd let my mum down. That's what bullying does to you—it makes you lose perspective.'

'So what did your mum do?'

'She let rip at the school, and before I knew it she had pulled me out of school and decided we were moving to Italy, that we were changing our name to her maiden name, Petrovelli.'

'So that was why you had a new start.'

'That's why. Mum's new relationship didn't work out, but she said it didn't matter because she fell in love with Italy instead. We all did. So it all worked out.'

Suddenly he halted and turned so they faced each other, took her other hand in his as well. 'I'd like it to work out for you too. Don't let Howard ruin your chance to do something you want to do with your photography. Don't believe his words.'

'It's not that easy.'

'I know,' he said softly, and she wondered if he still believed the words of those bullies so long ago. Still believed it was his fault his father had left. 'But you can try.'

Emily took a deep breath. 'OK. I'll try. I'll think about the idea of a Jalpura documentary.' For a long moment they stood, hands linked, and a strange trickle of warmth, of hope, of lightness ran through her. Until finally the hustle and bustle of people urged them to keep walking and Luca pointed to a nearby food stall.

'Shall we try that one? I am suddenly ravenous. And we need to eat before the dance.'

'Me too. That one sounds perfect.' And as he tugged her towards the enticing aroma she realised she was smiling.

Luca swallowed the last delicious mouthful of *biriani* and they started to walk towards the temple where the dance was going to take place.

'I am very excited about this,' Emily said. 'I've always wanted to see Kathakali performed.'

'Kathakali?'

'Yes, Samar and Shamini mentioned it earlier, after you'd gone. My dad told me about it. It's a dance that tells a story. It literally means story play. The dancers have years and years of training because it's so hard. The whole story is conveyed through gesture and facial expression and colour. The make-up is exquisite and basically different colours represent different characters and characteristics. It's amazingly complex and the story is usually epic. The performances can go on throughout the night.' She glanced up at him and gave a gurgle of laughter. 'Not today, though. Today is one scene from the story of Nala and Damayanti. It's a love story, but they have a pretty torturous path with demons and battles and magic and snakes before they get their happy ending.'

She broke off. 'Sorry. I am boring on.'

'Nope. You aren't.' He grinned at her. 'I think you'd have made a natural Kathakali dancer.'

'Hah. Just because I move my hands around a bit when I talk.'

'There's that, but it's also the way your nose crinkles when you dislike something and the crease on your forehead when you are focusing.' He studied each feature and his fingers tingled with a desire to smooth his fingers against her brow, to move down the bridge of her nose. 'Then there's your smile.'

He heard her intake of breath at his words, a sound she turned into a shaky laugh. 'I think you need more than a few wrinkles to be a Kathakali dancer.'

As she spoke they reached their destination, saw Samar and Shamini waiting for them, and now they turned their attention to the performance.

'Part of the whole experience is to watch the dancers transform,' Samar explained, and they watched a dancer lie prostrate as other members of the troupe applied a complicated *maquillage*. 'He is the main dancer, he is Nala, so he has the most complicated make-up.'

A few minutes later the performance began, the dancers assembled around a large multi-wicked bell metal lamp. Bare-chested musicians encircled the actors, drums to hand.

Luca's eyes widened as he witnessed the intricacies, the grace, the drama, the wealth of detailed movement that told the story. The scene showed Nala finally defeated by an evil demon who poisoned his character, made him into a gambler who wagered away his kingdom and deserted his wife. Perhaps that was what had happened to his father, Luca thought; his Achilles heel, his greed, had been exploited by a demon woman who would stop at nothing to get him.

Emily's words of earlier rang through his head. *'The very act of living your life as you have, of being a true family with your mum and Jodi, all you have achieved despite what he did to you all—that is success and you mustn't let anything take that away from you.'*

He turned to look at her as she stared wide-eyed and rapt at the stage; he'd swear he saw the suspicion of tears in her eyes as she swayed to the evocative beat of the drums, as the wife Damayanti wept as Nala crept into the night.

Looking down, he saw that at some stage in the proceedings he'd taken her hand in his. For a moment he considered releasing his grip, knew he didn't want to, told himself that it was all to do with the atmosphere, the beat of the drum, the flare of the fires that had sprung up throughout the grounds.

The applause was long and soon after the performers melted away. 'Now it's over to us,' Shamini said. 'I think we should dance the *kolkali*.'

They watched as groups of men and women formed circles; from somewhere came a supply of sticks that were passed around and both he and Emily gripped them. Other people held instruments, drums and cymbals. Luca looked to Emily for elucidation but she shrugged her shoulders. 'I have no idea how to do this.' Worry clouded her eyes as she looked down at the stick and Luca wanted to dispel it.

'Then let's just go with it,' he said, and a sudden exhilaration raced through him as he held out a hand to her. 'Together.' Because he wanted to dance with her, wanted her to abandon herself to the sound of the drums as she had for scant seconds back in Silvio's in Turin. Perhaps it would give her a release from the doubts and sadness he knew she carried, would lighten the load.

Surprise lit her eyes along with a second of hesitation and then she tucked a strand of hair behind her ear and placed her hand in his with a shy smile. 'Let's do it.'

The feel of her hand in his again brought a smile to his face and he squeezed it slightly, caught his breath as she moved closer to him, and he felt intoxicated by her proximity, her scent, her warmth.

Within minutes the music started, the beat slow at first, and the group began to move in a circle striking the sticks against each other, whilst keeping rhythm with different steps. Luca released Emily's hand but stayed close as they both tried to follow along, and soon enough they were swept up in the rhythm. Yet Luca was only aware of Emily, the rest of the crowd a mere backdrop against this entrancing woman, the sway and curve of her body, the grace of her movements and the expression on her face, her eyes focused on him.

The music increased in tempo and volume, and the movements became faster and faster as the circle of dancers expanded and contracted, the sticks a blur in the moonlight, and through it all Emily weaved and turned, the dance bringing her so tantalisingly close and then pulling her away, and it seemed to him that they danced for each other and each other alone.

Then another dancer tripped, lost his balance and stumbled into Emily's path; she tried to dodge but her body twisted at an awkward angle and instantly Luca moved to catch her and then there she was in his arms. 'Are you OK?'

'I think so. Yes. Thank you.' Her voice was breathless as she looked up at him and now his chest constricted at her beauty, dark hair wild around her flushed face, her brown eyes warm and alive with laughter and passion, and now he knew that she had danced for him, had been as caught in the spell as he was. Knew too he should let her go but instead his arms tightened around her as he told himself she might be hurt, might need his support. For a timeless instant they stood, and his head whirled as he saw desire spark in her eyes, her lips parted, and he couldn't help himself. Oblivious to the dancers around them, he lowered his head and kissed her.

CHAPTER TWELVE

THE TOUCH OF Luca's lips blew Emily's mind, cascaded her with feeling, made her feel alive for the first time in such a long, long time and she gave in to it. To the sheer raw visceral passion his lips aroused in her. She revelled in it as he deepened the kiss and wrapped his hands in her hair so that she let out a small moan of sheer unadulterated pleasure, pressed harder against him, wanting more. Wanting the barriers of the soft cotton T-shirt to be gone. Pleasure and frustration vied inside her in a whirling, squirming, hot mess of desire.

Until she knew she couldn't take any more. 'We need to go,' she said.

He nodded. There was no need for words, their sole focus now on assuaging the churn of need. All thoughts of one moment in time gone, discarded, abandoned without question. She was no longer capable of rational thought, her whole being motivated by desire for this man.

'We need to find Samar and Shamini.'

Luca dropped a curse but then nodded and somehow they got through the goodbyes, the necessary chit-chat, and then they were half walking, half running back to the resort. All that mattered now was getting to the hotel. A journey achieved in near silence, though his hand remained firmly clasped around hers. Almost as though, if they broke the link, common sense would weasel its way back in, and she gripped his fingers with equal fervour. Every so often he would brush his lips against hers and anticipation surged through her until her head whirled.

Then finally—finally—they got to the hotel and she followed him blindly to his thatched cottage, simply because it was nearest. He closed the door, moved to the windows and pulled the blinds down so the room was cocooned in cool dusky darkness.

For one fleeting moment a sudden panic touched her, a wonder if her body could do this, could remember how. Whether after the ordeal she'd been through she could expose herself. One hand smoothed over her now flat stomach and a pang of sadness touched her.

As if he sensed her change he stilled, slowed down and she looked up at him, his face shadowed now, but she could see concern dawn in his eyes. 'We don't have to do this, Emily. If you've changed your mind, that's fine.'

Had she? Or could she allow herself this? Set aside grief for a short while. He watched her, his gaze steady and full of reassurance, and she knew if she backed off he would fall in with her wishes without recrimination and with a level of understanding. His concern added a new layer of sweetness, and a different kind of warmth touched her senses. 'I haven't changed my mind.'

And this time the kiss was different, soft and sweet and almost tentative and it felt, oh, so completely right, and now as they walked backwards towards the bed and he lowered her gently down she smiled at him. Knew in that moment that she was in safe hands and she reached up to tug him down next to her. Then all doubts vanished as his lips covered hers and with tantalising slowness and exquisite promise he unbuttoned the front of her dress.

Then all thought stopped and she lost herself in the

vortex of need and want, of laughter and pleasure; the feel of skin on skin, the touch of his fingers, the sweep of his back, the scent of citrus and bergamot and Luca all assailed her senses.

Luca opened his eyes, instantly aware of Emily in the crook of his arm, and he made sure to remain still, wanted to let her sleep. As he looked at her, eyes closed, the curve of her eyelashes against her cheek, the silken tangle of her hair, a strange sense of wonder shivered through him. He lay back and stared up at the white of the ceiling, heard the sound of a bird from outside and luxuriated in the sheer magic of this moment.

On that thought she opened her eyes and he watched, revelled in the sheer intimacy of watching. Her small puzzled frown, her lazy smile as memory dawned and then she rolled away from him, sat bolt upright, sheet clutched to her chest.

'Oh…' she said. 'It really happened.'

'It really did.' He couldn't help but smile and she smiled back, a small shy smile but a smile none the less and, encouraged, he wriggled up the headboard so he was next to her, side by side, their legs pressed together in the warm aftermath of intimacy. Perhaps he should feel regret for the previous night but he didn't, perhaps he should also feel worry or concern about the next steps but right now he couldn't muster up the energy.

'I don't know what to say,' she said finally. 'I really don't. I mean, this is exactly what we were trying to avoid but…'

'It's a bit difficult right now to figure out why.'

'That's for sure.' There was a silence and then she tucked the sheet more securely round herself, moved even closer to him. 'I do have an idea.'

'Go ahead.'

'We both know this can't go anywhere. I don't want your type of relationship and you don't want mine. In truth right now I am too hurt to even contemplate a relationship anyway. But last night was…'

'Magical, amazing, glorious…'

Now she laughed, a small gurgle of a chuckle. 'All of those things. And I don't really see the point in shutting the stable door after the horse has bolted.'

'So you are suggesting we stay in the stable and bolt it from the inside?'

'Something like that. I'm saying that whilst we are here on Jalpura we should keep doing…' she gestured over the bed '…this. Maybe see this as a bubble in time. I'd like that—a bubble where I can insulate myself from the real world.' For a second, sadness flitted across her face and he wondered what secrets she still held to her.

'A time to just experience the moment?' he asked.

'Yes. And once we go home it all comes to a natural end. I'll deal with your marketing team then anyway, so our paths don't even need to cross. But *now* is a time to be happy and enjoy what's on offer.' Now she turned slightly so she was looking into his eyes. 'And I do understand what is on offer. Nothing heavy. All your usual caveats are in place. No expectations, no clinginess. Low-key, not intense. Fun and easy.'

Luca recognised his own words and a qualm hit him; was that what he wanted with Emily? The question jolted him with panic and he focused on keeping his expression neutral as she continued to speak.

'I know I don't match a lot of your other criteria.' He couldn't help his slight flinch—somehow the idea of criteria didn't seem as…valid…as it had a few nights ago. 'But that's OK, because this is a strictly short-term arrangement. I guess you'll have to think of me as an anomaly.'

More qualms hit him—this was breaking all his rules and he was suddenly scared he couldn't handle it, because his thoughts were spinning out of control. She was so near, so beautiful, so… Emily and he was scared that he'd let her too close.

'If that works for you?' Her voice went small and he knew that she feared rejection, could read his doubts.

Chill, Luca.

This was an overreaction. Because the bottom line was that he and Emily wanted different things—she did not want a long-term arrangement on his terms, she wanted a husband and a family and that was a no-go area for him. So she was right. This was a bubble, a blip if you will, and if Emily wanted fun and joy and magic then that was what he would provide.

'It completely works for me. You are a beautiful, magical anomaly,' he said and was rewarded with a smile. 'As long as you are sure this…' and now he gestured around '…is what you want.'

'I'm sure.' Her voice held certainty, and he saw nothing in her eyes to cast doubt on her word, though he still sensed a vulnerability, a fragility to her desire for a few days of happiness. And in that moment he vowed he would do all in his power to give her that; there could be no harm in that.

'Then how about we start right now with a little bit of this?' With a big grin on his face he tugged at the sheet, was rewarded by a small shriek from Emily as she reached for it.

'Hey, give that back.'

Now his grin broadened. 'Make me.'

With a breathless laugh she lunged for it and he moved

beneath her, caught her into an embrace, so she sat astride him, looking down, her glorious hair loose, the tips tickling his chest. Then she leaned down and kissed him and the sheet dropped from his hand forgotten as he kissed her right back.

An hour later they lay entwined and tangled in the sheets and Luca marvelled at how he and Emily had come to this. No rules, no regulations and right now he didn't care, because this felt like the most natural thing in the world.

He dropped a kiss on the top of her head, revelled in the feel of her silken hair. 'So what's the plan for the day?'

'Breakfast. I am ravenous. Then later today I'm going to take the family picture for Shamini and then I thought we'd stick to plan. Go for a walk and see the sunset at the summit—I think it may be a good location for the shoot?'

'Sounds like a plan.'

She rolled a little away from him and propped herself up on her elbow. 'Also I thought we could go through some photos. If you like. To take with you to your meeting with the royal representative.' Her smile was a little shy and he could sense the sudden tension in her body. 'I thought you could show them to him and suggest a quid pro quo. They endorse your chocolate and we'll make sure Jalpura is advertised as an amazing tourist destination as part of the campaign.'

Luca sat up, leaned against the headboard and she followed suit. As he put an arm around her shoulders a conflict of emotions coursed through him. 'Thank you.' He knew how hard it was for her to show off her work, knew how much the offer meant. 'That is an excellent idea.' But alongside pride in Emily was discomfort at his own actions. After all, his main goal of the meeting was to find out information about Jodi. Luca hesitated, his brain whirring—surely he could trust her to keep Jodi's situation confidential…surely it couldn't harm to share some information? But if he did that Emily would ask questions…and who knew what she'd find out? And it wasn't his business to share. Yet it felt wrong to lie, even if the lie was only one of omission. Especially when she was willing to go so far out of her own comfort zone to help him.

Before he could decide her phone rang; she picked it up from the bedside drawer and glanced down, then back up at him. 'It's Ava. It's probably her daily check-in, about the wedding plans.'

The words pulled him back to reality—saved by the bell. Emily was Ava's best friend, the reminder one he shouldn't even need. Quickly he moved away, swung his legs over the side of the bed. 'I'll go and sort out some breakfast. You talk to Ava,' he said.

'OK.' A pause, then she said his name and he turned to face her. 'I won't tell Ava about us. This is between you and me. There is no need for her to know.'

'Agreed.' Her words, a reassurance, tipped the scales towards the possibility of confidence. 'I won't be long.'

She nodded. 'Cool. Thank you.'

He returned half an hour later, pushed a trolley through the door. In his absence she'd pulled on one of his T-shirts and was curled up in one of the wicker chairs. For a moment he wondered if he should ask about Ava, decided to avoid it. Somehow the idea that she was keeping them a secret made him feel a little uncomfortable. A reminder of why he'd vowed not to get involved with Emily. But that ship had sailed and he couldn't bring himself to regret it.

He gestured to the bed. 'I thought we'd have breakfast in bed?'

Her eyes widened as she surveyed the laden trolley.

'*Dosas*, *idlis*, vegetable curry with egg, and masala potatoes and, of course, some coffee.' All her favourites.

'We can't eat that in bed. We'll make a mess.'

'That's the fun of it,' he said. 'We can get as messy...' and now he smiled at her '...or as dirty as we want.' He wiggled his eyebrows and she gave a low, sweet laugh.

'I'm in.'

And soon they were back in the bed, plates on their knees.

'This feels ridiculously decadent,' she said. 'We should be working...'

'Work-schmerk. We'll get plenty of that done later. Right now you need to taste this.' Carefully he scooped up some potatoes in a piece of *dosa* and obediently she opened her mouth so he could pop it in.

'My God, that is incredible.' She closed her eyes and he watched as she savoured the taste, felt a warmth of intimacy as they continued to eat, fed each other pieces of fruit until they were replete.

'I don't think I'll ever eat again,' she said. 'Or at least till lunchtime.'

There was a pause and then she took a deep breath, glanced sideways at him. 'Ava said to say hi.'

Luca realised he had no idea what to say. He settled for, 'Say hi back.'

'Also, Ava asked me to ask you something. She doesn't want to put you on the spot by asking herself. I don't want to wait to tell you so...'

'Go ahead.' Foreboding touched him.

'Would you walk her down the aisle at her wedding?'

The question came from nowhere and he knew the shock must show on his face.

'She knows it is a big ask but she just wants you to think about it. You don't have to answer now.'

'I can answer now. I don't think that would work.' The idea of taking on the role that James Casseveti would have done with such pride and joy and love seemed impossible to even contemplate, brought a complex swirl of emotion to the surface. He swung himself out of bed, pulled on his chinos and started to pace. 'I am surprised Ava would even want that.'

Emily joined him, dressed in his T-shirt that fell to below her knees; she placed a hand on his arm. 'You're her brother. Her family.'

'No.' Luca closed his eyes, then opened them again. 'Ava's life and mine have been carried out separately and apart—we are only "family" because we chance to share a "father". It is blood, not family. Family is about the bond you feel with people you grow up with and care about and who care for you. I like Ava but I can't make her into real family.' He saw a flash of sadness cross her face. 'I'm sorry.'

Emily shook her head. 'But you could get to know her, forge a bond with her. Of course, it would be different from your bond with your mother and Jodi, but it would still be real.'

'There is too much history between us.' He kept his voice gentle. 'I know it is not Ava's fault what her father, our father did. But it will always be there.' The knowledge that she had been chosen over him, had kept James Casseveti's love in a way Luca hadn't. That was his real failure and he had no need of any reminders.

'I understand that. But I still think you should try, otherwise your father's actions are still affecting the present, preventing you and Ava from developing a relationship.' She stepped forward and now her brown eyes held a plea. 'You have a choice. I get it would be hard but...'

Anger flickered into being; how could Emily get it? 'That is easy to say.'

Reading his expression, she reached out and took his hand, the touch warm and sweet, and it soothed the anger as she led him over to the wicker sofa. They sat down, still hand in hand. 'I *do* get it. I get how hard it is to accept the favoured child, the one who actually grows up with a parent, sees them every day, is part of their real family.'

Her words were sincere and he studied her face, saw genuine empathy there, and the penny dropped. Emily had spoken of her dad's second family, the brood of children. 'You speak of your father's second family?'

'Yes.'

'That is different. You have known those half-siblings all their life. You have a relationship with your dad.'

'Yes. But it is dilute, a shadow of what he has with my half-siblings. Don't get me wrong—he is fond of me. But I come second, I am of less importance. That's natural—he sees me twice a year, for a week at a time. He lives with his other kids, is there for all the milestones. I get I'm lucky he saw me at all, but growing up it affected how I feel about my siblings. Part of me resented them, even though I know it's not their fault.'

No, it had been her father's fault. Perhaps he could have done things differently, made an effort to see Emily on his own, made some time for her to forge their own separate bond. And now another penny clanged down. That was exactly what Emily was asking him to do now with Ava. He put that thought aside for the moment, wanting to know more about Emily.

'Do you still visit your family now?'

'I haven't for a while. In a way it still feels now how it did then. I wasn't part of their unit and I couldn't figure out how to infiltrate it. I was surplus to requirements.'

'So you watched from the sidelines?'

'Yes.'

'*I get that.*' He could picture a younger Emily, dark eyes wide and serious, at a busy bustling dinner table, listening to family 'jokes' she didn't understand, trying to work out what to say or do, how to get her dad's attention. And it sent a jolt of pain to his chest. 'I used to read all the celebrity magazines that followed Ava's lifestyle; I watched from the sidelines as well.' He'd studied the pictures with such intensity, looking for clues, hoping he'd see something in his father's expression that showed he felt regret, but all he'd seen was a father's love for his daughter.

'I'm sorry. That must have been difficult, to have to see and watch. At least I was part of my father's life.' She shook her head. 'I used to take photos of them all. It gave me something to do and later on I'd study them, try to work out what to do. Maybe if I did my hair like my younger sister, if I started to like superhero comics like my brother, would it help?'

'Did it?'

'Nope. In the end I figured it was best to stay invisible. And now it is all too late. They are still all a unit. They still have each other and they still don't need me. I have tried, truly I have, but I still can't figure out how. The bottom line is that they aren't really interested in me. That is their choice.'

'Maybe that will change, perhaps it's not too late— to forge some sort of bond. For you,' he added hastily.

'Then why is it too late for you? I know you don't need to. You and Jodi have each other, are a unit. But maybe you and Ava could form some kind of bond.'

'I don't think I can.' He heard the sadness in his own voice. 'There *is* too much history between Ava and me, even if we only met recently. Too much of that history is still with us. Ava loved her dad, loved and respected a man who tore my mother's life apart and deserted his children. There is no getting past that fact.'

'Not unless you want to,' Emily said softly. 'Unless you make the choice to try.' As her siblings hadn't. 'Because otherwise Ava is being punished for something she didn't do. And so are you. Missing out on getting to know someone who is your family by blood.'

As her siblings were missing out on a chance to know this woman.

'Look, please think about it. Not walking her down the aisle, but maybe just meeting up for a cup of coffee next time you are in London.'

'I'll think about it.'

'Good.' Her smile was so sweet and full of satisfaction that he couldn't help but smile back and then her smile widened. 'And now I think reality has intruded enough. I think we should go back to bed.' Now *she* wiggled her eyebrows. 'We've been messy. Now let's get dirty.' The words were said with an exaggerated huskiness, and without further ado he rose and pulled her to her feet and swept her up in his arms and carried her to the bed.

CHAPTER THIRTEEN

LATER THAT DAY Emily glanced across at Luca as a car drove them out to the cocoa-bean farm, felt a sense of replete satisfaction mixed with the surreal. As she studied the strength of his face, his sculpted body, the shape of his hands she gave a small shiver of remembered pleasure. He turned his head and she saw his eyes darken, knew he could read her expression. Though that was hardly surprising; there was every chance she was drooling.

The car pulled to a stop and they climbed out with a quick thank you to the driver and headed towards the house. Emily smiled as Shamini pulled the door open with a welcoming smile. 'Come in. We are so happy you are doing this for us.'

Emily clocked the quick glance the older woman darted between her and Luca and wondered if she'd seen the kiss at the dance. 'So where would you like the photograph to be taken?' she said hurriedly.

'Let me make you a cup of tea and I'll explain my ideas. Luca, you can head to the lounge, where the family is gathering.'

As they headed into the cool interior a small girl hurtled towards Shamini and wrapped her arms around her legs in a hug. 'This is my granddaughter, Amelia,' she said. The girl peeped up shyly and then hid her face in the folds of Shamini's brightly coloured sari.

Emily glanced round the whitewashed kitchen, with its stone worktops and swept tiled floor and the lingering scent of spice in the air. Pans hung from the ceiling and she glimpsed a larder with jars full of rice and dried lentils and herbs.

Once tea was made she followed Shamini and Amelia into a large lounge.

'I think the photo should be in here, as it is here we have most space.'

Emily blinked—she knew that Samar and Shamini had four children and eight grandchildren, but knowing and seeing were two different things. The room was a hubbub of noise and children, a bright swirl of saris and western dress. Until Samar spotted them, picked up a bell and rang it loudly.

The noise levels subsided and everyone turned to the doorway.

'This is Emily, who has very kindly agreed to take our picture. Emily, what would you like us to do? We're still waiting for my youngest daughter and her family, but we can get started.'

About ten minutes later Emily had sorted people out into a group and figured out lighting and backdrops, moved various things around and taken a few informal shots to warm everyone up.

The peal of the doorbell indicated the arrival of the final participants and minutes later a young couple walked in. 'I am so sorry we are late. Amitabh needed a nappy-change just when we were ready to leave,' the dark-haired woman said.

Emily saw now that the man held a baby in his arms

and Shamini swept forward and took the baby, presented him proudly to Emily.

'The latest addition to the family.'

Emily gazed at the baby and from nowhere grief screamed towards her, hit her so hard that she almost stepped back. This was what her baby would have looked like. Her baby who had kicked inside her, the baby she had wanted so badly, had already loved so much.

'He's beautiful. How old is he?' Her voice was slightly strangled and she sensed Luca glance at her.

'Ten months. He started to crawl a few weeks ago.' The baby gurgled and then tilted forward, arms outstretched towards Emily. 'He likes you.' Shamini held the baby out and Emily could feel her body temperature plunge. Her skin felt clammy with a sudden sheen of panic and the reek of sadness, all the worse because it was so unexpected, had pelted in out of nowhere and struck.

Would her baby have started to crawl yet, weighed the same as this little one, would he too have had a shock of black hair or would his head have been downy with little wisps? The baby regarded her with immense solemnity and then grabbed her finger and started to chew it. A tsunami of grief swept through her as she held this warm, living miracle of existence in her arms. Sorrow underlaid with anger. Why had it happened to her? And guilt. What had she done wrong?

A part of her wanted to hold onto this baby and turn and run, go somewhere where the baby was hers, where the world had been different, where she could simply have the future she'd envisioned, with her child.

Then all of a sudden Luca was by her side; his sheer strength and bulk, full of reassurance, pulled her back to reality. His gaze rested on her, concern and care evident.

For one brief moment she allowed herself to breathe

in the baby smell and then she gathered a smile together as she carefully handed Amitabh back to his mum, then turned away, pushed down the grief into the expanse of ache inside her.

'Right.' Picking up her camera, she said, 'Let's get this show on the road.'

And soon she looked through the lens at the grouped ensemble, this family standing together, a family who lived together clearly in harmony and friendship and love.

The knowledge that this couldn't happen for her clogged her throat, and she focused on the welcome familiarity of the camera's cold touch in her hand, channelled her everything into this. Perhaps she couldn't have it but she wouldn't grudge it to this family and she would do her best to provide them with a picture they could cherish, a picture that showed their bond, their connection and their love. In the way the grandmother held her granddaughter's hand, in the pride of a father in his children, in a wife's look of love to her husband and the respect and affection to her mother-in-law.

Once done, she found it in herself to mingle, chat to everyone, play with the children, all with a smile on her face. And through it all she was aware of Luca's gaze on her, the question and concern in his eyes, aware too that he was making this easier for her, just through his presence, the way he deflected conversation, the knowledge that she could lean against his strength if need be.

Whoa. No leaning, remember? No clinginess or emotional need. That was the deal—Luca had no wish to be exposed to another's pain or vulnerabilities. However understanding he'd already proven to be, this all ended in a few days. So she mustn't let herself get close on any other level.

Finally it was time to leave, to start their trek to the

summit of a local mountain to see the sunset, check out
the place as a possible photo shoot. Goodbyes said, they
left the house, turned to wave at the family grouped outside and headed for the car.

'What's wrong?' Once they were in the cool of the air-
conditioned car Luca turned to face Emily, scooted across
the seat to take her hands in his. He knew something was
wrong, had seen such intense pain in her eyes that his
own soul had shrivelled slightly and all he'd wanted was
to shield her. 'Would you prefer to go back to the resort?'

Emily shook her head. 'I'm fine.' For a moment he
almost believed her. Almost but not quite; her voice was
too tight and he knew what he'd seen. 'And I have high
hopes of this as a good location.' Her voice held a bright-
ness stark in its falsity and the contrast to the dull shadows, the ache in her brown eyes.

He hesitated, wondered if he should push it, but Emily
launched a flow of bright inconsequential chatter as they
climbed, interspersed with the constant click of her camera. Not that he could blame her for taking photos; the
trek showcased scenery so lushly beautiful it took his
breath away.

At one point they made their way through a cardamom
plantation. The scent of the spice pervaded the air, supplanted by the waft of tea as they walked through fields
of tea. As they got higher a haze of mist added extra atmosphere to the undulating rise and fall of the surrounding hills and valleys.

Once at the peak they sank down, breathless from
the walk, and gazed out over the spectacular panoramic
view that encompassed so many of Nature's wonders. The
flashing blue of a wide river, dense forests that lined the
mountain slopes, and the immensity of the sky.

'This is stunning. The sky feels so close that I feel like if I reach up, I can touch it.'

He studied her expression, saw appreciation in her gaze but sadness still shimmered through.

'Emily, tell me what's wrong—I know something has caused you sadness.'

She shook her head. 'It's OK, Luca. I know you don't like to get involved in the emotional side of things. And I *want* to play by your rulebook, want a fun, carefree, magical bubble of time. Turns out it's not that easy to escape reality. What with Ava and now this. But I'll be OK.' She smiled a smile that tore his heartstrings. 'Being up here, the walk, this vista, all seem to bring a tranquillity.'

Luca stilled, listened to her quote his own criteria back at him and castigated himself for being a selfish schmuck. Was that what he wanted from life, to protect himself from another's vulnerability? 'It's not OK,' he said quietly. 'I don't want to play by the rulebook. We have already agreed you are an anomaly. An anomaly in a bubble. So, if you wish to, if I can help, please tell me what has happened.'

There was a silence and as she looked out he knew she was coming to some sort of inner decision.

'Thank you. I would like to tell you; I haven't talked to anyone and up here it feels right to remember what happened.'

Shifting slightly, she leant against him, faced the view, as if she were also sharing her story with the universe. 'I lost my baby,' she said. 'I had a late miscarriage. I was six months pregnant. I thought I was safe, I'd felt him kick, talked to him, played him music. But then I lost him. If I'd gone to term he would have been ten months now, the same age as Amitabh. That's what set me off.'

'I am so sorry.' The words were so inadequate and he

pulled her closer, tried to convey his sympathy through the warmth of his body, through closeness. 'I cannot imagine how you must have felt. How you are still feeling.' A year wasn't long enough to get over something like that, if you ever did. 'I am so sorry. For you and for Howard.' The man was a bully, but he didn't deserve to lose a child.

'Howard didn't care—he didn't even want the baby.' Now her face looked pinched, white with remembered strain. 'The baby was an accident but for me he was a happy one. Sure, I had planned to wait a few years, we'd only just got married, but I was still ecstatic. Howard wasn't. He wasn't happy at all. Said it was too early, that a baby would interfere with our happiness. I think he wanted me to consider a termination, but he knew there was no way I would do it. But he resented the baby, hated me being pregnant. The put-downs became more barbed and he kept finding fault with my appearance. Particularly my weight, my skin; the morning sickness disgusted him; he hated that I was tired. He didn't even want anyone to know, said he had an upcoming book release and he didn't want anything to detract from that. So I had to hide the pregnancy.' Now she turned wide eyes onto him. 'And now I keep thinking did I do something wrong? Did I cause the miscarriage by pushing myself when I was tired? By hiding the pregnancy? By dressing wrong—there was a time a few weeks before when I wore high heels. What if that was part of it? If I did something wrong?'

His heart turned in his chest and for a moment anger consumed him, anger at the callous selfishness of her ex-husband. An anger he pushed aside as he heard the torment of guilt in her voice, the fear that it had somehow been her fault.

'Emily, I wasn't there but I know you. You would never put your baby at risk. I bet you did everything right, didn't touch alcohol, ate all the right food, did everything. When my mother was pregnant with Jodi she was exhausted all the time and she pushed and pushed herself.'

'She had to.' Emily's voice was small. 'Maybe I should have stood up to Howard, instead of running around desperately trying to be the perfect wife. I wanted to show him that the baby didn't have to be a bad change in our lives. I thought he loved me.'

Luca pulled her closer to him, could hear the pain and devastation in her voice.

'It turned out he was having an affair. It started whilst I was pregnant—he justified it by saying I had become unattractive, overweight and selfish. I couldn't believe I'd been so stupid. That it had happened to me, that I had believed in him. How could I not have seen the signs? When I watched my mother go through marriage after marriage, I thought I could spot a lie at one hundred paces. But I truly had no idea. How dumb am I?'

'You aren't dumb. Sometimes we believe what we want to believe.'

'Then that makes me a double fool. I grew up watching my mother do that time and again. Believing this man was the one, believing she was loved. And I fell into the same trap. Blown away by the idea that Howard loved the real me. Was interested in me, my photography, my personality—nothing to do with my parents. I thought he loved me for me.'

Luca searched for words of comfort. 'Perhaps he did. My dad loved my mum. Just not enough.'

Emily shook her head. 'Howard didn't love me; I think Howard only loves himself. He wanted the perfect adoring wife. The only reason I believed he loved me was because at least he genuinely didn't care about my parents' fame or fortune. I'd already shown him I was more than ready to adore him, look up to him, listen to him. Then I fell pregnant and he knew he wouldn't be the centre of my world any more. So he cheated on me.'

'Was he sorry?'

'Nope. When I found out I did confront him—he seemed to think his actions were justified as I was no longer attractive. We had a stand-up row. He left and I lost the baby two weeks later.' Now guilt shadowed her eyes again. 'Maybe the row made the difference. I don't know, but I didn't see him again. When I lost the baby it was as if the world collapsed on me. I lost it completely. The past months have been like some sort of nightmare. Howard wanted out, a painless divorce, and I agreed to everything. Then I pretty much went to bed, pulled the duvet over my head and blocked out the world. Turns out you can't do that. Reality creeps in, there are bills to pay and I realised I had to get myself up and going again. The problem is I can't always keep the grief at bay, or the questions. Then I panic. I want to turn the clock back, make different decisions, figure out what I did wrong and fix it.'

'Emily, you did nothing wrong. I know that, I swear it to you. You cannot torture yourself, trying to turn time back, or reliving the past.' He wanted Emily to know he understood. 'When my dad left I spent years trying to figure out why. What I did wrong. All I wanted was a chance to make it right, to turn back time and somehow make him stay. Then I thought if I could figure it out maybe he'd at least visit, call, send a postcard.'

'You did nothing wrong. He did.'

'But it didn't feel like that. Because I know he did love me. I remember the love, sitting on his shoulders, being swung up in the air, bedtime stories, walking along holding his hand. So how could he stop loving me so easily? I must have done something.'

'But you didn't.'

'You didn't do anything wrong either.' Turning away from the view, he focused on her, held her arms gently as she faced him, wanting that connection. 'I know you didn't. You can't second-guess yourself, can't torture yourself with the what-ifs and might-have-beens. Because you can't turn back time, you can't change what happened. But you can remember your baby, honour and cherish his memory. And the joy you felt in him.' Just as perhaps he should cherish his own memories with his dad, the knowledge that for five years he had been loved.

'I did feel joy.' Her eyes were wide now. 'When I knew I was pregnant I felt panic but mostly I felt awe, a deep awe that there was the beginning of a tiny living being growing inside me. I loved tracing his progress, the first small swell of my tummy, the idea that what I ate and drank was helping my baby to develop. Then there was the first time he kicked, the first time I played music to him. I loved him very much. I will always cherish his memory. And however sad I am I need to remember he also gave me joy.' She turned to Luca. 'And I believe your father loved you—you know that, you have all those memories that prove it. You did nothing wrong either, Luca—he did, and I think he regretted it all the days of his life. Yes, he lavished love on Ava, because he didn't want to make the same mistake again. I think he left you and Jodi shares in Dolci in a clumsy way to try to show love and make amends.'

Luca turned and pulled her into a close embrace, touched beyond all reason that in her own pain she could find words to give him comfort. She pulled away gently and said, 'Look.'

He turned his head and watched as the sun started to dip, streaked the sky in a glorious medley of orange and red against the panoramic background of a cloud-streaked sky. The colours seemed to light up the world, dapple and reflect the peaks and valleys, surround them in a magnificent aura of hues and tints.

He moved to pass her the camera but she shook her head. 'I just want to experience this moment. With you.'

So they sat hand in hand and watched the sun set before returning down the slopes, through the plantations and back to the resort and bed, where they held each other in their arms and created a different type of magic.

CHAPTER FOURTEEN

EMILY OPENED HER eyes aware that something wasn't quite right, something was missing. Luca. Groggily she reached out, realised he wasn't there and, after a night spent curled up in his arms or with her head on his chest or spooned up against him with his arm protectively around her, already her body protested at the lack of his skin against hers.

'Hey, sleepyhead.' His deep voice came from the end of the bed and she saw that he was up and dressed in a lightweight suit.

'Good morning.' She stretched. 'It's the meeting with the royal representative,' she remembered.

'That's the one.'

She frowned as she blinked away the last vestiges of sleep. 'You look nervous.' The idea was incongruous—it was hard to imagine nerves daring to impinge anxiety on Luca.

'I've never met a royal rep. But it's not that—I wanted to make sure you're OK before I leave. Tell you thank you for sharing with me yesterday and I hope you don't regret it.'

Did she? How could she, when he'd shown such understanding, known when to hold her and when to speak, shared his own trauma and loss and feelings with her?

Who would have thought it? 'No regrets,' she said. 'So go. You don't want to be late. And good luck—I know this is important to you and I'm sure you'll blow him away.'

Now she'd swear Luca looked…discomfited, uncomfortable, hesitant. Emily propped herself up, her forehead creased in a small frown. 'Is something wrong? You are nervous, aren't you?'

Quickly she swung her legs out of bed, walked towards him, even now revelled in the fact she wore one of his T-shirts, the idea both sexy and intimate. 'Hey. You don't need to worry. I know this endorsement is important to you but I bet you'll nail it.' She reached him and placed her hand on his arm, looked up at him, wanted her words to matter, touched at this unexpected vulnerability. 'Truly. Your chocolate is fabulous and endorsing it will give the royal family and Jalpura some great publicity. All you need to do is tell the truth.'

She'd swear he flinched, the idea confirmed as he took a step back, away from her touch, and a sudden hurt mingled with foreboding.

'Luca? Did I say something wrong?'

A succinct curse dropped from his lips. 'No. You said nothing wrong at all. You're right,' he said. 'I do need to tell the truth. To you.'

'What do you mean?'

He gestured to the table by the window. 'Why don't we sit?'

Emily frowned and the temptation to refuse, to simply cover her ears and go *la-la-la*, nigh on overwhelmed her. But instead she leant down, scooped up the trousers she'd discarded the night before and pulled them on, suddenly feeling at a disadvantage in the T-shirt.

She followed him to the table and sat in the wicker chair opposite him.

'I don't understand. What truth?'

'My meeting with the royal representative. I didn't make it to get an endorsement for my chocolate.' His voice was even, matter of fact, as if now he had decided to tell the truth, whatever that meant, he would do so calmly. The only tell was the clench of his jaw, and the hand through his hair. 'Or rather that isn't my prime objective.'

'Then what is?' Emily closed her eyes for a second, tried to figure out what the hell was going on. A sense of foreboding rippled in her gut, one she tried to calm. There would be an explanation for this, a good one, one that would assuage the sense of doom.

'I want to find out some information about Jodi.'

'Your sister Jodi? I'm still not with you.' What did Jodi have to do with anything?

'Jodi was badly impacted by our father's death. She decided to take some time out and go travelling and to begin with she loved it. She kept in touch, sent photos, we called regularly. Then she came to Jalpura, visited the cocoa farm, and got involved in organising the film festival. Then everything changed, her messages became less frequent and she sounded different. I can't explain it, but I knew something was wrong even if she wouldn't admit it. Then she left Jalpura and pretty much went incommunicado. She said she needed some space and I shouldn't worry or pull any big-brother shit.'

Now concern for Jodi outweighed her own confusion. 'So have you found out anything about Jodi? When did you last hear from her?'

'All I found out was that whilst she was working on the film festival she made friends with royalty. A princess.'

Emily raised her eyebrows. 'So either Princess Alisha or Princess Riya. I did some research partly to help you with the endorsement, but also as part of my plan to bring a flavour of royalty into the campaign.'

'Yes, that's what I figure. So I was hoping Pradesh Patankar could shed some light, maybe give me an idea of what happened to Jodi.'

The idea that he was willing to do all this for his sister touched her, more so because she knew no one in her family would ever do that for her. 'So you came to Jalpura to find out what happened.' Her voice was small, because, however much she lauded his concern for his sister, Luca had lied to her by omission. Worse. 'The advertising campaign was a cover.'

'No. The campaign is real.'

'But you only did it now because it gave you a reason to come to Jalpura.'

He hesitated, rocked back on his feet as he looked away from her and then back. 'Yes.'

'Why didn't you tell me?'

'Because I couldn't betray Jodi's trust; she would hate for me to discuss her private stuff with anyone, let alone…'

'Ava's best friend,' Emily completed. And in a way she could see that, understood that he couldn't possibly have told her about this when he first met her. But it still didn't make sense. 'In which case, why me? Why did you bring me here? Why would *you* employ Ava's best friend? Then bring me here.'

She stared at him, saw the discomfort in his stance, in his expression, and once again he looked away.

'Luca?'

Now cold hard premonition froze inside her and she wrapped her arms around herself, knew that, bad as this already was, it was about to become worse.

'I thought your name would help.'

'My name?' The penny dropped with a resounding leaden clang as everything fell into place. It all made sense now. Why Luca was neither bothered about seeing her portfolio nor cared about her lack of experience. 'You hired me for my name.' She started to pace, needed to move, to stoke the anger that she knew preceded the burn of utter, complete humiliation. 'It wouldn't have mattered how useless a photographer I was, you needed me here, on Jalpura, because of my name. You thought it would open doors for you.' Hurt began to cascade through her along with mortification. Luca hadn't believed in her talent, hadn't hired her because of her photography skills. He'd hired her because her name might have helped in his quest for Jodi.

Her brain clouded, fogged with hurt, and she tried to cleave through. Luca had decided to come to Jalpura to look for his sister, had decided to come here under cover of a photo shoot and bring Emily Khatri with him. In case she could be of use. Correction. In case her name could be of use. However, he'd failed to apprise her of the fact and she hadn't realised that was part of the deal.

What a fool she was, to have believed the whole spiel. Had she really believed that Luca's judgement was correct, could miraculously negate Howard's? Howard had been a cheat and a liar, turned out so was Luca.

'Why?' she asked quietly now. 'Why did you sleep with me, Luca? What was that? Some sort of bonus, a way of passing time in between your investigations? A way of distracting me in case I figured something out?' Because with hindsight she could see that he hadn't ever really engaged with the campaign. They'd visited locations but they'd never sat down and discussed ideas or brainstormed. Instead they'd spent their time talking, getting up close and personal.

'No. This. Us. It's real.' He gestured between them, his voice taut.

She shook her head, as a memory engulfed her of Howard being confronted with his infidelity and the way he had dismissed it. *'Lucille was an interim woman. Whilst you're pregnant. She doesn't mean anything. You. Me. We're real.'*

Disbelief at her own stupidity churned her tummy. Again—she'd done it again. Been taken in by an illusion. With Howard she'd believed he loved her for herself. With Luca she'd believed he'd employed her because he had faith in her talent, in her photographic skills. Had also believed he cared, that these days were magical. In reality they had been just another arrangement.

With Howard she'd believed in their marriage, been worried about how he was adjusting to fatherhood, run around trying to make things right. Whilst all the time he'd been sleeping with someone else. With Luca she'd believed in his ad campaign, was convinced he'd believed in her. Humiliation, mortification at her own stupidity, roiled over her skin, tinged and patched it with cold, and she rubbed her hands up and down her arms. Oh, God, she'd confided in him, slept with him…trusted him with her deepest emotions. Told him about her baby. She came to a halt in front of where he stood.

'No, it's not real, Luca.' Any more than her marriage had been. 'Everything, all of this, what happened between us, is fake. Founded on a lie.' She shook her head. 'I need to go.' She'd reached the door when she heard his voice.

'Emily. No. Wait. Please.'

From somewhere Luca found his voice. For the past minutes he'd been rooted to the spot, frozen as her words punched into him, each one a sucker punch to his ribs, his chest, his heart. Regret, panic and a fear he couldn't understand all churned inside him as the impact of his actions washed over him in a cold wave.

Slowly she turned and he took a step towards her, stopped at her instinctive recoil. How could he blame her? He'd messed up big time and he had no idea how to put it right.

'I am sorry. So sorry. But when I met you and you came up with the idea for the ad to be shot on Jalpura it seemed like a brilliant idea. A win-win situation. A way to help Jodi and achieve an amazing ad campaign. That was always real, and I did believe you were the perfect person for the job.'

'Because of my name.' The bitterness in her voice was justified. And unanswerable and that knowledge unleashed a sense of panic inside him, a realisation that this was sliding out of his control. Had it been just hours ago that they had been lying entwined, she with her head on his chest, cocooned in his arms? Enough. Somehow he had to explain his actions, convince Emily what they had was real, that the bubble was intact.

'Yes, your name mattered, but the ad campaign is real—your talent is real.'

'But you wouldn't have hired me if it wasn't for my name.'

He could see the dullness in her eyes and he wished, how he wished, he could turn the clock back and make this right.

He exhaled, knew he owed her that truth. 'I don't know the answer to that. But if I hadn't it would have been because you are Ava's friend—not because I didn't believe you could do the job.'

'That makes it worse, Luca. All my life I've been

someone's something. My parents' daughter, Howard's wife. Ava's friend. I thought—' She broke off and lifted her hands to her cheeks.

He knew what she'd thought. 'You thought that with me you were yourself.'

'Yes, and now I know I wasn't.'

'But you were. The past few days—they have been magical. What happened between us is nothing to do with your name. Every word I said about your talent is the God's honest truth.'

'I want to believe you, but I don't. Not when the whole trip here was based on a lie.' She shook her head. 'I can just about understand why you did what you did at the start. I understand you love your sister and you put her first.' The words a stark reminder to him that no one ever put her first. Not her mother, or her father. Certainly not Howard. Had she believed Luca would? 'If you were going to keep that from me, then you shouldn't have got involved with me, shouldn't have let me think this was something it never was. I bared my soul to you—and the whole time you were lying to me.'

'I told you things I have never shared with anyone. The only thing I did not tell you about was Jodi.'

'But that omission made all the difference.'

She was right and the knowledge that he'd hurt a woman who was already hurting so much, added to the burden she already carried, twisted inside him. The realization he'd done it again—once again he'd pushed away a person he loved through his own misguided actions. Only this time he knew exactly what he'd done wrong and no amount of wishing could undo that.

Whoa. Love? The realisation caused him to let out a small sigh of disbelief even as he knew it to be true. He loved Emily and he'd screwed it up. Of course, he had.

Cold, clammy awareness roiled. This was exactly why he'd made rules and regulations, had only committed to those immutable long-term arrangements. Where he couldn't hurt anyone or get hurt himself. Because he'd known all along that he could not manage love, had no idea how to keep it, navigate it.

He'd already hurt Emily, in a few 'magical days'. Because now the magic had turned dark and God only knew what harm and pain he'd manage to inflict over time. This had to end, and end now.

'You're right. I messed up and I'm sorry. Sorry I hurt you and sorry I failed you. I know there is no need for you to believe this, but I do believe in your talent. I believe in you. Please don't let my stupidity hurt you and please take care of yourself.'

She nodded, ran her hands up and down her arms and he had to fight not to step forward and pull her into his arms.

'I hope you find Jodi and that she is OK.' She took a deep breath. 'If you need to use my name, use it. If you need me to do something to help you gain access to the royal family, then please let me know.' The idea that she would make this offer flayed him and he knew that not even for Jodi would he ask Emily to do that. The knowledge was both ironic and surprising. 'I will write up my ideas and a report for your marketing department to file away, should you ever decide to go ahead with the campaign.' Her words were as jerky and stilted as his had been and he clenched his hands into fists. 'There are plenty of photographers who will jump at the chance.'

He stood frozen to the spot as the door clicked shut and his heart cracked. Part of him wanted to run after her, to beg forgiveness, declare his love, but he knew there was no point. That way could only end in more hurt to Emily. And he'd hurt her enough. With his inadequacy, his sheer selfishness,. There was no defence for what he'd done. Yes, he had prioritised Jodi, because he had vowed he would never let his sister down as his father had done. But in so doing he had let Emily down instead—a knowledge that seared him even as his whole being yearned for her. But there was no point. People he loved left him. End of.

He didn't know how long he remained there still and silent inhaling her elusive scent, the evocative floral tang that lingered in the air and filled him with an ache of regret and guilt. *Fool.* At some point he turned his head, caught a glimpse of her hairbrush on the bedside table and an image of her pulling it through the sheer satin of her hair caught his breath in bereft that he'd never see that again.

CHAPTER FIFTEEN

Five days later, Turin

LUCA SAT BEHIND his office desk and looked at the email, read it again.

Dear Luca

I wanted to let you know that I have found out some information about Jodi. After our conversation I contacted the royal representative and used my name to gain access to the Queen, who is a huge fan of my father. Whilst I was there I also met with the younger members of the family. I asked about Jodi but they all claimed not to have met her.

However, the following day Princess Alisha contacted me to tell me that in fact she does know Jodi. She was going under a different name of Gemma Lewes. The Princess only knows her real name because she sneaked a look at her passport. She says she and Jodi became good friends, but she left Jalpura very abruptly and has only responded to messages to thank Alisha for her friendship, apologise for leaving without saying goodbye and to say she will be in touch.

I hope Jodi is OK. I have posted you a report outlin-

ing my ideas for the ad campaign, a storyboard and a
selection of photographs.
Emily

As he gazed down at the screen instead of the text
he could see Emily's face, could picture her expression
as she typed, the fierce stare as she weighed each word,
the way she'd tuck her hair behind her ear. And now
memories streamed: the sweetness of her smile, the way
her eyes lit up with laughter, sparked with anger or desire. The way she crinkled her nose in question or doubt.
And then the memory of her face on that final morning
zinged into his mind, the hurt, the way she had wrapped
her arms around herself for protection. From the hurt
he'd caused.

Come on, Luca. Focus.

He forced his mind to Jodi, to his sister. To *his* meeting with the royal representative. Pradesh Patankar had
said he'd never heard of Jodi Petrovelli. That would be
explained by the alias that Jodi had for some reason assumed. But whatever his sister was doing it was clear
she wanted to be left alone by friends and family alike.
Exactly as she had said all along. Because Jodi knew she
could count on him, on their mother. If she needed them,
they would be there.

Emily didn't have that. Her parents were useless, prioritised others over her. She had Ava but she couldn't
turn to her because she'd promised not to tell Ava about
them and instinctively Luca knew she would keep that
promise.

Rising, he picked up his jacket and headed for the door,
phone in hand as he called an airline to book a flight to
London. A few hours later he approached Dolci headquarters, entered and was shown up to Ava's office.

'Luca?' Ava rose from behind her desk and walked round, a smile on her face, but worry in her eyes. 'Is everything OK? You said it was urgent.'

'It is to me. Thank you for seeing me at such short notice.'

'It's not a problem. You're family. Why don't you sit down? I'll grab us a coffee and you can tell me what is going on.'

Luca sat, knew that his own pride was a small price to pay. Ava was Emily's best friend and Emily deserved to have support from her. 'I messed up,' he told his sister. 'And I want to put it right. But now please go to Emily. I think she needs a friend.'

Emily sat at her desk in her London apartment and looked down at the photos spread out in front of her. The photos she'd taken in Jalpura. Taken *after* the last time with Luca, when she'd moved into a hostel for a few days, met with the royal representative, before she'd returned to London. In that time she'd taken refuge in photography, had taken photos to try and distract herself from the pain. To try to make her stop missing Luca.

Memories caused tears to sting her eyes and she tried for at least the millionth time to banish Luca from her mind. Didn't understand how Luca seemed to have distilled into her whole being. Why images of him continued to pervade her mind, waking and sleeping, memories to cascade through her. Of his smile, his touch, the spikiness of his hair, the feel of him… *Enough.* No more thoughts of Luca. He was not for her; he had lied to her.

For his sister.

Jeez, Emily. Stop thinking about the man. She didn't even understand why her deluded mind was making excuses for him.

Emily picked up her cup of tea and forced her attention to the photos. She focused on the simple picture of a Jalpuran woman teaching her child how to cook, and she felt a small curl of pride. The photograph conveyed so much—the love between mother and child, the simplicity of the earthenware pot, the youth of the child, the bright colour of the lentils being measured into the pan, the light and heat reflected off the stainless-steel plates.

A photo she would never have had the courage to take if it weren't for Luca.

Her eyes scanned the remaining photos and her gut told her she'd done something good, captured an essence of Jalpura and the richness of its life, culture and people. But then doubt surfaced—how could she trust her gut when she'd been so wrong about Luca? His voice rang in her head. 'Believe in yourself.' Wasn't that what they had both told each other?

The ring of her doorbell interrupted her thoughts. Who could that be? Stupid hope touched her that it would be Luca. *Ridiculous.* Luca would be on Jalpura now, talking to the Princess, tracking Jodi down.

Rising, she went to the door and pulled it open. 'Ava?'

'Hello, lovely. Are you OK? I came as soon as Luca told me.'

Emily froze. 'Luca told you what?' she said cautiously.

'He turned up at my office, said he'd messed up, he thought you may need a friend. That he needed to make it right. Then he left.'

'Left?'

'Yes.' Ava entered and enveloped her friend in a hug. 'Tell me what happened.'

Emily tried to think, hugged her friend back and then stepped back. What was going on? Why had Luca gone to Ava?

Ava studied her best friend's expression. 'OMG. Have you fallen for Luca? And vice versa?'

'No. Of course not.'

Had she? No, she'd fallen for an illusion, a fake. A man who'd only employed her for her name, had conned her. A man who had listened to her, encouraged her, held her whilst she cried and made love to her. Love…that was what it had felt like; their time together had felt full of love and caring and light and laughter. She loved him; it was so obvious, so clear…so disastrous. What was she going to do? Could something that had felt so real really have been nothing more than a con?

Ava stepped forward. 'Hey, it's going to be all right.'

Was it? And what had Luca meant about putting things right?

Luca rang the bell of the enormous whitewashed house, congratulated himself that he had managed to gain entry to the house of Rajiv Khatri. It had taken a certain level of determination to get through to the man himself but eventually he had succeeded, and once Rajiv believed he genuinely wanted to talk about Emily he had agreed to a meeting.

The door swung open to reveal a stately butler who studied Luca's credentials and then led the way through a spacious hallway to an enormous lounge, filled with sofas and family paraphernalia. The room was a mix of style and comfort.

Minutes later a tall slender Indian man walked in, dressed in jeans and a T-shirt, with a cautious smile on his face. 'Good morning.'

'Good morning.'

'Would you like refreshments? Tea? Coffee.'

Luca declined and the Bollywood actor gestured for

him to be seated and followed suit. 'So you wish to speak with me about Emily?'

'Yes.' Somewhat belatedly Luca realised he should maybe have prepared better for this, had been so focused on getting in front of Rajiv he hadn't planned what to say. 'When is the last time you saw her?'

The actor frowned. 'I am afraid I don't see what business it is of yours.'

Luca forced his body to relax; he was here to act as an intermediary, not an accuser. Part of him knew that he was maybe overstepping, but he knew Emily would never take either parent to task and someone had to.

'You're right and I apologise.' Luca inhaled deeply. 'I am here because recently I…got to know your daughter and I know it saddens her that…you aren't close. That because you have a second family who you live with, you never needed to get close to her.'

'That isn't tr—'

'Yes, it is.' A quiet voice intervened and, turning, Luca saw that a petite Indian woman had entered the room, dressed in a light blue patterned salwar kameez. 'Hello, Mr Petrovelli. I am Neela Khatri, mother to the second family.'

Rajiv rose when he saw his wife, but his expression was still one of anger. 'I have always treated Emily like family. She was only a baby when her mother and I split but I made sure I had proper visitation rights and when I moved back here…I…'

'Stop, Rajiv.' Neela spoke quietly as she moved over to her husband and took his hand in hers. 'Let us listen to what he has to say.' She gestured to Luca, who tried to gather his words together, as sudden panic assailed him. Perhaps he was making this worse, and Rajiv Khatri would withdraw all support.

'Please do not be angry with Emily. She has no idea I am here, so if I am speaking out of turn please blame me. Emily has not uttered a word of anger or blame. She is just sad. Sad that she can't be part of your extended family, doesn't have a close bond with any of you.'

Rajiv's expression changed, the frown indicative of a man who was listening, but it was Neela who spoke.

'I am sorry,' she said simply. 'Some of the blame is mine. To begin with I saw Emily as a threat, a reminder of Marigold, and I believed that you still loved her, had married me on the rebound.'

Now Rajiv took his wife's other hand in his and they exchanged a smile. 'And now?' he asked.

'Now I know you love me.' The look the couple exchanged was so full of love and understanding that Luca blinked, wondered if Emily's belief that this marriage was based on affection alone could be wrong. Neela smiled at her husband. 'But the pattern had been set and we were so caught up in our family that Emily must have felt excluded.'

Neela turned back to Luca. 'Please continue.'

'I think Emily would like to feel she is important to you, that she comes first, that she isn't on the sidelines of your lives. She has had a hard time lately and she could do with some support.'

Rajiv nodded his head. 'Thank you for this intervention. I will speak with Emily.' He shook his head. 'No, I will do better than that. I will go and see my daughter and try to make things right.'

Luca smiled, tried to imagine Emily's face when she saw her father, hoped with all his heart that they would work out a way to forge a new relationship. Hoped that when he met with Marigold, Emily's mother would react positively as well.

'Thank you,' he said.

Neela shook her head. 'It is we who thank you. For doing this for Emily.'

A week later

Emily tried to salvage as much of her courage as she could, even as nerves coiled inside her like a mass of writhing snakes. As her high heels clicked across the London street her heart pounded her ribs so hard she feared it would burst through.

Her mind still spun over the events of the past days. A few days after Ava's visit her doorbell had rung again and this time as she'd opened the door she'd nearly fainted. Had found it difficult to believe the evidence of her eyes, as she took in the identity of her visitors. Her parents, both of them *together* on the doorstep. The next hours had been both emotional and rewarding and had left her filled with hope that perhaps she and her parents could forge new bonds.

When they had left Emily had emailed Luca to thank him and he'd replied. The words were embossed on her mind.

Dear Emily,

I am glad that it worked out. I was wondering if you would be able to meet with me, though I will fully understand if that is not something you want to do. I would like to talk.

If you feel you can do this perhaps we could meet for a cocktail in London at your convenience?

Best wishes,

Luca

So here she was.

She slowed down as she reached her destination, knew that she would regret it to her dying day if she turned tail and ran now. A deep breath, and she pushed the door open, blinked as she entered the dimly lit interior and realised the place was empty.

No, not empty. As she approached the bar she saw Luca and her head whirled. She halted in her tracks, soaked in his sheer masculine beauty, every familiar angle and plane, the dark hair a little overlong now, his stance alert and almost primal as his eyes scanned the door.

'Luca.'

'Emily.'

Unbidden happiness fizzed inside her and she wanted to hurl herself into his arms, wanted to hold and be held, inhale his scent… Instead she stepped forward, approached the bar, half relieved, half disappointed at the barrier between them.

'I wasn't sure if you'd come.' His voice was low, deep and so wonderfully familiar.

'Neither was I. But…' she looked round '…where is everyone?'

Now he smiled and she was transported back to Jalpura, to Turin, to all the times his face had lit up her world. 'I've bought the bar.'

'You've bought it?'

'Yup. I am going to open a cocktail bar in London. Palazzo di Cioccolato is branching out. I listened to what you said, and I've done some serious thinking. I do want to launch in London and I will, but not yet. Perhaps when it is possible to come to a decision about Dolci, perhaps then. But in the meantime I realised I was so focused on rivalling Dolci that maybe I missed out on doing the other things I wanted to do. I like mixing cocktails, I enjoyed working at Silvio's. So here we are. Welcome to Teepee.'

Emily thought and smiled as she got it. 'Teepee—or TP as in Therese Petrovelli.'

'Yup. My mum loves the idea.'

'So do I.' Happiness for him swept through her, that he'd started to move on from revenge, from the emotional turmoil caused by James's actions in life and death. Yet the happiness was tinged with sadness, because she'd hoped Luca had wanted to see her for something different.

He cleared his throat. 'I hoped you would stay and have the very first cocktail served here.'

'I'd like that. I wanted to talk to you as well.' She sat down at the bar. 'I want to thank you. For going to my parents. I'm not sure exactly what you said but it's made a world of difference; opened up a whole new facet to my relationship with both of them.'

'I'm glad. Truly glad.'

'I think things will be different from now on. They actually turned up together, said it was their way of showing me that they truly wanted to try and change things up. I'm going to spend some time in Mumbai with my dad on our own and then stay with the family. My mum said she knows she can't change the past but she hopes she and I can spend a lot more time together and she offered to not go to Derek's—her current husband's—film premiere so she could be with me instead. I told her there was no need, but I appreciated the offer. Anyway, she took me on a girls' day out—hence the new look.' She glanced down at her outfit, aware she was talking too much but she couldn't stop. 'We had a lot of fun…massages, spa, shopping and lunch. So it's a start. Thank you.'

Because right now, whatever happened with her parents, she knew that Luca had gone the extra mile to do something for her. And that sent an appreciative glow through her veins.

'There is no need to thank me. I wanted to do that. For you.'

The expression on his face was so genuine, so warm, that something melted inside her, urged her to throw caution to the wind and vault over the bar into his arms. No way. That would embarrass them both and there had been enough mortification to last her a lifetime. She tucked a strand of hair behind her ear. 'I was wondering—have you managed to track Jodi down? Did you meet with the Princess?'

'No on both counts.'

Surprise widened her eyes. 'Oh… I assumed…'

'Once I got your email I realised exactly what I needed to do and I did it. I went to see Ava and then I flew to Mumbai to talk to your father, then I went to see your mother and here we are.'

'But…'

Luca shook his head. 'I will, of course, try to speak with the Princess and continue my search for Jodi. But in the end Jodi is an adult and she knows she can turn to me or our mum any time she needs to. I knew you were hurting and I wanted to—'

'Put me first.' The realisation cascaded over her skin and her heart sang.

'Yes. Because that's what you deserve, Emily. To be put first. And you didn't deserve what I did. I should have been upfront.'

Now she reached out, a small tentative touch of his arm, revelled in the familiar hardness of muscle under her fingers. 'It's OK. I understand why you did it. You love your sister and you couldn't take the risk that I wouldn't help.'

'That is the reason but that doesn't make it right. Not when it hurt you, not when it made you doubt that everything else between us was real. Because it was real, Emily. All of it. I meant every word. I believe in your talent, I believe in you. I hold your grief about your baby in my own heart. Because I love you.'

There was a silence and her heart fluttered in her chest. 'You love me?' The words seemed impossible, words she knew he'd vowed to never say again. Yet she knew them to be true, knew this man would never say those words unless he meant them with all his heart. Because he knew the power of love, the immensity of the gift and the responsibility that went with it. For Luca love meant a promise to never leave, never abandon the other.

'Yes, I do. I love you, with all my heart and soul. I know you may not love me back, but I want you to know how I feel. I love you. I love your courage and your strength in the face of the grief and pain you have faced. I love your sense of humour, your grace, the way you smile. I love how you feel in my arms when I wake up. I love how caring you are and how you see the world. Whether it is from behind a lens or not. I love you.'

Words welled up inside her, but she knew the most important ones. 'I love you too, Luca. With all my heart.'

She watched as he absorbed the words and then *he* vaulted across the bar and pulled her close, twirled her round and then gently placed her down, still safely encircled in his arms. 'Are you sure? After what I did?'

'I understand what you did. Yes, it was wrong, but you also did so much that was right—you started my healing process, you made me believe in myself, listened to me, held me and you made me happy.'

His silver-grey eyes lit up. 'I appreciate that—that you have found it in you to absolve me. Because I know what I did was indefensible; I regret it with all my heart. The idea that I hurt you, hurt the woman I love. It will not happen again. I promise you I will never lie to you again, not by omission or fact. If there is something difficult to face up to...'

'Then we will do it together.'

'Yes.'

'I did not know it was possible to be this happy.' He tipped her chin up with his finger. 'To know I will see your face every day when I wake up and last thing before I go to sleep.'

She looked up at him, gave a small mischievous smile. 'But surely you would prefer a different arrangement? One where we only see each other every blue moon.'

'No. I would emphatically not prefer that.' He tugged her closer. 'The idea makes my blood run cold.' Now his face became serious. 'You changed me, Emily. When my father died I felt such an influx of emotions, and I didn't know what to do with them. I wanted to bury them; you helped me to face them. I felt as though I had failed because I hadn't got my revenge. You showed me it was OK to feel and how to channel that emotion, to genuinely believe it wasn't my fault he left. You showed me that talking about how you feel is a good thing. That feeling is a good thing. You taught me that spending time with someone, getting closer, is a risk worth taking, is fun and rewarding. Today you have shown me it is possible for me to make a mistake, do wrong and still be loved. My actions did not drive you away for ever.'

'No. Because you also did so many caring things: you helped me grieve my baby, you convinced me that Howard was wrong about my talent, you showed me how to stand up to his voice in my head, you helped me move forward when I never thought I could. When we left London for Turin I panicked because I thought I couldn't leave my home, my grief—it felt like a betrayal of my baby. With you I learnt to laugh again, to dance, to work. To grow. You made me believe in myself, made me want to pursue my own dreams'

His arms tightened around her. 'I want to have children with you, when you're ready. I know it will take time. And we will never forget your first baby. I will cherish his memory with you. As I will always cherish you.'

Her heart seemed to wrench with happiness. 'And our children will be the luckiest in the world to have a dad like you. I know you will always be there for them, for every milestone.'

'We will be there for them and I think we will be the happiest family in the world. I love you, Emily.'

'I love you too, Luca.' She knew she would never get tired of saying the words of love.

'I think now is the perfect moment for that cocktail I promised you.' Taking her hand, he pulled her round to the opposite side of the bar. 'These are the ingredients. Tequila for strength, pineapple juice for sweetness, rum to add a little spice, and chilli for a bit of heat and some shavings of chocolate for extra sweetness.'

She watched as he expertly set to work, absorbed every deft movement as he mixed and shook the ingredients, allowed her gaze to linger on every inch of his glorious body, full of joy that this beautiful, generous, caring man was hers for life.

Now he smiled at her, the smile so full of love that she could feel it envelop her as he handed her the glass, expertly garnished and complete with an umbrella.

'Hold on. I need to get the *aperitivo*.' He returned a few minutes later. 'I thought we could have dessert first.'

His voice had a small catch in it and Emily glanced across at him, saw a sparkle in his eye, but also a hint of nerves as he placed down a plate with a variety of truffles, in individual paper cases, beautifully arranged in a pyramid.

He picked up his cocktail and they clinked glasses. 'To us,' he said.

'To us.' She looked at the drink. 'It's beautiful.'

'Yes. As is the woman who inspired it. Would you like to know what it is called?' His voice had dipped to a husky rumble that slid over her skin, made her giddy as it seemed so full of promise.

'What is it called?'

'Emily's proposal,' he said, and her heart beat a little faster as he nodded to the plate. 'Take the top chocolate.'

She did so, felt the weight of it and now her pulse rate notched up as she picked up the chocolate and gasped. Nestled in the paper case was a ring.

Luca reached out and took it, went down on one knee.

'Emily Khatri, I love you with all my heart. I swear to cherish and look after you, stand by your side through thick and thin, for the rest of my life. Will you marry me?'

Tears of happiness prickled her eyelids as she nodded. 'I will marry you, Luca. And I vow to always be there for you. For ever.'

He slipped the ring onto her finger and she gazed down at it. 'It's beautiful.' The glitter of white diamonds alternated with some brown gemstones she didn't recognise.

His grin widened. 'They are called chocolate diamonds,' he explained, and she gave a small gurgle of laughter.

'Of course, they are—and they are perfect.' Just as she knew their life together would be.

* * * * *

STARTING OVER
WITH THE SHERIFF

JUDY DUARTE

To Vickie Maltby,
who has purchased almost every book I've ever
written. Thanks for your love, support and prayers
over the years. I hope you enjoy this story, too!

Chapter One

Marissa Garcia stooped behind the cash register at Darla's Doughnuts, where she'd stashed her purse, reached inside and hunted for her cell phone.

Once she had it in hand, she straightened and sent a quick text message.

Any news yet?

She waited, and with no dots in response, she turned and placed the phone on the counter, next to the coffee maker. Surely she'd hear something soon.

The little bell on the front door jingled as it opened.

An elderly male voice called out, "It sure smells good in here. Makes me wish I could spend the day working with you, Marissa."

She laughed. "I know, right? I hate to leave, even when I'm off the clock."

In his mid-seventies and an army veteran and officer who'd served in two wars, Vietnam and Desert Storm, Carl Matheson was one of Fairborn's most interesting characters and her favorite customer. She offered him a warm smile. "Good morning, Colonel. How's it going?"

"I can't complain." The colonel, his face craggy, his blue eyes bright and his chin bristled, offered her a wink and a grin as he pushed his red walker into the small shop, slowly making his way to the front of the glass case. "I may not be getting around too good these days, but I'm still walking. And I'm on the right side of the grass." He nodded at the walker that held him steady. "And as long as I use my trusty little speedster, I manage to get my daily exercise."

Marissa bit back a chuckle. "Does your doctor know that your fitness routine is a four-block walk that ends at Darla's Doughnuts?"

The colonel scowled and let out a humph. "Oh, for cripe's sake. Doc Clemmons made me give up my Marlboros and Jack Daniel's. I've gotta reward my efforts somehow. Besides, a little sugar and caffeine never hurt anyone."

As Marissa poured a large coffee into a to-go cup, the colonel arched his neck and peered at the door that led to the small kitchen in back. "You running things on your own again today?"

"Yes, I am." This was the third morning Darla had asked her to manage the shop on her own. It was nice to know that her new employer trusted her to handle things while she was away.

"How's Darla's husband doing? Did Fred finally kick that infection?"

"I was just checking for a text. She took him to the doctor this morning, and I was waiting for an update. So far, no word from her."

"That's too bad," the colonel said. "I hope he doesn't end up losing his leg."

That's what had Darla so concerned. "Yeah, me, too." Marissa added, "So what can I get you today, sir?"

He eyed the variety of doughnuts and muffins, then tapped an arthritic finger against the glass case. "Gimme one of those bear claws and a maple bar. To go. And don't try to slip that fat-free creamer on me. I can tell the difference."

He certainly could. Marissa smiled. "I won't make that mistake again." As she added cream and sugar to his coffee, her cell phone rang. She glanced over her shoulder at the display, hoping to see Darla's name and to hear some good news.

Instead, she spotted an unfamiliar number with a San Diego area code.

"You gotta get that, sweetie? Go on, then."

"No. It's just a junk call." She silenced the ringer and let it roll to voice mail.

San Diego? She hadn't lived in Southern California since she was nineteen. And she hadn't been able to leave soon enough. It had taken her fifteen hundred miles, three different rental agreements in as many locales, and numerous temp jobs to end up in a place she could finally call home— Fairborn, Montana, with its quaint streets, colorful characters and small-town charm.

After placing the colonel's order into a bag, she tucked in a couple of napkins and set it next to the register.

"Don't forget the cream and sugar for my coffee," the colonel said.

"I've already added it—just the way you like it." She'd no more than popped on a lid when her cell phone dinged with a text, which had come from the same phone number. Only a portion of the message showed up on the display, just enough to cause her gut to clench.

Marissa? It's Erik…

Her heart dropped to the pit of her stomach. Her fingers trembled, and her grip loosened. She tried to steady the cup with both hands, only to fumble and drop it on the floor, splashing hot coffee everywhere and drenching the top of her once-white sneakers.

Her cheeks burned as if the coffee had splashed onto her face.

"Hey! You okay, hon?"

Marissa tore her gaze from the blasted phone and turned to the colonel, who stood near the register, his craggy brow furrowed in concern.

"Yes," she said. "I'm fine. Sorry. I'm just a little clumsy today, that's all."

"Join the club. Lately, I've been known to trip and drop things, too." The old soldier frowned, and the crease in his forehead deepened. "But you look like you just saw a ghost."

No. Just his text message.

Or a portion of it.

Erik Crowder. Her stepbrother, the jerk.

She hadn't seen or heard from him in years, and she'd hoped to never hear from him again. Hadn't he done enough to screw up her life? What made him think she'd even consider talking to him?

She'd have to block his number.

"Why are you so skittish?" the colonel asked.

"I…uh…" She glanced at the wet floor. What a mess. She threw a couple of hand towels over the spot and stepped on it, using her coffee-soaked foot to wipe the spill. Then she tucked a long strand of dark hair behind her ear and gathered her composure. "I'm just a little distracted this morning. Darla should have checked in by now, so each time my cell phone pings, I jump."

"She probably just got busy. Besides, she trusts you. I know you haven't worked for her very long, but you're the best employee she's had by far. You've always got a smile that makes the coffee and doughnuts taste better."

"Thanks for the vote of confidence. And you're probably right." But Marissa had learned that there were no certainties in this world. Not even when it came to people she'd once considered family. The hurt and humiliation of their final rejection still bore a hole through her heart.

As Marissa filled a replacement cup with the colonel's coffee, her hands continued to tremble, but she pushed through her uneasiness and, this time, securely snapped the lid in place. Then she put the cup in a cardboard carrier meant to hold four and set it and the white bag on the seat of his walker. "There you go. That'll be three dollars and twenty-five cents." She looked up and managed a smile. "The entertainment was on the house."

He chuckled and paid with a five. After she gave him his change, he stuck a dollar in her tip jar then turned toward the door.

"Thanks, Colonel." She walked to the front of

the shop and opened the door for him. "I'll see you tomorrow."

As the sweet old man began his walk home, her mind skipped back to the text message, and her heart continued to pound as if she'd just run a marathon.

Why on earth would Erik contact her? And why now, after all this time, after all he'd done?

Once back behind the counter, she stopped to pick up the rags she'd thrown on the coffee. She started to take them to the sink in back, but curiosity nagged at her until she picked up the cell phone to read the entire text.

Marissa? It's Erik. I need to talk to you. Please call me.

It would be a blustery winter day in hell before she called the guy who'd ruined her life.

And she'd be darned if she'd let Erik's text rent space in her head and ruin her morning. At least, not any more than it already had.

She carried the coffee-soaked towels to the kitchen. Then she grabbed a mop and returned to the front of the shop. She'd barely made a sweep across the floor when her phone dinged again, so she set the mop aside and snatched her cell from the counter.

This time, it *was* Darla who'd sent the text.

Sorry. My sister called this morning, and the time got away from me. How are things going?

Marissa had barely typed out *Okay* when the front door squeaked open and two preschoolers rushed into the shop, breathless and beaming.

"We beated him here," a towheaded little boy said.

"Yeah." The girl, her red curly hair pulled back into a ponytail, nodded. "He's a slowpoker."

Marissa broke into a smile. "Good morning. Who are you two winners racing?"

"Our daddy." The boy walked up to the display case and peered inside. "He said we could run ahead of him. And we did."

"We wanted ice cream," the red-haired girl said. "Aunt Carlene always takes us to Doc Creamer's after we go to the dentist or to the doctor or the appointment with Miss Shirley, but Daddy brung us this time 'cause the ice-cream place is closed right now."

Doc Creamer's Frozen Emporium was a popular place in town, but they didn't open until eleven or later.

"I really wanted a chocolate ice-cream cone," the boy said, "but doughnuts are good, too. Can I have that white one with the little brown candies on top?"

The girl gave him a nudge. "Jimmy, don't be bossy. You forgot to tell her *please*."

"Don't tell me what to do, Maddie. I was just going to say that." Jimmy, a cute little boy with a scatter of freckles across his nose, offered Marissa a smile. "Please can I have that doughnut? And my sister wants a pink one."

"Let's wait until your mommy and daddy get here," Marissa said.

"We don't have a mommy," the girl said. "Only a daddy."

Marissa sucked in a breath. Poor kids.

"But we got two aunties," the boy chimed in. "And they're just as good as two mommies. Huh, Maddie?"

"Yeah." Maddie nodded. "That's what Aunt Betty Sue told us."

"I'm sure she's right," Marissa said. "I don't have a mother, either. But I had an awesome daddy." Not a day went by that she didn't miss him, didn't wish she was still six years old and could crawl up on his lap and listen to his stories—those he read and those he created in his head.

"Our daddy is awesome, too," the girl said, and they exchanged a smile.

Marissa liked children, the younger the better. And she couldn't remember the last time she'd seen two who were cuter than these.

The bell on the door tinkled again, and a handsome, dark-haired man walked in—all buff and hunky. And far more gorgeous than a daddy had a right to be, especially when he shot Marissa a dimpled grin.

Dang. He was a gorgeous doppelgänger of Scott Eastwood, and if she didn't know any better, she'd think there must be a Hollywood film crew in town.

"I hope these little ragamuffins haven't been giving you any trouble," he said.

"Not at all." Marissa returned his smile.

"Now can we get our doughnuts?" Jimmy asked. "Please. And can I have a chocolate milk to drink?"

Maddie—his twin sister, she guessed—chimed in. "Me, too. Please."

Marissa glanced at Mr. Daddy for his okay. When he nodded, she said, "Two doughnuts and chocolate milks coming right up."

After retrieving the children's orders, she shot a smile at Mr. Daddy. "Can I get you something?"

"Coffee. Black." He gave her a quick once-over, then smiled. "You're new in town."

Apparently, he wasn't. And while she'd never offer up much about her past, she couldn't see any reason not to answer a simple question—honestly. "Yes. I moved here last month."

"Where are you from?"

"Originally? San Diego." She didn't need to tell him the roundabout way she'd come here.

"Nice city. Well, welcome to Fairborn."

"Thanks." She cast a glance at his left hand and noted the absence of a ring. So he hadn't remarried, although the kids mentioned not having a mom. Widowed? Divorced?

She glanced at the rest of him. Broad shoulders and bulging biceps suggested that he either had a well-used gym membership or a job that required strength and stamina. Maybe he worked in construction, although he was obviously off this morning.

Before either of them could speak, a thump sounded and the boy shrieked, drawing the adults' attention. Little Jimmy sat on the floor, his doughnut lying next to him—frosting-side down.

"Maddie!" he shouted, tears welling in his eyes. "Look what you made me do!"

"I didn't do anything," his sister said. "You shouldn't have stood on the chair."

Mr. Daddy was at his side in a minute. "You okay, Jimmy?"

"No. My elbow hurts. And now I don't have a doughnut."

Marissa snatched a fresh doughnut from the case—chocolate with white frosting and sprinkles. "You're in luck. I have another one just like it."

Daddy helped the boy get up, took a peek at

his elbow and then set the toppled chair upright. "What'd I tell you about feet belonging on the floor and not on the furniture? There's a good reason for the rules we have. Do you need a time-out to help you to remember?"

"No. I'm sorry."

"Don't do it again," the dad said, kissing the boy's forehead. "And your elbow is fine."

Marissa scooped the remainder of the downed doughnut into her hands and carried it to the trash can. Then she reached for a damp rag and returned to the accident site, where she wiped up all traces of frosting and crumbs.

"I'm sorry that I made your chair fall down," Jimmy said to Marissa.

"No problem, honey. Accidents happen. In fact, I spilled some coffee myself earlier." She pointed the toe of her stained sneaker at him.

They shared a smile.

Seeing her coffee-stained shoe jogged her memory. She looked at the boy's dad. "Speaking of coffee, let me get that for you."

"It's no problem. Thanks so much for your help." He tossed her a heart-strumming grin. "I can take it to go."

So he didn't plan to stay. Not that she'd expected him to, but… Well, she'd kind of like to get to know him and the kids a little better.

She filled his cup with coffee. "Cream and sugar?"

"No, thanks. Black." He grinned.

"Oh, right. You said that before. You got it." Now she sounded like a dingbat. Way to make a good impression… *Not.*

After handing him his coffee, she rang up the tab. "That'll be seven dollars and fifty cents."

He pulled a wallet from his hip pocket and withdrew a ten. "Here you go. Keep the change."

"You don't have to…" She caught herself. Not everyone who dangled money in front of her expected a favor, one that might backfire and give her a ton of grief.

"I know I don't need to. But—" he winked "—consider it a cleaning deposit. We'll be back, and who knows what'll happen next." Then he gathered up the kiddos and lovingly guided them out of the shop.

He took one last look over his shoulder at her and tossed her a smile before he shut the door behind him. He'd made a point of saying he'd come back. She certainly hoped it would be on a Tuesday or Thursday, the only mornings she worked here—unless Darla needed her.

It would be nice if he brought the kids with him. Whenever she saw a father who appeared to be devoted to his children, like her dad had been to her, it warmed her heart and sparked memories of the short time she'd had with him.

She'd never known her mom, but her dad had raised her until she was twelve. If the gentle giant hadn't died, her life, especially her teen years, would've been so much better.

Yet it was more than Mr. Daddy's paternal side that caused her heartbeat to kick its pace up a notch. It was his manly brawn and the dazzling pair of baby blues that made her feel like a woman in need of…

Well, she certainly didn't *need* a man in her life. She'd learned long ago not to rely on anyone other than herself. But it would be nice to get to know him better. And maybe even go out…

Oh, for Pete's sake. Her thoughts were spiraling. She'd have to put the whole dating thing on the back burner, especially when it came to Mr. Daddy.

Not that the kids were a problem. It was his marital status. Or lack of. Even if his wife had died, there had to be others on her side of the family, people ready to judge an outsider. And any sign of potential trouble like that would be a real game changer.

She knew that from experience.

On the drive to Tip Top Market, where Brandon Dodd would drop off the kids with his aunt and uncle, he glanced into the rearview mirror, where his four-year-olds were secured in their boosters in the back seat of his new Jeep Grand Cherokee. He always got a kick out of their childhood chatter, especially when they didn't know he was eavesdropping. Their take on life never ceased to amaze him.

"I like her," Maddie said. "Don't you, Jimmy?"

"Who?" her twin asked, as he held a red-caped superhero toy and zoomed it through the air.

"The doughnut lady. She smells good. Like Miss Cynthia at preschool."

"Yeah. She's nice. Nicer than Miss Cynthia. Because she didn't get mad at me when my chair fell down. At school, when it happened, I had to sit in time-out."

"I know," Maddie said. "And that nice lady gave you a free doughnut, too."

"Yep."

Brandon grinned. He liked the doughnut lady, too. And not just because she was attractive. He especially liked the fact that she'd been sweet and kind to the twins. He might be biased, but they were awesome kids—Jimmy with his scruffy, dusty-blond hair that seemed to have a mind of its own. That is, until Brandon helped him wet it down each morning. And Maddie, with her red curls that were just as wild. Fortunately, Brandon had learned to tame them using ribbons and barrettes—thanks to the help of the preschool director, who had noticed her crazy hair and given him some hands-on help. He wasn't a natural, but for a single dad? His hairdressing skills were improving.

He smiled again at Jimmy and Maddie. Sure, they could both be naughty sometimes, but hey. What kids weren't?

His mood darkened. He wondered if their mother ever thought about them, if she ever felt the least bit guilty about giving them up so easily.

Probably not. But her loss was his gain. He had no idea what his life would be like without them.

"Daddy," Maddie said, "what's the doughnut lady's name?"

"I don't know, honey." Brandon should have asked her when he'd had the chance, and while loading the kids into their booster seats, he'd kicked himself for leaving without doing so. But it'd be easy enough to find out. "I agree with you, honey. She was very nice."

"She's pretty like a princess," Maddie added, as she ran a pink toy comb through her dolly's curls, catching a snag.

No argument there. With long wavy dark hair and warm brown eyes, the doughnut lady didn't need a tiara or a gown to draw a man's attention. And the fact that she seemed to have a way with kids was a plus. Not that he planned to introduce a woman into their lives yet—much to the cha-grin of his great-aunt, Betty Sue.

You're too young and good-looking to be sin-gle, Betty Sue had told him time and again. *It isn't natural for a man your age to be celibate.*

Brandon wasn't exactly celibate, although it felt like that sometimes. But he wasn't about to discuss his love life, as rare as it might be, with one of his relatives, especially a woman in her mid-seventies.

"Daddy," Jimmy said, "how come we can't go to the park? It's not a school day."

"That would be fun, sport. But I have an im-portant meeting at lunchtime, so I have to take you back to the market."

Brandon had been depending upon his aunt and uncle to watch the twins since the day he'd packed them both in rear-facing car seats and brought them home from college, along with a bachelor's degree in criminal justice.

Brandon had hated to ask his aunt and uncle, Ralph and Carlene Tipton, to babysit since run-ning the market kept them both busy. But they'd jumped at the chance and were delighted to help out.

When Brandon had been in the seventh grade, his parents had gone through a nasty divorce. They'd barely been able to take care of them-selves, let alone provide him with a stable home, so he'd contacted his uncle and told him how he was being left alone for days on end.

While Aunt Carlene watched the market, Uncle Ralph drove most of the night to pick him up. After being confronted about their neglect, Brandon's mom and dad had willingly signed over custody to the Tiptons. Then Ralph took Brandon home with him to live in Fairborn. The way Brandon saw it, they'd saved his life.

You couldn't find two finer people than his aunt and uncle, even though they did get a little too opinionated, especially when it came to his personal life.

"Stop it, Jimmy. You poked me."

"I didn't. Super Dude did it."

Brandon glanced in the rearview mirror. "If Super Dude can't respect his own airspace, I'm going to take him away from you."

Jimmy scowled at his sister. "I don't tell on your princess doll when she pokes me."

Brandon fought the smile that tugged at his lips, then, taking note of his son's scruffy hair, said, "I think it's time for a visit to The Mane Event, Jimmy."

"I don't wanna get my hair cut. How come I always have to go and Maddie doesn't?"

"Because," his sister said, "I keep my hair out of my face with barrettes and ribbons. And you don't."

"That's because I'm a boy."

"I'll tell you what," Brandon said, as he turned into the graveled drive and parked in front of the market. "I don't have to work tomorrow. So we'll get Jimmy's hair cut. And afterward, why don't we stop by Darla's for another doughnut? How does that sound?"

"Good!" Maddie said.

"Can we get the doughnut first?" Jimmy asked. "And then get a haircut?"

"Sorry, son. That's not how rewards work."

"That's how I think it should work," Jimmy muttered.

For a guy who wasn't all that big on sweets, Brandon had a real hankering for a bear claw. Hopefully, the pretty woman who his kids called the doughnut lady would be working tomorrow morning. And he'd learn a little more about her, starting with her name.

Marissa closed up the doughnut shop at two, then she headed back to Rancho Esperanza, where she'd been staying for the past few days. It had been a godsend when Alana Perez offered her room and board if she'd help with the gardening, canning and baking. Marissa needed to build up her savings account, which wasn't growing fast enough for the plans she'd made.

She'd only managed to find part-time positions—one at Darla's and another as a reception-ist at The Mane Event. She had higher hopes for herself than just working for someone else, but for now, it was okay. Plus, on the upside, those two employers hadn't asked for references—or run a background check.

Besides, Alana kept her pretty busy at the ranch. It took a lot of work to get ready for the farmers market on the weekends. And since Cal-lie, who'd lived at the ranch until she married Mayor Ramon Cruz, had moved to town, Alana needed all the help she could get. Besides, she really enjoyed working with her new landlady.

Marissa had just turned onto the county road in the ten-year-old sedan she'd named Prudence when her cell phone rang. Ever since Erik had tried to contact her, she'd been careful about checking to see who might be looking for her. There was no way she'd talk to the guy. Even if he only wanted to explain or apologize for what he'd done, she wouldn't accept it. Not after what he'd put her through.

Fortunately, this call was from Alana. She tapped the speaker icon on the screen.

"Hey," Marissa said. "What's up?"

"Are you still in town?"

"No. I'm about ten minutes away from the ranch. Why?"

"Because I'm elbows-deep in bread dough for

the cinnamon rolls I'm making. I thought they might go over well at the farmers market and wanted to try the recipe first. But I just realized I'm out of powdered sugar."

"I'll turn around," Marissa said.

"No, you don't need to do that. Just stop at Tip Top Market. It's only about a mile down the road from here."

"Do you need anything else while I'm there?"

"Not that I can think of. But then again, I can't believe how forgetful I've been lately. I think the hormones have made my brain go wonky."

A smile tugged at Marissa's lips. "I've heard pregnancy will do that to you."

"It's a little annoying, but I'm so glad to be pregnant I don't care."

"And just think. You'll have a baby boy in a few short months."

"I think about that all the time. So I'm even grateful for all the little annoyances."

Alana and her fiancé, Clay Hastings, were looking forward to getting married next month, and they'd agreed to let Marissa plan their wedding. If everything went according to plan, and Marissa was able to build up her meager savings, she'd eventually be able to give notice to her employers and launch a brand-new career as a wedding planner. She even had a name for it: White Lace and Promises.

When she spotted the Tip Top Market and Casino sign up ahead, she pulled into the graveled driveway and parked near the front door. It didn't look like there were too many customers, so she ought to be in and out quickly.

She reached for her purse, locked the car door and headed inside.

Marissa had met Carlene Tipton at Callie's baby shower, but she hadn't stopped at the market before today. She'd passed this place several times and was curious about it.

Once inside, she scanned the interior. The market carried all the basics, including snacks and canned goods. It also boasted a pair of slot machines that sat to the right of the checkstand. Country music played on a radio behind a glass-front counter.

"Hey!" A little girl's voice rang out. "Jimmy, look who's here! The doughnut lady!"

"Uh-oh. Oops!"

Before Marissa could turn around, pain exploded in her forehead.

Chapter Two

Marissa gasped, rubbing her forehead and glancing around for the object that had narrowly missed her eye. There, down on the green tile floor, lay a little action figure wearing a red cape, its head dangling to the side.

"Jimmy!" the girl called out. "You're gonna get in trouble. I'm telling Uncle Ralph you hit a customer."

Tears welled in the boy's eyes. "I didn't mean to."

Marissa again touched her forehead, which still stung from the impact, then she stooped to pick up the plastic toy and made her way to where Jimmy stood. "I think this belongs to you."

"I'm sorry, Doughnut Lady." The boy bit down on his bottom lip, then took the toy from her. He looked at the wobbly head, which listed to the side. "Oh, no. And I killed Super Dude."

"It looks like he and I were both injured in a midair collision," Marissa said. "Accidents happen, right?"

At that, an elderly woman wearing a lime-green scarf as a headband approached. It was Betty Lou—no, that wasn't right. It was Betty Sue.

She raised her finger, the nail painted a bright red, and pointed it at the boy. "Jimmy, what did we tell you about throwing things indoors? You have a playroom in the back of the store. It looks like you need to spend a little thinking time in the corner." Then she turned to Marissa and sighed. "I'm sorry about that. I'm afraid my nephew is a little impulsive at times. Probably takes after me."

"No harm done," Marissa said.

A bright smile lit Betty Sue's blue eyes and softened the lines on her face. "Hey. I know you. We met at Callie's baby shower."

"Yes, we did." Marissa wasn't surprised to see Betty Sue at the market. After all, she lived with the Tiptons, who were the owners. But she hadn't expected to see the twins here. Was their daddy here, too?

"You're the doughnut lady," Maddie said, as

she turned to Betty Sue. "Isn't she pretty? Daddy thinks so, too."

Betty Sue brightened. "You don't say. I always knew that man had good taste. And a good eye."

"He's gotta have good eyes," Jimmy said. "And he's gotta be strong and a fast runner. That's why he goes to the gym."

"Yeah," Maddie said. "He's a hero."

"That he is, sweet pea." Betty Sue placed a hand on Jimmy's shoulder. "Uncle Ralph is a whiz at fixing things. If you take Super Dude to him, I'll bet he'll have his head upright in no time at all."

"Okay. Come on, Maddie."

As the children headed to the back of the market, Betty Sue leaned toward Marissa, cupped her hand around her mouth and lowered her voice. "Their father is a hero, but the most heroic thing he's ever done was to take responsibility of two babies, twins not even a year old. And for a man who grew up as an only child, he's done an amazing job of it. 'Course, Brandon's got me, Ralph and Carlene to help out."

"Hello, there." An older man wearing a green shopkeeper's apron approached the register with a broom, the twins tagging along behind him. "I'm sorry about the...um...mishap. Jimmy means well."

"Mr. Tipton?" Marissa asked.

"Yes, that's me."

"It's nice to meet you." She held out a hand to greet him. "I'm Marissa Garcia. I'm living with Alana at Rancho Esperanza."

"And she's the doughnut lady I told you about," Maddie added. "Doesn't she look like a princess?"

Marissa flushed. "I don't know about that." Other than her father, no one else had ever thought she had a drop of royal blood, although it was sweet that Maddie did.

"Can I help you find something?" Mr. Tipton asked.

Yes, she thought. *Where is the children's father?* Instead, she said, "I stopped to buy powdered sugar."

"It's in aisle three."

Marissa nodded. "Thank you."

"Ralph," Betty Sue said, "you can go back to what you were doing—and supervising Jimmy's time-out. I'll man the cash register for you. It'll give me time to get to know our new neighbor a little better."

Marissa would like to quiz Betty Sue further, too, but she'd better be subtle. She didn't want anyone to suspect she was curious about the heroic single daddy. At least she'd learned something.

His name was Brandon. And it would seem that his wife, the twins' mother, had died. Or else she was unfit for one reason or another. Ei-

ther way, the mom and her family weren't helping very much—if at all. So, if that was the case,
maybe she shouldn't write off the single daddy
completely.

Brandon had barely stepped foot into the Tip
Top Market to pick up the kids when Betty Sue
jumped up from her seat in front of her favorite
slot machine, nearly knocking over the stool. Then
she hurried toward him, while adjusting the green
scarf she used to hold her red curls in place.

"Slow down," he said. "I don't want you falling and screwing up your knee again."

"I'm just as steady on my feet as ever. Don't
worry about me. Besides, Ralph sold the motor-
cycle, remember?"

After she'd taken off on the bike, she'd spun
out in the gravel and wrenched her right knee.

"Oh, that Ralph." Betty Sue huffed. "It was just
an accident. I was perfectly fine driving around
that red hot mama."

Brandon grinned. "Ralph was only looking out
for you."

"And I'm looking out for you." She pointed a
finger at him and burst into a bright-eyed grin.
"I've got some news you need to hear."

Brandon wasn't so sure about that. His great-
aunt always seemed to have wild ideas.

"What's up?" he asked, hoping her so-called

news didn't have anything to do with Jimmy and Maddie.

"We had a visitor this afternoon."

"Oh, yeah?" Brandon scanned the market, looking for the twins.

"Her name is Marissa Garcia. And I can give you the 4-1-1 on her."

"Who?" He wasn't following her. But then again, it wasn't always easy to tune in to his great-aunt's wavelength.

"Marissa. The kids call her the doughnut lady. The pretty princess who works at Darla's Dough-nuts."

At that, Brandon tuned right in. "How do you know her?"

"I met her at Callie's baby shower. And then I saw her again today when she stopped in to buy powdered sugar. The kids told me they like her. And that you do, too."

He'd liked her, all right. He'd also felt a hormonal rush he hadn't had since the kids' mother had left him three years ago. "She was nice to the twins. And she didn't blink an eye when Jimmy knocked over his chair."

"I'm not surprised." Betty Sue chuckled. "She was fairly calm this afternoon when Jimmy launched Super Dude across three aisles and accidentally nailed her in the head."

"Oh, no. Was she hurt?"

"Nope. Just a little bump on the noggin. Unfortunately, I can't say the same for Super Dude, who lost his head." Betty Sue laughed, her eyes sparkling with mirth. "Anyway, Marissa is twenty-five. She's originally from San Diego, but we're in luck. She plans to stay in Fairborn."

Interesting, he thought. But he kept his facial expression in check. Betty Sue didn't need any encouragement. She was a romantic at heart, which was a little surprising since she'd never been married.

"Just so you know," Betty Sue added, "Marissa works at the doughnut store a couple days a week. Usually on Tuesdays and Thursdays. She's also answering phones at that new hair salon on Wednesdays and Fridays."

How about that? Brandon's plan to get Jimmy a haircut had moved up on his priority list, although he kept that to himself, too.

"And speaking of hair salons, you really ought to make an appointment with someone there at The Mane Event. They'll do a much nicer job than the barber you see in Kalispell." Betty Sue clucked her tongue. "Why you men favor those short military cuts is beyond me. Most women like it long. That's why Jason Momoa is so popular. Talk about a gorgeous hunk. Every one of my friends on social media drool over him."

"I don't think I'd like to have women drooling over me."

"Oh, come on. They already do. In case you didn't notice, you're considered one of Fairborn's most eligible bachelors."

He'd noticed. And up until now, he hadn't given his so-called eligibility much thought.

"Marissa is also taking a business class at the junior college," Betty Sue added.

"She is?" He picked up a copy of the local paper that was sitting on the counter and pretended to scan the front page.

"Up until last weekend, she was living in a studio apartment in town, but she just moved to the Lazy M, which is going through a renovation of some kind."

Brandon knew the place well. Jack McGee had owned it, and right before he passed, he'd changed his will and left it to Alana Perez, the granddaughter he hadn't known he'd had. The women who lived there referred to it as Rancho Esperanza these days, although the folks in town hadn't gotten used to the name change yet.

"You haven't asked me if Marissa is single," Betty Sue added, "but I've got the scoop on that. She's not even dating anyone, but that's not going to last for very long. So if you've got your eye on her, you'd better make a move. And a quick one."

Brandon laughed off the comment, but Betty

Sue was right on all counts. He *was* interested in Marissa. But was he up to dating anyone right now?

Ever since he'd moved back to Fairborn toting a baby carrier in each hand, he'd been dragging his feet about doing any serious dating. Life was complicated enough running around after the twins. At least, that had always been his default excuse. His smile faded as he thought back to the day Julie had stood in the hallway of the small on-campus apartment they'd shared, a suitcase in hand.

I'm sorry, she'd said. *I didn't mean for this to happen. But he's...my soul mate.*

What am I? Besides stupid, he'd thought.

She flicked a strand of long blond hair behind her shoulder and blew out a weary sigh. *I didn't think you'd understand.*

Brandon had held his hands at his side, fists clenched, keeping his mouth shut and his temper in check. He'd known Julie had once been involved with a guy who'd landed in prison. But he hadn't expected her to hook up with him after he was paroled. *What about the babies?*

This is your night to watch them. So I'll come back for them later.

The hell she would. *I'm the one they've bonded with. You've been too damned busy to be a mother.*

I'll call you after I get settled.

For the next couple of weeks, they'd shared

baby duties, although he'd kept the twins most of the time since she'd always had one excuse or another for changing the plan. On the days leading up to graduation, he'd finally asked her what it would take for her to sign over full custody to him.

She seemed to think about it for the longest time. *I have student loans that'll take time to pay off...*

Done. I'll have the papers drawn up.

He'd had to go to his aunt and uncle for help—mostly with childcare. But he'd paid the cost. Every dime.

And he'd never heard from her again.

Back then, Brandon had been hurt and angry, but his feelings for Julie had dissipated with time and distance. Any residual resentment he held now was on Jimmy and Maddie's behalf. It killed him to think that their mother had abandoned them, like his parents had done to him.

But hey. Live and learn. Besides, he was smart enough to know that not all women were alike. And up until now, he simply hadn't had the time or the desire to date again—at least, not when it came to pursuing a serious relationship with someone in particular.

"So...?" Betty Sue said. "What are you going to do about Marissa?"

Brandon bent and placed a kiss on his great-aunt's brow. "Thanks for the report. I'll give it some thought."

But he wouldn't be thinking too long.

Marissa didn't mind handling the phones and setting appointments at the salon. The additional work would help her build up her savings account. And thanks to Alana's friendship and her offer of room and board in lieu of work on Rancho Esperanza, Marissa no longer had to set aside the funds for rent, which meant that she'd able to move forward on her business plan to start White Lace and Promises sooner than she'd once hoped.

When the telephone rang, Marissa answered in a chipper voice, one that came naturally on such a nice Montana blue-sky day. "The Mane Event. How may I help you?"

"This is Marianne Posey. I'd like to make an appointment on Saturday with Hailey. Does she have time for a touch-up and a trim?"

"Possibly. Let me check." Saturdays were always busy at the salon, but Marissa might be able to find a time for Marianne. Hailey, who looked like she could be Taylor Swift's younger sister, was one of the newest hairstylists Tameka Miller, the owner, had hired. Fresh out of beauty school, Hailey was still trying to build up her clientele.

"Can you come in at three o'clock?" Marissa asked.

"Yes, I can. That'll work perfectly. Thank you."

She'd no more than ended the call and penciled in Marianne Posey's name when the salon door opened. Marissa glanced up to see Mr. Daddy, otherwise known as Brandon, walk in looking like a dream come true—a six-foot-tall hunk, with green eyes and neatly trimmed light brown hair. He certainly didn't need an appointment, but he had little Jimmy in tow.

"Good morning," she said with a smile. "What a surprise." And a very nice one.

He tossed a boyish grin right back at her, setting her heart strumming and knocking her a little off stride.

"Jimmy needs a haircut," Brandon said. "Is there any chance we can get it done today?"

Marissa double-checked with the salon's second-newest stylist, hired just a week before Hailey. "You're in luck." Marissa said. "Robin's available now."

"Does she give lollipops to good kids?" Jimmy asked. "The barber that Uncle Ralph takes me to does."

"Actually," Marissa said, "I'm the one who passes out the candy at this salon. I even have dog treats."

The little towhead's big blue peepers widened. "Do dogs get their haircuts here, too?"

"No, but they sometimes come in with their

owners, although they have to wait outside for them. And if they're good and wait patiently on their leashes, they get a treat, too."

As Robin approached the front of the salon, Marissa tossed a grin at Jimmy and winked. "Should I tell her to duck in case there are any superheroes flying through the air?"

"Nope. I don't even have a toy with me." Jimmy's expression sobered, and he bit down on his bottom lip.

Brandon gave him a little nudge. "Don't you have something to say to Marissa?"

The boy nodded. "I'm sorry that I hit you with my toy yesterday."

"It only hurt for a minute." She pointed to her forehead and showed him the redness hadn't lasted. "See? All better."

"Yep." Jimmy looked up at his father. "I told you she didn't get hurt too bad."

"That's not the point, son. I hope that time-out Uncle Ralph gave you will help you remember not to throw things indoors, especially in the market. And to be more careful with your toys."

"It did, Daddy."

What a good father, Marissa thought. Teaching his son right from wrong. To be kind. And thoughtful.

"Hey, there," Robin said in her gravelly former-smoker's voice. When she reached the front desk, she greeted Jimmy first, then Brandon. "What're we doing to his hair today, Dad?"

"Just a trim. Nothing fancy."

"You've got it." Robin took Jimmy by the hand. "Come on, sweetie."

Marissa expected Brandon to follow his son to Robin's chair, but he didn't, which pleased her in an unexpected way.

"My aunt told me that you're living at Alana's ranch these days. How are things going?"

"Great. We've been making cherry jam and baking bread. We've been selling produce and baked goods at the farmers market on the weekend."

"How's it going?"

"Great. We usually sell out."

"I'm glad to hear it."

"It keeps us busy. But it's been fun working as a team." Marissa tucked a strand of hair behind her ear. "I'm also helping Alana get ready for her wedding. She and Clay are getting married in a few weeks. On the ranch. And I'm helping them with the details."

"Oh, yeah? Isn't her future husband living in Texas?"

"Not anymore. Clay lives at the ranch now. And he's helping Alana with the repairs. He's also studying for the Montana bar, so he'll be able to open a practice here."

"That's good. Henry Dahlberg just retired, so it will be nice to have a new attorney in town."

"I think so, too." Marissa's eyes brightened, her excitement at planning her very first wedding impossible to hide. "Mr. Hastings, Clay's father, had expected them to get married at a fancy country club in Texas and wanted to pull out all the stops. But Alana and Clay want an outdoor wedding on Rancho Esperanza. And I think that's a perfect choice for them."

"Betty Sue said you'd like to start your own business as a wedding planner, so that sounds like a great project for you."

"Yes, that's true." The conversation flowed easily between them, and Marissa found herself opening up to him. "In fact, if I get off early, which probably won't happen today, I thought about stopping by the Petal Pusher to get some ideas about flowers so I can make suggestions."

"Sounds like it'll be a nice wedding." Brandon studied her for a moment, as if he could see something deep inside her that others were too busy to notice. "It also sounds like you're a true romantic."

"I don't know about that. I'm good at organizing parties and events."

"Does that mean you already have your own wedding all planned out?"

"Oh, no." She lifted her hand, palm-side out as

if to halt that thought. "I mean, maybe. Someday. But I've yet to meet a man I can trust."

Brandon sobered. "That's too bad."

She hadn't meant to use the word *trust*, although it was definitely fitting. But she didn't want to come across as a battered butterfly on its last wing. Even if she *had* been let down again and again. "What I meant to say was I haven't found the right man. And I'm really not looking."

Before Brandon could respond, his cell phone rang. He whipped it out of his pocket and glanced at the display. "I'm sorry," he said. "I have to take this."

"Of course."

Brandon walked outside, where he paced near the front window.

She wondered who'd called him. It sounded important. And he clearly wanted a private conversation.

Before she could give it much thought, the salon phone rang, and she went back to work. Still, she found herself stealing a peek out the window at Brandon every now and then—until he caught her. He grinned, and her cheeks flushed.

What a dingbat. Get a grip, Marissa. Don't let him think you're crushing on him, even if you are.

Five minutes later, Brandon stepped back into the salon, just as Jimmy ran up to the front desk and announced, "I'm all done."

"Don't you look handsome!" Marissa said.

"And she said I was good." Jimmy turned to Robin for validation. "Right?"

"He certainly was."

Brandon handed the stylist a five-dollar tip. "Thanks for squeezing us in."

"No problem. Thanks for letting me cut your little guy's hair."

Marissa reached into the drawer, pulled out a small basket filled with lollipops. She lowered it for Jimmy to see. "Why don't you choose one for you—and one for your sister, too."

He reached for a green one, then, after a little thought, he withdrew a red one. "Thank you." He paused for a moment, then looked up at Marissa and grinned. "You know what? You're really nice."

Marissa returned his smile. "And you're sweet. So is Maddie."

"When I get home, I'm going to tell my sister that you're a doughnut lady *and* a lollipop lady."

"I suppose you can say that," she said. "But you can call me Marissa. That is, if you want to."

"Okay. Can Maddie call you that, too?"

"Of course."

As Jimmy tore into the lollipop wrapper, Brandon leaned toward her, close enough for her to catch a whiff of his mountain-fresh cologne laced with a manly soap, and said, "I have to admit that the twins' nicknames for you seem suitable."

"How's that?"

"Doughnuts and lollipops are both sweet." Coming from anyone else, she might have found that line to be sappy or cheesy—or both. But the way Brandon said it, the way he looked at her with sincerity and attraction dancing in his eyes, touched her in an unexpected way, causing her cheeks to warm and her heart to flutter.

"Thanks for being so nice to my kids." Appreciation glistened in his eyes—something else, too. But she didn't dare make any assumptions. "We'll see you around."

Marissa sure hoped so. Because Brandon seemed like a sweet guy, too. The kind a woman who'd had her hopes and trust shattered could count on.

Chapter Three

Brandon didn't make rash decisions, but he'd had a few days to consider the best way to ask Marissa out—and where he should take her. His first thought was something simple and safe, like going to Doc Creamer's Frozen Emporium for an ice-cream sundae. But that seemed a little too family-like, the kind of place parents took their kids. He didn't want her to think he was looking for a mother for the twins.

Going to the movies wouldn't give them an opportunity to talk. Plus, The Reel Deal, the dollar theater in Fairborn, might make him look like a cheapskate. So if he went that route, he'd have to take her into Kalispell. He could always suggest they have dinner before or afterward, but any of the local restaurants were out. He might like the residents of Fairborn, but there'd be talk. And he'd never enjoyed being a hot topic on the rumor mill.

After racking his brain, he'd come up with a great idea. There was a law-enforcement dinner coming up next weekend, with dinner and music. He could invite her to attend with him, telling her that he needed a plus-one, which might play down the whole date thing.

And today was the perfect day to ask her.

After dropping off the kids at the Tiny Tykes Preschool, he drove down Elmwood Drive on his way home. As he neared the drugstore, he spotted a white pickup double-parked in front. He was off duty today, but both his job and town safety were always his priority. So he pulled into a newly vacated parking space two cars down—and next to his aunt Carlene's blue minivan. She must have left Uncle Ralph at the market to run some errands in town.

Brandon shut off the ignition and got out of his Jeep, just as a young man hurried out of the drugstore with his keys in hand and approached the truck he'd left unattended.

"Sir," Brandon called out, "you're double-parked. I'm not in uniform, but I can still cite you."

"I'm sorry," the man in his twenties said. "I couldn't find a parking space, and I knew I wouldn't be long. I had to pick up an antibiotic and a pain reliever for my baby boy. He's got a fever and an ear infection."

When it came to sick kids, Brandon had been there, done that. He certainly understood the worry, the need to make things better.

"Consider this a warning," he told the harried daddy.

"I will. Thank you, Officer." The man opened the door and climbed inside. He drove off, just as Aunt Carlene walked out of the drugstore, a frantic look on her face, as she scanned the sidewalk in both directions.

"Carlene," Brandon said, "what's the matter?"

"Betty Sue took off again. And I've looked all over for her."

"She's not in the drugstore?"

"No, not anymore. She was standing beside me while my friend Sharon and I were talking about the police dinner you're going to attend, then Betty Sue said she wanted to check something out. But when I went to look for her, she was gone." Carlene snapped her fingers. "Just like that."

"Okay, don't panic." His aunt and uncle were the best of folks. After taking custody of Brandon when he was thirteen, they'd treated him as their own son. And when he'd returned from college with the two babies, they welcomed him home. They also looked after the twins whenever he was on duty.

So it wasn't a surprise that, without hesitation, they'd taken in Betty Sue, Ralph's aunt, an older woman with a tendency to wander. Like his Uncle Ralph always said, "We'll never turn our back on family."

"Don't worry," Brandon said. "I'll look for her. She couldn't have gone far."

He'd no more than opened the driver's door to climb into his vehicle when his cell phone rang. He looked on the console where he'd left it and spotted Betty Sue's name on the display. He answered quickly. "Hey, Auntie. Where are you?"

"I got a little light-headed and figured that my blood-sugar level had dropped."

Brandon sucked in a deep breath, then slowly let it out. "So you left the drugstore?" That wasn't good. Someone would have been able to help her there, but not if she collapsed on the sidewalk. "Where are you?"

"I'm on my way to Darla's. I figure you're still in town after dropping off the kids at preschool. So why don't you join me? There's a nice table by the window. When you get here, I'll treat you to a jelly doughnut."

Had it been a Tuesday or Thursday, Brandon

would have jumped at the chance to see Marissa again. "I'll pass on the doughnut," he said. "I'm not big on sweets. But don't go anywhere. I'm coming to get you."

While wiping down the counter at the doughnut shop, Marissa noticed Betty Sue rushing past the front window as if she was on a mission, which was a little unexpected. It was even more surprising when the bell over the door jingled as she entered, her dyed-red curls held away from her face with a long, sunflower-print scarf.

She'd dressed colorfully again today, choosing a lemon yellow tunic over a pair of green polyester slacks and navy blue sneakers. A beaded, macramé purse hung from her shoulder.

"Good morning, Betty Sue." Marissa glanced out the window, wondering if someone was with her. From what she'd seen, the Tiptons kept a pretty close eye on her, especially Carlene. "It's nice to see you in town."

"Ever since Ralph took the car keys from me and then sold the moped, I don't get out this way very often. But Carlene had an errand to run today, so I rode with her." A rebellious glimmer in her eyes softened the wrinkles on her face. "I didn't know you worked on Mondays."

"Darla's husband had a doctor's appointment

this morning. She's going to relieve me around ten or eleven."

Betty Sue moseyed toward the display case and studied the doughnuts, Danishes, muffins and cinnamon rolls. "Is that cherry filling in those jelly doughnuts?"

"Yes, it is."

"Good. I love cherries. And Doc Clemmons told me I should be eating more fruit."

Marissa stifled a grin. "How can I help you?"

The older woman looked up and smiled. "Hopefully, I can help *you*."

Marissa had no idea what she meant by that, but before she could ask, Betty Sue turned away and craned her neck to peer out the window that faced Elmwood Drive.

Her behavior seemed a little odd today, but then again, from what Marissa had seen and heard, Betty Sue was a bit of a novelty.

"Are you waiting for Carlene to join you?" Marissa asked.

"She could show up, I suppose. And she'll probably be a little snippy-snappy when she does." Betty Sue headed for one of the white café-style tables near the window, pulled out a chair and took a seat. "I was at the drugstore a few minutes ago. While I was looking for my favorite brand of hair color, I ran into Darla. She was waiting on a prescription for her hubby and mentioned you were working today, which surprised me."

"Actually, I help Darla out whenever I can."

"Aren't you a sweetheart." Betty Sue looped the strap of her purse over the back of her chair and let it hang. "I noticed someone put out a water bowl on the sidewalk. I figured it was you."

"A lot of pet owners walk their dogs up and down this street," Marissa said. "And I thought the dogs might appreciate a drink."

"Like I always say, someone who's kind to animals and children must have a pure heart."

Marissa would like to think so, even though there were people in her past who'd questioned her heart. "Can I get you something to drink while you wait, Betty Sue?"

"Sure. I'd like a large hot chocolate with extra whipped cream."

"You got it."

"You told me you were single," Betty Sue said. "That hasn't changed, has it? I mean, you haven't started dating anyone yet?"

Why the curiosity? Had Brandon sent her on a fact-finding mission? And if so, should she be flattered?

On the other hand, maybe Betty Sue was just inquisitive, if not outright nosy.

"No, I'm still not dating anyone." Marissa turned her back and began to fill Betty Sue's order. She had no more than squirted an extra dollop of whipped cream into the hot chocolate when the bell on the front door jingled again. A familiar voice sounded, and her heart took off like a shot, and she froze.

"Aunt Betty," Brandon said, "Carlene's been calling you. She was worried when you left the drugstore without telling her. And even more so when you didn't answer her call."

"Oops. I must have had the ringer on silent, Brandon. Sorry about that. You remember my friend Marissa, don't you?"

Marissa slowly turned around, a disposable cup of hot cocoa in her hand.

At that, Brandon spun around and faced the display case. A slow, endearing smile stretched across his face and dimpled his cheeks.

"Hey," he said. "I didn't expect to see you here."

"Brandon," Betty Sue said, "don't just stand there gawking at the pretty woman. Tell her what you'd like to order."

He blew out a weary sigh. "I wasn't gawking. I was just surprised to see her, that's all." He sat at the table, across from Betty Sue, then turned to Marissa. "I'll have a large coffee. Black."

Marissa nodded, glad to have something to do because he *had* been gawking, at least a little. Hadn't he? She proceeded to pour his drink into a to-go cup. Then she took it to the table, just in time to catch a furrow on Brandon's brow and a mischievous twinkle in Betty Sue's eyes.

As she placed the drinks in front of them, Brandon offered Marissa an apologetic grin, although she wasn't sure what he had to be sorry for—other than being too darned gorgeous for a woman's own good.

She might be wrong, but it seemed as if Betty Sue was trying to set the two of them up, although she wasn't very smooth.

She ought to be annoyed, she supposed, but it was kind of cute. And if truth be told, the fact that someone in Brandon's family seemed to like her was a huge relief.

But did *he* like her?

The bell jingled, the door swung open again and Carlene entered, scanning the room until her gaze landed on her aunt.

"Oh, for goodness sake," Carlene said, her voice laced with both frustration and relief. "You scared the ever lovin' liver out of me again. Please, please, *please* stop taking off on a tangent without telling me where you're going."

Betty Sue rolled her eyes. "I would, but I can't very well do that when I'm not sure where I'm heading."

Marissa, who stood silent while watching the scene unfold, glanced at Brandon. When their eyes met, they shared a mutual moment of silent laughter.

Betty Sue whispered something to Brandon, then gave him a nudge before getting to her feet. She made her way to the front of the store, where her niece stood. "I love you, Carlene. And I'm sorry I worried you. Where's your car?"

"It's parked in front of the drugstore, right where I left it."

"Good. Let's go home. Do you want any coffee or hot cocoa to go? Maybe a bag of doughnut holes we can share during the drive?"

Carlene let out a weary sigh. "Sure, Auntie."

Marissa kept quiet as she filled the order: coffee with cream and sugar and a dozen doughnut holes.

"Did you still want a jelly doughnut?" Marissa asked the older woman.

"You bet I do. Doctor's orders and all." She winked, then reached into her macramé bag, pulled out a black wallet with a peace-sign appliqué on it and withdrew a twenty-dollar bill. "I'm springing for Brandon's coffee, too. And once I get our doughnuts, Carlene and I will leave you two alone."

Marissa would be happy to be left alone with Brandon. And if her luck held out, she wouldn't have another customer for a while.

* * *

Betty Sue sat in the passenger side of the mini-van, munching on the jelly doughnut and preparing herself for a scolding. She'd always been a rebel, which had set off her parents more times than not. And since Carlene seemed to have taken on that same role with her, she couldn't help being troublesome.

"I need you to stop wandering," Carlene said. "You scared me half to death!"

"I'm sorry. I guess you could say that I just get a wild hair every once in a while." Betty Sue stuck her finger in her mouth and sucked off the sugary glaze. Mmm. Darla served a mean doughnut.

"Mama told me that you were the most strong-willed and adventurous woman she'd ever known."

True.

"Ralph and I worry about you," Carlene added. "You're not as young as you used to be, Auntie."

Betty found that it was usually in her best interest to keep quiet at times like this. When she did, her niece and nephew usually just let it go and chalked it up to Betty just being Betty, always marching to her own drummer. Everyone had been shocked when she'd agreed to move in with her niece and her husband. But she'd tried living in one of those so-called active-senior facilities and had been terribly disappointed to find that there'd been very little to no action there.

Just a lot of old people, shuffling around waiting for the next bingo game. But Betty wasn't ready for that.

Besides, it was nice to be around family, especially since she'd never had kids. Of course, neither had Ralph and Carlene. But they'd raised Brandon ever since he was thirteen. And speaking of Brandon…she hoped that he was happy now that he was sitting with that lovely doughnut lady.

Once Betty Sue and Carlene left the doughnut shop, Marissa turned to Brandon. "Betty Sue is a real hoot. I really like her."

"She's hard not to like, but she really frustrates Carlene. To be honest, I think she does it on purpose. Betty Sue has always been an independent woman, and she's not ready to hand over control to anyone, especially Carlene."

"I'm sure it must be hard to give up your independence." Marissa paused, then bit down on her bottom lip. Should she address the subject that had grown clearer and more obvious as the last few minutes had worn on?

She may as well. Brandon had to have noticed it, too. "I don't know about you, but it seems to me that Betty Sue is trying to do a little matchmaking."

"She wasn't very subtle, was she?" He scooted his chair away from the table, then made his way to the front counter. "But I *would* like to ask you out."

Okay, she thought, as she leaned in to him, waiting. Wanting.

"There's a special dinner to honor law-enforcement officers in the county on Saturday night. And I wondered if you'd like to go with me. As my plus-one."

Her gut clenched, and the heat that had begun to simmer in her body cooled. *Law-enforcement officers?* Why would Brandon be attending an event like that? Was he an attorney? Or…

Her cheeks warmed, her mind screamed no and her heart spun in her chest like the tires of a car stuck in the mud. Surely, he wasn't a member of the police force. Was he?

He had to be. Right?

If the words hadn't stalled in her throat, she would have asked him flat out if he was a cop.

"That is," he said, "unless you're seeing someone."

She sucked in a wobbly breath. "No."

"No, you aren't seeing someone? Or no, you're not interested in going to that dinner?"

Both. How did she tell him she'd be a hot mess if she was expected to eat and socialize with a roomful of law-enforcement officers?

And what would he say if she told him why?

She sucked in a breath. Okay. Enough. It was

time to put the past behind her, right? She wasn't a frightened teenager anymore, with nowhere to go, no one to turn to.

But she couldn't. Instead, she said, "I'm sorry, Brandon. It sounds like a nice evening, but I already have plans for Saturday night."

He looked a little surprised, if not deflated. And she felt crappy, as if she'd lied to him. But she hadn't. Neither had she been forthright. Should she say something? Or keep her secret to herself?

Not that it was anyone's business. "Then maybe another time," Brandon said, his cheeks a little rosy as if he'd been a high-school freshman who'd asked the prom queen out on a date, only to be rejected.

She felt his embarrassment, which drew her sympathy and battered her resolve.

"Sure," she said. "Maybe another time."

A slow grin spread across his face. "All right." He nodded, took a step back, then turned and walked out the door.

She watched him go, her heart racing, thumping like the frantic footsteps of someone resisting arrest. At the same time, her heart crumpled.

There went a great guy with the wrong job. Brandon was out of her league on so many levels—his community standing, for one. Financial security for another. And even if that didn't matter to him, there was no way a former felon ought to even consider dating a cop.

Chapter Four

Marissa hadn't seen Brandon in nearly a week, but she'd soon learned why he'd invited her to a law-enforcement dinner. He was a deputy sheriff, one of several who patrolled the Fairborn city streets.

If he'd had another job—anything other than one that sometimes locked up innocent people—she would've been happy, maybe even excited, to go out with him. To dinner or anywhere. But there was no way she'd consider dating anyone remotely connected to the criminal-justice system, no matter how hot he was. And Deputy Brandon Dodd, with those broad shoulders, lively green eyes and square-cut chin, was a definite hottie. But Marissa's experience with the police, lawyers and correctional guards tipped the scales out of his favor. Way out of his favor.

She hadn't heard from him since, so she figured he'd gotten the message and realized she was reluctant to date him. But the following Tuesday morning, while she was working at Darla's, he showed up in uniform.

Just the sight of him sauntering in the door sent a rush of adrenaline through her veins, kicking up a fight-or-flight response.

Calm down, girl. You haven't done anything wrong.

"Good morning," Brandon said with a charming grin that was a little disarming.

She managed a smile and said hello in a voice that came out a little too squeaky for comfort.

Her attempt to act normal and unaffected must have failed, because his happy expression shifted to a furrowed brow, and he zeroed in on her like a cop cornering a suspect.

"What's the matter?" he asked.

Unwarranted guilt swept over her as if he'd just caught her robbing the till, but she shook it off the best she could. She *wasn't* guilty of anything. Not now, and certainly not before.

"Nothing's wrong. What can I get for you?

Coffee? You take it black, right? Maybe a jelly doughnut?"

"Yes. And just coffee, please. But that's not why I'm here."

Uh-oh. Was he here on official business?

"What's up?" she asked.

"I wondered if you could answer a couple of questions."

Her heart pounded. Did she need a lawyer? She hadn't done anything wrong, but she'd learned the hard way that innocence didn't matter if no one believed her. "Officially?"

"Sort of."

Her heart hammered harder and louder, as if trying to escape. Had he somehow found out about her past? It was doubtful, she supposed. But she didn't dare ask.

"You're here alone, right?"

"Yes. Is that against some town ordinance? Am I in some kind of trouble?" she asked. *Darn it. What was the matter with her?* She hadn't meant to look or sound guilty.

He stammered. "I didn't mean to imply that I was here in an official capacity."

Was this some kind of *Bachelor Cop* reality show? "I'm sorry. Your uniform kind of threw me off."

He tugged at his collar and cleared his throat. "Damn. This is going badly. I'm sorry. I haven't done this sort of thing in years. And it's definitely not like riding a bike."

His nervous response downsized her apprehension. He was right. This was going badly.

"I'd like to go out with you," he said. "And I thought we were both on the same page. But when I asked you to attend that dinner with me last Monday, I got the feeling that you weren't interested in going out with me. And I just wanted to clear the air."

She couldn't blame him for that. If she intended to be a permanent resident and businesswoman in Fairborn, she'd need to tamp down her nervousness around him and anyone else who worked in law enforcement.

"I have a lot on my plate right now," she said. "Two jobs, an online college course, helping Alana get ready for the farmers market, then manning the booth with her on the weekends. There's also the wedding I'm planning, which is really important to me. So I'll need to help Alana choose a florist, a baker. And since Callie, her best friend, is about to give birth to twins, I might have to go shopping with her to pick out a dress."

She heard herself rambling, but what other tasks could she throw at the guy so she could dodge a more truthful answer? Ordering tables and chairs from a party-rental place in Kalispell? No, that'd be too much.

"I'm sure you're busy," he said. "But please be honest. Are the kids a problem for you?"

At that, her lips parted, and her bluster fizzled. "No, of course not. You have great kids. Cute, sweet."

"Then, it's me?"

No. It wasn't that…

"It's *me*," she said. "You're a great guy, Brandon. Handsome. Bright. Easy to talk to. And your kids are…" Oh, for Pete's sake. Now she was talking herself into it!

She threw up her hands, as if in surrender, and conjured another, more believable excuse. "I'm coming off a breakup, so I'm not up for getting involved with anyone so soon." Not that she and Steven had been all that invested, romantically speaking, and the decision to split had been mutual. On top of that truth, mocking her lame excuse, last summer wasn't all that recent.

The longer he stood there, studying her with a sympathetic eye, the more she began to regret telling him she'd had plans last Saturday night. Not that she would have gone to that police dinner with him. She would have felt as out of place as a pole dancer at a ballet recital.

The door jingled, and two middle-aged women entered. When they spotted Brandon, they both broke into broad smiles. The tallest one, a brunette, said, "Good morning, Sheriff. I can see you're here for your doughnut fix."

Brandon gave them each a polite nod. "Hello, Sharon. Danielle. I'm actually a deputy. The sheriff is an elected position. And that would be my boss."

"I know," the brunette said, "but Danielle was just telling me that she heard Sheriff Beaumont is thinking about retirement and that you'd like to take his place."

"That's just a passing thought."

"Well, you'd have our vote," the blonde— Danielle—said.

The women approached the display case, where Marissa stood rooted in place.

"Good morning," Marissa said, shaking off the idea of deputies and sheriffs and elections—oh, my. "What will it be today?"

The brunette, Sharon, glanced at Brandon. "I'm sorry. We didn't mean to take cuts, Deputy Sheriff."

The other chuckled. "That's right. We know how important a doughnut break is to you guys."

"Go right ahead," he told them. "I've already had my break. I was just leaving. Have a good day, ladies."

He tossed Marissa a parting grin, one that didn't seem to reach his eyes. Then he walked out the door.

Sharon nudged her friend, then winked at Marissa. "All in a day's work, huh?"

But it wasn't. Not really. And when Deputy Dodd sauntered into Darla's, whether with his kids or on duty, it was never a typical day.

Brandon climbed behind the wheel of the squad car, shut the driver's door and blew out a sigh of frustration. He hated stereotypes, yet he'd just validated the one about cops and doughnuts. The only reason he'd gone to Darla's today, for a fix he didn't need, was because it was Tuesday.

And he knew Marissa would be there.

Only trouble was, after focusing his life on his kids, he was a little rusty at dating. Still he'd given it his best shot this morning. Apparently, the question had stunned Marissa, and he wasn't sure why. He'd assumed she'd felt that same little zing he'd felt, the same attraction.

But he did understand how a recent breakup might cause her to drag her feet, fearing she might make the same mistake again. Hell, he was still reluctant to get involved with anyone, and his split with Julie had been three years ago.

Marissa also might have shied away from him because of his job. If that was the case, it would have been nice if she would've just leveled with him.

It was also possible that she wasn't ready to go with him to something so formal. Then again, maybe he'd read way too much into her pretty smile and her kindness to his kids. Maybe she just wasn't that interested in him, after all.

He'd always prided himself on being observant and a good judge of character. Or course, that instinct had let him down when it came to dating Julie.

But his gut told him Marissa wasn't like that. She couldn't be. Jimmy and Maddie had taken to her right away. She put out bowls of water on the sidewalk for the dogs whose owners walked them past Darla's.

Either way, he thought as he backed out of the parking spot and headed down Elmwood Drive, he'd tripped up somehow.

And to make matters worse, he was in such a hurry to hightail it out of the shop, he'd left without taking his cup of coffee.

The trusty, old maroon Honda Civic had well over a hundred thousand miles on it when Marissa bought it six years ago, and up until now, it had been dependable, getting her from San Diego to Montana, so she couldn't complain. But she had a feeling there were some big repair bills coming her way.

The battery had been dead this morning, and she'd needed a jump start. And even after she'd gotten on the road and started the twenty-minute drive to town, she hadn't been able to go any faster than forty miles an hour.

The air-conditioning hadn't ever worked, not since she bought the car, and so she'd rolled down the windows. But the weatherman had predicted a warmer than usual summer day, so she'd dressed appropriately—a white scoop-neck blouse with lace trim, black shorts and a pair of sandals. She'd also put her hair in a ponytail. But she'd begun to perspire. Even the soft rock playing on the radio failed to keep her mind off her growing discomfort.

As she turned off the county road and onto Fairborn Drive, the engine rattled and chugged.

Now what?

She turned off the radio so she could pay more attention to the noise under the hood. She'd need to explain it to the mechanic at Don's Auto Works.

Would she even make it there? She had her doubts.

At the intersection, she stopped and waited for the red light to turn green. Once it did, she pressed down on the gas pedal, but instead of taking off, the car inched forward, chugging and sputtering as it did.

"Darn it," she uttered as she urged it across the intersection and to the side of the road, where it conked out completely.

At least she only had a couple of miles to walk.

She grabbed her purse, as well as her water bottle, and got out of the car. No need to lock it, since there was nothing of value inside—and it wasn't going anywhere. Then she started her trek into town. She'd barely gotten a hundred yards when she spotted a squad car up ahead.

Apparently, the officer—Brandon Dodd, she assumed—spotted her, too, because he turned around and drove her way.

Sure enough. It was Officer Hottie. He rolled down the window. "Car trouble?"

"Yes. I'm afraid so. I was going to walk to Don's Auto Works. Hopefully, they'll have a tow truck available." She tucked a loose strand of hair behind her ear. "Is it okay that I left my car on the side of the road? I mean, I don't want to get a ticket. I can try to push it to a better spot."

"It's okay where it is. But there's no need for you to walk. Get in. I'll give you a ride."

She hesitated as she eyed the vehicle, with its red light on the top and caged back seat. She hadn't ridden in one of those in years, and she didn't plan to ever again.

"It's okay. I don't mind walking. I can use the exercise."

"Don't be silly. It's going to be warm today."

It wasn't just warm, it was supposed to be a scorcher. And she'd be a sweaty mess by the time she got to the repair shop.

"Climb in," he said.

"Front or back?"

He laughed as if he didn't know she'd been half-serious. "The front, of course."

Reluctantly, she opened the passenger door and got into the squad car. In spite of all the gadgets on the dash, which were a bit disconcerting, the cool air blowing through the vent welcomed her, urging her to relax and accept the ride he'd offered her and the comfort it provided.

As Brandon pulled back onto the road and headed toward town, he said, "I hope my aunt's attempt at matchmaking didn't bother you too much."

"It didn't. In fact, I get a kick out of her. She's one of a kind."

"You can say that again!" He chuckled. "Betty Sue is actually my great-aunt. On Ralph's side."

Marissa wasn't sure how those relationships worked.

"Family is family," she said, although hers had never really counted her as such.

"My aunt and uncle watch the twins for me when I'm on duty," he added. "And now they're looking after Betty Sue."

"They seem like wonderful people."

"They're more like a mom and dad to me," he said.

She was tempted to ask what happened to his

parents, but she wasn't up to sharing her own past with him. So she kept quiet.

"I put Maddie and Jimmy into preschool three days a week, in part to give my aunt and uncle a break, even though they insist they don't need one."

Hoping to dig for a little more information, she asked, "Does their mother help out with them?"

"She's not involved in their lives. I have full custody."

Wow. She hadn't seen that coming.

"So what about you?" he asked. "Do you have family?"

"We've never been very close."

"That's too bad," he said.

She didn't see it that way. Having no family—or an estranged one—was better than claiming the lousy one she'd once had. She'd rather not explain why her family had turned their backs on her—and why she'd cut them out of her life after that. But maybe she'd better explain, at least a little.

"My mother died when I was a baby," she offered. "And my father died in a freak industrial accident when I was twelve."

Brandon inhaled, looking surprised. "I'm sorry. That must have been a tough loss. Did you have any extended family members who took you in?"

"No. Not really." She would have been better off if there had been aunts, uncles, grandparents...

"My dad remarried a couple years before he died, so my stepmother raised me." No need to go into any more detail than that.

"I'm lucky," he said. "My parents split up, and the divorce sent them both into tailspins. If I had stayed with either of them, there's no telling how I might have turned out. But I was lucky. I moved in with Ralph and Carlene, and they showed me what a real family was like."

"That's cool." It was too bad Marissa hadn't had her own extended family who'd taken custody of her when her father had died.

Maybe, instead of spending time behind bars and being uneasy around judges, attorneys and the like, she might have ended up patrolling the city streets like Brandon did.

As they neared the auto-repair shop, Brandon shot a glance across the seat. "Do you have a ride home?"

"Actually, I'm working an extra shift at the salon today. It's only a couple of blocks away from the auto repair shop, so I'll walk."

"And after that? What if your car isn't ready?"

She'd figure something out. Maybe ask someone to give her a ride.

Before she could respond, he said, "I'll tell you what. I'll stop by the salon later this afternoon and make sure you have transportation."

"You don't need to do that."

"I know. But I'm off duty at five thirty. And then I'm going to drive out to the market to get the kids. So it's right on the way."

Dang. Did Officer Hottie have to be such a regular guy? And so darn thoughtful?

"Sure. Thanks. That'd be nice. I have a feeling my car will be in the shop for a long time."

As she slid out of the passenger seat, he said, "One more thing. Would you be opposed to going out to lunch with me? Not today, of course."

Seriously? That sounded tempting, but she was too stunned to speak.

"If that seems too much like a date," he added, "how about a picnic with the kids at the park?"

To be completely honest, the thought of packing a picnic basket and taking Jimmy and Maddie to the park was really appealing. She'd like to watch them run and play, push them on the swings, stand at the foot of the slide and cheer them on the ride down…

"That sounds fun," she said. Besides, an outing like that would also be a lot safer because it would take the focus off them as a couple.

And it wouldn't feel like a date.

By the time six o'clock rolled around, the salon had closed, and the stylists had all left. Tameka was in the back room, talking to her husband on the phone.

Marissa was just restocking the inventory that was displayed next to the front desk when Brandon knocked at the locked front door. She'd expected him to drive up in his squad car and show up in his uniform, but he was dressed in a pair of worn jeans and a black T-shirt. It was a surprisingly normal ensemble that, along with a dimpled grin, set off a swish and a flutter in her chest.

She placed the last of the conditioner on the glass shelf, then she opened the door and let the gorgeous deputy inside the shop.

"What did you find out about your car?" he asked.

She blew out a sigh. "I'll be on foot or borrowed wheels for a while. At least a week."

"That's too bad," he said. "Are you ready to go?"

"Yes. I just need to let Tameka know I'm leaving. She's in the back room, tallying up the receipts for the day." Marissa left Brandon at the front of the store, then slipped into the back room, where Tameka had just zipped the cash bag shut. "The shelves are all restocked. Do you need me to do anything else?"

"No, I've got things under control. Thanks again for coming in on your day off, Marissa. And you've been a lifesaver on Wednesdays and

Fridays. I might even need you to work on Saturday afternoons—if you're available."

She helped Alana at the farmers market on the weekends, but Alana would understand if she had to leave early. "Just let me know when you'd like me to start. Have a good evening."

"You, too."

Marissa headed back to the front of the shop. And to her ride home.

Moments later, she was opening the passenger door of Brandon's personal vehicle—a white late-model Jeep Grand Cherokee that had two boosters secured in the back seat.

But what surprised her was a cardboard pet carrier resting between them. A whimper sounded from within.

"What's this?"

"A puppy. I just picked him up a couple of minutes ago. The kids have been begging for a pet, and I found him wandering around this morning. His fur was so dirty and matted that it looked like he'd been on the street for a long time. So I took him to the groomer, a friend of mine from high school. She's a real dog lover. After she fed him and gave him a bath, she had the vet who volunteers at a rescue center check him out. He's healthy, but a little underweight. And since he doesn't have a microchip, we have no way of finding his owner. So I plan to surprise the kids."

"Lucky dog," she said. And she meant that. The puppy was going to live with a great family.

Marissa had always wanted a pet, although her stepmother had refused to even consider it. But she would have settled for a nice family. As it turned out, she hadn't gotten one of those, either.

"Do you mind if I take him out of the box? I don't imagine he likes being caged." Marissa certainly hadn't liked it.

"Sure. Go ahead."

After loosening the lid, she reached in and pulled out a small black-and-white cocker spaniel mix. "Oh, my gosh! He's so cute."

The pup squirmed in her arms, but only so he could reach up and give her a long, appreciative lick on the cheek.

"What are you going to do with him when you work and the kids are at preschool?" she asked.

"Mrs. Hendrix, my neighbor, is a dog lover. I called her and asked if she'd be interested in being a puppy-sitter, and she was more than a little enthusiastic. So I've got that covered."

She wasn't surprised that he had it all figured out. To be honest, she wouldn't mind puppy-sitting, either. That is, if he ever was in a jam. But she didn't dare offer. She'd have to be careful about getting too close to him and his family.

"Are you in a hurry to get home?" he asked.

The question took her aback. "Why? What do you have in mind?"

"I can't wait to surprise Maddie and Jimmy. So I thought I'd stop at the market first, give them the puppy, and then the kids and I can drop you off at the ranch before the three of us head home."

"Where is home?" she asked.

"The kids and I live in town, over on Second Avenue. When the sheriff's office hired me, I bought a house with a big backyard. I even built them a playhouse. They love it there, and so do I. But they don't get to spend as much time there as I'd like them to."

"Because of childcare?"

"Yes. I mean, they love Uncle Ralph and Aunt Carlene. And they've got a playroom in the back of the market. But it's…"

"Not home," Marissa supplied.

"No, it's not. But there are a lot of other single parents doing the best they can to create a home. The twins are happy and healthy, so we're doing okay."

Marissa had to admit, she'd begun to like the man behind the badge, even if she was still a little uneasy around him. There was just something about the way he looked at her that made her wonder if maybe…if there was a chance that her past wouldn't freak him out.

"So what do you say?" he asked. "Would you

rather have me drop you off first? Or do you want to see the kids go crazy over their new pet?"

Part of her, the part that wanted a man like Brandon to like her and to include her in a family activity, wanted to say yes. But the other part—the part that would never forget the time she'd spent in jail—insisted that she hold her tongue.

What would he think if he knew of her arrest? Would he, like her so-called family and most of the people she used to know, believe that a conviction in and of itself automatically meant guilt?

But when she looked into his warm gaze, her fear and questions seemed to dissipate into the pheromones dancing in the cab of the Jeep, along with the scent of his mountain-fresh cologne.

A deputy sheriff was bad enough. But he was running for county sheriff. An elected position, with the respect of everyone in the community. She ought to decline, but in spite of her better judgment, she wanted to share in the children's delight, so she said, "Sure. Let's take this sweet bundle of fluff to meet his new family."

Chapter Five

Brandon gripped the steering wheel and studied the road ahead as he drove to the market to pick up the twins. He was glad Marissa had agreed to ride along with him. She seemed eager to introduce the puppy to the kids, but she'd been giving him mixed signals when it came to going out with him.

He glanced across the console at her striking profile, as her big brown eyes gazed out the windshield. She wore red lipstick today, instead of the simple pink gloss she favored when working at Darla's. And her hair, which she often pulled up in a twist of some kind, hung soft and loose, the glossy curls tumbling over her shoulders. She looked classy but casual.

Beautiful.

He sucked in a breath. She'd probably be a knockout no matter how she dressed. Even stepping out of the shower, her face clean, hair dripping wet, her skin…

Whoa. Now, there was an image he'd like to see. And one he was going to have a hell of a time getting out of his head. Not that he planned to work too hard at it.

Up ahead, a Greyhound bus pulled off the side of the road in front of them. It stopped near the awning-covered bus stop. Several passengers got on, while a woman, a blonde with long, stringy hair, got off carrying a small, black canvas tote. She had on a bulky, oversize gray sweatshirt and a pair of baggy jeans.

Marissa craned her neck, as if checking out the new arrival.

"See someone you know?" he asked.

She turned and cast him a wistful smile. "No. Not really. Just someone traveling alone. And no one was waiting for her."

He'd noticed that, too. In his line of work, being observant was critical.

"Why did she catch your attention?" He assumed Marissa might have once traveled alone, once been nervous or scared to embark on a journey to a new life in an unfamiliar community.

She shrugged. "No reason. It's just that she seemed…kind of sad, I guess. That's all." She lifted the puppy and snuggled it. "I guess it's because I have a heart for strays."

"Like Alana," he said. The woman she lived with, the one who'd inherited the Lazy M, renamed it Rancho Esperanza and had let various people move in with her, all of them having a need of one kind or another.

"Alana has a big heart, and she's been a good friend. It's hard not to smile when she's around, and more so now. She's in love and excited to be getting married."

Alana was a little too trusting, if you asked him. But he wasn't one to warm up to people too quickly. As a cop, he'd learned to be skeptical at first. Of course, his experience with Julie had led him to be cautious, too.

"Speaking of marriage," he said, "how are the wedding plans coming along?"

At that, Marissa's somber expression brightened. "So far, so good. Alana liked my idea of placing a gazebo near a weeping willow tree on the property, and Clay has already purchased the lumber and materials to build it. He can afford to hire someone, but he wants to do it himself and plans to start work on it this weekend."

Brandon—like a lot of men he knew—didn't see the point in having big weddings. It seemed to him that the enormous amount of money spent on a party could be put to better use. But most women seemed to make a big deal out of them—planning them, dressing up to attend one.

His mood darkened. Not Julie, though. When she told him she was pregnant with the twins, he'd offered to marry her, but she'd turned him down, saying she didn't see any reason for it, that it wasn't necessary. And, as things panned out, that decision had ended up for the best. A divorce would've made their split much harder. And more complicated.

He wondered where she was. Still in New York, he imagined. She never called, never asked about the kids. That was for the best, too, he supposed. But it ate at him to think she'd just walked away from them, abandoning them completely.

Minutes later, he and Marissa arrived at Tip Top Market, which was about to close. Brandon assumed his aunt and uncle were getting ready to lock up and go into the back room to count the day's receipts. That would leave Betty Sue and the kids alone in the house. He always tried to pick up the kids and be home before his great-aunt was left alone with them, but stopping by the salon and waiting for Marissa had taken a little more time than he'd expected.

Not that he was overly worried about the twins. Carlene was the one who'd mentioned her concern about Betty Sue, especially as she was growing older. But the kids adored Auntie, and she loved them, too.

He swung along the back side of the store and drove down the short, blacktop-paved lane that led to the modest, three-bedroom house where his aunt and uncle lived.

"So this is where you grew up?" she asked.

"I spent my teen years here."

"Where were you before?" She kissed the top of the puppy's head, then quickly added, "I'm sorry. That's none of my business."

He wasn't sure why he felt compelled to open up, to share his past with her, but she was easy to talk to, and he couldn't see any reason to keep it from her. "Up until I was thirteen, I lived with my mom and dad. He was verbally abusive, and they both had drinking problems. They probably still do. I decided I wanted more out of life than a crappy past and an unpleasant future. So I called Uncle Ralph and asked if I could move in with him and Carlene. They'd never had kids of their own and didn't blink an eye at taking me in."

"I'm impressed that you made such a wise decision when you were still a kid."

He shrugged, unwilling to mention that his

mother, like Julie, had let him go without much of a thought.

"I'm sure you've made Ralph and Carlene proud," Marissa added, her voice soft, almost wistful.

"I tried." He didn't usually talk about it to people who didn't already know, but… "During my junior year in college, Uncle Ralph was in a car accident and almost died. I quit school and came home to help Carlene with the market."

"You didn't graduate?" she asked.

"I did, eventually. Uncle Ralph was out of commission for nearly a year and had to go through extensive rehab. Once he was able to spend a full day at the market, he and Carlene insisted that I go back and get my degree. I'd wanted to complete my education, too, so I appreciated their full support."

He'd no more than parked in front of the house, when Maddie ran outside, the screen door slamming behind her. "Daddy!" she squealed in glee. "You're home! Come see what we made."

Brandon glanced at Marissa and winked. "Welcome to my world. And just to warn you, whatever they made probably resulted in a huge mess. According to Maddie and Jimmy, they love being left with Betty Sue because she's the only grownup who has time to play with them."

"That's sweet." Marissa reached for the cardboard carrier. "Do you want me to put the puppy in the box so you can surprise them?"

"No. I doubt that little guy wants to go back in."

"You're right." Marissa opened the passenger door and got out of the Jeep.

"Jimmy!" Maddie hollered into the house. "Come quick. Daddy brought the doughnut lady here!"

At that, her brother ran out onto the front porch, with Betty Sue on his heels. The moment they spotted the black fur ball in Marissa's arms, their eyes widened.

"You got a puppy!" Maddie said.

"Can we play with it?" Jimmy asked.

Marissa shot a glance at Brandon, allowing him to share the news with his kids, then she set the little pup on the ground.

"I found this little guy on the side of the road," Brandon said. "He doesn't have a home, so I thought we might want to keep him."

Both kids gasped, then raced to where the puppy sniffed, checking out his surroundings. Jimmy was the first to reach the little stray and knelt beside it. Maddie, as usual, was a bit more reserved. "We get to keep it? For reals?"

Brandon nodded his agreement. "Yes, for *reals*. But having a pet is a big responsibility. So I asked Mrs. Hendrix if she'd watch him for us when you're in school and I'm at work."

"I love dogs," Betty Sue said. "I had three of them when I lived in Missoula. I also volunteered at the Humane Society. The puppy will be in good hands with me."

Brandon didn't doubt that for a minute. "Thanks, Auntie. We can bring the pup here once in a while. But Mrs. Hendrix lost her dog last spring, so she's looking forward to having a puppy to look after and to keep her company."

Betty Sue began to kneel beside the kids, then straightened and grimaced as if her arthritis objected to childish enthusiasm. "So what are we going to name him?" she asked the children.

Maddie, who was in a real princess phase, plopped down in the dirt, between her brother and the little stray. "If he was a *she*, we could give her a name like Ariel or Jasmine or Belle or…"

"Oh, no." Jimmy picked up the dog and gave it a hug. "He's not a princess. He needs a boy name. Like Thor."

"He does *not*." Maddie placed her hands on her hips. "He needs a *dog* name, like…" She bit down on her bottom lip, then looked at Betty Sue. "Help us."

Clearly delighted to be asked, Betty Sue beamed. "Your favorite book is *Where the Wild Things Are*. So how about Max?"

"I *love* that name," Maddie said. "And I love our new dog."

"Me, too." Jimmy giggled when Max licked his face. "Hey. He loves me back."

"Let's go, kids. I need to drop Marissa off at Rancho Esperanza, then we'll take Max home and help him get settled."

Moments later, the kids were secured in their booster seats, the dog resting beside them.

"I wanna hold Max," Jimmy said.

Maddie objected. "You got to pick him up first, so I get to hold him in the car."

Before Brandon could settle the dispute, Marissa said, "Why don't you take turns? Maybe you can trade off every five minutes."

Brandon tossed her a smile. "Great idea. You're a good referee."

"I suspect anyone who's around these two very long would have to be." She laughed, then climbed into the passenger seat.

He was glad she'd been a part of his surprise for the twins. In fact, there was a lot to like about her, but she'd made it clear that he'd have to take things slowly.

Five minutes later, as Brandon turned into the drive that led to the ranch, Marissa said, "Time's up."

The twins giggled and passed Max between them.

Brandon's time with Marissa was nearly up, too, he thought as he pulled into the yard at

Rancho Esperanza and put the Jeep in Park. He glanced in the rearview mirror, where the kids seemed oblivious to anything other than Max.

He hadn't planned to walk Marissa to the door, but... On the other hand, why not? It would give them another chance to talk one on one, without little ears listening. So with the engine running and the air conditioner on low, he left the kids and the puppy in the car. "I'll just be a minute," he told them.

Then he and Marissa got out of the Jeep and walked up the steps and onto the front porch, where he could still keep an eye on the twins.

"Thanks for bringing me home." She offered him a shy smile that damn near turned him inside out.

"No problem. And thanks for holding Max. And being the timekeeper for the kids."

At that, her smile broadened, lighting up those golden-brown eyes and sparking something inside him, something warm and blood-stirring. He reached up and cupped her jaw. His thumb brushed her cheek, and her lips parted as if she sensed he was about to kiss her. He waited a beat, but she gave him no indication that she was going to object.

He might regret it later, but he brushed his lips across hers. He hadn't meant to do more than give her a sweet good-night kiss, but when her lips parted, he was toast. It must have affected her in the same way, because the kiss exploded into an array of fireworks that could put the Fourth of July to shame.

She placed her hand on his chest, then slowly drew her mouth from his. "That's not taking things slow."

No, it wasn't. He might have pulled her back into his arms and kissed her again, but he had two curious children in the back seat who might see them.

"You're right." But he wasn't about to apologize. And he didn't think she expected to him to. "I'll talk to you later. When the kids aren't with me. Neither of them can keep a secret."

Then he gave her a parting grin and returned to the Jeep.

And speaking of secrets…

When it came to his feelings for Marissa, he knew he'd better keep them close to the vest until he found out whether she felt the same way about him.

The next day, Marissa went to work at Darla's. Each time the door opened, she looked up, expecting to see Brandon walk into the shop. He'd told her they'd talk later, and she'd been dreading that little chat, especially if he brought up the kiss they'd shared.

The truth of the matter was, she'd enjoyed it. Way too much. And her hormones had nearly run amok.

It was amazing how one sweet but alluring kiss could be so tempting. Nevertheless, she wasn't about to get romantically involved with a police officer, no matter how sexy he was or what a good kisser he was.

After spending the morning serving dough-nuts and coffee at Darla's, Marissa walked to the deli down the street. She planned to meet Alana at the Petal Pusher so they could pick out flowers for the wedding. She had an hour to kill, so she decided to buy a sandwich and eat it at the park across the street.

She'd no more than walked into the eatery when she noticed a blonde with long, scraggly hair checking out the menu that was posted on the wall. The twenty-something woman wore a gray, oversize sweatshirt—the same one she had on when she'd gotten off the bus last night.

It had to be the woman she'd seen when she was with Brandon. But what she hadn't been close enough to notice yesterday was a red, swollen gash on the side of her head and a thick coating of makeup that didn't do a very good job of hid-ing a black eye.

As she began to count out her change, Marissa said, "Hi, there. You must be new in town."

The woman nearly jumped out of her skin. Then she glanced over her shoulder apprehensively. When her tentative eyes met Marissa's, she offered a frail smile. "Yes. Sort of. But I'm... really just passing through."

Marissa nodded, as if that made perfect sense. She'd felt the same way when she'd arrived in Bakersfield, California. And then again in both Reno and Boise as she made her way to the perfect place to start a new life.

She suspected the blonde wasn't just passing through. Running away was more likely. And probably from the person who'd caused her injuries.

Marissa didn't like to make assumptions about people she didn't know, but she couldn't tamp down the sympathy for the skittish drifter that sprang up from the depths of her own battered soul.

The woman reached into the front pocket of her jeans and pulled out a couple of wrinkled bills and a handful of change. As she began counting it out, Marissa said, "Put your money away. Your lunch is my treat."

Her lips parted, and her brow furrowed. "You don't need to do that."

"Yes, I do. On my first day in town, a nice man purchased my lunch and told me it was his way of welcoming me to Fairborn. So I want to pay his kindness forward. And maybe someday, if you get the chance, you can do the same for somebody else."

"I…" Her apprehensive, disbelieving expression morphed into one of relief. "Thanks. I don't know what to say."

"You don't have to say anything. My name is Marissa. What's yours?"

"Ella."

After purchasing turkey sandwiches, potato chips and apple juice for both of them, Marissa suggested they eat at the park. When Ella agreed, they crossed the street and found an unoccupied picnic table under the shade of an elm.

"You don't owe me any explanations," Marissa said. "But I have a feeling you're running away. And if someone hurt you, I don't blame you at all."

Ella keep her gaze down as she continued to unwrap her sandwich.

"I ran away from someone, too," Marissa added. "And it took me five years and three different towns before I found the perfect place to call home."

Ella cut a glance her way. "Someone hurt you?"

"Pain and abuse isn't always physical." Marissa unscrewed the lid of her apple juice and took a swig.

Ella remained quiet for the longest time, then she said, "It was my husband. I vowed to love him in sickness and health—and all that stuff. So I took his anger and beatings for as long as I could. Besides, he told me if I ever left, he'd kill me. And I didn't doubt him. But two nights ago, he came home drunk and…" She took a deep breath and slowly let it out. "I swore that would be the last time he hit me. So when he fell asleep on the sofa, I took the keys to his pickup, grabbed what little I could carry and climbed out the bedroom window. After throwing his keys down the well, I made it to the bus depot and spent half the money to buy a one-way ticket as far as I could get."

"And now you're in Fairborn."

Ella nodded. "But it's not far enough. I'm scared to death that he's going to find me…"

Marissa didn't doubt her fear for a second. When she'd spent time in jail, she'd met a woman who'd been charged with murder after killing her abuser because she'd felt as though it was her only escape. "Do you have a plan? Someplace to go?"

Ella slowly shook her head. "Not really. He'd look for me at my mother's house first. And he knows my friends."

"Have you called the police?"

Ella shook her head. "He's a cop, and those guys tend to stick together. I know most of them are good people and have a high sense of morals and ethics. But anytime I see a man in uniform, I cringe."

Marissa's gut clenched. She knew exactly how Ella felt. Not the physical abuse. But the uneasiness around police officers. "I don't want to get into it now, but I know what you're saying, and I can relate." They exchanged a smile, and that gave them a bond of some kind.

"Maybe I can help you. Give me a minute." Marissa got to her feet, and as she walked a short distance away, she reached into her purse and pulled out her cell phone. Then she called Alana.

When her friend answered, Marissa told her about Ella and her need to find a place to hide.

Just as she'd expected, Alana said, "I'm heading to town. But we're not going to meet at the Petal Pusher. Wedding flowers can wait. Meet me at The Mane Event. A complete makeover is in order."

"Agreed." Marissa ended the call and returned to the table. She placed a gentle hand on Ella's shoulder. "I've got your back, honey."

Tears welled in Ella's eyes. "Why are you helping me? And being so nice? You don't even know me."

"Because women stick together. And it's the right thing to do."

Fifteen minutes later, Ella and Marissa—once strangers but quickly becoming comrades-in-arms—entered the salon, where Tameka was manning the front desk.

"Does someone have time for a color and a cut?" Marissa asked. "My friend wants a brand-new look. And it's my treat."

As soon as Alana arrived at the salon, Marissa introduced her to Ella, who was waiting for Robin to finish combing out her client before taking Ella back to her station.

"I've talked it over with my fiancé," Alana said. "You're welcome to stay with us. But you'll need to clean up after yourself. And there'll be no drug use, no boyfriends…"

"You don't have to worry about that," Ella said. "I've never used drugs and don't intend to start now. And I doubt if I'll ever trust another man again."

"Then, it's a deal," Alana said. "Welcome to Rancho Esperanza."

Then they left Ella in Robin's capable hands and walked to the florist, where they studied an array of blooms and photos. They even found time to stop at Patty Cakes, the bakery on Elmwood Drive, where they set up a tasting.

An hour and a half later, they returned to the salon, where Ella's long blond hair had been dyed black and cut in a short pixie style. Bangs hid the injury on her forehead. The only thing that re-mained the least bit familiar was a pair of cautious blue eyes, a smudge of makeup hiding the bruise under one of them.

"Ella," Marissa said, "you look amazing." Then she turned to Robin. "You're a whiz. I'm so glad you had time for her."

"Me, too," the stylist said. "We've had a busy afternoon, and we're really going to be slammed until we close."

Marissa handed Robin a twenty-dollar tip. "I'll settle up with Tameka."

Ella smiled shyly. "This is the first time I've felt remotely safe, Marissa. Thank you so much. I promise to pay you back."

"Don't worry about it. It was my pleasure." Various people along the way had supported Marissa, in one way or another, on her journey from felon to future businesswoman. She reached into her purse, pulled out her wallet, removed her ATM and handed it to Tameka. "Here you go."

As Tameka ran the card, she asked, "Would you mind watching the phones for me, Marissa? I just cracked a crown, and it's super sensitive. The dentist is going to fit me in. If you can't do it, that's okay. I'll see if my sister can cover for me while I'm gone."

"I'd be happy to help out, but..." Marissa shot a glance at Alana, who was going to take her home since the car was still in the shop.

"No problem," Alana said. "I don't mind waiting. There's something else I'd like to do while we're in town."

"Oh, I almost forgot," Tameka said before stepping away from the counter. "I'm going to need you to work on Thursday afternoon along with your regular shift on Friday. Are you available?"

"Yes."

"That's great. I don't want to stretch you—or my budget—too much. So why don't you take tomorrow off?"

"All right." That would give her and Alana time to address and mail out the invitations, along with taking care of several other items on her wedding to-do list.

While Tameka headed toward the back of the shop, where she always parked, Marissa stepped behind the counter. "Thanks, Alana."

"No problem. Ella and I are going to take a walk down to Wear It Again, Sam."

Ella appeared confused. *"Where?"*

"It's a consignment clothing store," Alana explained. "They carry some neat stuff, and you're going to need a few outfits."

"But I don't…" Ella sucked in a shaky breath. "I mean…"

"Don't worry, honey." Alana took Ella by the arm. "It's what we do at Rancho Esperanza. We help each other out." As they started for the door, Alana glanced over her shoulder. "We'll be back in an hour or so. If you get out sooner than that, meet us there." Then she led Ella out of the salon.

After they left, The Mane Event continued its buzz of activity, with clients coming and going. A sign out front announced that walk-ins were welcome, but the three hairstylists, as well as the manicurist, were booked back-to-back for the rest of the afternoon, so if anyone showed up, hoping to get in today, they were out of luck.

Of her two part-time jobs, Marissa enjoyed this one the most. It was cool to see people coming in haggard or scruffy, only to walk out looking their best.

The time flew as Marissa juggled appointments, purchases and departing clients. She'd barely gotten a moment to breathe when she saw Carlene Tipton entering the salon with Betty Sue. Carlene looked rather plain in a pair of jeans and a plaid blouse. But the older woman practically lit the room. A coral-and-green-striped scarf held her wild red curls away from her sparkling eyes. She wore a multicolored bohemian skirt and a white top with a large flamingo appliqué on the front. A pair of bejeweled slippers rounded out the eye-catching ensemble.

Marissa greeted them with a smile. "Good afternoon, ladies."

"I'm here for a manicure and a pedicure," Carlene said. "And my aunt has an appointment with Hailey for color."

"Jordan, the manicurist, took a short break between clients, but she should be here any minute." Marissa turned and surveyed the back of the busy shop, where Hailey stood at her station, blow-drying a woman's hair. "I'm afraid you'll both have to wait. But it won't be long."

"I see an empty chair back there," Betty Sue said. "I'll just sit myself down and watch the activity until Hailey's ready for me."

"Auntie," Carlene said, "I think it'd be better if you sat up front with me."

Betty waved her off. "You and I are all talked out after our drive to town. I'd like to chat with someone else for a change."

Carlene let out a sigh. "Okay. That's fine. But don't leave the salon."

Betty Sue let out a humph. "Would it be okay if I went to the bathroom?"

"Auntie, you went before we left home."

"I don't have to go *now*. Not yet, anyway." Betty Sue looked around and said in a loud whisper, "But I took a laxative this morning."

Carlene cleared her throat. "Of course you can go to the bathroom. But will you give me a heads-up first?"

Betty Sue laughed. "Sure. No problem. Thank you for your interest in my plumbing." The older woman winked, then made her way to the back of the salon, where she took a seat next to the shampoo bowls.

Carlene leaned forward, resting her arm on the reception desk, and spoke quietly. "I hope you don't think I'm mean or short-tempered. I'm usually very patient. But Betty Sue exasperates me at times. I know she means well, but…"

"I understand," Marissa said, although she did think that Carlene seemed pretty irritable when she was with her aunt. She probably ought to loosen up a bit.

Carlene blew out a sigh. "Betty Sue begged me to get her a hair appointment, but when I did, she made me change it several times for silly reasons. I mean, why should it matter when my nephew is on duty? It's not like my husband can't handle babysitting the kids and running the store. Ralph's got things under control—and most of the time, better than I do."

"Maybe you need a break," Marissa said. "Or some help. You've got a lot on your plate—running the store, chasing after two sweet but active preschoolers, not to mention Betty Sue."

"You're probably right. I even thought it might help to hire someone to work at the market, although it's such a big part of our lives that I hate to take a step back."

"Well, you're here now," Marissa said. "So

relax and enjoy. Maybe, while you're waiting, you can look at the display of polish on the wall and pick a color."

As Carlene walked away, compassion washed over Marissa, and she wished there was a way for her to help. It had to be difficult to run a store, babysit a couple of adorable but precocious preschoolers and keep up with Betty Sue. Yet a bit of envy struck her, too. It would be nice to belong to a family—one that cared for each other and had each other's backs. There was a time she would have given anything to belong to a family like Brandon's, even if they were all a little unusual.

Carlene returned to the desk, holding a bottle of red polish, and lowered her voice. "And do you know what else? I don't even need to get my nails done today, but I didn't dare leave my aunt here on her own. With my luck, I'd come back to find she'd hitchhiked to New York to attend a Woodstock reunion. Or go try to find another moped. And to make matters worse, she would never pull one of those stunts on Ralph!"

Betty Sue was quite the rebel. Marissa smiled and said, "I'll keep an eye on your aunt so you can kick back and enjoy your beauty treatment."

As if on cue, Hailey's last client approached the desk to pay for her treatment, which meant Betty Sue was next.

Several minutes later, Jordan returned from her

break and took Carlene to her station for the manicure and pedicure. So Marissa got back to work, collecting payments from customers, answering calls and making appointments.

Periodically, she glanced at Hailey's station, where Betty Sue's color was applied. So far, so good. Marissa looked at Carlene, who was getting her pedicure while waiting for her fingernail polish to dry, and gave her a thumbs-up. Then she got back to work, organizing the products on the shelf next to the cash drawer.

That is, until one client let out a shriek. "Hey! My casino winnings are gone!" Still draped in a black robe to protect her clothing, her hair wrapped in a towel, the fifty-something woman marched up to the reception desk, her finger pointed at Marissa. "Someone got into my purse while I was at the shampoo bowl!"

Marissa's heart pounded in a primal beat—a flight-or-fight response. She threw up her empty hands, almost in surrender. "I didn't take anything. I haven't even left this desk."

"I know that. I wasn't accusing you, honey." The client waved her off, then jabbed her index finger at the telephone. "You need to do something."

"I'll do it," Betty Sue hollered from the back of the salon. "My nephew will get to the bottom of this."

Marissa had absolutely no reason to feel guilty. Or nervous. But tell that to her raging heart rate.

But all this didn't make sense. Who would've stolen money from that woman's purse?

And why did Brandon have to be on duty today?

Chapter Six

Dispatch sent Brandon to The Mane Event to check out a reported theft. Since Marissa didn't work on Tuesdays, he hadn't expected to see her there. But when he walked inside and spotted her standing behind the front counter, looking especially pretty with her hair pulled up in a messy topknot and her lipstick worn down to faint pink tinge, time stalled until he realized that he was damn near gaping at her, and he snapped back to reality.

"What's going on?" he asked.

"One of our clients said someone stole money from her purse." Marissa pointed to where a frowning woman in her fifties sat in a chair near the front window, her cheeks flushed, her graying hair wet and stringy.

Betty Sue, whose red curls had been styled neatly, was sitting in a seat next to the alleged victim, clutching her macramé purse in her lap. A few steps away, Carlene lounged at the pedicure station, her bare feet outstretched, rolled tissue between her toes, the nails lacquered in bright red polish.

Were his aunts involved?

The woman, who still wore a protective black cape over her shoulders, got to her feet and placed her hands on her hips. "I'm glad you're here, Deputy. Someone stole my casino winnings—nearly five hundred dollars!—while I was at the shampoo bowl. I was going to show Robin pictures of my new grandbaby, and when I dug through my wallet, I noticed my money was gone. I'd counted it earlier today, so I know it was in there. And now it's not."

"No one has left the salon yet," Marissa said.

Unless the thief had slipped in and out the back entrance, then he or she was still on-site.

"If someone got into my purse," Betty Sue said, "I'd look to see if I'd misplaced my money before making a big stink."

That certainly was possible. His great-aunt was

a little absentminded at times and often misplaced her things.

The victim tossed his aunt a dirty look. "Mind your own business, Betty Sue."

Clearly, the two women knew each other.

"Aw, come on, Rosanna." Betty Sue clicked her tongue. "Last week, when we played bingo, you couldn't find your wallet in that big ol' suitcase you call a purse. And then come to find out it was there all along."

"That's an expensive designer bag, I'll have you know."

"It's a knockoff."

"That's enough, ladies." Brandon glanced at Rosanna's feet, where an oversize jungle-print tote rested. Then he met her gaze. "Is that your purse, ma'am?"

The woman nodded. "Yes, it is."

"Do you mind if I look inside?" he asked.

Somewhat miffed, she reached for the leather handle and handed over the bag. "Knock yourself out."

Damn. It weighed a ton. Betty Sue was right. He opened it to look inside and dug through a slew of things like chewing gum, loose coins and safety pins, a small pack of tissues, breath mints and a roll of antacids. He even found two sets of car keys, not to mention a crossword-puzzle book and a small box of chocolate-covered raisins. He finally found her wallet at the bottom, and like she said, there wasn't any cash in there.

He then unzipped a side pocket, reached into it and pulled out several folded hundred-dollar bills and some twenties. "Is this the money you were talking about?"

She flushed a dark shade of scarlet. "Um… Yeah. That's it."

Betty Sue rolled her eyes. "Another mystery solved."

Brandon hated to add insult to injury, but he couldn't help it. "Ma'am, you really ought to take the time to search your belongings before accusing someone of stealing. It could lead to hurt feelings and other unintended consequences."

The woman nodded, grabbed her purse from Brandon, then walked out of the salon, her hair wet and stringy, her shoulders still draped in the black cape.

"Look at that," Betty Sue said. "Now who's the thief? She didn't pay for her haircut. And she's wearing the salon's cape. Want me to chase her down?"

"That's not necessary." Brandon figured she'd return the cape and pay for her cut as soon as her embarrassment died down.

"Betty Sue," Carlene said, "why in the world would you call 9-1-1 when a simple search of that woman's purse would've put the issue to rest?

Brandon has more important things to do than to chase after imaginary thieves."

Betty Sue had been the one to call dispatch? His aunt was truly something else.

Betty Sue's smile slipped into one of wide-eyed surprise. "Uh-oh. Nature's calling." Then she hurried to the back and disappeared into the bathroom.

Carlene blew out an exasperated sigh. "I'm sorry about that, Brandon. But you know how she is."

"No problem. Not every call I get ends up with an arrest." He turned to Marissa, who appeared to be a little unsettled by the incident. "I'm just glad Rosanna found her money."

"Me, too," Marissa said. "It's nice to know there isn't a thief in our midst."

"For the most part, you'll find the people who live in Fairborn are law-abiding and trustworthy."

She fingered her necklace, a small silver heart on a delicate chain.

"Are you okay?" he asked.

She blinked and dropped her hand. "Yes, of course." Her smile and sweet demeanor returned. "Thanks for responding so quickly."

"All in a day's work." Which reminded him. He was still on duty and had a job to do. So he tore his gaze from hers. He turned toward the door.

Then he had a second thought. "I've been meaning to ask. What'd you find out about your car?"

She rolled her eyes and blew out a sigh. "Besides needing a new battery and a starter, replacing the spark plugs and a few other things? Let's just say that Prudence will be in the shop for a while."

"*Prudence?* You named your car?"

She gave a little shrug. "Why not?"

"No reason, I guess." Actually, it was kind of cute. His gaze swept over her. In fact, everything about her was cute.

"I told the mechanic to go ahead and fix it," she said. "My only other option is to buy another vehicle that has fewer miles on it. So I'll be catching a ride to town for a few days."

He'd seen her car, and poor Prudence had seen a lot of miles and better days. "How'd you get here today?"

"Clay, Alana's fiancé, brought me. And Alana is going to drive me home. She's just down the street. Shopping."

"Good. I'm glad you've got it covered. When do you have to work in town again?"

"Not until Thursday. If my car isn't ready by then, I'll ask either Clay or Alana to bring me to work."

"No need. I'm going to drop off the kids at the market early that morning. You can ride with me."

Her lips parted, and she slowly shook her head. "You don't need to do that."

"But I'd like to. Besides, it's not out of the way."

She thought about it for a moment, then she seemed to see the rationale. "Are you sure you don't mind?"

"Not at all." There was nothing Brandon wanted to do more than to spend some time alone with her. To let her know he wasn't like the guy she'd once been involved with, the guy who'd broken her heart and betrayed her trust.

And he hoped to set a date when the two of them could go out, no matter if it was at dinner or lunch.

A real date—and without the twins.

While Carlene drove the family minivan back to the ranch, Betty Sue lowered the passenger-seat visor, lifted the curls off her forehead and peered at her reflection, checking out the residual dye on her forehead. It was her fault, though. When Rosanna had freaked out, Betty Sue hadn't been able to stay seated, so she'd jumped up before the stylist had time to clean it. She'd wanted to be where the action was.

Hmm. Next time she was at the salon, she'd have to tell the stylist not to take too much off the top. Her curls got a little wild sometimes, so they needed to be tamed. But she didn't want them whacked off.

"Betty Sue," Carlene said, drawing her attention from her reflection, "how do you know that woman who thought her money was stolen?"

"Rosanna? She plays bingo on Wednesday nights." The woman had also made a brazen play for Earl Hoffman, the bartender who worked all the events held at the Grange Hall. And Betty Sue had already made her interest in him known. So she and Rosanna had some heated words about it a time or two.

"I got the feeling that you suspected Rosanna might've forgotten where she'd stashed her cash."

That's because it had happened to her a few times before. "Rosanna's a little ditzy, which is why she can't keep a boyfriend."

"Boyfriend? What are you talking about?"

"Oh, nothing. But let's just say her card is a B-12 short of a Bingo."

Carlene clicked her tongue. "If you knew she was that ditzy, why did you call 9-1-1 as if there'd been an armed holdup in the salon?"

Betty Sue chuckled. "I wouldn't have made a fuss if Brandon wasn't working today."

"Oh, for goodness sake. You did it on purpose? Are you trying to set him up with Marissa?"

"She's a nice girl."

"You hardly know her."

"I get vibes about people." Betty Sue closed the mirror and raised the visor. "And I have a *real* good one about her. She's not ditzy like Rosanna."

"You can be a little ditzy yourself," Carlene said.

Hmm. Maybe. But at least Betty Sue could still pull the wool over Carlene's eyes. Because her bossy niece believed that Wednesday nights at the Grange was called Bargain Bingo, when it was actually High Roller Bingo, with a cash bar. And both Betty Sue and Rosanna had hit it big last Wednesday.

"Don't you ever get feelings about people?" Betty Sue asked, although she knew the answer. Her niece was about as observant of her surroundings as someone playing six different cards during Blackout Bingo.

Carlene blew out a sigh. "I wish I did. But I don't. About six or eight weeks ago, we had a customer come into the market. He bought a pack of cigarettes and a couple of lollipops. I assumed he had kids and pegged him for a decent sort. But it turned out that he and a buddy assaulted Clay Hastings, stole his car and left the poor man for dead. And I never saw *that* coming."

"From what I heard, neither did Clay." Betty Sue chuckled at her dark-humored quip.

Carlene chuffed. "Oh, Betty Sue. Really! But I won't argue with you about Marissa. She seems to be a nice woman. And the twins like her, which is a plus. But please don't interfere in Brandon's love life."

"I was just trying to help."

"You don't need to. And if you promise to back off, I'll let you in on a little secret."

Betty Sue loved secrets. "What's that?"

"I talked to Ralph last night. And he assured me that Brandon likes Marissa and plans to ask her out. But if you don't stop interfering, you're likely to put a stop to things before they're off and running."

Betty Sue lifted her hand in a Boy Scout salute. "It's a deal. But will you and Ralph please keep me in the loop? I love hearing about budding romances." Especially when her vibes told her that a man and woman were perfect for each other.

And, in that case, there was no harm in helping the relationship along.

As soon as Tameka returned to The Mane Event, she thanked Marissa for covering for her while she was away. "The receptionist at my dental office said she'd squeeze me in, but I had no idea it would take so long."

"No need to apologize. I'm glad I was able to help." Marissa reached for her purse. "It's never fun to sit in a dental chair, but it's better than having a toothache."

"Don't I know it?" Tameka placed her own purse where Marissa's had been, on the top shelf, under the front counter. "I assume everything went smoothly while I was gone."

"Sort of." As she and the salon owner traded places, Marissa shared the details of Rosanna's mistaken claim and Betty Sue's knee-jerk reaction that had led to the deputy's arrival.

"Oh, boy." Tameka rolled her eyes. "I'm glad I missed the excitement. Thank you so much for handling it."

"All in a day's work," Marissa said, inadvertently repeating the response Brandon had made earlier.

"Thanks again," Tameka said.

"You're welcome. I'll see you on Thursday." Marissa pushed open the salon door and stepped onto the sidewalk.

Alana and Ella hadn't returned yet, so she began the walk to the consignment store, planning to join them unless she met them along the way. She'd only gotten two blocks down the street when she spotted Alana and Ella up ahead, chatting away like two old friends. Ella carried a bulging white bag, filled with her purchases.

The three met on the sidewalk in front of the two-story redbrick building that housed Fairborn Savings and Trust, the bank that occupied the entire first floor.

Ella reached up to tuck a strand of hair behind her ear, a habit she'd undoubtedly acquired before cutting it short. Her hand dropped back to her side, and she looked first at Alana, then at Marissa. "I don't know how to thank you guys for all you've done for me."

"We've both had people help us along the way," Alana said. "So we like to do the same for others whenever we can. Come on. Let's go home."

At that, they walked to Alana's car, a brand-new one Clay had recently purchased for her to replace the old ranch pickup she used to drive.

As they approached the white SUV, Ella said, "You have no idea how long it's been since I've had someone in my corner."

Marissa could certainly relate to that.

"Maybe now you can stop looking over your shoulder," Alana said.

"I wish I could. It's just that the last time I ran away, Doug found me two blocks from the bus depot. He grabbed me from behind and dragged me to his truck. And when we got home, he beat the crap out of me and swore he'd kill me if I ever tried a stunt like that again. And I had no reason to doubt him. I just couldn't take it anymore."

"You'll be safe at Rancho Esperanza," Alana said.

True. But it would probably take a while for Ella's fear to die down. She might have undergone a makeover that left her looking much different on the outside, but on the inside, where she bore the emotional scars of her abuse, it would take time to heal and move on.

Marissa ought to know. She still carried a few emotional scars, even if no one had physically abused her.

She'd no more than reached the passenger door when a barrage of memories struck, one after the other. She squeezed her eyes shut, hoping that might block out the painful images.

A drug-sniffing dog.

Police officers swarming the car.

Her hands pulled behind her back, handcuffs snapping shut, the metal cold and tight against her skin.

It's not mine, Marissa had cried. *I don't know where it came from.*

But no one had believed her, least of all her so-called family. Nor had they cared enough to come to court during the trial, let alone pay for a decent lawyer. The public defender had taken very little interest in fighting for justice in her case.

Needless to say, once she'd served her time and completed her probation requirements, she'd left San Diego and her past behind. But it had taken nearly five years and several moves for her to finally find a place where she could put down roots. And she'd never looked back.

Well, not until Erik's text a couple of weeks ago.

Damn you, Erik, she thought. *And damn your father and my stepmother, too. I never want to hear from any of you again.*

That night, as Marissa was crossing the living room on her way to the kitchen to help Alana prepare dinner, her cell phone dinged, alerting her to an incoming text. She reached into her back pocket and pulled out the smartphone. When she glanced at the lighted display and spotted the 619 San Diego area code, she froze in her tracks.

Call me. It's important.

Oh, no. Not again.

She'd yet to open the text completely, but she'd seen enough to know that Erik hadn't given up on his attempt to contact her. She'd meant to block his number, but she'd gotten so busy that she'd forgotten. Before she could read the rest of his message or get into her settings to block him now, the doorbell sounded.

"I'll get it," she called out.

She was still stunned by Erik's text when she swung open the door, only to find Brandon standing on the stoop and sporting a dimpled smile.

She glanced around the porch. "Where are the kids?"

"I left them and Max with Mrs. Hendrix, my neighbor." He took a step back. "Can I talk to you? Alone?"

"I…uh… Sure." She tried her best to return his grin with one that was unaffected, but she doubted that she'd been able to completely pull it off. Nevertheless, she walked out onto the porch, the screen door closing behind her. The sun had just begun to drop into the west, streaking the Montana sky in swatches of pink and lavender.

"What's up?" she asked.

"I wanted to talk to you, but I didn't want to do it while you were at work or in front of an audience." He glanced at the living-room window, just as Ella was walking through the room, probably on her way to help Alana in the kitchen.

"Who's that?" he asked.

"Her name is Ella. She's staying here for a while."

"Oh, yeah? Is she a friend?"

Did it matter? "Just someone we're helping out right now."

Brandon scrunched his brow. "You don't have any qualms about inviting a stranger to live with you?"

"Yes, but not Ella."

"Why not?" His eyes bore down on her.

"Because. We just don't."

"Based on what?"

Marissa wasn't usually so trusting. Heck, she'd had a good reason not to be. But Alana had been so good to her that her pay-it-forward philosophy was hard to ignore. And Ella definitely needed a friend right now. "Just call it gut instinct. She needed a place to live, and we want to help."

"Con artists are experts at making you feel comfortable before they pounce. I can run a check on her through the database."

Is that what he'd done with her? Did he already know about her record?

No. He would have said something, right? And he certainly wouldn't have asked her out.

"Thanks," she said. "I appreciate your concern, but there's no need to run her through your database. Ella's fine. And so are we."

"I'm just trying to look out for you."

And she appreciated that. It wasn't often that anyone had cared about her enough to do that.

She studied the handsome deputy, who'd shed his uniform for a pair of worn jeans and a white, crisply pressed button-down shirt, the sleeves rolled up.

"Are you always so trusting?" he asked.

"Are you always so skeptical?"

"I have to be."

She supposed he did. She'd crossed paths with a lot of skeptics when she'd gone through the criminal-justice system. And while she understood they were just doing their jobs, their suspicious natures made her a little skittish.

"I didn't mean to question your judgment," Brandon said.

He had a point, though. "No offense taken."

"I came here to ask you a question."

"What's that?"

"I'd like to take you to dinner. There's a nice steak house in Kalispell. It's got great reviews, and I'd like to try it out, but I don't want to go alone."

"Are the kids going, too?" she asked.

His smile fell. "It's not a kid-friendly place."

"I thought we were going to take things slow. And that our first... I mean, what happened to the picnic at the park we'd talked about?"

"Don't you think that, before we involve the kids, we should take time to get to know each other a little better?"

She supposed that made sense. He probably didn't want to risk confusing the children if their...date—or whatever it was—didn't work out.

"We can always take the kids on a picnic some other time," he added.

She hadn't gone out to a nice dinner in ages. Not since her father died. She wasn't even sure she had anything appropriate to wear. She could probably find something, though.

Yet her reluctance to date a police officer

wouldn't let her speak, even though he looked like a regular guy right now, one who was more handsome than a man had a right to be.

Would going out with him be so bad? What was she really afraid of? He might be a deputy sheriff, but it's not like he'd been her arresting officer.

His expression sobered. "Why don't you sleep on it? I'll see you later."

Then he turned and headed for his Jeep, looking a little dejected. She had half a notion to call him back, but she remained on the porch, watching him go.

As he pulled out of the yard, a heavy blanket of guilt draped over her.

If Erik hadn't just sent her that text, dredging up old memories and throwing her off balance, she might have agreed—whether Maddie and Jimmy went with them or not.

Truth be told, she liked Brandon. And she liked his kids, too. Their family didn't include a mommy, but that didn't mean they hadn't made the best of it. They were happy.

She and her father hadn't needed a mother, either. They'd been happy, too, until Suzanne entered the picture. Fake tan, fake blond, fake boobs, all of which could be forgiven. But not the fake smiles she had for Marissa whenever Daddy was around.

Thank God those miserable days were over.

Maybe that's what drew her to Brandon—in addition to sexual attraction. His family. And he was offering her a chance to get to know them, too—if not to become a part of it. And then, there was that kiss… That amazing, heart-strumming kiss.

She slapped her forehead. What a dingbat. She was going to jinx things if she wasn't careful. Sure, she might have a past, but if she wanted to put it behind her, she'd have to embrace the future. And that meant taking a risk.

So how did she make things right with him?

She supposed she could start by telling him about her conviction and the time she'd spent in jail—before he decided to run her name through his database. And if he still wanted to date her, then she'd go to dinner with him on Saturday night.

Feeling better already, she returned to the house with a spring in her step and tomorrow's game plan in mind.

Chapter Seven

When Brandon left Rancho Esperanza after talking to Marissa, he wanted to go anywhere but home. Thirty minutes earlier, he'd left the twins and their puppy with Leanne Hendrix, the rosy-cheeked widow who lived three doors down from him. Leanne had moved in six months ago, and she'd already proved to be a good neighbor—one of the best.

"I'm going to see a friend," he'd told her before leaving his house. "So I might not get home until late. There's leftover spaghetti in the refrigerator."

"I brought some homemade chocolate-chip cookies for dessert. So don't worry about us. And don't rush on my account. If you're not home before eight, I'll get them ready for bed. Then I'll watch TV until you get back." She scanned the living room. "Where are the little munchkins?"

"They're in the backyard, playing with Max. I've already told them I'm leaving."

"So get going." She lifted her hands and shooed him toward the door. "I'm glad that you're finally getting out. You need to do that more often. I just hope that friend is a lady."

His smile had given his secret away, but that hadn't concerned him. Leanne Hendrix was more discreet than most of the people who took a personal interest in his love life. And another plus, she didn't socialize with either Carlene or Betty Sue.

They'd be all over him, wondering what had happened, how his new romance was unfolding. But whatever he'd thought was happening between them had hit the wall.

Sure, the kiss they'd shared had convinced him that they had chemistry, but it hadn't swayed Marissa at all. He'd left the ranch feeling confused, frustrated and embarrassed. But rather than go home early and let Leanne know that he'd crashed and burned, he'd stopped by Sully's Pub to kill some time.

He'd no more than stepped in the door when his good friend and local firefighter spotted him.

"Hey, Dodd!" Greg Duran called out, as he motioned for him to join him at his table. "I thought you'd given up the party life for good."

When they were teenagers, neither of them had been what you'd call party animals. They'd both played football for Fairborn High and had tried to stick to a healthy regimen as student athletes. Brandon had graduated as the valedictorian, while Greg had come in a close second. Then they'd both gone on to the University of Wyoming, where they'd kicked up their boots a bit. But in their junior year, Uncle Ralph had suffered his serious injury, and Brandon had filed an incomplete and gone home to help at the market.

Now, as Brandon pulled out a chair at Greg's table, he asked, "What are you doing? Are you all by yourself?"

"I met Joel Braddock here, but he got a call from his wife, and she wasn't very happy that he'd forgotten their anniversary was tonight. I figured I'd finish my beer, then go home." Greg motioned for the waitress to return to the table. "How're the kids doing?"

"They're doing great." Brandon wasn't at all surprised that Greg would ask. Not just because they were friends, but Greg and his sister Nancy were the twins' godparents. "I left them at home with a sitter. I figured I'd…slip away for a while."

The waitress, a tall blonde in her mid-thirties

stopped by and offered Brandon a welcoming grin. "What can I get you?"

"I'll have a Corona and lime."

He and Greg made small talk for a while, about the weather and the latest playoff game, until the cocktail waitress delivered his beer.

"I put an offer in on a house on Cherrywood, and it was accepted." Greg rested his elbow on the table, then leaned back in his seat. "I'm tired of paying off my landlord's mortgage and decided it was time to buy a place of my own."

"Congratulations," Brandon said, although he couldn't quite shake his somber mood.

"I've been dating Shelley Whitaker," Greg said. "Her sister Melanie is going through a divorce. She used to have a crush on you in school. Want me to set something up?"

"No."

"Wow. The twins' mother must have really done a number on you. I can't believe Brandon Dodd is still unattached. And for some reason, he's happy about it."

"I used to be."

"Something changed? What's up?" Greg lifted his glass mug and took a swig of beer.

"Nothing." Brandon fingered the condensation on his bottle.

"You can't fool me, dude." Greg lifted his nearly empty glass and pointed it at him. "You look like you're stewing about something. What is it?"

Brandon sucked in a deep breath, then slowly let it out. "There's a woman who's caught my eye. I know she's feeling something for me. But she doesn't want to date me."

"Hmm. Why's that? You're not too ugly. And you seem like a decent sort." Greg chuckled at his dumb attempt at humor.

"We've got chemistry, that's for sure. When I kissed her the other night, it was off the charts."

"What'd she do? Slap you?"

"No. She enjoyed it every bit as much as I did. At least, I thought she did."

Greg finally seemed to get it, to see the seriousness and realize how much it bothered Brandon.

"I told her to sleep on the idea of going out with me, but that was more or less a parting shot. I really don't expect her to change her mind."

"So what's her problem?" Greg asked. "Do you think it's the kids?"

"At first, I thought it was. I mean, some women might find a single dad with two four-year-olds complicated and someone to steer clear of. But Marissa is great with Maddie and Jimmy. You can sense when someone doesn't like kids. And that woman clearly enjoys being around them. She likes dogs, too. She really took to Max, our new puppy."

"You're right," Greg said. "That doesn't compute."

"I know." And Brandon didn't like the way the numbers were adding up.

"Could it be your job? I mean, a lot of women can't hack the fact that bad guys might shoot at police officers. We both know that the crimes in Fairborn are pretty tame, but not always. You know that. And some women might worry."

It was sure beginning to look like Marissa might be the kind of woman who'd stress about something like that. "You know, when I first asked her out, it was to a law-enforcement dinner. She said no. And when I showed up at her workplace in uniform, she froze up. She claims it's because she's getting over a broken heart, but I don't know about that. I guess I'm not buying it."

"Maybe it *is* you, dude." Greg chuckled, then slowly shook his head in disbelief.

"That's possible, I guess. But I really don't think that's it. Sometimes, I feel like I've known her forever. Then at other times? It's almost as if she's afraid to date me. I'm in law enforcement. I can read people. And it doesn't make sense."

They each took a drink of beer. Then Greg said, "What you're saying is that something about her doesn't feel right."

Brandon hated to admit it, but yeah. He'd nailed it. "Maybe so."

"Have you thought about doing a background check on her?" Greg asked.

"No. I can't do that. I mean, who runs the woman he's interested in through the database?"

"I get that," Greg said, "but I can talk to a friend of mine who's a private investigator. He'd do it as a favor to me."

"I'm definitely curious." After all, she was new in town and didn't seem to have family here. "But I don't know if that's a good idea."

"It's not a bad one," Greg said. "You have two adorable kids, and you need to be careful about who you let into their lives. Plus, you're thinking about running for sheriff, right?"

"I haven't decided to throw my hat in the ring yet." But he'd certainly considered it.

"You'll need campaign donors, and you sure don't want any skeletons coming out of the closet, even if they belong to the woman you're dating."

"The woman I'm *thinking* about dating. I haven't even taken her out once yet. She's dragging her feet, remember?"

"Dude, you're a catch. Why wouldn't she say yes?"

Brandon hadn't planned to check into Marissa's past. Why should he? She was so sweet, so nice, that he didn't think he had anything to worry about. But Greg was right. He did have the twins to consider. And he'd trusted the wrong woman once.

Oh, what the hell. "Go ahead. Talk to your PI friend." Then in spite of his initial reluctance, he added, "Her name is Marissa Garcia, and she's from San Diego. She works at Darla's a couple days a week and also at the salon. She must have a driver's license, and she's taking a class or two at Fairborn Junior College, so they'd have her social security number."

"Got it. I'll let you know what I find out." Greg typed the info into his phone.

Brandon glanced at the clock on the wall, next to a stag's head. "I gotta get out of here." He reached into his wallet, pulled out a ten and laid it on the table. "I'll talk to you later."

Then he headed home. And if Leanne, bless her ever lovin' heart, asked him how his visit had gone, he'd respond with a thumbs-up.

Who said a hand couldn't lie?

With the wedding a mere ten days away, Marissa had planned to get the rest of the details taken care of on Wednesday. But Darla had called last night at six o'clock, saying her husband's doctor had ordered a bone scan at nine the next morning, along with a couple of follow-up tests.

"I'm feeling fine," Fred hollered in the background. "I don't know what all the fuss is about. Or why it has to be done tomorrow. My leg feels fine."

"He does seem to be okay," Darla admitted. "So he's probably right. But I worry about him. And I think the doctor just wants to rule out any problems in the bone."

"I swear," Fred said loud enough for Marissa to hear, "my wife would pack me in bubble wrap if I'd let her."

"It's only because I love you," Darla told him. Then she cleared her throat. "Anyway, is there any chance you can relieve me by seven o'clock, Marissa? I'll have plenty of doughnuts made by then to last all day."

"No problem. I'll be there."

Now here Marissa was, working at Darla's on a busy Wednesday morning. She'd hardly had a chance to breathe, but she did manage to answer a couple of confirmation emails. One was from the party-rental place for the tables and chairs she'd ordered, and another from the florist saying she could definitely provide the flowers and greenery for decorating the white gazebo Clay built. Everything was scheduled to be delivered to Rancho Esperanza the day before the wedding.

At a quarter to nine, Carl Matheson, the elderly veteran and her favorite customer, opened the door. He'd no more than taken a step inside when he spotted her behind the counter. A slow grin stretched across his craggy face. "Well, I'll be damned. You're a nice surprise. And on a Wednesday, no less."

She returned his smile. "Good morning. How's it going, Colonel?"

"I can't complain." The elderly gent continued into the shop, his blue eyes bright, his cane tapping against the tile floor. "I finally got rid of the walker, but I still have to use this." He lifted the cane in the air and waved it like a sword. "At least I can ward off any muggers who don't know who or what they're messing with."

She laughed. "Looks like you're getting back to your fighting weight. I'm glad that hip replacement didn't slow you down too much."

"Yeah, well, my doctor was a little surprised, too. He called me a tough old soldier. And that's true. At least, I'm healing. I might not be too steady on my feet yet, but I'm moving better."

"I'll get your usual, Colonel. Unless you'd like to mix it up."

"You know what? I'm feeling brave today. Give me a large coffee and one of those cream-cheese-filled pastries. And this time, I'll eat it here. I need to rest my bones before I try to walk home." He took a seat at the nearest table while she poured his coffee, adding his usual sugar and cream, and set his Danish on a plate.

As Marissa served him, she was about to ask if he wanted some company when the door jingled, and Ralph Tipton, Brandon's uncle, entered the shop. She didn't know the man very well, but she'd met him a couple of times.

"Good morning," Marissa said, a little more chipper than usual.

"Hi, there."

"Hey, Ralph," the colonel called out. "Are you driving that fancy new red pickup?"

Ralph grinned. "Yep. I bought it last week. What do you think?"

"Nice wheels."

"Thanks."

Marissa craned her neck and caught a glimpse of a shiny red truck.

"It's the first new vehicle I've purchased in a long time," Ralph added as he walked over to the display case and studied it carefully.

"What can I get you?" Marissa asked.

"I'll take one of those bear claws and a large cup of coffee with a splash of cream."

"Would you like it here or to go?" she asked.

"I'd better take it with me." He let out a weary sigh. "I just did the preschool run, but I need to get back to the market. We've got a delivery coming in, and... Well, things can get pretty hectic at times. Carlene and I are going to hire someone to come in and help out a few days a week. In fact, both Carlene and Betty Sue mentioned that you'd be a good fit and that you might be available."

"I wish I could. Between my work here, at the salon and at the ranch, I just don't have any more hours in the day." And that was too bad. Marissa would have jumped at the chance, but her time was stretched to the limit, especially with the upcoming wedding. Then a thought crossed her mind. "My friend Ella might be available. She lives with us at Rancho Esperanza."

"It wouldn't be a full-time position," Ralph said. "At least, not yet. But I'd like to talk to her—and the sooner the better."

"I'll mention it to her as soon as I get home. And if she's interested, I'll bring her by the market later today so you can meet her."

"That would be great. Thanks."

Maybe, if Marissa was lucky, she'd run into Brandon while she was at Tip Top Market. She'd apologize for her hesitation last night. And if he asked her out to dinner again? She swallowed, pondering the conversation she'd need to have with him about her time in jail. But if he was still game, so was she.

At the end of Brandon's shift, as he drove to the market to pick up the kids, the conversation he'd had with Greg just a few hours ago was weighing heavily on his mind.

"I hate to have to tell you this," Greg had said,

"but Marissa Garcia has a record. And she did jail time in San Diego."

"For what?"

"Drug charge. Transporting. A year in county jail. After her probation was up, she moved away from San Diego. She's lived in Bakersfield, as well as Reno and Boise, and eventually landed in Fairborn. And it looks like her family turned their backs on her."

Brandon felt like throwing up. He couldn't believe it. No wonder she seemed hesitant around a member of law enforcement.

She wasn't who he thought she was.

And why so many moves? Whatever her reason, the fact that she didn't stay in one place was another red flag.

He supposed he should be happy to get the real scoop, but it was a hard blow. He'd misjudged another woman, it seemed.

But what had happened? The crime took place several years ago. People could change, couldn't they? And apparently, Marissa hadn't been in trouble since.

Either way, dating a woman who'd been convicted of a crime was out of the question. He had two sweet kids to think about. And a possible campaign to run in the near future.

But that didn't make him feel any better about it. He'd liked Marissa. A lot.

When he pulled onto the parking lot, he noticed a familiar old pickup in front of the market. It had once belonged to Jack McGee, the late owner of the Lazy M, which was now known as Rancho Esperanza. He assumed that Alana Perez was picking up a few necessities. As he turned onto the easement that led to the house, he spotted Uncle Ralph's new pickup parked behind the store and smiled. The man had worked his butt off for years, and for the most part, he didn't treat himself to luxuries. So that Dodge Ram was well deserved. And now it was his pride and joy. *Good for you, Ralph*, he thought. *And heaven help anyone who dares to ding it.*

Brandon continued the short drive to his aunt and uncle's house, where Betty Sue sat on the front porch in one of two rocking chairs, watching the twins playing on the steps that led to the yard. They chattered between themselves while holding small chalkboards in their laps and yellow pieces of chalk in their hands. Max, his weary head resting on his paws, snoozed between them.

Marissa, who'd been seated in the rocker next to Betty Sue, got to her feet at his approach, and his gut clenched. He was going to have to talk to her, and if he could get her off to the side, he supposed now was as good a time as any. Betty Sue often said, "Everyone is redeemable, given enough love and understanding." But the cop in

Brandon, coupled with his experiences, made him question how often that actually happened.

Jimmy brightened and set his chalkboard aside. "Daddy! You're home! Auntie has a bag of lemon drops, and she shared 'em with us. You want one?"

"No, thanks. Not now."

"And guess who came to see us," Maddie added. "Marissa!"

"I see that," he said, unable to match his daughter's enthusiasm.

Marissa looked especially pretty today, with her glossy dark hair loose and tumbling over her shoulders, those caramel-colored eyes glistening. Her expression seemed shy. Apprehensive? Maybe even sad. It was hard to say, but as she closed the distance between them, she bit down on her bottom lip.

Her scent, something fresh and clean and floral, snaked around him, taunted him, tempting him to put off the conversation they needed to have.

Damn. It was almost as if she already knew what he was going to say, and she was prepared to state her defense. And when it came to putting her best foot forward, she'd pulled out all the stops.

Toughen up, he told himself. *You've got this. Confront her now.*

"Can I talk to you?" she asked. "Alone?"

"Yes. I'd like to talk to you, too. Let's take a walk."

She fell into step beside him, as they followed the pathway that led to Carlene's rose garden, where a cement bench rested under a mulberry tree, flanked by a couple of cherub statues.

They started to talk at the same time, then stopped.

"What did you want to talk to me about?" she asked.

"You first."

She tucked a glossy strand of hair behind her ear, revealing a small pair of earrings. Studs that glinted in the waning light. A golden gem of some kind. Topaz maybe. They looked nice against her olive complexion.

"Okay," she said. "I'm sorry that I was so hesitant when you asked me out to dinner last night."

He now had a pretty good idea why. "I understand."

"No," she said. "I don't think you do. There's something I need to tell you. When I was seventeen, I got arrested for something I didn't do. And no one—not the police, not the attorneys, not the judge and not even my so-called family believed me. I was convicted and served time, a little over a year, and I never even had a single visitor. So I guess you can say that I have trust issues with authority figures." She looked him up and down. "Like cops."

He hadn't seen that coming. But could he believe her? Especially when she claimed no one else had?

"I'm attracted to you," she admitted. "But when I realized you were a law-enforcement officer, I…"

"You didn't want to go out with me."

She nodded. "Yes. But that wasn't fair to you. I shouldn't have judged you based on my experience. I was only seventeen and had to face the criminal-justice system on my own."

"That had to be tough."

"You have no idea how hard it was."

He hoped what she was saying was true. And he wanted to believe her, but… He glanced at the porch, where Maddie giggled at something Jimmy had sketched on his chalkboard.

He had two kids to think about.

"So," Marissa said, her eyes zeroing in on his, "now that you know about my record, you might not want to ask me out again. And I would understand."

"I…I know about your record," he admitted. "About the drugs in your possession and the intention to sell. About your time at the Las Colinas Detention Facility."

Her expression morphed from shy and hopeful to one of surprise and then annoyance. "You already knew? How?"

His cheeks burned, and he shrugged.

"You ran a background check on me?"

"A buddy offered to run it for me, and I didn't stop him."

"Why?"

"I could have accepted the fact that you weren't interested in me. But there was something there. And it seemed like you were almost afraid to go out with me for some reason, and that didn't compute. I had to know why."

Marissa plopped down on the bench, next to a cherub. He'd checked up on her. It was enough to make her want to move far away, to find another place to set down roots. But her past would always come back to haunt her. And Brandon did have two small children to think about, even if there was no way in the world Marissa would be a threat to them.

She supposed he wouldn't know that, though. All he knew so far was whatever legal crap he'd gleaned from his buddy's research. And now her carefully hidden secret, her lousy past, was about to collide with the present. She just hoped it wouldn't knock the bright future she'd planned for herself out of reach.

I had to know why.

"Do you want to hear my side of the story?" she asked. "Because you won't find it in my file."

"If you'd like to tell me."

At this point, she didn't see why not. "My mom died when I was just a baby, so for the first ten years of my life, it was just my dad and me. We were super close, but then he remarried. I actually thought it might be cool to have a mother, like my friends, but it didn't turn out that way. From the day they got home from their honeymoon, it seemed that she and I were always competing for Daddy's attention. Then, two years later, my father died in an industrial accident at work. There was a settlement of some kind, but to this day, I've never seen a penny of it.

"My stepmom became my legal guardian, which wasn't too bad until she remarried a guy who had a son, Erik, who was two years older than me. I never could understand why she seemed to connect more with Erik than she did with me, but he was always kissing up to her, and it worked. I tried to be his friend, but that was a big mistake. He used me. As it turned out, he was a drug dealer. At least, he must have been. That's the only explanation I have for what happened."

"What did he do?" Brandon asked.

"He was a freshman in college, but he lived at home. One day, he invited me to go to a party on campus with him. I was a high-school senior, and I jumped at the chance to hang with him and his friends. Then he told me to get ready and to meet him outside.

"I wanted to make a good impression, so I hurried upstairs, changed clothes and put on some makeup. When I got outside, he told me we'd have to take my car. He wanted me to drive, since he planned on getting high. And heck, I didn't drink anyway, so I agreed.

"When we got there, he spent more time outdoors than he did inside. But I didn't care. People were pretty cool, and I liked learning about college life. After a while, he told me it was time to go. I wasn't ready, but I could tell he'd been drinking. So we left.

"Apparently, the cops got word about drugs going down at that party, and they set up a sobriety checkpoint. I wasn't worried about driving because I'd only been drinking soda pop. But when we rounded the corner and saw the police cars and an officer signaling cars to pull over, Erik jumped out of the passenger seat and ran away. I couldn't go around. I had to go forward, but I wasn't afraid. I hadn't done anything wrong."

She dug her toe in the soft dirt, her gaze on the ground as she relived that night.

"One of the officers had a drug-sniffing dog that started barking at my car. And come to find out, my trunk looked like it belonged to a pharmaceutical sales rep who liked to smoke pot. At the time, I didn't know what the pills were. Later, when I was arrested, I found out it was Ecstasy."

"And Erik never confessed?" Brandon asked, as if he might believe her story when no one else did.

"No. I should have known better than to trust him—or to expect him to come clean before I was officially charged. But no such luck. And for some dumb reason, my stepmom decided to show me tough love so I'd learn my lesson, which meant she refused to bail me out or to pay for a lawyer. I ended up with a public defender who didn't take my claims seriously."

"So you were convicted."

"Yes. And Erik transferred to an out-of-state college, while I went to jail. After I got out, I was sent to a halfway house until I'd finished my probation. Then I moved as far from San Diego as I could."

"And you never contacted them? Your family?"

She chuffed. "No. I kept thinking that someone would try and find me, that they'd apologize and beg for forgiveness. But when that never happened, I wrote them all off and put them and that ugly memory as far away as possible."

She nearly mentioned the texts she'd gotten from Erik, but there was no reason to. It was too late. She wasn't looking for his apology because she wasn't going to forgive him after all this time.

"What about your friends?" Brandon asked. "Didn't they offer you any support?"

"I'd thought they would. But they were all going to college, and most of them had been offered academic scholarships. So they shut me out of their lives after my arrest." And she really couldn't blame them. Who'd want to stay in touch with a convicted criminal, especially when her own family had turned their backs on her?

She slowly shook her head. It was hard to use the word *family* to describe the people she'd once lived with, the people who'd refused to believe or defend her.

Erik's lie had led to her yearlong incarceration and branded her a convicted felon for the rest of her life.

If her daddy had been alive when she'd been falsely convicted of a crime she hadn't committed, he would've moved heaven and earth to help her.

She looked up at Brandon, hoping he would understand. "Do you believe me?" The question came out with a quiver, her voice faint and shaking.

He didn't answer for what seemed like a lifetime. Instead, he studied her as if he was dissecting her story, looking for something that might contradict whatever he'd learned when he'd run that background search.

"I understand." She got to her feet. "I'll stay away from you and your kids. You don't have to worry about me."

Chapter Eight

Did he believe her?

Brandon wasn't entirely sure, but he sure wanted to believe she was telling the truth. Still, the question hung in the air until she got to her feet. He wasn't ready to see her go, so he reached for her hand. "Wait, Marissa. Sit down."

She complied, and they remained in the rose garden for a while, his hand still holding hers.

He'd learned to be skeptical, first when dealing with any excuse one of his irresponsible parents gave him, then when Julie ditched him for her former boyfriend—her so-called soul mate.

And now his job demanded that he question every story, every defense, against hard evidence.

She cleared her throat. "Say something, Brandon."

He turned in his seat, his knee brushing hers and sparking a warmth, even in the chill of the evening.

She gazed at him like a fragile bird. "Do you believe me or not?"

His skepticism faded, and the urge to protect her took its place, whether warranted or not.

"Yes," he said. "I do."

Her shoulders slumped in relief, and she blew out a pent-up sigh. "I was afraid you were going to be like everyone else."

He understood her fear. If what she'd told him was true—and he wanted to believe that it was— she'd only been seventeen and had to face a horrible situation on her own.

"So," she said, "now what?"

He wasn't sure. "Take things slow. See where this goes." Whatever *this* was.

She gave his hand a gentle squeeze before releasing it. "I hoped you'd say that. Do you still want to have that picnic or go out to dinner? If you do, then I'm game. But if not, or if you'd rather wait awhile, I'm okay with that, too."

Once he'd gotten over his initial shock, his gut insisted that she was innocent. That she'd gone through hell without any support from her family or friends. Maybe that's why she'd gravitated toward Alana and the women who lived at Rancho Esperanza. To get the friendship and acceptance she deserved. To find a family, even if they weren't blood-related. To give all that she'd never received.

"I'd still like to go out with you," he said.

"I'm glad to hear that." Her soft, orange-blossom scent stirred in the evening air, surrounding him with wholesome thoughts of goodness. Did that equate to innocence?

"Let's leave the kids out for now and start by having dinner." He didn't want to add them into the mix yet. "Just you and me."

"Okay."

"Does Saturday night work for you?"

She smiled, her eyes sparkling in relief. Or maybe unadulterated hope. "Yes. I'd like that."

"All right, then. I'll pick you up at six."

"I'll be ready."

He was going to suggest that they return to the house, but before he could utter a word, her gaze locked on his. "Your turn. What was it that you had to say to me?"

"We've already talked about it, actually. And I'm glad we did." He turned in the cold, concrete seat, and his knee pressed against hers again, this time sending a spiral of heat through his blood.

Damn, she wasn't just attractive. She looked vulnerable, and he had the strangest compulsion to protect her.

He placed his hand along her jawline, his thumb caressing her cheek. So soft. So… Her lips parted again, and he leaned in to give her a chaste let's-start-over-and-be-friends kiss. At least, that had been his plan until she slipped into his arms, leaned into him and kissed him back.

She had a sweet, lemon-drop taste he found intoxicating. She was intoxicating, and he couldn't seem to get enough of her. He could have kissed her until they were both breathless, but they were too close to the house, and he didn't want the kids to come looking for them and find them in a heated embrace. So he reluctantly ended the kiss.

"I thought you wanted to take things day by day," she said softly, her cheeks flushed.

She was right. And if he dared to kiss her again, he'd be tempted to jump headfirst into the deep end. And if that was to happen, he'd better hope and pray he wasn't making another big mistake in misjudging a woman's character.

Betty Sue sat on the black swivel chair at her favorite slot machine, but her eyes were on the woman Ralph and Carlene had hired to work at the market. There was something about her that didn't seem right. Not that anyone else seemed to notice.

Ella was in her mid-twenties with short jet-black hair—the color that usually came from a bottle. She was of medium height, neither tall nor short, but a little too thin—like a bird. She was skittish like a little sparrow, too. Earlier this morning, Betty accidentally dropped a roll of quarters, and the poor girl nearly jumped a foot.

Sure, some people had quick reactions, but Ella had actually flinched. She also had a tendency to look over her shoulder whenever the door to the store opened. And when she did, she seemed to freeze, and her expression appeared to be more fearful than curious. Betty Sue had no idea what her story was, but she'd bet a nickel to a dollar that it wasn't pretty.

As luck would have it, the Jensen Dairy refrigerated delivery truck pulled into the yard and parked in back of the market. Carlene and Ralph both left Ella in charge so they could meet with the driver, a man they knew from their high-school days. And Betty Sue took the opportunity to quiz Ella.

She slid off her seat, taking care not to trip, and made her way to the front counter, where the little gal stood near the register. "Do you mind if I ask you a personal question, Ella?"

The poor thing stiffened. "Wh-what's that?"

"Don't worry. You don't have anything to fret about. You're doing a good job. And you're a hard worker. My niece and nephew are pleased that they hired you. But someone I once knew used to move around like you do—always afraid someone might sneak up on her, and I can't help noticing the similarities between her and you."

Ella grew troubled and worried her bottom lip. She stole a glance first at the front door, then at the grocery aisle that led to the back of the market. "I don't know what you're talking about." Then she turned and straightened the packs of cigarettes in the tall glass display case behind the register, which didn't need straightening.

Betty Sue placed a gentle hand on her shoulder. "Who hurt you?"

"I… He…" Tears welled in her eyes, and she used the back of her hand to swipe them away, removing a swatch of makeup in the process and revealing a shiner, albeit one that was fading. "Doug. My husband."

Betty eyed her carefully. "You afraid he'll come looking for you?"

She nodded. "Without a doubt. The last time I left, he swore he'd kill me if I ever tried a stunt like that again."

"Did you call the police?"

"I was afraid to. He's a cop. Or at least, he used to be. He's on a medical leave of absence. But he has friends on the force. He's also from a prominent family in the community. He told me no one would believe me, and I knew that was true."

"Cuts and bruises can provide a strong witness. But at least you're safe now."

"I hope so. I cut my hair short and dyed it. He probably has no idea where I ended up, but I still can't help being afraid that he'll figure it out and find me."

"You have family in Fairborn?"

"No. But he knew how much money I had and how far the bus would take me. He's mean as heck, but he's not stupid."

"What does he look like?" Betty Sue asked.

"Doug has brown hair and wears it kind of short. He's not super tall, but he still looks like a big man. He played football in college. And he works out a lot. He's proud of the result and wears a lot of sleeveless T-shirts. He also drives a red pickup with gun racks."

Betty Sue eased close to her slowly, in the way she might have approached a wounded stray dog. "Do Ralph and Carlene know?"

Ella slowly shook her head. "I was afraid they wouldn't hire me if they thought there'd be trouble on the horizon."

"I won't say a word," Betty Sue said. "Your secret is safe with me. But you need to relax. If you're not careful, your jumpiness is going to set off alarms. And in case Doug does show up—and I *don't* think he will—someone might say something that could tip him off."

"Thank you for understanding. And for the advice." Tears welled in her eyes again. And she used her fingers to clear them away.

"I'll watch the store. You go on back to the restroom and reapply that makeup. The bruise is a little more prominent now."

"Thanks." She sniffled, then reached for her purse, which she kept under the counter. She started to walk toward the restroom, then paused. "The woman you knew. Was she able to start a new life? Did she stay safe?"

After she shot the bastard. Betty Sue nodded. "She never had to deal with him again."

"And she was your friend?"

"She was me."

Brandon had heard a lot of great things about Feliciano's, the new steak house in Kalispell, which is why he chose to take Marissa there on their first date. But no one had told him about the romantic ambience.

The hostess, a tall brunette in her forties, carried leather-bound menus as she led him and Marissa to their table. They continued past an indoor water fountain, the gurgling sounds drowning out the voices of other diners, and approached a colorful mural of a vineyard on the back wall. Marissa's black heels clicked on the distressed hardwood floor as she walked beside him, her arm brushing against his.

"This place is amazing," she said. "I can see why you didn't want to bring the kids here."

That wasn't his only reason for leaving them with Mrs. Hendrix. Even though she was great with his children, he wanted to get to know Marissa better before he included her in any more family activities.

"You've got that right," he said. "I can imagine Jimmy spilling his milk, and then Maddie scolding him for not being more careful."

"Do they mind staying with a sitter?" she asked.

"Not when it's Mrs. Hendrix. They really like her."

The hostess stopped at a table for two that had been draped with white linen and topped with a flickering candle and a single red rose in a crystal bud vase.

Yet more moving, more stunning, than the setting and atmosphere was his lovely date, who wore a simple, sleeveless black dress and carried a matching wrap. She'd woven her dark locks into a stylish twist that revealed the same yellow-stone studs he'd noticed before.

She looked especially pretty tonight. He'd told

her that when he'd picked her up, but here, in such a romantic setting, she really stood out.

He pulled out her chair, and she thanked him before taking a seat and placing her clutch purse on the table. Then she let her wrap fall from her shoulders behind her. He caught his breath at the sight of her smooth, bronze-colored skin. The soft candlelight cast a magical glow on her lovely face.

"Those are pretty earrings."

"Thank you." She fingered her earlobes. "They're topaz. My birthstone. My father gave them to me when I turned twelve."

That must have been right before he died, Brandon thought. Assuming her story was true. But why wouldn't it be?

"That's a nice way to remember your dad."

She smiled. "I think so. I wear them a lot."

Rather than let the conversation slip into something sad or wistful, he changed the subject to a happier one.

"So," he said, "how are the wedding plans coming along?"

"Great." Her warm, brown eyes glimmered in the candlelight, her pride and enthusiasm shining through. "The wedding is next week. The cake is ordered, and so are the flowers. The gazebo is going to be beautiful. And Alana bought the perfect dress. We're only missing one thing. Or rather two."

"What's that?"

"Did Ramon contact you?" she asked.

"Yes." The Fairborn mayor and Brandon were friends and had known each other for years. "Ramon sent me a text and asked if I'd let Jimmy and Maddie take part in the wedding. As the ring bearer and flower girl."

"What did you say?"

"I told him I'd think about it."

Her brow furrowed, and her head tilted slightly to the side. "What's your concern?"

"Actually, I thought it was kind of weird that the twins' names came up. I mean, I really don't know the bride very well. And I only know the groom in a professional capacity." Brandon didn't want her to think Alana's husband had committed a crime, so he added, "Clay was carjacked and assaulted. And I took part in the arrest of the perp."

"Yes, of course."

"Don't Clay and Alana have anyone else that could do it?" he asked. "Like the kids of a friend or family member?"

"Actually, they don't. Do you know Ramon's wife?"

"Of course. Callie."

"She's Alana's best friend and the matron of honor. Alana mentioned that the only thing missing was a ring bearer and flower girl, and when

Callie suggested Jimmy and Maddie, we all thought it was a wonderful idea."

"Ramon and I are pretty tight, so I guess that makes sense."

The waiter, a tall balding man wearing black slacks and a crisply pressed white shirt, stopped by to introduce himself and to take their orders. They decided on a bottle of a Napa Valley merlot to start and the chateaubriand for two. Once he'd walked away from the table, Marissa leaned forward. "So what do you say? Can the kids be in the wedding?" She paused. "I'm sorry. Am I being too pushy? I don't want you to do something you're uncomfortable with."

If his agreement would keep her smiling for the rest of the evening, how could he say no? Besides, he knew how important the wedding plans were to her. So he said, "All right."

"Great. I assume you got your invitation?"

"I did," Brandon said. It was a small town, and people usually included everyone.

"Good. And with the twins in the ceremony, you should attend the rehearsal dinner the night before. But just so you know, having the kids take part won't cost you anything. Clay will pay to rent a little tuxedo for Jimmy, so all you'd need to do is take Jimmy to the Tux Shop and have him measured—and the sooner the better. Clay is also going to buy Maddie's dress. I've already picked out the perfect little gown. I'm sure a size four will fit her. If not, we can have it altered."

Brandon didn't like other people picking up the tab for him or his children. "I'll pay for the dress and tux."

"You really don't have to. Clay was prepared to spend a fortune on the wedding, although Alana insisted upon keeping it simple. And for the most part, that's the plan. It'll be an outdoor event with a country theme. And really, your kids are going to look so cute."

Marissa definitely had things all planned out, but Brandon knew things rarely went the way he expected, especially when it came to his children. "I have to warn you, Jimmy isn't keen on baths or dressing up. But if a fancy dress is involved, Maddie will be all over it. She's really into all things royal these days, so she'll be thrilled to wear what she's going to consider a princess costume."

"Then, maybe I'd better look for a small tiara she can wear, although I was thinking a headband made of real flowers." She lifted her finger, the nail painted pink, and tapped her chin, as if her creative brain was working hard to figure it out.

Brandon couldn't help smiling. "Maddie will be happy either way."

"I'm sure she will, but I want everything to be perfect." Marissa took a deep breath, then slowly let it out. "I think I have everything under control, but there's just one thing that might go wrong."

"What's that?"

"Callie is eight months pregnant and expecting twins. The doctor thinks she will go into labor anytime. I just hope it doesn't happen before next Saturday. Or during the wedding. Can you imagine?"

"That would be a complication." But that wasn't the only thing that could go wrong. Jimmy could lose the ring. Or accidentally knock over the cake. And Maddie could trip on her way down the aisle and burst into tears...

He glanced at the happy wedding planner. Hopefully, she'd still be happy after the ceremony, no matter what went south. Because with his twins involved, anything could go wrong.

As Marissa and Brandon left the restaurant and headed toward his Jeep, she said, "Thank you for a lovely evening. The food was to die for. And the candles and roses, that amazing fountain, the excellent service. I've never been to such a nice restaurant before. Except once." She touched her earrings. "When my dad gave these to me, he took me to a fancy restaurant on the top floor of a building that looked out over San Diego. It was for brunch, and I still remember I had pancakes and fruit salad."

"I'm glad you enjoyed it."

She really had, so much so that she wished the night would never end, but he had children at home. And a babysitter to relieve.

He opened the passenger door for her, and she slid onto the seat. Then he circled the car and got behind the wheel.

Once he started the engine, backed out of the parking space and pulled onto the street, she said, "Tell me about Mrs. Hendrix. And why do the kids like her so much?"

"She's our neighbor—and a widow. Her kids live out of state, and they're building careers. They haven't started families yet, so she's kind of adopted Jimmy and Maddie. Whenever she bakes cookies, she always brings some to us."

"They're lucky," Marissa said, wishing she'd had a grandmotherly neighbor or someone who'd taken an interest in her when she'd been a child.

"And Mrs. Hendrix is lucky to have them, too. She's going to start watching them on the days they're not in preschool and when I'm on duty. She didn't want me to pay her, but I told her that's the only way I'd agree to the arrangement." He chuckled. "She said I drove a hard bargain."

"So they won't be staying with Carlene and Ralph anymore?"

"No," he said. "I'm trying to give my aunt and uncle a bit of a break."

"Are the kids too much for them?"

"They said no, but they're getting older, and they refuse to retire. They have a lot of responsibilities with the store. And they admit that Betty Sue and the twins keep them busy. We'll still visit them regularly. Only now they won't have to worry about messes and discipline."

"I'm glad they'll still get to spend time with you and the kids."

"Me, too. I'd like to see them take a vacation someday. In fact, they finally hired a part-time employee to help at the market. I hope that works out for them."

He was talking about Ella. Marissa nearly told him that she'd been instrumental in making the introductions, but she didn't want to come across as prideful or tooting her own horn. She'd rather earn Brandon's trust and respect by being herself and not for what she may or may not have done for his family.

As Brandon turned onto the country road that would take Marissa back to Rancho Esperanza, he said, "And believe it or not, Betty Sue can be pretty fussy at times. But she seems to like the woman they hired. That'll be helpful since Carlene and Ralph will probably ask her to keep an eye on Betty Sue once in a while. Don't get me wrong. I love my great-aunt, but she can be a handful sometimes."

"I'm glad things are working out for everyone involved." She was also happy to know that she'd helped Ella create a new start, a better life and a safer environment.

"I haven't met the woman yet, but my aunt and uncle assured me that she's been very helpful and that she tries hard." Brandon cut a glance across the seat. "By the way, what's the dress code for that wedding?"

"You can wear a jacket if you want to, but slacks and a button-down shirt should be okay. I'll be wearing a dress, of course. And working behind the scenes."

"Good to know."

They continued to chat for the rest of the twenty-minute ride about nothing in particular and everything in general. The dashboard lights lit his face, and Marissa liked the way his eyes crinkled at the corners when he smiled.

"Was it hard to return to town after college? With the twins and no wife?"

He shrugged. "I wasn't embarrassed by it, if that's what you mean. And my family was great. I don't know what I would have done without my aunt and uncle."

Marissa remained quiet for a while, happy for him. It must be nice to have a loving, accepting family. Her life certainly would have been a lot easier if she'd had someone to lean on, someone who'd loved her.

As Brandon turned into the long driveway that led to the ranch house, ending the memorable evening, Marissa again thanked him.

"You're welcome. I'm glad you went with me to check out Feliciano's. That's not the kind of place a guy would want to go alone."

Maybe not, but Brandon wouldn't have had any trouble finding another woman to date. He had to be one of the most eligible bachelors in the county. And she was happy that he'd chosen her. She was also relieved to know that he believed in her innocence, that he believed in *her*.

He parked, and as she opened the passenger door, he got out of the Jeep, too. Then they walked together to the porch, where an outdoor light bathed them in a soft, yellow glow.

Would he kiss her again? She hoped he would. Ever since the last time, she'd been thinking and dreaming about it. She paused before the screen door, but it seemed silly to thank him yet again, so she said, "I guess I'll see you at the rehearsal dinner. Friday, at six o'clock. At the ranch."

"Yes, I'll see you then. If not before."

Then he kissed her, slowly at first. Sweetly. But as his woodsy scent caressed her, she reached up and slipped her arms around his neck and kissed him back—full throttle.

Her lips parted, allowing his tongue to seek hers, to meet and mate. Their hands stroked, caressed and explored each other, the fabric of his shirt and her dress preventing any skin-to-skin contact. If she didn't live with a houseful of people, she'd be tempted to invite him inside for coffee, a nightcap or…whatever. But it probably wouldn't be very wise for her to do, anyway.

So she reluctantly lowered her arms and withdrew her mouth from his.

"Damn," he said. "That was one hot good-night kiss."

Ditto, she thought. The sparks of heat darn near lit up the night sky.

"I'll talk to you later," he said.

"Sounds good." She had no idea what he meant by *later*, but she certainly hoped it was soon. And before the rehearsal dinner.

Chapter Nine

As it turned out, Marissa didn't see Brandon that next week, which had been a little disappointing, but she'd kept busy with the wedding plans.

By the time Friday rolled around, the evening before the wedding, the party-rental company had made their delivery. They'd set up the chairs the way Marissa had instructed, with an aisle down the middle, in front of the new white gazebo, which had turned out beautifully, even though it hadn't been decorated yet. The florist would bring the flowers and greenery tomorrow morning. But for now, everything was ready for the wedding party, who'd be coming soon.

As the sun dipped low in the western sky, Marissa stood in the yard, making one final assessment for tonight's event. Two large tables sat at the side of the house on the lawn. In keeping with Alana and Clay's country-wedding theme, each had been adorned with yellow tablecloths and multiple bouquets of wildflowers arranged in quart-size mason jars, each trimmed with multicolored ribbons. Mini-lanterns and string lights crisscrossed above the tables, providing romantic lighting.

Pleased with the setup, Marissa returned to the kitchen, where Ella had been cooking up a storm, the results filling the house with the aroma of savory beef, roasting vegetables and herbs. The first whiff reminded her of the restaurant Brandon had taken her to last week, high-end and outrageously delicious.

Their new roommate hadn't lived on the ranch for a full twenty-four hours when they learned that she was a whiz at cooking—and not just for small groups. So even though Clay had offered to hire a catering company to provide the wedding meal, he and Alana had asked Ella to prepare tonight's rehearsal dinner. She wasn't going to accept payment, but Clay insisted.

Marissa made her way to the counter, where Ella was placing plastic wrap over the top of the salad bowl. "That looks amazing. What all did you put in it?"

"Besides the greens? There's goat cheese, toasted walnuts, pumpkin seeds and figs." Ella smiled proudly. "Plus my secret homemade dressing, which is already in the fridge."

In addition to that yummy salad and roasted veggies, tonight's menu would also consist of a choice of petite filets of beef with a balsamic demi-glace and breast of chicken sautéed in marsala wine sauce, with an option for the vegetarians—pumpkin and butternut-squash ravioli. Dessert would be make-it-yourself ice-cream sundaes.

Tomorrow, a caterer would show up with a specialized chuck wagon, where he would grill Santa Maria–style tri tip on-site. To go with it, Ella would make red potatoes and a southwestern green salad with another of her secret dressings.

"Everything smells so good," Marissa said. "I knew the meals would be delicious, but where did you learn to balance out all the kitchen chores like this?"

"My grandmother used to be a caterer, and when I was a teenager, she let me help."

"She certainly taught you a lot." Marissa glanced at the luscious fruit salad that filled a large hollowed-out watermelon that had been carved to look like a fancy basket.

"I'm also addicted to the Food Network,"

Ella added. "I would've loved to attend culinary school, but… Well, I got married, and then my life plans sort of stalled." She fingered a fading bruise on her neck. With a nervous laugh, she added, "Then it went into a tailspin."

"Well, you're safe now," Marissa said. "It's time to make your happiness a priority. You can still go to school—if you want to."

"Maybe." Ella shrugged. "Wouldn't that be something?"

"Yes. Something you absolutely can do." Marissa glanced at the clock on the oven. The pastor and his wife would be arriving soon. Clay's father, Mr. Hastings, too. Her heartbeat skipped. And Brandon.

"Did you do anything special for the kids?" Marissa asked. "I should have asked their father if they were fussy eaters."

"I have some chicken tenders and macaroni and cheese on hand. So if they don't want an adult meal, it won't be a problem."

"Perfect. I'll check with Brandon as soon as he arrives." Marissa scanned the kitchen, which was surprisingly tidy. "Is there anything I can do to help?"

"Not that I can think of. I've got everything under control. And the table settings are gorgeous."

And that meant that—so far, and fingers

crossed—Marissa had the entire evening under control. She began mentally checking off her last-minute to-do list. Hmm. "Maybe I should make seating assignments."

"I don't think that's necessary. There's not that many people coming."

"You're probably right. I have both tables side by side and set them for twelve."

"Isn't that too many?" Ella asked. "I made enough food, but I didn't think either of Clay's brothers would be arriving from Texas until tomorrow."

"Let's see." Marissa began counting them off. "There's the bride and groom, matron of honor and best man. Then there's Mr. Hastings. Pastor Jennings and his wife. Brandon and the twins. You and me. That makes twelve."

"I won't be joining you guys for the rehearsal or the dinner. I'll just serve the meals and then come back to the kitchen and clean up."

Marissa was about to object, to insist that Ella join them, but the doorbell rang, and she hurried to greet the first arrivals. It might be the pastor and his wife. Or maybe Callie and Ramon. But it could just as easily be Brandon and the kids, who she was most eager to see. So she kicked up her pace as she crossed the living room. When she opened the door and spotted Brandon and the twins standing on the stoop, her heart took a tumble, and a warm smile stretched across her face. "Come on in, guys. I'm so glad you're here."

She stepped aside, and as the kids entered the living room, Marissa's eyes locked on the gorgeous daddy. The deputy looked incredibly nice tonight in a pair of black jeans and a white button-down shirt. He smelled good, too.

He stepped through the door, the scent of soap and a masculine cologne trailing behind him, setting her senses on high alert.

"I never got to go to a wedding before," Maddie said, drawing Marissa's attention. "Daddy said I get to be the flower girl and wear a princess dress."

"Yeah," Jimmy said. "And I get to be the ring boy."

"Can I wear the dress now?" Maddie asked.

Marissa's heart melted. What a sweet *ring boy* and flower girl.

"I'll let you see the dress, but you'll need to wait until tomorrow to wear it. You'll even get to take it home with you."

Clearly disappointed, the little girl scrunched her face.

Before Marissa could show her the child-size gown, the doorbell sounded.

"I'd better get that," she said. It was probably the minister and his wife.

Instead, it was Adam Hastings, Clay's father. Marissa invited him in.

Mr. Hastings wasn't a tall man, but the wealthy Texas rancher carried himself in a way that commanded respect. He removed his cowboy hat when he entered. "You must be the wedding planner."

A sense of pride settled over her, and she offered the older man a smile. "Yes, I am. Marissa Garcia. Please come in and make yourself comfortable."

She'd no more than closed the door when she heard footsteps approaching from down the hall. She looked over her shoulder to see Clay and Alana, who'd been talking privately in the ranch office. She had no idea what they'd been discussing, but it must have been something happy because they were all smiles.

Marissa had hardly taken a breath, when the matron of honor and the best man arrived. Callie had a healthy glow as she waddled inside, her husband, Ramon, at her side.

Moments later, the pastor and his wife entered the house, and the rehearsal was on.

So much for having any time to spend with Brandon and his sweet son and daughter. And tomorrow would be another busy day. But that didn't matter. Marissa had planned the perfect wedding, and if everything went as it was supposed to, she'd be one step closer to opening White Lace and Promises.

The rehearsal had been a success, and Saturday dawned bright and warm. Marissa couldn't be happier with the way Alana and Clay's wedding had come together. The gazebo, now adorned in greenery and an array of colorful blooms, most of them sunflowers, sat in front of a copse of weeping willows. A pond to the side provided a lovely view of the countryside.

Rows of rented white chairs flanked a white carpeted aisle the bridal party would walk down. And the guests would start arriving soon.

With Alana marrying an attorney whose family had more money than they knew what to do with, they could have pulled out all the stops in planning their ceremony, even though they had a baby on the way and had opted to marry quickly. Clay's father had wanted to invite hundreds of his friends and associates, which both the bride and groom nixed. From what Marissa had heard, Adam Hastings was used to getting his way, so the fact that he'd pretty much folded on the idea said a lot about his willingness to build a better, more respectful relationship with his youngest son.

"Marissa!"

She turned at the sound of the child's voice and

spotted the adorable little red-haired girl dressed in a princess-style gown and her dapper twin brother rocking a little tuxedo and tugging at his bow tie. A smile that began in her heart spread across her face as she started toward them, her gaze bursting with appreciation for the flower girl and the ring boy, not to mention the daddy who'd done his best to get them ready.

"Maddie, you look beautiful—a perfect little princess. And, Jimmy, aren't you handsome in that grown-up suit and tie."

The girl beamed, while her brother scrunched his face. "Do I have to wear this thing? Bows are for girls."

"Maybe, if it's okay with your dad, you can take if off after the ceremony." Marissa turned to the handsome daddy, who wore a pair of black slacks, a pale blue button-down shirt and a smile that nearly stole her breath away. She preferred the deputy in civilian clothes, either casual or dressy. But she had to admit, even in his uniform, he looked nice.

Brandon placed his hand on Jimmy's small shoulder. "I'd agree with that. You can ditch the tie after the wedding." He scanned the parking lot. "My uncle and aunts are coming, but I haven't seen them yet."

Marissa glanced toward the area they'd set

aside as a parking lot. "There's a shiny new pickup. Isn't that him now?"

"Yes, that's him. He loves that truck. He has a friend who now works at the dealership, and he got a good deal."

"Who wouldn't love a deal like that?" Marissa scanned the grounds, checking out the gazebo, the caterers setting up the tables, the pastor wiping his brow with a white handkerchief. She wasn't wearing a watch, but the clock was ticking. "I'd love to hang with you guys a little longer, but I need to go inside and check on the bride and her matron of honor."

"Do what you need to do." Brandon flashed her a smile. "Now that it's getting down to the wire, you've got your work cut out for you. And so do I." He nodded toward the twins. "I need to keep these two little munchkins clean and presentable for the next twenty minutes."

What a good daddy. And a wonderful man. She took one last moment to admire the handsome deputy she'd come to trust. With all the love and romance in the air today, it'd be in her best interest to do her job and keep her mind on the couple who'd soon be tying the knot.

Still, when she approached the French doors at the back end of the house that led to the master bedroom, she stole one last glance over her shoulder at Brandon. He stood near the gazebo, where a few women had already gathered around him, fawning over the kids. And clearly fawning over him, too.

A pang of jealousy hit, and she did her best to tamp it down. She had no reason to feel the least bit possessive. Not yet, anyway. But the way things seemed to be going, maybe it was just a matter of time.

When Carlene and Ralph stopped to talk to Eddie Cruz, Ramon's father, and his date—Helena Somebody-or-other—Betty Sue took the opportunity to slip away and head to the small orchard, where she plucked some ripe cherries from the tree and stashed them in her purse to eat later. She'd attended plenty of weddings in her day, although never her own. But very few of them served a meal on time.

As she headed back to the festivities, where people were beginning to take their seats, she scanned the small crowd, looking for Ella. The other day, at the market, Ella had mentioned that she was preparing tonight's food. Poor thing was probably slaving in the kitchen. Betty Sue had promised to look out for her, and she'd meant it. Even if that meant washing dishes or serving meals.

So she circled the ranch house, like some of the later arrivals, and entered through the back door.

She spotted the frail little thing in the kitchen, wearing a white, full-length apron and peering out the kitchen window and into the yard.

"What are you doing holed up in here?" Betty Sue asked.

Ella jumped, spun around and slapped a hand over her chest. "Oh, my gosh! You startled me."

With her black hair too dark against her fair skin, the short strands poking up like she'd stuck her finger in an electrical outlet, she looked scared to death. "Why aren't you outside with the others? I can see that you'd like to be out there."

Ella slowly shook her head. "I might be a little curious, but I'd rather stay inside. Weddings make me uneasy."

"Why's that?"

She shrugged. "My marriage was a nightmare. But it's over now. Well, it will be, once I can get a legal divorce. And that's not likely to happen anytime soon. There's no way I'd want Doug to find out where I am."

"I hear you."

Betty Sue eased forward and checked out the dessert tray Ella was filling with a variety of sweet treats—tiny little pies and cakes a person could eat in a single bite. "Did you make this fussy stuff for your husband?"

"No way. I tried it once, and he threw every single one of them at me. He's a meat-and-potatoes sort of guy. His favorite after-dinner treat was a twelve-pack of beer."

Booze and drugs could make a macho man mean as hell. They could also make him ugly.

"Don't you like to cook?" Ella asked.

"I used to. I even worked at a natural-food store once. In the bakery. But I got fired."

"Oh, no." Ella sobered. "What happened?"

"My special brownie recipe had always gone over big. I called them Brownie Boosters. So I whipped up a batch at home one day and took them to the store to see how the customers would like them."

"I'm sure the store owner was concerned about health regulations."

Betty Sue lifted her hand and waved her off. "That wasn't the problem. Hell, people couldn't get enough of them, although I had to sell them under the counter."

Ella's eyebrows rose, and her eyes grew wide. "Brownie *Boosters*? You mean, you put marijuana in them?"

Betty Sue nodded proudly.

Ella chuckled. "And I thought you were a sweet old lady."

"Honey, you have no idea how sweet I am. I'm also very resourceful. Anyway, when word got out, the bakery's sales and profits shot through the roof."

"So the owner got a cut?"

"Of course. I'm no thief."

"Then, why did you get fired?"

"One Sunday morning before church, Pastor Babbitt stopped in the store and ordered a bagful. He'd always had a sweet tooth. I suspect he ate them all, because mid-sermon the boost hit him. He'd just launched into the fire-and-brimstone part when he got the giggles and couldn't stop." Betty Sue smirked and folded her arms across her chest. "I'm not a churchgoer, so I wasn't there. But folks said he wrapped up the sermon and said, 'Let's start the potluck. I'm starving.'"

Ella placed a hand over her mouth to staunch her laughter. "You're funny."

"Maybe so. And you're not the only one who's mentioned it. Too bad my family can't connect with my sense of humor."

Ella's expression turned serious. "Tell me something. When we were talking at the market the other day, you said that you'd been abused, too. But the minute Carlene returned from the back room, you dropped the subject. That was okay with me, because I didn't want her to learn about my situation, either. I like my job and the Tiptons. And I don't want to give them any reason to fire me."

"I kept my beatings quiet, too," Betty Sue said. "Ashamed, I guess. But at least I wasn't married to my abuser. 'Course, that didn't mean there weren't legal repercussions. And a trial."

"Do you mind telling me about it?" Ella asked.

If Betty Sue was going to talk to anyone about that day back in 1968—August the fourth, to be exact—it would be the shy kid hanging on her every word. She glanced at the doorway that led to the front part of the house, as well as the doorway to the mudroom. A glance out the kitchen window let her know that the guests had begun to take their seats.

"I'd better tell you later," Betty Sue said. "Carlene will be calling 9-1-1 if I don't get out there and take my seat. But I swore I'd never let anyone lay a hand on me again."

"Thanks for being my friend." Ella closed the distance between them and gave Betty Sue a hug that damn near knocked her to her knees, as scarred and arthritic as they were.

It was the first adult-size hug Betty Sue had been given in ages, and it made her tear up. Still, she held Ella tight, stroking her back, the bony vertebrae revealing just how thin the poor kid was. Who would have guessed that this frail, frightened little gal would be the first real friend she'd had in a long, long time?

Alana was the epitome of the blushing bride, yet even the pink tint on her olive complexion looked as if it had been professionally applied by an experienced makeup artist. And her dress was perfect: ivory-colored, knee-length, with a sweetheart-lace bodice, a scoop neck and elbow-length sleeves. Her baby bump refused to hide under the material that gathered under her bust-line. It was almost as if her son, who wouldn't arrive for another three months, was determined to take part in the wedding that would join his happy parents in marriage.

Callie, the matron of honor, was just as lovely in a similarly styled maternity dress. Her light brown hair had been swept up in a bun, adorned with a crown of yellow roses to match her dress. She looked a little uncomfortable, though. But who wouldn't be? She was about to have twins, and those active little ones had stretched the soft, jersey-like fabric around her belly.

While the bride and her matron of honor did a last-minute makeup check, Marissa couldn't help but stand beside the two pregnant friends, marveling at how close they were, how supportive they were of each other.

The two women had been friends ever since they met as teenagers. And while Marissa was happy for them, she couldn't help feeling a wee bit envious. Maybe, one of these days, she would have her very own BFF.

"You both look beautiful," Marissa said.

"Should I let the pastor know that we're ready to start the ceremony?"

"Yes, we're ready." Alana gave Callie a warm hug. "Let's do this."

As Marissa turned to leave, she'd barely taken two steps toward the door when Callie cried out, "Uh-oh."

Alana let out a loud gasp, and Marissa spun around to see both women staring at Callie's high heels and a puddle on the floor.

Marissa's eyes widened, and she pointed. "Is that…?"

Callie nodded. "I'm afraid so. My water broke."

Too stunned to speak, let alone move, Marissa's mind began spinning a mile a minute as she tried to make sense of what had happened. What it meant.

What would a seasoned wedding planner do at a time like this?

Her first thought was to ask the pastor to speed up the ceremony, but that wouldn't work. Callie was expecting twins, and anything could go wrong at this point.

"Will you please get my husband?" Callie said.

"Yes. Of course." Marissa hurried out the bedroom door. The last time she checked on the groom and his best man, they'd been downing a beer in the guest room down the hall.

She knocked at the door, then opened it and entered without waiting for an invitation. Both men stopped chuckling at whatever they'd been talking about.

"We've got a problem," she said.

Clay got to his feet. "Don't tell me my father is barking out orders again. Dammit. We talked about that, and he promised—"

"No, he's fine. A perfect gentleman." She turned to Ramon, who appeared to be kicking back until their gazes met. "Callie's in labor. Her water just broke."

The new mayor jumped to his feet. "Oh, man. Is she okay?"

"Yes. I mean, so far. But—"

"I'm on it." Ramon turned to Clay. "I'm sorry, man. I hate to leave at a time like this, but the doctor told us not to drag our feet if something like this happened. She's already dilated, and one baby wasn't in an optimum position."

"Go," Clay said. "But drive carefully."

Ramon tossed him an unsteady grin. "Don't worry. I will. I've got precious cargo on board."

As he dashed off, Marissa crossed her arms and blew out a sigh. "I know you're not supposed to see the bride before the ceremony, but maybe we ought to make an exception in this case. I'd like to know if you guys want to proceed with just the two of you, postpone things or—"

Clay shook his head. "Alana won't want to postpone the ceremony. And I don't, either. Let's talk to her and see what she has to say. I want this day to be perfect for her."

"It'll definitely be memorable."

Five minutes later, Marissa went outside, where Brandon stood with the twins, attempting to keep them in line until they got the cue to start the walk down the aisle.

Maddie, a basket of flower petals in her hand, spotted Marissa first. "Is it time yet?"

"Yeah," Jimmy said. "I want to take off my bow. And I can't do it until after that man and lady kiss."

Rather than answer the twins, Marissa turned to their daddy, who was probably ready to get this show on the road, too. "I'm afraid there's a problem. Not a bad one. A joyful one. Sort of. I'm sure everything will be okay…" She was rambling, and she knew it.

"What's going on?" he asked.

"Callie's water just broke, and Ramon has taken her to the hospital."

"Wow." Brandon combed his hand through his hair, leaving it looking stylishly mussed instead of military crisp.

"Did she get cut really bad?" Jimmy asked. "When the glass broke and she spilled the water?"

Marissa placed a hand on his head. "No, honey. She didn't get cut. She's going to the hospital because it's time for her to have her babies."

Brandon blew out a sigh. "Is there something I can do?"

"Actually, there is."

"I'm not on duty, but I can call the substation and get them a police escort."

"I think Ramon beat you to that." She took a deep, fortifying breath. "We need a stand-in for the best man."

Brandon furrowed his brow. "Surely you don't mean *me*?"

"Yes, I do. I'm going to cover for Callie. And Ramon has already handled all the best man duties. So all you have to do is stand next to Clay at the gazebo and look supportive and happy for him."

"I *am* happy for him, but what about one of Clay's Texas friends? Or even one of the other attorneys in his firm? Hell, he's got two brothers here. Why not ask one of them?"

"I suggested those alternatives, too. But Clay wanted to keep the wedding fairly small, so he didn't invite any of his friends. And he was in private practice, so he doesn't have any coworkers. On top of that, he isn't very close to either of his brothers and, even if he was, he doesn't want to choose one over the other. He'd prefer to have a local friend."

Brandon couldn't hide his disbelief. "But I'm *not* a friend."

"Not yet. But he's a great guy. And now that he and Alana own the neighboring ranch, he's a big landowner in town. I'm sure you'll be friends before you know it. So what do you say?"

Brandon had no idea what to say, but he knew how important this event was to her. And they'd just lost the best man and the matron of honor in one fell swoop. But if the wedding was a success in spite of that, word would spread in the community, and she'd earn a name for herself as a wedding planner.

He glanced down at the twins, who were gazing at him as if he had all the answers. He looked at the anxious wedding planner, then checked his wristwatch. "The ceremony should be taking place right now. I'm not dressed appropriately, and it's too late for me to find a tux."

"You look fine. Nice. Perfect."

A guitar sounded from the gazebo, where the pastor's wife sat off to the side, providing soft music.

Brandon let out a sigh. He guessed he'd have to take one for the team. "What do I have to do?" he asked.

"You attended the rehearsal last night. So all you need to do is to join Clay inside the house. The two of you will stroll out to the gazebo together. I'll take the twins inside and tell Alana it's time to walk down the aisle. Then I'll pick up Callie's bouquet, and the rest will go on as planned."

And she was right. Minutes later, Clay had loaned Brandon a black bolo tie. And now they both stood in front of the gazebo, to the left of the Pastor Jennings, a tall, jovial young minister in his early thirties.

As Maddie and Jimmy walked down the aisle, just like they'd practiced last night, Brandon damn near popped a button on his white shirt, even though Maddie was dropping clumps of flower petals instead of tossing them lightly, and the satin pillow Jimmy held listed to the side. Fortunately someone had tied the ring on top.

Marissa followed the twins, smiling as if she didn't have a care in the world. But heck, why shouldn't she be happy? She'd just handled her first mishap, and no one outside of the wedding party was the wiser.

She looked lovely today in a summery sundress with a pale green background and a floral print. Her hair was swept up in an intricate twist, revealing two sparkling studs—the topaz gemstones her father had given her. She whispered a silent thank-you to Brandon when she reached the front.

He might have continued to gawk at her, but Stacy, Pastor Jennings's wife, got to her feet and struck a different guitar chord, alerting the crowd that the bride was coming. Instead of the traditional wedding march, she played "Forever and Ever, Amen," a classic country tune made popular by Randy Travis.

Adam Hastings walked Alana down the aisle, and the ceremony began.

Moments later, after Pastor Jennings pronounced Clay and Alana husband and wife, they kissed—sweetly, lovingly and with the promise of a long and happy life together. Then they proceeded down the aisle. Brandon offered Marissa his arm, and she took it. As they followed the bride and groom, it took all he had not to glance over his shoulder to make sure Maddie and Jimmy were taking up the rear, just as they'd practiced.

They'd no more than reached the last row of chairs when Jimmy let out a happy shriek. "Whoo-hoo! We did it! Daddy and Marissa got married, too."

The wedding guests burst into laughs and giggles. And Brandon merely shook his head. He never knew what one of his youngsters was going to say next. He'd have to correct that misunderstanding before the Fairborn rumor mill kicked into high gear.

But with all the excitement, not to mention the love in the air, he couldn't help having a few romantic thoughts of his own. He turned to Marissa, her fingers still holding his arm, and smiled. "Do you have plans for tomorrow?"

"What do you have in mind?" she asked.

"How about a picnic at the park. With the kids."

Her golden-brown eyes lit up, and a smile spread across her pretty face, dimpling her cheeks. "I'd love that."

So would Brandon.

Chapter Ten

The wedding had gone off without a hitch, other than the mad dash Ramon and Callie had made to the hospital. By the time the cake had been cut, Ramon called to let Alana know that his and Callie's newborns had arrived, and that mama and babies were doing great. Talk about happy endings! And new beginnings, Brandon thought the next afternoon, as he and Marissa watched Maddie and Jimmy play at the park. A warm, bright sun and a cool breeze made it a perfect day for a picnic. He would have picked up hamburgers or a pizza, but Marissa had insisted on making their lunch: turkey sandwiches for the adults and peanut butter and jelly for the kids. She'd also packed a thermos of iced tea, juice boxes, fruit slices and homemade chocolate-chip cookies for dessert.

Maddie and Jimmy had played for a while, eaten lunch and then run back to the playground, where they were now taking turns going up and down the slide.

Brandon stole a glance at Marissa, who sat beside him on a blanket she'd spread on the grass. She wore a red top and a pair of white shorts that revealed shapely, tanned legs. Yet it was the expression on her pretty face that caught his rapt attention, the delight she seemed to take in watching his children play. Then her smile faded, and she turned to him.

The breeze whipped a couple strands of dark hair across her eyes, and she brushed them aside. "Alana and Clay will be in Hawaii for the next two weeks. While they're gone, would you mind if I invited Jimmy and Maddie to spend a day with me at the ranch? I could show them the horses, dogs and chickens. And maybe we could make cookies."

She wanted to spend the day with the twins? She hadn't included him, so the question surprised him, and he didn't immediately respond.

"If you're not ready for something like that," she said, "I understand. And we don't need to set a date. Maybe sometime. I mean, in the future."

"Sure. Someday. If you're sure they won't be too much for you."

"Seriously? I'd really enjoy having them around. We could play games. And color pictures. Whatever."

"They'd probably like that," he said.

She nodded, then returned her gaze to the playground, where Maddie and Jimmy had moved from the slide to a dome-shaped jungle gym, but her expression remained pensive. He was tempted to say something that might draw another wistful smile. But before he could come up with something, she turned to him and asked, "Are the kids ever too much for you?"

"I must admit, when they were babies, it wasn't easy, and I hardly slept. And even now, they can be a handful at times. They really keep me hopping, especially with all their questions. But I can't imagine what my life would be without them."

"Lonely, I suppose."

"You got that right." He shot another glance her way, wondering if maybe she was lonely at times, if that's what she'd been thinking about. Growing up without a sibling. Losing her father. Facing the criminal-justice system on her own.

At times, he supposed, he was lonely, too. Not that he didn't have a loving family. He stole another look at Marissa. What would his life be like if she were to become a part of it, even just a small part?

"Will you tell me about their mother?" she asked.

He hadn't been prepared to talk about Julie. And most people, other than his family, had never asked.

"I don't mean to be nosy," Marissa added. "I just…wondered about her."

"She was a fine-arts major. I met her after my return to college. I'd just changed my major from business to criminal justice." It had been a better fit for a guy who had a protective streak and who believed in truth and justice.

"Did you love her?" Marissa asked. "I guess that's pretty obvious that you did."

"I thought so. But in retrospect, it was lust." And on both of their parts. The beautiful, sexy, blonde city girl had swept him off his cowboy boots. "When she got pregnant, I offered to marry her, but she refused. I stuck by her during her pregnancy and was at the hospital when the twins were born."

"You're a wonderful father."

He shrugged. "I try to be."

"You really are. I've seen you interact with them. I suspect that on your worst day, you're better than most parents on their best."

He hoped so. "Thanks for the vote of confidence."

"It's hard to imagine you, as a college student, raising two newborns on your own."

"Julie was more involved back then. At first, anyway. And I tried to do my best to help her—and not just financially. I watched the babies for her whenever she was in class. In fact, after a while, I realized that I had them more often than she did." Damn, he loved those kids. Even when they were crying and he couldn't figure out why. Walking the floor with them. Talking to tiny babies who didn't understand a word he said but seemed to feel what was in his heart. "I could never understand why she wasn't as attached to them as I was."

He shot another glance at Marissa, saw the way she'd scrunched her brow in thought. "Does she come around to see them? To visit?"

"No, she's not involved with them at all." He still found it hard to believe Julie could just walk away from her babies the way she had. "Right before their first birthday, she told me she'd hooked up with an old boyfriend, a guy who'd spent time in jail and had just been released."

"That must have been a tough blow," Marissa said, her tone soft, compassionate. Yet her brow remained furrowed, her demeanor pensive.

"My aunt and uncle believed children needed

both a mother and a father. I agreed, at least in theory. But in this case, I knew what my children didn't need. And that was a stepfather prone to criminal behavior."

Marissa nodded her agreement.

Still, Brandon hadn't meant to dwell on the past, to spill his guts like that. So he changed the subject. "Hey, did you hear they're opening up a new organic grocery in town?"

"Oh, really?"

Before either of them could continue the small talk, the twins ran up and asked if they could have another cookie. Marissa looked at Brandon, waiting for his approval.

"Sure," he said.

Marissa reached into the basket she'd brought and passed out two more cookies, and the kids dashed off. But for the rest of the afternoon, she remained fairly quiet. He supposed she was probably thinking about Julie, about the relationship they'd had, the way it had ended. And to be honest, the past was weighing on his mind, too.

Thankfully, Marissa hadn't let her pensive mood affect her interactions with Jimmy and Maddie. She continued to answer their questions and be attentive to their chatter. So he didn't let the fact that she'd clammed up when it came to their adult interactions bother him too much.

At least, when it did, he didn't let it show.

* * *

Marissa spent a lonely evening by herself at the ranch. With Alana and Clay on their honeymoon, the house was quiet. Even Ella, who'd moved in a couple of weeks ago, was either working or visiting a friend, although Marissa wasn't sure who it was. Just that it was someone she'd met at the market.

And since Katie Johnson, the young college student who lived in one of the outbuildings with her two younger brothers, had taken the boys to Missoula for a short summer vacation, Marissa was the only one at home.

There was nothing to distract her from thinking about the afternoon she'd spent with Brandon and his sweet kids. Jimmy and Maddie had tugged at her heartstrings, and for the first time, Brandon was opening up about being a single dad. But then she'd let her curiosity blow the day all to heck. Why in the world had she brought up the twins' mother? His response had sent her into a blue funk that was nearly impossible to kick.

She'd been able to handle the fact that he'd once cared about the woman. He'd stuck by her, even when she hadn't stuck by her own children. But when Brandon admitted that he hadn't wanted the felon the kids' mother loved to have any influence over Maddie and Jimmy, it felt as if her whole world, all her hopes and dreams, had suddenly fallen apart.

And while Marissa could certainly understand his concern, she'd realized that he might never fully trust her. Had he truly believed her explanation about her own incarceration?

When she'd asked about having the children spend the day with her at the ranch, for example, he hadn't jumped on the idea. And she wasn't going to bring it up again.

Monday was just as quiet and lonely, but she spent the day doing chores around the house and taking care of the garden—watering, weeding and picking the produce. She'd hoped Brandon would call her, but he hadn't. And she wasn't about to make the mistake of calling him.

There was no getting away from her past, she told herself as she stabbed a tool into a flower bed's soil. If Brandon couldn't deal with her unwarranted time in jail, well, okay. She'd need to accept it and move on. But truth be told, she didn't want to.

On Tuesday, as usual, she spent the morning working at Darla's. As soon as she arrived at the doughnut shop, her boss removed her apron. "I'm glad you're here. I have plenty of doughnuts, pastries and sweets made to last the morning, so I hope you don't mind if I cut out early. I have a migraine coming on. I need to go home, take some medication and try to sleep it off."

"No problem." Marissa had never been prone to headaches, but she'd heard migraines could be brutal. "I'll cover for you. And I'll lock up at two."

The morning began as usual, until a FedEx truck pulled up in front. The driver delivered an overnight delivery, a legal-size envelope addressed to Fred Garrison, Darla's husband. Marissa signed for it, then called Darla's house.

Fred answered on the second ring, the television blaring in the background. "Hello? Marissa? Hang on just a minute while I turn down the TV."

When the volume lowered, he asked if something was wrong.

"No," Marissa said. "Everything is fine here at the shop. But FedEx just delivered a large envelope for you. It looks important."

"You don't say." Fred cleared his throat. "I wasn't expecting that paperwork until later this week. But I'm glad it's there."

"I'd be happy to bring it to you after I lock up for the day," Marissa said. "Unless it can't wait. I can lock up the shop temporarily. Otherwise, I'll drop it off around two fifteen."

"It can wait until then. And thanks for bringing it to me. I'd really appreciate that. I'm supposed to stay off my foot, and Darla's taking a nap."

"Can she sleep through the telephone and television noise?"

"Yep. She's upstairs and all the way down the hall."

Good to know. "All right, then. I'll see you this afternoon."

As planned, Marissa locked up the doughnut shop a couple of minutes after two. Then, since she was still borrowing the ranch pickup until tomorrow, she drove the short distance to the Garrisons' house, which was located in a fairly new development, just off Oak Tree Drive.

She pulled along the curb, parked in front of Darla and Fred's two-story home and carried the package to the front door. Instead of ringing the bell, she knocked lightly.

"Come on in," Fred hollered.

Marissa opened the door and stepped into the spacious living room, where Fred sat in a brown leather recliner, his feet elevated. She crossed the room and handed him the envelope. "Here you go, Fred."

He thanked her, then proceeded to open it.

Marissa scanned the living room, noting the TV tray that sat next to Fred, the empty water glass, the dirty plate that must have held his lunch. "Can I get you anything while I'm here? A fresh glass of water?"

He looked up from his reading. "That'd sure be nice. Thank you."

She nodded, then scooped up the dishes and carried them to the kitchen, which was more than a little untidy. She prepared a glass of ice water, then after delivering it to Fred, she returned to clean up the mess neither Fred nor Darla should worry about today. She loaded the dishwasher, then filled the sink with hot soapy water and washed the pots and pans.

After she tidied up the kitchen, she used the soapy water in the sink to wipe down the counters. When she was satisfied with her work, she noticed a glass vase next to the stovetop.

A wistful smile crossed her lips. Her dad used to have one like that. A cut-glass Waterford vase that had been a wedding present. She wondered what had become of it. Suzanne had probably kept it without considering Marissa might want it to remember her parents by.

Oh, well. There wasn't anything she could do about that. But nevertheless, Darla's vase deserved to shine. The bouquet of flowers it once held had left a green, grungy film on the inside. So she carried it to the sink. As she lowered it into the water, it slipped from her grasp. She tried to catch it as it dropped, but it hit the edge of the sink and broke upon impact.

"Shoot!"

When she fished the broken pieces from the water, she cut her hand and pain seared through her. "Ow! Dang it."

She snatched her hand from the sink, but not before realizing the cut was deep. The water was tinged pink. She reached for a wad of paper towels and held them to the wound, but it bled through immediately. "Oh, man." She applied pressure over the one-inch gash to the side of her right hand, hoping that would help.

It didn't take a paramedic or a triage nurse to tell her she needed stitches. And that she'd have to drive herself to the clinic.

What luck. And now she'd need to tap into her savings to pay a medical bill. She'd also have to replace the vase. Could this week get any worse?

After settling a public disturbance at Town Square Park, which turned out to be an angry mother of a teenage boy challenging a bigger boy who'd been bullying him, Brandon headed toward his squad car, which he'd parked along the curb near the ball fields.

He was about to climb behind the wheel when he glanced across the street and spotted a familiar old pickup in one of the last parking spaces in front of the two-story redbrick medical building. Any of the Fairborn locals would recognize Jack McGee's old truck anywhere. If Alana was in Hawaii with her new husband, there was only one other person who might be driving it. His assumption proved true when he spotted Marissa heading toward the pickup, a purse slung over her shoulder.

They hadn't talked since the picnic on Sunday, and while he'd been a little hesitant in calling her afterward, he couldn't very well ignore her now. Neither did he want to. Instead of climbing into his squad car, he crossed the street and approached her.

"Hey," he called out.

She looked up and froze in mid-step. When their eyes met, she wore a suspect-in-the-headlights expression. He'd seen others do the same thing when they spotted him in uniform, most of them guilty about something. Odd, he thought. Then again, it probably had more to do with the conversation they'd had on Sunday afternoon.

His gaze lowered, and he noticed that she was holding a gauze-covered hand protectively against her chest. She'd apparently been hurt and must have come out of one of the medical offices.

His brow furrowed. "What happened?"

Her expression softened. She removed her injured hand from her chest. While holding it upright, she turned it slightly and looked at it. "This? Cut it on broken glass. It's not serious, but it needed a few stitches."

"Are you able to drive?" he asked.

"It's not a stick shift, so I can manage." She offered him a weak smile, yet her stance remained a little stiff. A little cool. Apparently, whatever had unsettled her on Sunday still bothered her.

"Is everything okay?" he asked.

"Sure." She offered up a smile. A really fake one.

Something was definitely off. Or rather, it was still off. She'd been pretty quiet on the ride home from the picnic, although she'd responded to the kids. Yet whatever had been wrong a couple of days ago seemed worse now, and he couldn't help thinking he was to blame.

Dammit. He should have called. It's not like he hadn't thought about her constantly.

Should he let her go? The radio he wore clipped to his belt squawked, signaling an incoming police call.

"You're busy," she said. "I'll see you around."

"We'll talk later, okay?"

"You bet." She didn't look at him, though. She just dug into her purse and pulled out the keys with her good hand.

He let her go. For now, anyway. Hell, he didn't have another choice. But tonight, after he got off duty, picked up the kids from preschool and asked Mrs. Hendrix to feed them dinner, he'd go to Rancho Esperanza and talk to her.

He answered the call and half listened as he watched her walk away, her steps quick. She unlocked the pickup and climbed inside.

It was time to have the chat with Marissa that he should have had before now.

Betty Sue had been seated in front of her favorite slot machine when Ralph came in and surprised the hell out of everyone at the market.

"Come on, honey. It's time. Please don't argue with me." Ralph slipped his arms around his wife and nuzzled her neck. "Let's trade in that minivan you've been driving and buy a new car for you."

Betty Sue damn near fell off her stool. "Well, run me over with an Oscar Mayer Wienermobile."

"Honey," Carlene said, "I really appreciate your suggestion. But I have two kids to haul around."

"You don't need a school bus to do that," Ralph said.

"Can I help you pick it out?" Betty Sue asked. "Carlene needs something red and sporty. Like a Porsche or a Corvette."

"Absolutely not," Carlene said. "But maybe something safe with a big back seat."

Yee-haw! Betty reached for her purse. "I'll go with you."

"Actually," Ralph said, "I'd rather you stayed here with Ella. I want to take Carlene to a late lunch."

Fair enough, Betty thought, although she didn't need a caretaker. If it was anyone other than Ella, she might have raised a stink. But she and the young woman had a connection.

So off the two lovebirds went. Betty Sue returned to her slot machine, and Ella straightened the shelves and rang up what few customers came in.

About forty-five minutes later, Ella said, "I'm going to the stockroom, Betty Sue. Will you watch the register for me?"

"You bet I will, sweetie." That's what Betty Sue liked about Ella. She didn't treat her with kid gloves, didn't treat her as if she was old and unable to look out for herself.

Betty Sue slid off her stool and made her way to the front counter. She'd no more than reached the register when a red pickup drove up. It had gun racks in back, which wasn't at all unusual around here. But when she spotted the driver, a big bulky guy wearing a sleeveless shirt, a chill wriggled down her spine. Apparently, his phone rang, and when he took a moment to answer it, Betty Sue snapped a picture of the guy with her cell, then she opened the register and removed a handful of cash and Ralph's extra set of keys. Then she hurried as fast as her arthritic knees would allow, ignoring the pain, and made it to the stockroom seconds later, huffing and puffing like an antique steam engine.

Ella looked up, the start of a smile forming on her face until she spotted Betty Sue. "What's wrong?"

"I think your jerk of a husband is out front." She showed the girl the picture.

Ella's face, as fair as she was, drained of color. "Oh, my god. He found me."

"That's what I thought." Betty Sue shoved Ralph's key fob into Ella's hand. "Get your purse, go into the bathroom and climb out the window. Take that truck and drive to the airport. Then use the cash to buy a ticket on the first flight out of Kalispell you can find. You're always welcome to come back when you feel safe."

Ella's whole body, as slender and frail as it was, shook so hard she could hardly grip the black fob. She started to move to the restroom, then hesitated. "I don't want to leave you here with him."

Betty Sue waved her off. "Get out of here. Stick Ralph's keys under the floor mat, and call me when you get someplace safe. I'll take care of things here."

Ella didn't argue. She took her bag from the shelf and slung it across her body. Then she stuffed the cash inside.

"Now, get a move on," Betty Sue said. "Circle around back and take the north road."

Ella hurried to the restroom with Betty Sue hobbling to keep up with her and watching as she tried to open the window. "Go. And be careful."

"It won't open."

The window was stuck. As Ella desperately tried to force it open, the glass broke. A shard nicked her hand as it fell to the floor. "Ow!"

"Dammit. Told you to be careful." Betty Sue took off her headscarf and wrapped it around Ella's palm. "I'll clean up. Get that dang window open and skedaddle."

Ella fought with the window frame until it finally gave way, providing an escape route. As she scurried out, Betty Sue closed the bathroom door and hobbled back to the front of the store, where the big ol' brute stood at the counter. "Hello, sir. How can I help you?"

"I'm looking for a woman."

"Sorry. Don't let the slot machine fool you. This isn't that kind of place."

"I'm not looking for *that* kind of woman." He handed over a photograph of Ella, blond hair hanging loose and free. "Have you seen *this* one?"

"Hmmm." Betty Sue pretended to study it long and hard. Ella had made some changes to her hair color and had cut it, but someone might still recognize the resemblance. "I think…maybe I did. A little gal who looked a lot like this stopped in a couple weeks ago. She asked for directions to Canada. Said she got a job and was relocating."

Ella's abuser glanced at the open register. In Betty's haste to grab the hundreds and fifties from under the till, she'd left the damned thing open. Plenty of fives, tens and twenties were still there, free for the taking.

Did the big brute plan to rob the market? Just in case, Betty reached for the gun Ralph kept behind the counter. Before she could raise it to scare him off, he grabbed it from her and gave her a shove. She lost her balance and fell. Her head struck the cigarette case hard and… She saw a glitter of stars until the lights went out completely.

Chapter Eleven

Brandon didn't get flustered during a crime report and investigation, but this was different. This was his aunt and uncle and the only real family he had.

When Dispatch had called him and reported Tip Top Market had been robbed and that one of the clerks, a female, had been assaulted and was unconscious, his heart nearly dropped to the pavement, and he couldn't get into his squad car fast enough.

Brandon arrived at the market just as the ambulance was pulling out. When he saw his aunt and uncle standing in the yard watching the paramedics pull away, lights flashing, siren roaring, he was relieved. Thank God the injured clerk wasn't Carlene. It must be the new woman they'd hired.

He felt badly that their new employee had been injured. Maybe her job application would reveal her next of kin, someone who would be worried about her.

Carlene was in tears, and she slumped into Ralph's embrace. Money and stolen property could be replaced. He was glad the couple was safe. And that they had each other to lean on at a time like this.

As Brandon got out of the squad car, Ralph, his lip quivering, said, "I'm glad you're the one on duty today. When I asked the 9-1-1 operator who would be coming, she wouldn't say."

"What happened?"

"We left Ella, our new employee, in charge of the store and Betty Sue," Ralph said. "Then we came home to find Betty Sue bleeding and unconscious. Ella's gone. And so is my new truck. There's money missing from the register."

Ella? The woman his aunt and uncle insisted was working out well? That she tried hard, that she was good to Aunt Betty Sue?

He'd had a weird vibe about Ella when he learned Marissa and Alana had let a virtual stranger move in with them. "Did you talk to the references she listed on her job application? Did they give you any reason to be leery about hiring her?"

"I… Well, we didn't call anyone. Marissa vouched for her, and that seemed good enough for us."

"You should have called me," Brandon said.

"We didn't want to bother you. You've got the kids, a house, a job."

But background checks were a big part of his job.

"I never imagined this could happen," Carlene said. "Ella seemed to be responsible."

She certainly *did* seem responsible.

"All the large bills were stolen," Ralph said, "as well as some of the small ones. She took my keys, too."

"Who? Ella?" Brandon's brow furrowed.

Carlene clicked her tongue. "We aren't sure who did this. I just can't believe it was Ella. She wouldn't hurt Betty Sue. The two of them have gotten very close. In fact, Ella even comes to visit Betty Sue at the house. I know that there's a fifty-year age difference between them, but they like to go for walks together or hang out in Betty Sue's bedroom and chat and laugh."

Ralph huffed. "Maybe Ella was planning this all along, and Betty Sue got in the way. You just never know about people."

"No," Carlene said. "It wasn't her. Those two are kind of like a couple of teenage friends."

"*Friends* don't do things like this, honey."

Brandon agreed, but he kept his thoughts to himself.

Ralph placed a kiss on Carlene's brow. "I love you to pieces, but you've always been a little too trusting."

Brandon scanned the parking lot. The only vehicle there was a red Lexus SUV, the registration still taped to the windshield. "Whose car is that?"

"Your aunt's," Ralph said. "I just bought it for her today. That's where we were when this happened. At the dealership in Kalispell. Then we had lunch at a little French café she likes. When we got back here, we found Betty Sue unconscious and bleeding. Damn."

Right now, the perp was looking at charges of robbery, felony assault and grand theft auto. And, if Betty Sue died—God forbid—there'd be a felony murder charge. And like it or not, Ella, Betty Sue's new BFF, was a suspect. That is, unless the culprit had taken Ella with him against her will.

Brandon called Dispatch and asked them to send the crime-scene investigator out, then he told his aunt and uncle to wait in the parking lot while he entered the market.

Inside, he spotted the register, the till wide open. A few bills had been scattered on the floor.

Broken glass from the cigarette cabinet glistened in the overhead light. His stomach twisted. A puddle of Betty Sue's blood covered the floor.

Ralph's gun lay next to where Betty Sue had landed. Why hadn't the perp taken it? Had Betty Sue tried to use it in an attempt to defend herself?

Brandon made his way through the market, walking up and down the aisles. Nothing seemed to be out of place. He then entered the stockroom, which looked okay. The playroom his aunt and uncle had created for the kids appeared tidy.

He opened the bathroom door. The window was busted open. Most of the glass was outside, which meant whoever broke it was in the bathroom at the time. Why'd the perp exit that way? To avoid any possible surveillance cameras?

Too bad there weren't any. Brandon had wanted Ralph to put in a system, but he'd refused, saying they didn't need one, that folks around here were trustworthy.

It was also possible that a customer had driven up during the robbery and the perp or kidnapper wanted to escape unnoticed. Then again, why hadn't that customer called 9-1-1?

He stepped closer to the window and spotted blood on the glass, which meant the crime-scene investigator would swab it for DNA, as well as dusting for fingerprints.

He returned to the parking lot, where he found

his aunt and uncle. Ralph had just ended a phone call. His face was white, and his hands shook. "That was the ER doctor. Aunt Betty Sue suffered a very serious injury. They're still running tests, but they'll be putting her into a drug-induced coma to allow her brain to heal."

Carlene covered her mouth and choked back a sob. "I need to be at the hospital. I want to be there when she wakes up."

At her age, a fall and an injury like that could be life-altering, if not fatal.

"What do you know about your new employee?" he asked.

"Her name is Ella Perry," Ralph said. "She's twenty-seven. I'll get her job application for you. I can't remember where she came from, but she lives at Rancho Esperanza now."

He'd planned to stop by the ranch after work today so he could talk to Marissa. But he'd be heading over there now—on an official visit.

Before arriving at Rancho Esperanza, Brandon had gone over the job application Ella had filled out. But when he tried to verify her previous address and other significant details, he came up empty-handed. Ella Perry, if that was her real name, had lied. And sadly, his aunt and uncle had failed to call any of her references, which was too bad because she'd made them all up—names, addresses and phone numbers.

He'd been tempted to scold them for both being too trusting, for not being more careful, but a lot of good that would do after the fact. Besides, he should have been more involved in their hiring practices. He would have, if he hadn't cut back on their childcare hours. He'd thought he'd been doing them a favor.

Damn. Who asked for references, then failed to follow through on contacting them?

Either way, he was at Rancho Esperanza now. He knocked at the door, and moments later Marissa answered. Her pretty eyes widened at the sight of him, and while he felt an initial compulsion to offer her a friendly smile, this visit wasn't likely to be very friendly.

"I'm looking for Ella Perry," he said.

Marissa stiffened. "Is she in some kind of trouble?"

"I'm not sure. She's a person of interest in a robbery and an assault."

"Ella wouldn't do that," Marissa said.

"How do you know?"

"I just do. She's sweet and gentle to the point of almost being timid. If I'd had even the slightest concern about her honesty, I wouldn't have taken her to meet your aunt and uncle."

Was Marissa somehow involved? He hated to

think that, but he had to put his personal feelings aside and do his job.

He thought about the background check Greg had his P.I. friend run on her.

I hate to have to tell you this, Greg had said, *but Marissa Garcia has a record... Drug charge. Transporting. A year in county jail. After her probation was up, she moved away from San Diego. She's lived in Bakersfield, as well as Reno and Boise, and eventually landed in Fairborn.*

The same questions Brandon had that night came to mind. Why had she made so many moves? Why hadn't she stayed in one place very long?

Marissa opened the screen door and walked out onto the porch. Was there a reason she hadn't invited him in? One that had nothing to do with the chill he'd sensed when they'd gone to the park with the kids?

He glanced at her bandaged hand. Earlier today, before the call came in, he'd asked her what had happened.

Cut it on broken glass. It's not serious, but it needed a few stitches.

But what kind of glass? Had it been a broken window?

Could she be involved in the robbery at the market? With Ella?

No, that wasn't possible. Was it?

"Where were you this afternoon?" he asked. "Before you cut your hand?"

She paled, the color draining from her face, and her lips parted. "What are you suggesting, Brandon?"

"Someone robbed the market today."

Her jaw dropped. "And you think *I* was involved?"

"I'm just doing my job, Marissa. I'm investigating a robbery and an assault."

She swallowed, and her brow furrowed. "Who was assaulted?"

"Betty Sue. Someone knocked her unconscious, robbed the till and took off in my uncle's new truck."

"Oh, no! Not Betty Sue." Sympathy for the elderly woman soon gave way to the realization of what he'd implied. "And you actually think *I* had something to do with her getting hurt?"

"All I know is that Ella is missing. She's your friend, and you helped her get the job at the market. And there was a broken, blood-smeared window that was all in one piece when Ralph and Carlene left Ella in charge."

Marissa lifted her injured hand and shook it at him. "I worked at Darla's this morning. And when I locked up the shop, I delivered some paperwork to her husband, Fred. While I was there, I tidied up the kitchen and broke a crystal vase. So I have a valid alibi, Officer. Darla had gone to bed with a migraine and was asleep, but Fred Garrison can vouch for my whereabouts earlier today. He can also tell you how and where I cut my hand."

"All right," he said. "I'll talk to him. While I'm here, would you mind stepping aside and letting me take a look in Ella's room?"

She stiffened and folded her arms across her chest, taking care not to bump her bad hand. "Where's your warrant?"

"You don't have to get so defensive. I'm just doing my job. And looking out for my family."

"I got that. Loud and clear. So unless you have any other questions, Officer Dodd, I'm going to go back inside the house."

If she was as innocent as she claimed, he wouldn't blame her for being mad. But he still had to check out her alibi to be sure. He didn't mean to upset her, but he couldn't give her a free pass until his job was done.

Marissa felt like slamming the door in Brandon's face, but she kept her cool. Once it clicked shut and she turned the dead bolt, tears filled her eyes and streamed down her face.

He'd actually thought she might be involved in a robbery and an assault. But then again, why wouldn't he question her now? He'd run a background check on her already. Once a criminal, always a criminal, right?

She leaned her back against the door and slid down to the floor.

The cold, hard truth hit her like an avalanche, crushing her, making it hard to breathe. Brandon hadn't believed her when she'd told him she hadn't committed a crime. Clearly, he was never going to trust or believe her. And worse, anytime a crime happened in Fairborn, Marissa would be his first suspect. Always.

She'd paid her debt to society, one she'd never owed. Yet that didn't matter to Brandon.

And to think she'd actually flirted with the idea of dating him, of falling in love with him.

The ache in her heart tightened into a knot. Who was she kidding? She'd been dangerously close to falling in love with him, and even now, she couldn't ignore that fact. She shook her head. No, she was in love with him already. Dang it.

But Brandon had just burst her dream as if he'd poked a needle into a bright red balloon.

Marissa stood and wiped her face with her sleeves. She and Brandon were over. So she just had to put it behind her like every other unfair thing that had happened to her. But that wouldn't be easy. This betrayal, this pain was different. And she feared she would carry the heartache for a long, long time.

And what was more, Ella was missing. Betty Sue was gravely injured. And in her heart of hearts, Marissa knew Ella would never injure her friend.

It might be dinnertime, but she'd just lost her appetite.

A glass of wine sounded good. Not that she'd drown her sorrows. As she headed for the kitchen, her cell phone rang. She snatched it off the counter, not even bothering to look at the display. She assumed it was Brandon and answered without saying hello. "There's nothing to talk about."

"Yes, there is," Erik said. "Please don't hang up, Marissa."

Her blasted stepbrother. What was he doing calling her? Her fingers trembled, and she nearly dropped the phone. Erik had always been a charmer with a wild side. He'd been so good at snowballing their parents, and they'd never suspected a thing. Still, she'd actually looked up to the guy back then. That is, before he let her take the heat for a crime he'd committed.

"What do you want, Erik? I should just hang up on you."

"Please don't. I know you hate me, and I don't blame you. It was so wrong, so very wrong, for me to let you take the heat for the pills and the pot in the trunk. I had a serious drug problem back then, but last year, I joined Narcotics Anonymous."

Good for you, jerk. You didn't just ruin a year of my life, you've screwed up my future, too.

"I'm following the 12-Step Program. And I'd like to make amends with the people I've hurt—you being the one I hurt the most."

Great. Now he was using her to feel better about what he'd done. As if *I'm sorry* would erase all she'd gone through and the harm he'd caused.

"You're forgiven," she snapped. Now maybe he'd leave her alone. If he didn't, she'd change her number.

"Thanks. I know you'll need time to process this, and you may never truly forgive me. Maybe we can talk more about it at another time. But don't hang up. That's not the only reason I called."

Did Suzanne or his father die? Did he want to invite her to the funeral? Ha! Fat chance of that. She wouldn't attend, even if they lived across town, rather than fifteen hundred miles away.

Erik continued. "Did you know your father had set up an irrevocable life-insurance trust for you before he died?"

Her brow furrowed, and she clutched the cell tight. "What are you talking about?"

"Your dad's attorney called Suzanne. Once you turned twenty-five, the money was to be divided between the two of you."

"I had no idea." With the phone still pressed

against her ear, she walked to the sofa and plopped down.

"The lawyer said your father was well aware of the fact that you and Suzanne didn't get along very well."

"To say the least."

"Apparently," Erik said, "the trust was created out of your father's life-insurance policy. Your share is one hundred thousand dollars. But the money can't be divided until you both contact the bank in San Diego."

"Is this a joke? Another one of your schemes?"

"No, it's real." He paused. "I'm not like that anymore. I'm not."

She didn't respond. She wanted to believe him, but she couldn't make the leap.

After a few seconds of silence, he said, "Marissa? You still there?"

"Yeah, I need to wrap my head around this," Marissa said. "Can I give you a call tomorrow?"

"Sure. Anytime. I'll forward the info to you. What's your email address?"

She gave it to him, then he added, "Like I said, I'm really sorry."

"I heard you." It was the best response she could come up with since forgiveness wouldn't come easily.

She ended the call, trying to grasp all that Erik had told her, not just his admission of guilt and his apology. Had her father left her an unexpected gift?

Erik might be blowing smoke, but he'd seemed sincere. And the news finally began to sink in. One hundred thousand dollars.

If what he'd just told her was true, and that was still a big *if*, she'd have the money to pursue her dream of becoming a wedding planner. White Lace and Promises would soon become a reality, which was timely since she'd be able to build on the momentum from Alana and Clay's lovely wedding.

But the memory of Brandon standing on her porch in his sheriff uniform—and of his accusing gaze—washed over her. And she couldn't seem to muster any enthusiasm. Thanks to Brandon and his distrust of her, she couldn't join the Fairborn Chamber of Commerce because in a small town, the gossip would always be there. *Oh, Marissa Garcia? The woman Brandon dumped when he learned she'd spent time in jail? A criminal, no doubt.*

How could she possibly continue to live in Fairborn? This was Brandon's turf. And even if she could make a go of her business, even if she achieved success and community acceptance, she'd always be a criminal in the local deputy's eyes.

Marissa let out a groan and rubbed her eyes. Whine time. And time for a glass of wine.

She'd barely walked into the kitchen when her focus shifted from herself and anger at Brandon and Erik to concern for Ella.

The poor, battered woman. Was she safe?

Deep in Marissa's heart, she knew Ella wouldn't hurt Betty Sue. And she wasn't a thief. There had to be another explanation. Had someone else robbed the store and taken Ella hostage? That was possible, and Brandon had lost valuable time by not looking for her.

Then again, Doug Perry, Ella's abusive husband, might have found her. And if so, she was afraid he'd kill her, just as he swore he'd do if she ever left him again. Had she run away from him in desperation?

Marissa should have mentioned Ella's abuse to Brandon. Maybe she should call him now.

But what would she tell him? That Ella might be in jeopardy? That she wanted to file a missing-person report?

Yet that wouldn't explain the fact that Betty Sue had been severely injured. And that there'd been a robbery.

Her cell phone rang, drawing her from her thoughts. This time, she checked the display before answering.

"Thank God," Marissa uttered when she saw Ella's name. She didn't bother to say hello. "Where are you?"

"I'm in Seattle. I guess Betty Sue told you what happened. I was supposed to call her when I was safe, but her phone keeps rolling over to voice mail."

"Betty Sue is in the hospital. That's why she isn't answering."

Ella gasped. "Oh, no! What happened?"

"What do you mean *what happened?* I was going to ask you. You were there."

"She was fine when I left. Is she going to be okay?"

"I hope so. It's a head injury. I think it's pretty serious." Marissa let out a weary sigh. "What happened at the market today?"

Ella revealed the details, telling Marissa about Doug's arrival at the market, about Betty Sue warning her and insisting that she take Ralph's truck.

"I was so scared he would kill me. I would have frozen in fear, but Betty Sue took charge and told me what to do. Can you please let Ralph know that I left the pickup in the parking lot at the airport in Kalispell? Stall fifty-five. The keys are under the floor mat."

"Yes, of course. I'll tell him." Marissa combed the fingers of her good hand through her hair. "Brandon is investigating the incident as a robbery and an assault."

"Doug may be a brute, and he might have hurt

Betty Sue, but he's not a thief. At least, I don't think so."

"You have to call Brandon and explain what happened."

"I can't. My phone is about to die, and I don't have a charger. I'll have to buy one."

"Okay. But can you describe Doug? Do you know where he might have gone?"

Marissa took notes while Ella provided Doug's full name, date of birth and address. "I'll text you pictures of him standing beside his pickup truck. Hopefully, the license plate will be visible. You can also check Betty Sue's cell phone. She took a picture of him while he was outside the market."

"I'll handle it. Did you get a hotel room?"

No answer. "Ella?"

Ella's phone was dead. But thank God *she* was alive. That was the best news Marissa had heard all day. She now had the information Brandon needed to find the real culprit and to clear Ella's name. And hers, too.

But it wouldn't repair Marissa's relationship with Brandon. Or allow her to remain in Fairborn any longer. At this point, she needed another fresh start.

Chapter Twelve

Brandon had just put the twins to bed when he got a call from Marissa. He had no idea what she had on her mind, although he hoped she'd tell him she was sorry she'd gotten angry at him and that she understood he was just investigating a crime in which the victims had been his family members.

Okay. Maybe he hadn't handled the interview very well. But getting the facts sometimes meant being tough.

"Hey," he said. "What's up?"

"I heard from Ella. She left your uncle's pickup

in the parking lot at the airport in Kalispell. The keys are under the mat."

Brandon hadn't seen that coming. "Ralph will be happy to hear that."

"She also told me what went down at the market today, although I doubt you'll take my word for it."

He probably ought to apologize, but he wasn't sorry for doing his job. "Why don't you start by telling me her version of the story." Of course, at this point, Ella's version was the only one he had to go on.

"I'll start by telling you that Ella is a victim of domestic violence. Her husband used to beat the crap out of her, and a couple of weeks ago, she finally ran away from him. But he came looking for her. Focus your investigation on Douglas Raymond Perry, who lives in Coeur d'Alene, Idaho. And if you don't want to take Ella's word for it, check Betty Sue's cell phone. Your aunt took a picture of him while he was standing outside the market. And once Ella is able to recharge her cell phone, she's going to send me some pictures of him. When she does, I'll forward them to you."

"Are you saying Ella's husband is responsible for the robbery?"

"I don't know about that. There might not have been a robbery. Ella said Betty Sue gave her the cash to escape, along with your uncle's keys. I have no idea what happened after that, but my guess is that Betty Sue and Doug Perry had a run-in at the cash register."

"I'll get right on it."

A cool silence filled the line until Marissa asked, "How's Betty Sue? Is she doing any better?"

"No. I talked to Ralph earlier. She's still in a medically induced coma, but the doctor mentioned that they may bring her out of it in a couple of days."

"I'm praying for her."

"Thank you. We appreciate that." He paused for a moment, trying to gather his thoughts, to say the right thing in the right way. Then he blew out a sigh. "I'm sorry if I hurt your feelings. It wasn't personal."

She waited a beat, then said, "It was personal for me. Apparently, you don't know me as well as you think you do."

Maybe not, but from what he'd learned so far, she'd been honest with him all along. And he hadn't trusted her.

"Like I said, I was just doing my job."

"Today, maybe. But running a background check on a woman you wanted to date? I think that's a little over the top. Maybe that's common procedure for cops, but it doesn't work for me."

It had been Greg's idea. But Brandon wasn't

going to blame anyone other than himself. He'd given Greg the okay. And any other excuse he might have had at the time escaped him now. "I'm sorry, Marissa. I was wrong."

"Yes, you were. Someday you're going to make a mistake, and when that happens, hopefully, whoever you've wronged will have a bigger heart than you have. And they'll be more willing to forgive."

"Can we start over?" he asked.

"We never got started," she said, her soft and weary tone tearing at his heart. "Good night, Brandon."

The line disconnected before he could respond.

The next morning, Marissa purchased an airline ticket and told Erik she was on her way. Even though she saw the flight to San Diego as a business trip and wasn't excited about sitting down in the same room with Suzanne, it was a good excuse to get out of town.

She packed light, since she wasn't going to stay any longer than necessary. After placing a second pair of jeans into her overnight bag, she reached into the closet to remove a white blouse. She'd just begun to fold it when her cell phone rang. A glance at the display told her it was Brandon. She was tempted to let it roll over to voice mail, but she answered it anyway, her tone revealing her pain and disappointment. Then she put it on speaker so she could finish packing.

"What's up?" she asked.

"Douglas Perry was arrested last night," Brandon said. "For assault and, depending upon what the crime-scene investigators learn about his intent, he could be charged with attempted murder."

"Good." At least Brandon had listened to her and followed through accordingly.

"Perry also had an outstanding warrant for his arrest. He was out on bail and wasn't supposed to leave the state."

"What was he arrested for?"

"A couple of weeks ago, after Ella left him, he went to a bar and downed more than his share of whiskey. On his way home, he was involved in an accident. It wasn't his first DUI, and he failed to show up for court-ordered rehab. So he'll be locked up for a while."

Thank goodness. "Ella will be relieved to hear that."

"Will you let her know that it's safe for her to return to Fairborn now?"

"Sure." Marissa placed a plastic bag filled with her makeup and toiletries into her carry-on. "How's Betty Sue? Is she doing any better?"

"She's not fully conscious yet, but she's responsive. So the doctors are optimistic."

"I'm glad to hear that." She zipped her bag shut. "I'd like to visit her when I get back."

"Where are you going?"

It really wasn't his business, but there was no reason to be rude or snarky. "San Diego."

"To see your family?"

"It's not a social visit, but I'll see them while I'm in town."

"How long will you be gone?" he asked.

It didn't really matter. Even when she returned to Fairborn, she wouldn't stay in town much longer. "A couple of days."

"When you get back, I'd like to take you to lunch. Or maybe meet you for coffee. We need to talk."

She blew out a weary sigh. "There's nothing to talk about. I've already told you how I feel. Besides, I won't have time. Katie Johnson, who lives here with her younger brothers, and I volunteered to watch the ranch and feed the stock while Alana is on her honeymoon. I'm not going to dump the full responsibility on Katie, but as soon as Alana and Clay return, I'm leaving town. I've already given notice to Darla and Tameka."

"Please don't go. That's not necessary. I was wrong, and I'm sorry. You've proven time and again that you're loyal. And you have a kind heart."

Marissa sucked in a deep breath, then slowly

blew it out. "I accept your apology, Brandon. But whatever we may have had or tiptoed around is over. You'll never really trust me. You'll always be a cop, and you'll never forget that I'm a convicted felon."

"That's not true."

"Oh, no? You wouldn't even let me be around your kids without a chaperone present." And the fact that he didn't trust her to be good to those two precious kids had crushed her.

He didn't respond right away, probably chewing on the truth. But she didn't have time to defend herself or to state her case.

"I need to go, Brandon. I have a plane to catch." Then she ended the call. And ended things with him once and for all.

Last night, after Brandon fed the kids dinner, supervised their baths and got them ready for bed, Marissa had remained on his mind. Even the bedtime story Jimmy and Maddie had chosen for him to read was about a cat named Marissa. Who in the hell would dub a cat with that name?

There's nothing to talk about.

I'm leaving town.

Whatever we had is over.

The thought of her leaving hit him like a rock to the solar plexus. And he'd slept like hell.

After dropping off the twins at preschool, he

called his uncle to ask if Betty Sue was doing any better.

"The nurse told me she had a good night," Ralph said. "She's conscious now. So Carlene is going to watch the market, and I'm going to the hospital. Visiting hours start at eleven."

"Want to meet me for a cup of coffee before then?" Brandon asked.

"Sure. I'll see you at The Jumping Bean in an hour."

An hour later, as Brandon and Ralph shared an outdoor table at Fairborn's newest coffee shop, Brandon tried to figure out a way to bring up the subject of Marissa and his feelings about her. But all he ended up doing was fussing with a paper napkin, rolling a corner up, then unrolling it.

"Something on your mind?" Ralph asked.

"Is it that obvious?"

"On you? Yes, it is." Ralph opened a sugar packet and poured it into his heat-resistant paper cup. "You've always been good at keeping your thoughts and feelings close to the vest. But you're perplexed about something."

Brandon blew out a sigh. "It's Marissa. We've been...sort of seeing each other. But I'm afraid I've really botched things up with her." He went on to explain what he'd done—the background check, the false assumption he'd made about her being involved in a robbery that never actually happened. And he didn't hold back.

"A relationship requires trust," Ralph said. "And sometimes that means choosing to trust, even when you have reason not to."

"I'm not sure I'm following you."

Ralph took a deep breath, then slowly let it out. "About twenty years ago, I had an affair."

Seriously? "I had no idea."

"No, why would you? I'm not proud of it. I can try to explain what I did and why, but I can't. It was a horrible mistake." Ralph sat back in his seat, his shoulders slumping at the guilty admission that he clearly hated to make.

"What caused you to do it?" Brandon asked.

"It happened during a time our marriage was a little shaky. Your aunt and I had been arguing a lot, and she said she needed some time away. A cooling-off period. So she went to visit a friend in Missoula. I went to Sully's Pub one evening, and I met a woman. She had a nice smile and was a good listener. She made me feel special. And one thing led to another." Ralph gave a little shrug. "It just happened."

"And Carlene found out?"

Ralph nodded. "One of the women in her bridge group spotted me with someone else and told her. I figured all hell was going to break loose when she found out. We'd had some loud arguments in the past, but not that time. Carlene was crushed, which only made me feel guiltier than ever."

"How did you earn her trust again?"

"She eventually forgave me, but the trust? It was shattered. I could have apologized until the birds flew south for the winter, but Carlene—God bless her—chose to trust me. And I gotta tell you, I've spent the last twenty years proving to her that she made the right decision."

Brandon took a sip of coffee, letting his uncle's confession seep in.

"Take it from me," Ralph added, "we all make mistakes, son. If you love Marissa, you'll have to go hat in hand and ask her to forgive you. And if she turns you away, try again. Because true love is worth fighting for."

"As long as I don't turn into a stalker."

Ralph laughed. "You won't. I suspect from the way she looks at you, she feels the same way."

"Maybe." Did he love her?

If he didn't, then why did it hurt so bad to lose her?

He'd have to convince her that he trusted her completely. He just wasn't quite sure how to go about it, especially since she had every reason to believe he'd betray her again.

Marissa's flight to San Diego arrived on time. After making her way through the airport with her carry-on, she waited at the curb until Erik picked her up. She had to admit, he looked a lot better than he had the last time she'd seen him—the day she'd been arrested and he'd clammed up and refused to take personal responsibility.

He'd been too thin, and his otherwise-tanned complexion looked as if he'd hibernated all winter in a bat cave. He was bulkier now. Healthier, it seemed. He appeared calmer, too. Before, he'd either been hyper or sullen and moody. Today he was neither.

They didn't talk much as he drove her downtown, where she was to meet Suzanne at the attorney's office. She wasn't looking forward to seeing her stepmother again, but she was ready to put this part of her life behind her.

She'd told Erik that she forgave him, but she still felt resentful. And doubtful. She'd never forget what he'd put her through and the blemish it had left on her reputation, the ugly mark it had left on her heart. He'd hidden his drug addiction from their family and left her to take the blame for his crime.

"We're here," he said, as he pulled into the driveway that led to an underground garage, and parked the older Toyota 4Runner. They didn't talk. After they entered the lobby, they took the elevator to the eighth floor.

When they reached the attorney's office, Marissa spotted Suzanne seated in a reception area and paused in the doorway. The tall blonde, her hair cut in a chic bob, stood and offered a weak smile. But Marissa couldn't seem to return it. Even a cool greeting would have been as fake as Suzanne's tan.

"It's nice to see you," Suzanne said. "I'm glad you're here."

Seriously? Was she actually glad to see Marissa? Or just eager to get her share of the trust?

"I bet you are," Marissa said, not looking at the woman. "Let's get this over with."

"I owe you an apology," Suzanne added. "I believed Erik when I shouldn't have. I don't blame you if you find it hard to forgive me. I'll never forgive myself." She reached into her purse, pulled out a business card and handed it to Marissa. "If you ever want to talk, you can reach me at my real-estate office."

Marissa glanced at the glossy card, and while she couldn't see any reason to ever contact her stepmother, she slipped it into the front pocket of her jeans. "Sure. Whatever."

Suzanne's lips pulled to the right, then to the left. "I'd like to take you to dinner tonight. I hope you'll agree. In the meantime, I'll leave you to talk to your father's attorney. I've already signed off on the paperwork. I want you to know, I'm not taking my share of the trust."

Marissa furrowed her brow. "Excuse me?"

"I'd like you to have it all. It won't make up for my lack of support during your trial and…and your incarceration, but I hope it will convince you of how very, very sorry I am."

Either this was some kind of scam or Marissa hadn't heard her right. She didn't know what to believe. Or what to say. *Thank you? I accept your apology? Dinner sounds great? What's in it for you?*

"You might find this hard to believe, Marissa. But I want nothing more than for you to forgive me. And I hope you'll call me. About dinner tonight."

Marissa gaped, didn't know how to respond. This turn of events had her mind wheeling.

"But whether you forgive me or not, I wish you the best." Suzanne offered another smile, this one stronger than the last. But was it sincere? Was it some kind of a trick?

She turned and walked out the door, her stilettos clicking down the hallway as she made her way to the elevator.

Erik touched her elbow. "She means it, Marissa. She's really sorry. And so am I. After everything that went down, I know we'll never be a real family again, but we can be civil."

Marissa stepped back. "I suppose. But I'm

not sure if I'll ever be able to trust either of you again."

"That's fair," Erik said.

A balding man in his fifties entered the reception area.

"Marissa Garcia?" he asked.

Words escaped her, but she nodded.

"I'm Grant Collins, your father's attorney and the trustee of the insurance trust. Come on back to my office. I have the documents ready for you to sign. My paralegal is also a notary, so once you have them in hand, you can go directly to the investment bank that holds the account. It's all yours. So you can either leave it invested or take the cash."

"All right." Marissa glanced at Erik, who took a seat next to the chair Suzanne had vacated.

"I'll wait here for you," he said. "Then I'll take you wherever you want to go."

Marissa had no idea where she wanted to go, or what she wanted to do. She had more options now than she'd ever had, and her mind was spinning. But in the meantime, she followed Mr. Collins to his office.

Betty Sue reached for the bedside remote and raised her head so she could get a better look at her new room. They'd moved her out of ICU earlier today, thank goodness. And if she was lucky, the doctor was going to release her to go home tomorrow.

Carlene, who was seated in the chair next to the bed, said, "I talked to Ella this morning. She told me how brave you were. She was able to escape thanks to your clear head. And then you went to face that horrible man by yourself. I'm proud of you."

"Oh, yeah?" Betty Sue chuckled. "I'm a tough old bird. So cut me some slack. And don't treat me like an invalid when I get home."

"I'll try to remember that." Her tone rang guilty, and she kept her focus on the speckled linoleum floor.

"Good." Betty Sue shrugged. "And I'll try not to wander without letting you know what I'm up to. Except when I go to the Grange Hall to play bingo. I've got my eye on Earl Hoffman, the bartender who works at most of the events held there. And I'd hate to have you mess things up for me."

Carlene raised her hand in Scout's-honor fashion. "I promise."

"Then, it's a deal." Betty Sue glanced at the doorway and spotted Marissa holding a flower arrangement and looking a little sheepish, like she wasn't sure if she should make her presence known or slip off and give them some privacy.

"Come on in," Betty Sue said. "Don't be shy, honey."

Marissa slowly made her way into the room. "I hope I'm not intruding."

"You aren't. We're just chatting. No big deal." Betty Sue reached for her glass of water and, using the straw, took a couple of sips. The white-board next to the television listed the date and the name of the nurse who was taking care of her today: Patricia M. "It's Thursday. Isn't that your day to work at the doughnut shop?"

"I took some time off," Marissa said. "I flew to San Diego for a night. I just got back and thought I'd stop by to see how you're doing."

"I'm a little banged up. But it's just a flesh wound. Seems like everyone thinks I nearly kicked the bucket, but I'm still here."

Marissa made her way to the tray table. "I brought you some roses. Would you like me to place them here? Or maybe near the sink, where you can see them?"

"Put them by the window." Betty Sue fingered the gauze bandage on her head, the badge of cour-age she'd received after her run-in with the brute who'd come looking for Ella. She would have shot him, but he got the jump on her. Twenty years ago—hell, five years ago—he wouldn't have stood a chance.

Someone rapped on the doorframe and cleared their throat. Betty Sue glanced up to see Bran-don wearing his uniform. He was a handsome man—and the kind a young woman could look up to even if she'd been pulled over for a traffic infraction.

"Looks like we're having a party. Come on in."

He stood in the doorway a moment. His gaze landed on Marissa's, and she stiffened.

Betty eyed them carefully. Hmm. Trouble in paradise, it seemed.

As Brandon made his way to Betty Sue's bedside, he offered her a grin. "How are you doing?"

"Not bad, although I'd feel a lot better if I was at home."

"I'm sure you would." Brandon returned his attention to pretty Marissa, whose skittish demeanor suggested she'd like an excuse to bolt.

Carlene got to her feet. "We're only supposed to have two visitors at a time, so—"

"I'll go," Marissa blurted out.

"No, you won't." Carlene started toward the door. "You just got here. I'll take off and come back this evening. Is there anything I can bring you, Betty Sue? Anything you need?"

A big ol' smirk stretched across Betty Sue's face. "How about a bottle of Jack Daniel's?"

"I'll bring a milkshake instead." Carlene chuckled as she walked out of the room.

"Extra whipped cream, then," Betty Sue called out.

They made idle chitchat for a couple of minutes, then Brandon said, "If you don't mind, I'd like to take Marissa outside. There's something I want to talk to her about."

"Feel free to have that little chat right here," Betty Sue said. "I'll ask the nurse to bring another chair."

"Thanks for the hospitality," Brandon said. "But I need to talk to her privately."

Marissa rolled her eyes.

Betty Sue figured the girl wasn't up to hearing whatever Brandon was about to say. She had no idea what Brandon had done, but from Marissa's huff, it was something he needed to apologize for.

"Go ahead, then." She waved them off. Then she crossed her fingers, hoping the boy made things right.

And that Marissa would forgive him.

Chapter Thirteen

Brandon hadn't expected to see Marissa at the hospital, but he was glad they'd run into each other. And he was relieved that she'd agreed to talk to him. He just wished he wasn't wearing his uniform. He knew that put her off.

As they left the room, their shoes tapping on the polished tile floor, he started to turn right and down the corridor, but Marissa stopped in her tracks. "Where are you going?"

"There's a memorial garden right off the lobby," Brandon said, expecting her to continue walking with him.

Marissa tucked a silky strand of hair behind her

ear, revealing the pretty topaz studs. "Whatever you have to say, you can say it here."

He stepped closer to her, and her alluring scent, something lightly floral and springtime fresh, filled the air, taunting him. Damn, she looked good today. She wasn't wearing anything fancy— just a white blouse and a pair of jeans that hugged her curves.

She eased away from him and said, "What is it you want to say?" A frown and her serious tone let him know how badly he'd hurt her.

"I…"

She folded her arms across her chest, protectively, blocking her heart. And shutting him out.

Okay. He got that. So he tried another tactic, a neutral one. "How was your trip to San Diego?"

Her stance softened. Slightly. "Better than I expected."

She looked away and nodded to a doctor passing by, a faint smile aimed at that guy.

She'd only been gone for a night, but he'd missed her something fierce. He'd never felt such a longing for a woman before, and it rocked him to his core. Had he lost her for good?

"I'm actually thinking about moving back home," she added.

He stiffened. "Home? As in San Diego?" He didn't want her moving anywhere, especially more than a thousand miles away. "I thought you left to get away from your family."

"I did. But they're trying to make amends."

"After all they did, all they didn't do, you can forgive them?"

"I've thought about it a lot. I should try. They gave me reason to believe they were truly sorry."

A glimmer of hope raced through him. Could he give her reason to believe *he* was truly sorry?

"So what did you want to talk to me about?" she asked, looking at her watch.

Okay, here goes. He sucked in a breath, then let it out slowly. "To tell you that I screwed up royally. I should have trusted you completely, and I promise to do that from now on. I hope you'll forgive me."

She glanced down at her feet and didn't respond. He didn't push. He let her have the time to think, to consider what he'd said. And, hopefully, time for her to soften even more.

She finally looked up and spoke. "Remember when I asked if I could take the kids to spend time with me on the ranch?"

He nodded.

"You didn't answer right away. And when you did, you said, 'Maybe. Someday.' I realized you weren't comfortable with me being alone with them, and that hurt."

He ran a hand through his hair. So that had

been the tipping point. At least he knew it now. Maybe he could explain in a way she'd understand. "Mostly, the question surprised me. And since my kids really like you, I didn't want them to feel badly if things didn't work out between us."

She clicked her tongue. "Be honest. You also didn't trust me."

True. And he couldn't argue. "I know I tend to be skeptical of people. It's who I am—and a result of my childhood. But it also comes with the job."

"I sensed that. Thanks for confirming it." She looked at her watch again.

He was losing her, and a sense of panic set in. "No, wait. I think you misunderstood me. I know you're a good person—honest, loyal and loving. And I trust you. Completely. Will you give me a chance to prove it?"

She slowly shook her head. "I'm sorry, Brandon. I can't give you that chance. I have too much going on in my life right now."

"Like what? Maybe I can help you find a balance. What are you dealing with?"

"I need to decide where to open my business. I want to be a wedding planner. And a party planner."

"Fairborn would be the perfect place. I've got some money saved. I'd be happy to invest in your venture. Or loan you the money." Hell, he'd even give it to her. He was getting desperate to make things right between them.

"I like you, Brandon. I might even love you. But I don't need your help." She waited a beat. "Or you."

His heart pounded. "Come on, please. You're giving your family a second chance. How about giving me one, too?"

"I'm sorry," she said, unfolding her arms. "I can't do this right now."

"Why not?"

She looked at him with beautiful, soulful eyes that glistened with hurt. "Because you broke my heart."

And now she was breaking his.

As they gazed at each other, he fought the urge to hold her in his arms to comfort her, but he'd blown his chances with her.

"Listen," she said, shaking her head as though to rid her emotions. "I need time. And space. It's not just you, it's me." She nodded down the hall, toward the elevator. "I'm going back to the ranch. Tell Betty Sue I said goodbye. I'll see her again before I leave town."

Brandon grabbed her arm, his grip firm at first, then loosening. "You go visit her. I'll give you the time you need. But know that I'll always be there for you. If you'll have me." Then he released her and walked away.

His steps echoed down the hall as he made his way to the elevator. She'd said she might even love him. So he might still have a chance to convince her.

Only trouble was he had no idea where to go from here.

When Brandon walked into the hospital room wearing his uniform, all Marissa could see was his badge—and the man behind it, the guy who'd always be a cop, who'd always be on the lookout for a crime ready to happen, a criminal to apprehend.

She'd wanted nothing more than to take him at his word, to know that he was truly sorry, that things would be different between them from here on out. But she knew that wasn't to be.

She let out a sigh and paused before the doorway to Betty Sue's room. Closing her eyes, she rested her forehead against the doorframe.

When a frail, wrinkled arm reached out and grabbed her hand, she nearly jumped out of her skin. "Betty Sue! You scared the heck out of me. What are you doing out of bed?"

"Listening in on the conversation you were having with my nephew. And planning to chase after you if I had to. Come in here, girl. We need to talk." The elderly woman held her IV pole in one hand and pulled Marissa into her room with the other. The strength of her grip was surprising.

"You're not supposed to be walking around. You just got out of the ICU. Do I have to call the front desk?"

"Don't be a tattletale. I'm fine. Patricia, my nurse, is a tiny little thing. She won't put up much of a fight. Besides, I'm just trying to take care of my family. Now, come in and sit down. You and I are going to have a little chat."

When Marissa was seated and Betty Sue had scrambled back into bed, all the anger, the sorrow, the grief she'd choked down over the years bubbled to the surface, and she couldn't hold in the tears any longer. "I'm sorry." She sniffled. "This is so unlike me. I don't usually cry. And certainly not in front of anyone."

"Let it out, honey. I get the feeling you have a lot to cry about."

As if finally having an opportunity to let it all loose, the words rolled right out of her mouth, and she told the elderly woman everything—about her dad's unexpected death, her stepmother's resentment, Erik's betrayal and her efforts to find a place where she could put down roots and start fresh.

She had to take a moment to catch her breath, to avoid hyperventilating after her long, rambling spiel. "I finally landed in Fairborn."

"Go on," Betty Sue said. "Don't stop now."

Marissa blew out a ragged sigh. "I've made friends here. I like living at Rancho Esperanza. But then…"

"Along came Brandon."

Marissa nodded. "I didn't realize he was a deputy sheriff. I just thought he was a gorgeous guy and a wonderful father. I adore the twins." She paused, wondering if Betty Sue would understand. Or if she'd take Brandon's side. After all, they were family, and blood ran deep.

But something told her Betty Sue wasn't a typical relative. She cut a glance at the woman sitting upright in her hospital bed, and the words, the hurt tumbled out again. "Did you know that he had the gall to run a background check on me? I mean, who does that to a woman he wants to date?"

Betty Sue clucked her tongue. "You got me there. No wonder you're mad at him. But don't forget Brandon is a cop. He's trained to look beyond the obvious. He has that sort of mind and the investigation tools at his disposal."

"So you're telling me he doesn't trust anyone?"

Betty Sue shrugged. "I think it's more like *Trust but verify.* He has two sweet kids. He's going to protect the public, but believe me, he's going to protect his family first."

"You're right. And I could have forgiven him for that, but after the so-called robbery and the assault, he came to the ranch and practically accused me of being a coconspirator with Ella." She lifted her injured hand, which bore only a regular bandage now and not one made of gauze. "He wanted to run a DNA test to see if it was my blood on the broken window at the market. Can you believe that?"

"He was doing his job. He obviously cares for you, so it must have been hard on him, too, don't you think?"

"I guess." Was she being self-centered and not taking into consideration how Brandon felt? How he had a job to do?

Betty Sue clicked her tongue and slowly shook her head. "So what are you going to do about your situation?"

"Relocate. I might even go back to San Diego. I was there yesterday, and my family... Well, they seem to be really sorry for what went down. And they're trying to make it up to me."

"Are you kidding? After all they did to you? You're thinking about forgiving them?"

"Yeah. Is that crazy?"

Betty Sue looked Marissa up and down. "It's actually very healthy as long as you don't get sucked back into their drama. But how about Brandon? Are you going to give him a chance?"

"I don't know. I feel so scattered and so broken

inside, I don't know what to do. All I know is that I can't deal with his trust issues."

"Maybe you have those issues, too. Consider trusting that what he says is true. You seem to be doing that with your family. It's called taking a leap of faith."

She had a point, Marissa supposed. "I just don't know if I can jump that high."

"Listen," Betty Sue said, "I'm going to tell you about the great love of my life. Like Ella, I was a battered woman, too. And I was able to escape. But I built a wall around my heart, determined not to trust the wrong guy again."

"The love of your life hit you?"

"No. Not him. But I was leery of trusting anyone ever again. So I broke up with my Mr. Right before he could do me wrong."

"There's nothing wrong with trying to protect yourself."

"True." Betty Sue crossed her arms. "But there is if you shut out true love. Rumor had it that my old lover took it hard, that my leaving town really tore him up. And eventually, I returned, thinking I'd give him another chance. But it was too late. He was with another woman, and she was obviously pregnant. With his baby."

"Maybe I need to go away for a while."

"Oh, for Pete's sake. You're going to run away? Don't do that. You're at a crossroads. It's called fight or flight. If Brandon was a grizzly bear—or God forbid, a brute like the one who used to beat on Ella—I'd say run like hell. But Brandon's not like that. He's also teachable. So in this case, I'd suggest you fight."

"Fight for him?"

"Heck, no. Don't fight *for* him. There's no one standing in the way other than you and him. So fight *with* him. Tell him how you feel. Tell him that he'd better cut the skepticism crap when it comes to you. Stand up for yourself. Demand respect. Brandon doesn't get to make all the rules, right?"

Marissa gazed at the wise woman: something warm and maternal burned bright in her. An understanding, a kindness and support that had always been lacking in Marissa's life. She'd never known her mom, and she'd once hoped to see something similar in Suzanne's eyes.

She brushed at the tears that began to slide down her cheeks, and she choked back a sob to no avail.

Betty Sue opened her arms, offering a hug. "Come here, honey. Let it out."

Marissa accepted her comforting embrace, and the sweet, quirky old woman held her while she cried. When her sobs finally subsided, Betty Sue released her.

"Thanks so much for listening to me. And for

your advice. Has anyone ever told you that you'd make a good counselor?"

"No one in my family. But I've always known it." Something wistful clouded her eyes, then she smiled. "Maybe I should go back to school."

Marissa wouldn't put anything past the spunky woman. "You don't need a degree to help people, Betty Sue."

"I know. But I may as well get one. I only have one more class to take for a master's degree in psychology."

"Seriously?"

Betty Sue chuffed. "I hate science, and there was a graduate-level human biology course I was supposed to take. But with my social security and pension, I can afford a tutor these days."

"You're something else."

"So are you, honey. And don't you ever forget it."

Marissa certainly would remember this conversation for the rest of her life. She just wasn't sure where she'd be spending it. Or if she'd be spending it with Brandon.

Brandon needed to talk to someone, a guy his age, a friend he respected. So while he was on his way to the preschool to pick up the twins, he called Mrs. Hendrix and asked if Maddie and Jimmy could have dinner with her.

"That would be great. I hate eating alone, and I love to cook. I'll think of something kid-friendly to make, like fried chicken. Would they like that?"

"Don't bother cooking tonight. I'll pick up a pizza on our way home."

"Do you have to work late?" his kindhearted neighbor asked.

"Actually, I need to talk to a friend. A guy I went to high school with."

"That's nice. Men like you need some downtime."

That was true. And boy oh boy, did Brandon need some downtime. He'd always been able to think himself out of a dilemma. But the one he was facing with Marissa was a biggie. Ralph had suggested that he keep at it, that he not give up. And that's what Brandon thought he'd been doing. But it hadn't worked. In fact, he'd probably made things worse outside the hospital room.

Damn. He needed a second opinion.

When the twins got into the car, Jimmy said, "I smell pizza."

Both kids clapped and cheered.

"I'm taking you over to Mrs. Hendrix's house for dinner. And you're going to stay with her for a while."

"Why?" Maddie asked. "Are you going to work?"

"No, I'm going to see Greg."

"You guys having a playdate?" Jimmy asked.

"Yeah. Something like that."

An hour later, after calling Greg and delivering the twins and the pizza to Mrs. Hendrix, he'd gone to his house, showered and put on his favorite pair of jeans and slipped on a T-shirt. Then he drove to Sully's Pub, where he found his buddy waiting, a longneck bottle of Corona in hand.

"Damn." Greg stretched out his long legs and crossed his ankles while watching Brandon take a seat across from him. "You might have showered and gotten comfortable, but you look like hell. What happened?"

"I crashed and burned with Marissa." Brandon motioned for the cocktail waitress. When she stopped by the table, he nodded at Greg's longneck bottle. "I'll have a beer, too."

Once she left them alone, he launched into the problem he had with Marissa, the wall she'd backed him into.

Greg let out a slow whistle. "I feel for you, man. Shelley just cut me loose, too."

"I'm sorry."

Greg waved him off. "No big. I'll get over it."

Brandon sat back in his seat and studied his friend. "You seem to be taking it well."

"Yeah, well, she said it was just a physical thing for her. And when push came to shove, it was for me, too. It still stung—if you know what I mean. No one likes to be used."

Brandon nodded, thinking about his ex and the kids' mom.

"But what the hell. Another woman will come along."

For Greg, maybe. But Brandon didn't think another woman would do the trick for him.

"Man." Greg leaned forward and scrunched his brow. "You look like someone kicked you to the curb."

Brandon blew out a sigh, then told his friend the entire saga, how Marissa had pushed him away at the hospital. "She gave me the standard woman's breakup lines—all of them. 'I need time. And space. It's not you, it's me.'"

"Ouch. So, it's over?"

"Yeah. Probably."

The cocktail waitress brought his beer, and he thanked her. Then he took a big, thirst-quenching, guilt-easing sip. But even that didn't help.

"Probably?" Greg sipped his beer. "There's hope somewhere in that story?"

"She said she thought she was in love with me."

Greg pointed his longneck bottle at Brandon. "Then, you have a chance."

Brandon looked up. "You think?"

"All you have do is prove to her that you trust her."

"How?" Brandon rolled his eyes. "I've told her a hundred times. She won't listen."

"I said *prove* it. Show her."

"How in the hell am I supposed to do that?"

Greg shrugged. "Wish I could tell you, bro. You know her better than I do."

Then an idea came to him. One that just might work.

Chapter Fourteen

By the time Brandon had emptied half his bottle
of beer, he was ready to leave Sully's Pub and put
his plan in motion. But he couldn't bail out now.
Not when he was the one who'd invited Greg to
meet for a drink. So he tried to focus on what his
buddy was saying.

"What this town needs is a gym," Greg said.
"Don't you agree?"

"Maybe so." Brandon stayed in shape by lift-
ing weights in his garage and running.

Greg, who stood six foot four and worked out
regularly, took a chug of beer. "I'm thinking about
opening one. You want to be a partner?"

"No, I don't think so." Brandon had offered to help Marissa open her business, and while she'd refused, he wanted his funds to be available in case she changed her mind. "But if you open one, I'll join."

"Okay. I've got a couple of other guys in mind."

About that time, the blonde cocktail waitress stopped by their table and offered Greg a bright-eyed smile. "Can I get you another round?"

"Sure." Greg glanced at Brandon.

He slowly shook his head. "No, thanks. Not for me."

"I'll take have another beer," Greg said. "And an order of buffalo wings."

"You got it." The blonde, who was actually quite pretty, lingered a moment longer, her gaze meeting Greg's.

When Brandon spotted a spark of mutual attraction and a flirtatious glimmer in his friend's eyes, he took the opportunity to cut out. So he got to his feet, reached into his back pocket and pulled out his wallet.

"Where are you going?" Greg asked.

"To prove myself to Marissa." Brandon glanced at the shapely, blue-eyed blonde. "Take care of my friend here."

"I sure will." She grinned from ear to ear. "My pleasure."

Brandon handed Greg a twenty to cover the

check. At least, the first round of beers and the buffalo wings.

"Good luck," Greg called to his back.

"Thanks." Brandon was going to need it.

Twenty minutes later, he arrived at Rancho Esperanza and parked in the yard. A soft light shone through the blinds in the living-room window. It was too early to turn in. Marissa must be watching TV. Or maybe she was reading.

He made his way to the front door and knocked. Moments later, she answered wearing a blue sundress, her feet bare. The sight of her took his breath away.

"Brandon," she said, her voice soft and laced with surprise.

"I hope I'm not bothering you, but we need to talk." He braced himself for the door to slam in his face, but she stepped aside instead and allowed him into the house.

That was a good sign.

He scanned the interior of the small living room—the scarred hardwood floor adorned with a blue rug, white walls sporting a fresh coat of paint and a rustic fireplace, the stones stained from smoke and soot, the mantel a rough-hewn beam.

"Have a seat," she said.

He glanced at the faded tweed recliner, then at the sofa. A bookmark peeked out of a novel that rested on the lamp table, next to where she must have been seated. He hated to push himself on her, but he hoped to have an honest, intimate conversation with her. So he bypassed the chair and chose the sofa, taking the side opposite where she'd been reading, leaving a cushion between them.

While she settled into her seat, he turned his gaze her way. Her dark hair, lush and glossy, tumbled over her shoulders, and he was tempted to touch it, to run his fingers through those curls. He waited for her to catch him looking at her, hoping she'd turn to him and smile, giving him a sign that all was right in her world.

Hell, if she could forgive her family, especially after they'd turned their backs on her when she'd needed them most, maybe that meant she'd forgive him, too. God, he sure hoped so.

"So what else did you want to talk about?" she asked.

"I told you that I trust you. And I want to prove it."

She merely studied him, looking soft and vulnerable. Yet doubtful.

"You can take Maddie and Jimmy anytime you want to have them. You can bring them here and keep them overnight—or all week. I won't even call or come by to check on them."

Her head tilted slightly. "You'd trust me with your most precious possessions?"

"Unconditionally. And if you'll let me back into your life, into your heart, you'll be just as precious to me."

She stared at him, lips parted. Soft, plump lips he'd give anything to kiss again.

"So what do you say?" he asked.

"You're serious?" she asked. "You'll let me take the kids? Unsupervised? You're not afraid I'll teach them to smoke or how to knock off a convenience store?"

He grinned. "Okay, I deserved that. Like I said, I trust you."

It would be so easy to say yes, to turn and embrace him, to thank him for giving her a chance to fit in... That is, until she recalled Betty Sue's advice.

Don't fight for him. Fight with him.

Tell him how you feel. Tell him that he'd better cut the skepticism crap when it comes to you. Stand up for yourself. Demand respect. Brandon doesn't get to make all the rules, right?

Marissa turned in her seat, her knee brushing his. She grew serious, lifted her finger and pointed it at him. "I'll consider forgiving you. But we need to get some things straight."

"I'm listening."

"Okay, then. First of all, I will *never* lie to you.

That said, you need to promise me that you will always believe me."

"No problem there. I promise."

"Secondly, I want you to forget about my record. I spent time in jail, but it was for something I didn't do. And if you don't believe me, I'll give you my stepbrother's phone number. He'll tell you those drugs were his."

"Don't need his number. I believe you, remember? We just covered that."

"All right. Then I want you to promise you'll forget about that conviction and my jail time."

"I'm afraid I can't. Not as long as you carry the pain and scars from it. That memory will be mine, too—until you're able to forget it and put it behind you."

Tears welled in her eyes, and her bravado faltered.

"Listen," he said, extending his arm to offer his hand. "Let's make a pact. Regarding our past— long past and recent past. No regrets. We won't bring it up, and we won't stew about it. No more worries. Just the here and now."

She nodded. "I like that." She shook his hand. "Agreed."

His expression turned serious. "There's one other thing. It's a big thing. Maybe. For you."

"Okay."

"I'm a deputy sheriff. I'm a good one, too. It's

what I do. And it's my career. Going forward, can you handle that?"

If he'd asked a few weeks ago, she'd have said no way. But now she realized she didn't need to run or hide anymore. This lawman was after her, and it was time to let him catch her. "Yes. I'll be honest, I'll always worry about you, but that'd be true even if you were an accountant."

"Good. Perfect." He eased closer to her on the sofa. "Is it okay if I promise something you haven't asked for?"

She nodded, shaking loose a tear that ran down her face. He reached over and wiped it away with a gentle hand. "Marissa, I promise to love you. Always. Unconditionally. And I promise to not only trust you with my kids, but with my whole heart. It's been battered in the past, first by my parents and then the twins' mother. But I can't think of entrusting it to anyone else but you."

Hope burned bright in his gaze, and any objection, any question she might have had, any condition she might have insisted upon, faded away.

"I love you, too, Brandon." Then she fell into his arms and kissed him. It began lightly at first, sweetly and with awe, then passion kicked in. She opened her mouth, and his tongue slid inside, mating with hers in a heated rush, twisting, tasting.

Her heart swelled with love for him, and her hormones spun out of control. She'd like to lead him back to her bedroom. But he had children at home, kids who needed him. Then again, maybe he had it covered.

She drew her lips from his and, resting her forehead against his, asked, "Can you stay for a while? Or do you have to go home now? I mean, are the kids okay?"

"They'll be fine until I get home."

"Good," she said. "I…um…I don't have any condoms, but for what it's worth, I'm on the pill. I was having some irregular periods, and the doctor prescribed it to straighten them out."

"And I was tested recently, when I had a department physical. All negative."

That's all she needed to know. "How long can you stay?"

"Are you inviting me for a sleepover? If so, all I have to do is make a phone call or two."

Heat rose from her toes to her nose. "I'd like nothing more than to have you spend the night."

"Then, give me a minute. I'll make that call."

After Brandon had called Mrs. Hendrix, he looked up at Marissa and winked. Then a slow smile slid across his gorgeous face.

She reached for his hand and led him down the hall and to the guest room, where she'd been staying. She'd yet to add any artwork or flowers or new bedding to make it her own, so the small, cozy room wasn't anything fancy—just a double bed, nightstand and dresser.

It certainly wasn't a honeymoon suite, even if at the moment it kind of felt like one. But Brandon wasn't a groom, and she wasn't his bride. Not yet, anyway.

But like a newlywed, she couldn't wait to make love with him, to celebrate the promises they'd made and their intentions to keep them from now on.

"This is it," she said, as they entered the room and approached the double bed covered with a blue-and-white-striped comforter.

Brandon drew her into his arms, bent his head and kissed her, slowly, thoroughly. Their mouths fit perfectly, as if they'd been made for each other. As their tongues continued to mate, their hands roamed each other's bodies, seeking, exploring, caressing.

When his fingers worked their way to her breast, his thumb skimmed across her nipple, and she whimpered. A yearning emptiness settled deep in her core. If they didn't pull back the sheets and move to the bed soon, she was going to melt into a puddle on the floor.

She slowly withdrew her lips from his, and as their gazes met, heat simmered in his eyes. He wanted her as badly as she wanted him. With a voice husky and laden with desire, she whispered,

"I want you to make love with me. Now." She turned her back to him and lifted her hair. "Will you unbutton me?"

"Gladly."

When her sundress gaped open and the cool air in the room chilled her skin, Brandon placed a kiss on her shoulders, singeing her with the warmth of his breath. She slowly turned around, removing her dress at the same time. She let it drop to the floor. Then she unhooked her bra and slipped out of it, too.

As she peeled off her panties, slowly revealing herself to him in a slow, deliberate fashion, their gazes met and locked.

"Marissa. Honey. You're more beautiful than I'd even imagined." He blessed her with a smile, then opened his arms, and she entered his embrace.

Never had she felt so loved, so cherished.

He kissed her again, and she leaned in to him, against his growing erection, and a surge of desire shot clear through her. The chemistry they shared grew stronger and even more amazing than before.

Could she ever love this man any more than she did right now?

Brandon kissed Marissa again, long and deep—savoring the taste of her, the feel of her naked body in his arms, the heat of her touch.

He slid his hands along the curve of her back and down the slope of her hips. So soft, so perfect.

He wanted her more than he'd ever wanted any other woman, and he couldn't wait to feel his bare skin against hers. He ended the kiss long enough to shuck his boots and jeans, to remove his shirt.

When they were both naked, she skimmed her nails across his chest, sending a shiver through his veins and a rush of heat through his blood. He bent and took one of her breasts in his mouth, laving the nipple, tasting her skin—the light, floral scent of her fading perfume.

He trailed kisses downward to her taut stomach, his thumbs stroking along her rib cage, as he tongued her belly button. When she let out a whimper, he raised his head and caught her eye, saw arousal written all over her pretty face.

As if on cue, she stepped back and moved to the bed, where he joined her. Then they continued to stroke, to touch, to taste until they were both nearly breathless with desire.

"I don't want to rush this," he said, as he hovered over her. "But I need to be inside you."

"There's nothing I'd like more." She reached for him, guiding his erection to where he wanted it to be.

He entered her slowly at first, but her body welcomed him with slick, liquid heat. As she arched up to meet each of his thrusts, his pace quickened.

He drove into her, in and out. She tightened her grip on his shoulders, breathing accelerated in loud gasps. She cried out as they came together in a sexual explosion that damned near took his breath away.

"I love you," he whispered. So very much. "And I love what we just did."

"Me, too. I… This was…"

When she stalled, looking for the right words, he provided them. "This was better than either of us hoped for. Did I get that right?"

She nodded. Yet neither of them moved. Brandon didn't dare. All he knew was that he wanted to hold on to her, on to this soul-stirring emotion forever.

Marissa wasn't very experienced when it came to sex, but she knew beyond a shadow of a doubt that the lovemaking she and Brandon had shared several times during the night had been incredible.

As the morning sun peered through the slats in the blinds, she rested her head on her lover's shoulder, relishing the feel of his body against hers.

"You know," Brandon said, "the twins have a birthday coming up. They're going to be five on the first of October, and I'm going to have a party for them."

"Can I help you plan it?" she asked.

"Absolutely. I hoped you would. I'm not sure how I'm going to please them both. Maddie's big on tiaras and princess gowns. And Jimmy loves superheroes."

"I'll come up with something. Don't worry."

"I don't care what it costs," he added. "But we don't need to get too fancy or carried away."

"It'll be a nice party. And lots of fun. I'll take plenty of pictures, too. I'd like to create a portfolio of parties and weddings I've planned to show future clients what they can expect from me."

"Speaking of your business plan, I've got some money put away. I mentioned it before, and you said no. But I'd really like to help you get started."

Marissa rolled to the side and braced herself on her elbow. "You won't have to help financially. I have my own money—a parting gift from my dad. He set up a trust fund for me. And that's why I went to San Diego."

Brandon turned to face her. "So that's why your stepmother and stepbrother want to make amends."

She arched a brow. "Always the cop, huh?"

"I'm sorry. I didn't mean to make you mad. I won't bring it up again. I'll trust that you know what you're doing."

A smile slid across her face. "Thanks for the vote of confidence. And just so you know, it was two hundred thousand dollars. Suzanne and I were supposed to split it equally. But she signed over her share to me. She said she was sorry she hadn't supported me through the trial or during the time I was in jail. So she wanted me to have it all."

"Wow. I wouldn't have seen that coming."

"I know. I hadn't expected that, either."

They lay there for a while, facing each other. Pondering the bond they'd created, the love they'd made.

Brandon trailed his fingers along her shoulder and down her arm. "Do you have any thoughts about that birthday party yet?"

"Don't worry. I'll have plenty of ideas. Just give me a little time. A cup of coffee should jump-start my creative process."

He chuckled. "Then, let's have breakfast, too."

"Sounds good. But what about Jimmy and Maddie? Do you need to check on them?"

"I'll call Mrs. Hendrix and tell her that we'll pick them up in an hour. Then I'll take you all to the Mulberry Café for breakfast. The kids love their pancakes."

"And I love you." Marissa brushed a kiss on Brandon's brow, then climbed out of bed. "I'll race you to the shower."

He threw off the covers and climbed out of

bed. "Is this what I can expect from now on? Fun and games?"

"Every day. For the rest of our lives."

Epilogue

It was a beautiful Saturday afternoon at Rancho Esperanza, and the twins' birthday party was in full swing. Marissa couldn't believe how well everything was going, especially considering she'd planned two separate parties and encouraged the children to all come in costume.

The adults sat at the ranch's picnic tables, and the party-rental company had brought child-size tables and chairs, along with two blow-up bouncy houses, one a castle for the girls and one a jungle gym of sorts for the boys. She'd assumed the girls would all come as a Disney princess, but one of them showed up as Princess Leia, along with a toy lightsaber. Upon arriving, they'd each hurried off to join their friends.

On the other hand, the cutest little Thor stood guard over the castle when he wasn't jumping with the princesses. It was nice to see the children intermingle like that.

"You've really outdone yourself this time," Alana said, as she approached. "Two parties in one."

Marissa turned and smiled at the woman who'd become a friend, not just a kindhearted roommate. "It's been more fun than work." She nodded at Alana's ever-expanding belly. At nearly eight months along, she would be giving birth soon. "How are you holding up?"

"Great. My feet are killing me, and my back aches. But I feel wonderful. Excited. I can't wait to have birthday parties. I never had one when I was a kid. And I've never been invited to attend one like this. It's so cool. All the parents seem to be having fun, too."

"I'd still love to plan a baby shower for you."

"Thank you, I know." Alana laughed. "I don't need one. Clay's dad has been sending daily surprises. Our little boy already has more clothes and toys than he needs. But maybe we can plan his first birthday."

"You've got a deal."

"If you'll excuse me," Alana said, "I'm going to head to the ladies' room—yet again."

Marissa laughed. "You do that. I'm going to check on the food."

As she glanced toward the house, she spotted Callie and Ramon Cruz heading toward one of the picnic tables. Ramon was pushing a twin stroller. They had the cutest little babies—a boy and a girl. And Marissa couldn't wait to see them again. Only trouble was she'd better help Ella, who'd recently returned to Rancho Esperanza after learning her abusive ex would be spending the next ten years in prison. One of the passengers in the vehicle he'd hit while driving under the influence had died.

Marissa shook her head. Such a waste and so tragic. But Ella was okay now. And healing, slowly but surely. She'd found a new home, too.

As Marissa made her way to the house, past the table where Betty Sue sat with a nice-looking man in his early seventies, with a sparkle in his blue eyes as he turned them on the older woman.

When Marissa stopped to say hello, Betty Sue beamed. "This is my friend Earl Hoffman."

She'd come with a date? You go, girl! Marissa greeted the smiling man. "It's nice to meet you. How did you two meet?"

"Playing bingo," Betty Sue said. "Earl tends bar at most of the events held at the Grange Hall. So if you ever need a bartender, he's a good one."

"That's great to know," Marissa said. "If you have a business card, I'd like it."

"Not with me." Earl nodded toward Betty Sue, their heads touching affectionately. "She'll know how to get a hold of me. Just give my gal here a ring."

Hmm. "Will do," Marissa said.

As she continued toward the house, she spotted Brandon on the back porch, talking to his friend Greg Duran. They were both tall and too handsome for their own good. But Greg was even taller, bulkier.

Marissa stopped to say hello to them, just as Greg asked Brandon, "Who's the cook? She's a cute one, but she sure jumped a mile when I said hello to her."

"Ella's not your type," Brandon said.

"What makes you think you know my type?"

"Just because." In a low voice he added, "Don't even think about asking her out." Brandon turned his focus on Marissa. "Honey, what else can I do to help?"

"I've got everything under control." She'd just turned toward the kitchen when Maddie and Jimmy came running up to her and their daddy.

"This is the bestest party ever," Jimmy said.

Maddie nodded. "I got my wish. A real castle."

"It sure looks like fun," Greg said. "And I see a big pile of presents on that table in the gazebo."

"Yeah," Jimmy said. "We can't wait to open them. But we already got the best present ever."

"Oh, yeah?" Greg asked. "What's that?"

"Daddy got us a mommy for our birthdays!" Jimmy said.

Brandon laughed. "I sure did."

"Marissa?" Maddie asked in a quiet voice. "Can we call you Mommy?"

Marissa's heart melted into a gooey mess. "Absolutely."

Maddie tugged at her brother's red cape. "Come on, Jimmy. There's Uncle Ralph and Aunt Carlene. Let's go tell them the good news. We got a mommy."

"Greg," Jimmy said, "you come, too. We want you to help us guard the castle for the girls."

"Okay, buddy," Greg said. "Always happy to help a damsel in distress."

As the kids and Greg dashed off, Brandon opened his arms, and Marissa stepped into his embrace.

"We've got a lot to celebrate," he said.

"And a lot to be thankful for." Marissa kissed the man who'd given her the world—his heart, his children and his unconditional love and trust—gifts she'd cherish forever.

* * * * *

COMING SOON!

We really hope you enjoyed reading this book. If you're looking for more romance, be sure to head to the shops when new books are available on

Thursday 24th June

To see which titles are coming soon, please visit

millsandboon.co.uk/nextmonth

LET'S TALK

Romance

For exclusive extracts, competitions and special offers, find us online:

MILLS & BOON

THE HEART OF ROMANCE

A ROMANCE FOR EVERY READER

MODERN

Prepare to be swept off your feet by sophisticated, sexy and seductive heroes, in some of the world's most glamourous and romantic locations, where power and passion collide.

HISTORICAL

Escape with historical heroes from time gone by. Whether your passion is for wicked Regency Rakes, muscled Vikings or rugged Highlanders, awaken the romance of the past.

MEDICAL

Set your pulse racing with dedicated, delectable doctors in the high-pressure world of medicine, where emotions run high and passion, comfort and love are the best medicine.

True Love

Celebrate true love with tender stories of heartfelt romance, from the rush of falling in love to the joy a new baby can bring, and a focus on the emotional heart of a relationship.

Desire

Indulge in secrets and scandal, intense drama and plenty of sizzling hot action with powerful and passionate heroes who have it all: wealth, status, good looks…everything but the right woman.

HEROES

Experience all the excitement of a gripping thriller, with an intense romance at its heart. Resourceful, true-to-life women and strong, fearless men face danger and desire - a killer combination!

To see which titles are coming soon, please visit

millsandboon.co.uk/nextmonth

JOIN US ON SOCIAL MEDIA!

Stay up to date with our latest releases, author news and gossip, special offers and discounts, and all the behind-the-scenes action from Mills & Boon...

 millsandboon

 millsandboonuk

 millsandboon

It might just be true love...

GET YOUR ROMANCE FIX!

MILLS & BOON
blog

Get the latest romance news, exclusive author interviews, story extracts and much more!

blog.millsandboon.co.uk

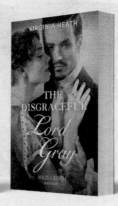

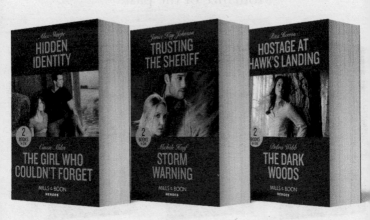

MILLS & BOON
MEDICAL
Pulse-Racing Passion

Set your pulse racing with dedicated, delectable doctors in the high-pressure world of medicine, where emotions run high and passion, comfort and love are the best medicine.

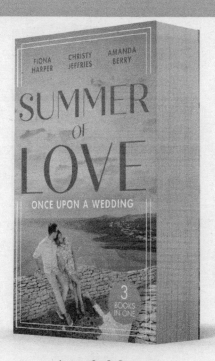